Take Me Home

Alex Hart has worked in the film and television industry for over twenty years, primarily in drama and factual development. When she isn't at her desk, spending time with her imaginary friends, she can often be found reading, paddle boarding, cycling, running and playing squash. She lives with her two Siberian cats, Lilya and Igor.

Take Me Home is her debut novel.

Find out more at:

🌐 www.alex-hart-author.com

🐦 @ alexhartauthor

Take Me Home

Alex Hart

ORION

An Orion paperback

First published in Great Britain in 2020
by Orion Fiction,
This paperback edition published in 2020
by Orion Fiction,
an imprint of The Orion Publishing Group Ltd.,
Carmelite House, 50 Victoria Embankment
London EC4Y 0DZ

An Hachette UK company

1 3 5 7 9 10 8 6 4 2

A CIP catalogue record for this book
is available from the British Library.

ISBN (Paperback) 978 1 4091 8907 7

Typeset at The Spartan Press Ltd,
Lymington, Hants

Printed and bound in Great Britain by Clays Ltd,
Elcograf S.p.A.

www.orionbooks.co.uk

In memory of Bear, and my dear friend Jane Harbord –
who rest on my shoulders as I write.
The world is considerably emptier without you both.

x

I

The signs were there. I simply ignored them. It's kind of my forte.

It may have been the menacing clouds looming outside the apartment window that gave me my first clue. Or perhaps it was the sharp pain in my skull. A result of too many beers the night before. However, the biggest indication today was going to get worse was the thundering fist on my front door. It caused the walls and my teeth to rattle in unison.

I knew who it was.

The whole apartment clattered with the banging.

'I know you in.' His voice boomed through the door.

I froze halfway between my bedroom and the living area.

I'd avoided him all week, but it seemed my time as a self-enforced fugitive was up.

'I go nowhere.' His voice, muffled.

I braced myself, pulled back my shoulders, took a deep breath and opened the door with a smile.

Standing in the hallway, my landlord, Artyom Mirzoyan. Dressed in his usual cheap suit, his black satin shirt undone to his bulbous stomach. Sweaty silvery hairs poked out, feathering the seam.

'Hey, Arty.' I attempted to sound breezy. The words caught in my throat.

'You got rent?' His Armenian accent thick like harissa.

'Nice suit,' I said.

He raised his eyebrows and twitched his cuffs.

My shoulders dropped. 'Sure. On my way to the bank now.'

'You say that four days ago.' He opened his arms wide, his palms face up.

'On my way now,' I said again, trying to sound convincing this time, despite the churning away of my insides.

'You pay rent today or you go.' He wagged his finger at me. Gold rings adorned his chubby digits.

'I know, Arty. I'm sorry.' And I am. He's been good to me.

He shrugged and shook his head.

'I will. I promise.'

'Today.' He pointed his finger again and slunk off along the hallway.

I needed money and I needed it fast.

I had attempted to get hold of my editor the past four days. If he ever checked his phone, he'd see three missed calls and two emails from me. He probably had and was ignoring me. When I first started out, I was the *go-to* photojournalist. But nowadays there were graduates armed with just a smartphone and willing to do the jobs for half the going rate, so guess who my editor chose?

I grabbed my cellphone and tried once again.

'Yeah?' Richard's gruff growl told me he was in no mood for crap, but at least he had answered this time.

'Hey, Richard.'

'Harper.'

He hadn't got time for me.

'I've been trying to call.'

'Right, well we're up against the usual deadline ...'

I cut straight in.

'Look, just wondering if there are any gigs? It's been pretty qui—'

'Harper, I'm sorry. There isn't much around. You know how it is. All the jobs are pretty much filled.'

I cleared my throat and, seeing how bright and breezy didn't work, I went for desperate. Which I am.

'I'm in a fix here, Richard.'

I caught the hustle and bustle of the newsroom behind him.

'Look, I get I'm not the only one on your books, but there's got to be something?' I pleaded.

I glanced around my apartment. Yesterday's papers sprawled across the tattered tan leatherette couch; a half-eaten pizza waiting to be cleared. A stack of bills, half of which I hadn't bothered to open, piled on top of the table. A siren wailed past the window.

Finally Richard spoke. 'There's a couple of small gigs.'

My heart soared.

'There's a fundraiser at The Bronx Zoo.'

'That it?' I asked, without trying to sound too bummed.

'Well ...' He cleared his throat. 'There's the Gala at *The Pierre* tonight. Greg was going to cover it, but seems he's suffering after a night out at Jimmy Chang's ...'

Like a roller coaster chugging up the hill, I felt the anticipation of a bigger gig, and all thanks to my new partners in crime, Salmonella and Jimmy Chang.

'... But Greg's hoping he'll be OK in a couple of hours. He's going to check in with me later,' Richard said.

Damn.

'Well, you know I'm good for it,' I said. There's bigger bucks in a front-page shot than some tiny picture of so-called cute

3

kids feeding a giraffe that no one except their parents will look at, never mind care about.

Richard let out a low, slow growl. 'You'll have to wear something fancy to do it. It's a high-end ball. I can't have you sticking out in your jeans and T-shirt? Have you got anything like that?'

I knew Richard was genuinely asking me. He's known me a long time and I don't think he's ever seen me in much else other than my usual jeans and T-shirt.

'Sure I do.' I struggled to swallow the lie, guessing he wouldn't swallow it either.

He grunted. 'Let's see what happens.' He cut the phone off before I had a chance to thank him.

Instead, I thanked Jimmy Chang.

I don't know why I bothered to look in my bedroom closet. I'm hardly going to open it and surprise myself. *Oh, hey, look at that fancy red dress.* I knew I was going to have to buy something. It wasn't that I simply didn't have the money, but the thought of buying a dress, and for what? To get a gig that'll only pay enough to cover it. But if I got this gig, Richard was more likely to give me others.

It was already afternoon and, ignoring my hangover, I grabbed my purse and checked my flexible friend Mr Visa was in there. I snatched the box of half-eaten pizza, left my apartment, shifted down the stairs and exited my building.

At the bottom of the stone steps was Walt. Caucasian, large bushy black eyebrows, steely white hair. He could be anything between fifty and seventy for all I knew. He sat cross-legged. A blue knit cap pulled low, half covered in soiled blankets, odd shoes on each foot, leaning against the iron railings at the front of the block.

'Hey, Walt.'

'Princess.'

We slapped our palms together.

I passed him the box of pizza. He flipped open the lid the second it was in his hands.

'You got damn chillies on it again, girl.'

I shrugged and grinned. He picked them off and flung them on the sidewalk.

I walked towards the subway and wondered if I didn't find some more gigs soon, whether that would be me. It wouldn't be the first time.

When I exited on 54th, the rain that had threatened to break teemed onto the sidewalk. A chill wind bit at my face. I zipped up my brown leather jacket and hopscotched to avoid the puddles. I aimed for the first entrance and shook myself off like a dog the second I was inside. I followed the hordes of people on the escalator and headed towards La Vida Loca.

I scanned the store for dresses and headed over to them. I grabbed a couple and made my way towards the fitting room.

I don't know who jumped first. The little girl or me. She couldn't have been more than five years old. She sat with her feet dangling over a seat, a furry Mickey Mouse tucked up on her lap. I gave her a half-smile and entered a vacant cubicle.

I wriggled out of my now-sodden clothes and slipped on the first dress. Already my skin itched at the idea of wearing it. I pulled up the back of my hair, glanced at the mirror and decided it would do. It was bad enough having to wear the damn thing, never mind wasting any more of my time trying on any others. If I was lucky, I could get away with poking the price label down the back and returning it to the store tomorrow. It was not like I was going to wear it again.

And that's when I looked at the price label.

Hellfire. Are they serious?

It was half a week's rent. I flipped the labels over on the other dresses. I vowed to ensure I would not get one single mark on it and tomorrow it'd be returned to its rightful place. Back on the store rail.

I exited the fitting room, glanced at the little girl, who I guessed was waiting for her mom, and made my way to the till.

A couple of women lined up in front of me, arms laden with purchases, their wallets at the ready. Two sales clerks stood at the counter chatting. The younger one chewed gum and nodded while the other rattled off her plans for the night. No urgency in finishing their conversation.

I coughed. Subtle, I know.

The older sales clerk peered towards me. With a kiss on her colleague's two cheeks, she grabbed her purse and left the store.

Gum Girl, who can't have been much more than seventeen, eventually got to me. She didn't glance my way. She scanned the label, folded the dress and shoved it in a paper bag.

'Two hundred seventy-nine dollars.' She blew a bubble, popped it and flipped out her hand for my credit card.

When I left the store, the rain had relented a little. I have to say, even with the weight of half my rent clasped in my fist, I felt pretty upbeat. With tonight's gig, I could net a nice sum, take the dress back, pay Arty and get into Richard's good books.

A little more relaxed, I took a seat on the subway.

I got to my stop and skipped up the steps.

My cellphone beeped.

I headed along the four blocks towards my apartment. I kept my eyes peeled for Arty. I might be able to pay him soon, but not yet. If he caught me with some overpriced dress in my bag, I could see him bursting out of his polyester suit with rage.

I dialed the voicemail, pressed the cellphone against my ear and waited to hear the message.

'Message received today at 15.47 – Hey, Harper, Greg's called in. He's fine for tonight, so I'm sorry, but I'm going to have to pull you off that gig…'

I swear, I almost kicked the dress to the curb.

'…Anyhow call me, there's still the zoo job if you're up for it.'

I texted back a reply and refrained from including the expletives spinning around in my head.

Fine. Send me details.

I didn't register the subway journey back to the store, I was so pent up.

I think the second the words 'We're closing' spilled out of Gum Girl's mouth, she detected the 'Don't even think about it' look on my face. She almost swallowed her gum whole. I flipped the bag onto the counter with a crackle. I shoved the receipt towards her, stood with my hands on my hips and tried to regulate my breathing.

'I need to return this,' I said.

For a moment, she appeared flustered. I admit, I did look like I was about to pull a gun out on her.

'Sorry,' I added. It's not like it was her fault the world was rallying against me. I just needed a break.

She flicked her fingers over the till buttons.

I glanced around the store, my attention caught by two tiny legs poking out from behind a clothes rail.

I looked at Gum Girl, who, as I said, can't have been much older than seventeen, and back at the kid. It was the same little girl from earlier.

'She yours?' I asked.

'Uh?'

'The kid. She yours?'

Gum Girl gave me a blank stare. She followed my gaze to the rear of the store. The little girl huddled behind some jackets, clinging on to her toy.

Gum Girl shook her head.

I walked to the back. I scanned left and right to see if I had missed seeing someone. There was no one other than us.

I crouched down to the kid.

She was dressed in a pink flowered frock. A thin gray button-up sweater over the top. Her silky dark hair cut in a stylish bob.

'Hey.' I didn't know what else to say to her.

The girl squinted at me and said nothing.

'What you doing?' I asked.

She kicked her feet together, not wanting to catch my eye.

'Where's your mom?'

She glimpsed at me and shrugged.

I heard the pop of a bubble. The gum girl approached from behind.

'So, we're closing.' She said it brightly, like I should thank her or something.

I turned and gave the sales clerk the same blank look the little girl had given me a second ago. I looked back to the kid.

'What's your name?'

'May.'

'I'm Harper.'

Gum Girl persisted. 'So, like, I need you to leave.' Intonation rising on the last word.

I placed my palms on my knees and lifted myself up.

'Right. So, what you going to do? Leave her here? Maybe

you've got a roll-down mat she could sleep on?' I shrugged, as if it was the only solution.

'What?'

Again, from her baffled expression, she must have thought I was serious.

'I don't know if you've noticed, but there's a little kid in your store. By herself. Without her mom or dad.'

'Right. OK. But I need to close up.' She glanced at her watch.

I peered towards the jelly sandals poking out of the bottom of the jacket rail. I looked back at Gum Girl and, realizing it was a lost cause, I crouched back down and took May's hand.

'Come on, let's go find your mom.'

Of course, at the time, I was sure it'd only take a minute to locate her. After all, she was probably bawling her eyes out at store security searching for her lost little girl.

How wrong could I be?

2

I led May to the security booth on the top floor and sat her on a nearby bucket bench.

I crouched and leaned on the back of my heels.

'OK, so listen, kid—'

May looked up at me with her large brown eyes. Her eyelashes curled against her lids.

'I'm going to ask security to give a call-out to your mom, let her know you're here.'

''K,' May said. She clung on to her furry Mickey Mouse toy, kicking her legs on the plastic seat.

'So did she say where she was going?'

May shook her head.

'And she left you in the store and said she was coming back?'

'No. Uncle Orange said she was coming to get me.'

'Wait, what?' My brow creased.

'Uncle Orange. He said Mommy was coming to get me.' May twisted Mickey's ear around in her tiny hand.

I perched next to her on the bench and turned her towards me.

'Let me get this straight. Your Uncle Orange dropped you at the store?'

May nodded and kicked her legs again. 'He said I had to go in and wait and she would come get me.'

'So where's Uncle Orange?'

May shrugged. 'Don't know.'

'He just left you?'

She nodded. 'Where's my mommy?' May's lower lip trembled.

I looked around me. The place was beginning to thin of shoppers.

A slight thrum of pain hammered on my temples. 'I don't know. Listen, who's Uncle Orange?'

'He's my daddy's friend.'

'Your daddy's friend.' I repeated it to myself, my brain whirring as fast as it could.

I glanced over to the security booth. All hopes lay with a guy who couldn't have been much over five seven, stocky with a paunch.

'Wait here.' I tapped May's knee and walked over to him.

I cleared my throat to get his attention.

The guy looked up and glanced down, and when I say down, I mean straight to my chest.

He looked back up and blushed.

'I've got a young girl here. Her mom is supposed to be picking her up from the store and she seems to be late. Can you make a call-out or something?'

His radio buzzed with interference and a voice came over the airways regarding a tussle on the first floor.

'Sorry, ma'am, I've got to deal with this.'

He made to leave.

I grabbed his arm. 'Wait. Did you hear me? I've got a young girl here who's lost her mom.'

Terence – 'Head of Security' as his name tag pinned on his grubby white shirt showed – sighed. He walked to the balcony and leaned over the metal railing, giving him a clear view of the first floor. He unclipped the walkie-talkie from his belt and pressed his mouth to it.

'Be right with you, Al.'

He glanced over to May on the bench and strolled over to his booth. He leaned over the counter. His stomach rested against the top, his shirt pulling out from his pants, exposing his flabby white skin. He grabbed a microphone.

'Er, there's a lost kid here. If you're looking for your lost kid, report to the security office on the fourth floor,' his voice whined through the speakers.

He made his way to the escalator. His walkie-talkie back up to his mouth, his neck craning over the side, looking to see if there was still a fight going on.

I sat back next to May.

'So, this Uncle Orange, he brought you here?'

'Yeah, he bought me candy and a donut.' May giggled.

'He did, huh.' I didn't like the feeling in my stomach. 'Your daddy wasn't with you?'

May shook her head.

'And where were you before you got to the store?'

May's brow creased in confusion.

'Did you come from home?'

'Yeah. We went on a really long ride and then we stopped because I felt sick, but Uncle Orange said that we were nearly there and then he said that when I felt better I could get some candy. And I felt better and we had a donut too.' May, excited by the memory, barely took a breath between the words.

I glanced at the security booth. There was no one around.

'And you're sure he said your mom was going to pick you up?'

The exhilaration of her adventure seemed to dissipate as soon as I mentioned her mom. Her eyes glistened with tears.

'I want my mommy.'

'I know, kid, I know.' I glanced at my watch. 'Do you know your mommy's name?' I asked her.

There was a pause and her brow crumpled. 'Mommy.'

'You know what your daddy calls her?'

Again a pause. 'Sweetie.'

I couldn't help but smile.

'What about your last name? You know what that is?'

May stared at me for a second. 'Brown.'

'Brown? Your last name is Brown?'

She nodded.

'How old are you?'

May looked at her tiny fingers. 'Four.' She held up her hand, showing me her fingers.

'That's pretty old,' I said.

I scanned the few shoppers left dawdling around the storefronts.

'Think you can you describe your mom for me?' I asked.

'Pretty.'

OK, this wasn't going well.

'Is she dark like you and me?' I pulled at my hair.

May shook her head.

'Blond like …' I glanced around us. 'Like that woman over there?' I pointed at two blond women staring at some shoes in one of the storefronts.

May nodded. 'She's pretty.'

Yeah, and she's missing, I thought to myself.

I guessed from the fact May had dark hair her mom may have had it bleached. I leaned over the metal rail to the lower floor. I scanned every blond woman who walked past to see if I could spot anyone with roots. But all the women I saw who fitted the description were laughing and joking around with friends. They clearly hadn't lost their daughter. They were stopping and staring in store windows seemingly without a care in the world. Hardly the mark of a mom with a missing kid.

I turned and spotted in my peripheral vision someone approaching the security booth. Anticipation soon turned to disappointment when I clocked it was Terence.

'No luck, huh?' he said, his nose wrinkling.

I didn't know how to answer that.

Terence flipped the walkie-talkie around in his right hand. He clipped it onto his belt, unclipped it and flipped it again. He covered it with his black uniform jacket and rested a hand on it, like he was packing heat. There was no doubt in my mind he'd practiced this move in the mirror. The sort of guy who dreamed of being the big hero, but when it came to it, he choked at the first hurdle. He liked wearing the uniform, but the doing was way beyond his reach.

I glanced at the time and back at Terence, who made a show of surveying the area.

I really didn't like the idea of a man having dropped May off at a store, leaving her all alone, saying she had to wait for her mom. No one would do that, surely?

'Can you do another call-out?' I asked Terence, in the hope the first one hadn't been heard by her mom. She might have been so frantic searching for her little girl, she could have blocked out all other noise.

'Well . . .' He said it slowly, as if considering other options. By the fact we had been sat here waiting, with no sign of her mom appearing, it seemed to me it was the only option.

Terence slipped into the booth and seated himself in front of the microphone and camera monitors.

'Hey, can I get a look at that?' I asked.

Terence did a double take. 'The cameras?'

'Yeah, see who dropped her off.'

'Listen, I'm sorry. I can't just show you—'

'Look, all I want is to find the kid's mom and be on my way, OK?'

I said it a little aggressively, but my patience was running thin. After the day I'd had, all I needed right now was to get to McKendrick's, have a few drinks and blow off some steam.

'I think you best take her to the cops,' Terence said.

My heart sank.

'Can't you do that? Or call them or something?'

'Well …' He winced and shook his head. 'Thing is, can't leave my post. Be quicker if you took her to the 63rd on Brooklyn Avenue.'

Crap. That was the last thing I wanted to do.

I gazed across at May, who appeared on the verge of tears.

The nearest precinct house was a couple of stops from the stores. If I wanted to miss the evening rush of drunks being checked into their cages, I needed to take her now.

Looking around me one last time in the vague hope her mom would miraculously materialize, I relented to the inevitable.

Clasping May's tiny hand in mine, all I could think as I led her out onto the street was – who in their right mind leaves a kid alone in New York City?

3

The first thing that hits you when you enter any precinct house isn't the huddle of drunks waiting to be booked. Or the noise from some rowdy hobos pleading their innocence after being caught with their hands in someone's pocket. It's the smell.

Holy crap, you don't know anything like it until you've been in one. The thick stench of ammonia and vomit, the rancid odor of men's sweat combined with stale beer and who knows what.

There's never been one precinct, and trust me I've been in a fair few, that hasn't had the same distinctive funk.

Seems I timed it wrong, thinking there'd be no line. In front of me, a line snaked around the front lobby. Bedraggled guys handcuffed to cops. A couple of women who scarcely looked like they had underwear on, never mind warm clothes. Their hair straggled. Eyes sunken. Twitching from one foot to the other, desperate for their next fix. Around the outer edges, seats occupied with the dregs of New York waited their turn or huddled in the relative warmth before they were kicked out onto the sidewalks.

May's hand squeezed mine tighter. I arched my neck to see towards the front desk. A short bald guy, approximately fifty years old, stood behind the counter. He barked at a skinny fella who leaned against it, barely able to keep himself upright.

I headed towards the front and the bleating started.

'Hey, you. Lady, you're cutting in.'

'Get back in line.'

'You want to cut in, you suck my dick first.'

I turned to them, 'Screw you,' and gave them the finger.

OK, so I forgot I had a kid with me, but still, screw them.

'Listen,' I said, trying to get the attention of the guy behind the desk. 'I've got a kid.' The bald guy didn't glance up from his computer.

'Good on you. Congratulations,' he said.

'She's lost.'

He still didn't look up. He tapped away at his keyboard.

'Her mom was supposed to be picking her up and she didn't show. I'm worried she was in an accident or something?'

'Listen, sweetheart . . .' The desk sergeant finally looked at me. Hackles rose on the back of my neck. 'This look like daycare to you? Look around. You wait in line like every other turd on this block and I'll see what I can do.' He air-swiped me as if to move me out of the way. 'Back of the line.'

If May's hand hadn't been in mine, I swear I would have punched him. Instead, I muttered 'asshole' loud enough for him to hear, but this time, not loud enough for little ears.

May yanked on my hand. 'We going home?'

I looked down at her and back around at the degenerates. I blew air out of my cheeks and headed towards the only vacant seats.

'Let's sit here a minute,' I said to her.

Slumped on my left, a man who looked close to eighty, asleep with his bearded chin resting on his chest.

I turned to May. 'Do you know your address?'

May looked at me, blank.

'OK, kid. What about Uncle Orange. He's daddy's friend?'

May nodded.

'And your daddy definitely wasn't with you?'

May shook her head.

'You know where daddy was?'

She shrugged a little. 'Daddy always working.'

'Know what he does?'

'Makes people happy,' she said, proud.

Makes people happy? 'Any idea how he does that?'

May shrugged.

Great.

'And your Uncle Orange? Is that his actual name?'

She shook her head. 'He always gives me an orange, silly.'

I wasn't sure where to go from here.

May yawned and pulled Mickey close to her.

'You tired?'

May nodded. 'I want to go home.'

'Yeah, me too, honey,' I replied. And a beer, I thought to myself. At this rate, not only would Jimmy be gone, but the bar would be shut.

She blinked at me and huddled up to my side. The old guy jumped himself awake like a car starting in winter. He gave out a low growl and, as quick as he woke up, his head fell back towards his chest.

Another hour drifted by. The ever-increasing line shuffled to the front. By the fact I was now accustomed to the smell around me, I knew too much time had passed.

May had fallen asleep. Her tiny body slumped on the seat and, like the guy next to us, her head rested on her chest. The toy dangled below her knees. Mickey's hand scraped the floor.

It was then it struck me what May was wearing. Her cotton dress, thin sweater and jelly sandals were hardly the appropriate outfit for a New York fall day.

Where was her mom? I'd been so sure when I'd taken her from the store that she'd turn up in minutes, it hadn't occurred to me I'd be here hours later, waiting in some pit to hand her over.

I ignored the whining coming from the line and headed back to the front desk.

'Excuse me, sir?

'Like I said, sweetheart, wait your turn.'

This time, I didn't have May's hand in mine to refrain me from pouncing over the counter and punching the guy sharp on the nose. Not wanting to spend the night in the cage, I somehow managed to unfurl my fists in time for me to take a deep breath and glance over to May. 'So, what happens if her mom or whoever doesn't turn up?' I asked him.

'What do you think? We put her to work here, lady.'

It took every ounce of energy not to do it. It would be worth a night in the cage to see him with a broken beak.

'Child and Family Services,' he said.

'What?' A thud hit my belly, like he'd got in there first and hit me right in the gut.

'Child and Family Services. They'll take her. Look, I've got a line of bookings and I'd like to get out of here before my retirement's due, so wait your turn and we'll see what we can do.'

I didn't listen to what he said. Instead, all I felt was the searing pain where his left hook had sucker-punched me with those four words.

Child and Family Services.

Not on my watch.

I turned back to May. Checking no one was looking, I grabbed her hand, and before anyone could stop me, we raced out and down the precinct house steps.

4

OK, so technically, in the eyes of the law, it was abduction. It may not have been the smartest move, but what the hell was I supposed to do? Wait around until some worn-out goody-two-shoes with a caseload of kids finally turned up to take her to some two-bit home for the night, while they worked out where the hell they were going to ship her?

I may not be a kid-type girl, but I'd spent enough of my life with so-called *Child and Family Services* to know I was not going to let this happen.

Thing is, you only needed to take one look at this kid and you could see she wasn't the usual clientele that ended up in some temporary home. She wouldn't last a night. She had been sat there with her glossy hair and soft skin, dressed in a pretty frock, matching jelly sandals, smelling like she had rolled in fresh strawberries and cream. And yes, she was sort of underdressed for the weather, but still, something didn't quite sit right. Why would someone drop her like that?

I clung on to May's little hand and headed west towards the nearest subway. My palms clammy, I walked a little too fast for her. I felt like any second now some cop was going to chase us until he'd got May securely locked up in some home that stank of other kids' urine. There was no way I could let her fall into the system, even if it was for one night.

'You're hurting my arm,' May said.

'Sorry, kid.' I let go of her hand and placed mine on her shoulder, guiding her towards the subway.

The subway platform was packed. The squeak and squeal of brakes of a train approaching on the other side echoed on the walls. Ours thundered through the tunnel. A newspaper on the tracks blew up into the warm air and fluttered down before being crushed by the wheels.

As we boarded, commuters stared at May clinging to her furry toy for a little warmth. Eyeballing them back, I unzipped my leather jacket and wrapped her in it. I thumbed some punk off who tried to take the only vacant seat. He slunk to the other side of the carriage. I sat May down and crouched beside her.

'We'll get you home soon enough.'

She twisted her mouth a little and blinked. She may well have believed it, I'm not sure I did. She glimpsed up at me with glassy eyes. A tear snaked its way down her plump cheek and soaked into Mickey's fur.

How do kids do that? Panic rose in my gut. If the girl began to wail for her mom, I had no idea what I was going to do. I needed to call around the local hospitals, make some inquiries. Maybe I was right and she'd been in some sort of accident and hadn't been able to pick her up. As sad as it seemed, at least this little mystery would be zipped up and shipped off before the bar called last orders.

The train shunted along the tracks, stopping and starting, squealing and screeching along the metal rails. The stench of compacted humans mingled with grease from the tracks.

Finally, we got to Sheepshead Bay. There was no way I was going to my apartment with Arty lurking. I needed to buy some time. Think things through. Make a few calls. Perhaps by then some alert would be out for the kid from her mom and I could roll up like I had just found her, and this nightmare of a day would be over.

I hadn't realized quite how much the warm air from the subway had enveloped us until we headed out of the tunnel into the now frigid night-time air. The wind blew in from the east. Goosebumps prickled on my bare arms. The streets filled up with the evening crowd, rushing to who knows where. The smell of Chinese spices clashed with the sweet chilli of enchiladas, perfumed with the distinct saltiness from the nearby bay.

I glanced down at May in my jacket. She looked a little like ET when Gertie dressed him up. It was no wonder we were getting stares.

'I'm hungry.' May tugged on my arm. The tears were gone, but I recognized a whine when I heard one.

'Me too, kid.' I knew just the place.

We headed along Shore Parkway and walked for ten minutes. The hum of the evening tide of people washed in from the city and pervaded the sea air.

I glanced at May. 'You recognize anything?'

May looked around, shook her head and gazed at the crowded streets.

We clambered up the steps to McKendrick's bar to the customary growl of Rat. A straggly biscuit-colored mutt stationed on the top step. A line of fishing rope tied to his collar wrapped around the iron railing. A mauled piece of rubber at his paws.

He jumped up at my legs and waited to be patted.

'Rat meet May. May meet Rat.' I rubbed the top of his head. May hid behind me as he slobbered on my jeans.

'Thanks for that,' I said. Warm saliva seeped through the denim.

I pressed on the door.

Oh, the sense of happiness I felt as the familiar smell of beer filled my nose. My pumps crunched underfoot from stray pistachio shells. It was almost as dark inside as it was outside. A low light highlighted Bill behind the bar.

'Hey.' A chorus of grunts came from all directions.

'Who's your friend?' A voice grumbled from somewhere.

I ignored them and walked towards Bill.

'Y'know, even in your leather jacket, I've got to say she looks a little too young, but nice try,' Bill said. A red and white striped dish towel over one shoulder, a grubby rag in the other.

'Bite me, wise-ass,' I said.

'I'll bite you,' Larry shouted over.

'You still got some grills?' Tom said to him.

I glanced over and shook my head. Larry smacked his gummy lips together and saluted me a hello.

I propped May up on a bar stool, unzipped my jacket from her and gave Bill a look which told him I was in no mood for his crap. He shrugged and wiped the rag across the surface in front of us.

Bill had run McKendrick's since I could remember. To me, he appeared the same as when I was a kid. Perhaps his hair a little thinner, but he never seemed to have much to start with.

'What can I get you ladies?' He leaned forward and placed both palms on the bar in front of us.

'Get the kid some fries and ...' I stumbled, 'a Coke, me a

Scotch.' OK, so I was in charge of a kid. But, you've got to agree, today hadn't been a walk in the park and I needed to relax, to think, work out what I was going to do next.

I turned on my stool to May. 'Let's get you something to eat, then we'll go look for your mom, all right?'

May nodded.

'You trust me, kid?'

She nodded again.

'Good.' I rubbed her back. If there was one thing I knew, it was the fear kids felt when they were with strangers. I'd spent enough of my time at her age being pushed from pillar to post, from one home to another, to know the pit in my stomach was something I had to accept or drown in. The last thing I wanted was for her to be feeling the same.

I scanned the bar. 'No TJ?'

'Nope,' Bill said. He placed a glass up to the optic.

May gazed wide-eyed around her and, for the first time, I saw my favorite dive in a different light. Even in the dingy glow, you could make out the cracked leather peeling away from the foam on the stools. The bar top covered in smeared stains. And as for the clientele, they would appear as comfortable waiting in a soup-kitchen line. Jimmy was over in the far corner nursing a Scotch, and by the hangdog look in his eyes, it wasn't his first. Tom and Larry occupied their usual spot by the TV, half-supped beers at their feet, the table laid clear for their cards and pistachios. They'd given up playing for money a long time ago, after one of them won the other's week's wages, which resulted in too many black eyes and broken jaws. Finally deciding, for the sake of friendship, to play for nuts, the local emergency room lost some business, but, hey, their families got to eat.

The crackled sounds of SBFM filtered through the speakers, competing with the volume of the large-screen TV.

If you were a stranger walking into this bar, you'd think it was full of no-hopers, but I'd grown up with these guys. I could have gone to any new bar in town, with their home-brewed beers and steel and oak surroundings, like they invented it, but there was no place quite like McKendrick's. I only needed to get a stray glance from some wayward douchebag who thought I was easy meat and these guys would be steering him out the door before the head on his beer had settled.

'Compliments of the chef.'

Bill shoved a red plastic basket of fries in front of May and threw two packets of ketchup beside it.

'Cheers,' I said. I nodded at him in appreciation, swigged my drink back in one and shoved the empty glass back across the bar. 'Don't ask,' I said.

Bill shrugged, flicked the dish towel over his shoulder and filled up the shot.

'Jimmy's paying,' I said, glancing towards him.

Jimmy raised his near-empty glass and nodded to Bill.

'Not eating?' I said to May. It took me a second to realize she was struggling to open the packets no smaller than her hands. I took them from her and ripped open the tops. I doused the fries in the sauce and waited until she dug in.

I licked my sour fingers clean and took a swig of my drink. I swilled the contents of my glass around. I spotted my reflection in the mirror behind the bar and noticed May was doing the same. I tucked my hair behind my ears and she followed suit. Watching her reflection, I picked up one of the fries. She copied me. I tried hard to keep the smile off my face, but when I stuck my thumb up to my nose and waggled my fingers, I couldn't help but break into a laugh.

'Watch this.'

I winked at her and swiveled around on my stool.

'Fancy a game, Jimmy?' I nodded towards the pool table.

Looking at the way Jimmy swayed on his chair, hovering over his glass, I knew it would be an easy win. A few years back, he'd been hard to hustle. But since Lou-Ann had left him, he nursed the Scotch like it was a long-lost dog and I got a fair few drinks paid for, care of his bad judgment and my misspent youth.

I turned and heard Bill whistle. He shook his head at me, a dirty grin peeled back to show his rotten teeth.

Come on, it's not like he didn't take my money when he wasn't so addled by booze.

All's fair in love and pool, right?

Jimmy, his skin shiny from alcohol-induced sweat, swigged back the last of his drink. He leaned forward, placed his hands on both of his knees to steady himself and sauntered across to the pool table.

I glanced back at May. She gulped down her Coke.

I picked up the cue, knowing, if nothing else was going to go right today, at least my weekend tab was about to be paid for.

I let Jimmy break and listened to the soft clunk of the balls hit the sides with as much force as a kitten with a ball of wool.

'Nice move, Jimmy.'

He grunted in response and propped himself on the nearby table to steady his swaying mass.

I leaned over the green, took aim, and boom, fired two solids into the pockets with one shot. Pop. Pop. Pop.

As I say, a misspent youth. Don't underestimate it.

★

It can't have taken more than ten minutes to secure my bar check, and with a shrug from Jimmy, my tab was safe.

'A beer for me, and a Coke for…'

The heady rush from the two glasses of Scotch and an easy win soon turned to bile and swam up my throat.

'Shit. Where'd she go?' I stared at the empty stool next to the half-eaten fries and back up to Bill.

He shrugged at me and nodded towards the restroom. 'How do I know? I look like Mary Poppins?'

I raced into the restroom. The fluorescent light from the one bulb that worked flickered and, for a moment, blinded me. The odor of chemical blocks Bill shoved down the cisterns to try and mask the smell of stale urine filled my lungs the second I entered. Instead of a mirror on the wall, which had, a long time ago, been smashed in some fight, read some graffiti, which some smart-ass had daubed with their lipstick. 'You look like shit. No one cares.'

I slammed all the stall doors open. They bounced back with a thump.

Empty.

I ran back into the bar, adjusted my eyes to the dark and crouched towards the sticky floor. I searched under the pool table, behind the chairs, over in the far right-hand corner, where crumpled boxes of potato chips lay unevenly stacked.

Nothing.

Mother of God, I could only have taken my eye off her for a second. OK, maybe a while longer, but I didn't think I could lose her. I'd been so occupied whipping Jimmy's ass, too concerned about my bar check, to notice if anyone had come into the bar. They could have taken her without so much as a blink from the regulars, who were too busy downing their dregs, winning their hands of poker or watching the game.

Figuring she was no longer in the bar, I sped towards the exit. I crashed open the front door. My heart thundered in my chest as I took in the scene.

5

May was huddled on the top step, Rat curled up beside her, her tiny pink hand stroking his wiry fur. Startled at the speed of me exiting the bar, May's big brown eyes opened wide.

Taking a deep breath, I squatted beside them.

'Don't move,' I said. I pointed my finger at her and at Rat.

Leaning back up, I entered the bar, grabbed my jacket and, with a brief wave, said my goodbyes.

'Time to go, Rat. I'll be back.'

Rat raised his head and rested his chin back on May's knee.

'Doggy,' May said.

'Yeah, doggy. But we've got to go, kid.' I placed my jacket over May's shoulders and stepped between them to get past. I turned and grabbed May's free hand. 'Come on.'

'Bye, doggy.' May patted the top of his head.

I needed to take her somewhere safe and quiet, a place I could make calls to the local hospitals.

We headed left, back towards Emmons Avenue. The neighborhood filled up with the evening crowd. Music streamed out from the restaurants lined along the street.

A patrol car cruised by. The brief sound of radio chatter spilled through the open window. My hand tensed in May's.

'We going home?' May asked.

'Not yet, but we will,' I lied. I watched the patrol car drive off into the distance.

We turned down Haring Street. The hustle and bustle quietened a little. On the other side of the sidewalk, a couple of kids hovered close to what I guessed from the boarded-up windows was a trap house. One kid, dressed in black, a hood pulled up tight, a baseball cap drawn low over his face, nodded to two guys as they approached. With the swift slap of the hands, a wrap of something that would render them useless for the rest of the evening was exchanged. They clambered up the steps to an open door hung unevenly and disappeared inside, their coma awaiting.

I knew these streets like the back of my hand. The sidewalks, uneven and cracked. Electric cables zipped to and fro above our heads. Nineteen-twenties timber houses overlooking newer apartment buildings stood like old wooden pegs below the overhead telephone lines. Iron fences caged each building, claiming every inch of space. The Star-Spangled Banner hung limp from a number of homes.

We carried on straight down. I knew I couldn't go back to mine with Arty on the warpath.

I turned and faced a small one-story wooden building. The house was pitch-black. A gate dangled on its hinges, half open. A couple of concrete steps led up to the front doorway. A tattered, faded striped awning over the porchway.

Still holding May's hand in mine, we stepped up towards the front door. I leaned in and pressed my face against the cool glass.

The house was still.

'Stay here. Don't move.'

I let go of her hand and scuttled back down the steps. I turned to my left, into the front yard. Without wanting to be seen by any neighbors, I scrambled along the small alleyway to the backyard gate. Seizing a trash can, I heaved it up to the fence, stepped my right foot onto it and grabbed the top. Easing myself up, I flipped over and jumped down to the back. A cat hurtled across the yard. It stopped and stared. For a few seconds, we held each other's guilty gaze. Surrendering, the cat retreated through some open wire into the neighbor's yard. Standing still, I listened for any movement. I heard nothing but a rustle from the wooded shrubs. I edged myself to the back door and tried the handle. Locked. I leaned into the window and tried to detect any movement. Nothing. I shifted my fingertips around the wooden frame. It loosened a little. Cracked yellowing paint crinkled in my hand. I dug my fingers into my pants pocket and took out my wallet. I flicked it open and removed my trusty credit card. I edged it around the seal of the frame and bent it towards the hook. With a satisfying ping, the hook snapped off and, hey presto, the window opened.

Wasting no time, I eased myself in. I flung my legs over and slid off the kitchen surface into the darkened room. Shuttling through to the front of the house, I opened the door.

May stood where I had left her.

Surprised, she blinked at me a few times.

'This your home?' she said.

'Not quite. Let's just say I'm borrowing it.' I didn't want to confuse the kid with details. I grabbed her arm and tugged her in, shutting the door quietly behind her.

I led her into the living area, switched on a side lamp and scanned the room for the remote. A tattered beige couch took up most of the space. A cheap wooden cabinet on the far wall littered with crap. A table piled with betting slips, old TV guides and car magazines to the right. An armchair which didn't match anything, to the left. Locating the remote, I flicked on the TV and pointed to the couch. May jumped up onto it and within seconds was fixated with whatever crap was on the screen.

I went back into the kitchen, shut the window and switched on the light. Dirty dishes lay in graying greasy water. A dented saucepan, half full of some gloop, sat on the counter. I opened the refrigerator door. A few leftovers in plastic tubs that had seen better days cluttered the top shelf. Beer bottles, the second. I grabbed one and, with a thump of the lid on the lip of the kitchen table, I heard a satisfying sizzle. I turned off the kitchen light and returned to the living room, taking a long, slow gulp of beer.

I slumped into the armchair facing the front. The windows dressed with a sheer blind. Shadows shivered outside under the streetlight. A couple of people passed by and then there was nothing.

Taking May's lead, I stared at the screen, but my mind was whirring. I was beginning to regret the drinks at the bar. I stood and walked over to the cabinet and riffled through the drawers. Lifting out the telephone directory, I flicked through to the letter B and down to the name 'Brown'.

There were thousands. It would take weeks to call every one.

I turned to the letter 'O'. My finger swept along the page to 'Orange'. Perhaps it was his real name. There were at least a couple of hundred of them in New York. I didn't know where to begin.

Exhaustion and frustration swept over me.

I ran through everything in my head. She said her uncle had dropped her at the store, saying her mom was going to pick her up. The only conclusion I could come to was that something must have happened to her mom. Else, if she was running late, seeing the store was closed, she would have gone to security and, finding out I'd gone to the cops, she would have followed me there.

Perhaps I should have stayed at the precinct house. But if her mom hadn't have turned up, May would have been taken by Family Services. Despite their name, I knew they were anything but.

And there was the question of her 'uncle' dropping her off. No one leaves a kid her age unattended and certainly not in Brooklyn. My teeth clenched at the thought. Why would a man who she said is her 'daddy's friend' do that? And where was her dad in all of this?

I didn't like where my mind was going. I'd seen enough kids in my time who'd had their so-called uncle 'take care of them'. It was why they'd ended up in the foster homes in the first place. But those kids had a glazed look in their eye. If you didn't know better, you'd miss it, but if you'd been around enough of them, you could spot it in a second. It was like the light had been turned off inside of them. Now, I didn't know May from the next kid, but I wasn't convinced either way. What I did know was, I had a four-year-old in my care and I needed to get her home.

I glanced from the TV to May. She was slumped on the couch, fast asleep. Not wanting to wake her, I flicked off the TV and the side lamp and covered her in a blanket.

I hunkered in the dark. The buzz of the refrigerator next door, the only sound in the house. My head throbbed at the temples. Tension burned in my shoulders. I closed my eyes and curled up in the chair.

I don't know if it was the alcohol I had consumed or the sheer exhaustion of the day, but, regardless, I sure as shit should have heard a key rattling in the door.

Instead, all I heard was the distinct click, click of a gun clip loading.

Startled, I opened my eyes.

It was pointed right at me.

6

'Jesus, Harper, you trying to give an old man a cardiac arrest?'

I took a moment as he lowered the gun.

'Hey, TJ, what's up?' I gave him a half-smile.

He released the gun clip and, in the moonlight, relief washed over his face.

'Can't you call, like everyone else?' he said.

Without noticing May curled up under the blanket, he headed straight through to the kitchen. He flicked on the light.

I glanced down at her. Still fast asleep.

I followed TJ into the kitchen and shut the door behind me.

He wore a pair of slacks, smarter than his usual attire. Under his sports jacket, a pressed white shirt pulled tight over his ample stomach.

'Since when did you pick up the phone? And you seriously need to fix that window,' I said. I'd bought him a cellphone way back and he never switched it on, never mind charged it.

'I got all the security I need.' TJ placed the gun on the kitchen counter with a clunk. He patted down the few hairs he had left on his head and removed his jacket.

I'd known TJ since I was a kid. He'd chased me across Brooklyn more times than either he or I could remember. Every time I'd gone missing from some home, he made it his mission to root me out, unearth my hiding places and drag me back. But not without feeding me up first. He'd been a beat cop for most of his career, shunning desk jobs and promotions to keep on the street. That's where the real police work was done, he always said. Knocking on doors, getting to know people, keeping your ear to the ground. The service was his life. And judging by the state of the kitchen, he wasn't taking to retirement too well.

He opened the refrigerator door. He pulled out two beers and passed one to me.

'You been on a date?' I asked.

'No.' He answered a little too quick.

'So why you got lipstick on your cheek?'

TJ wiped the back of his hand across his skin and looked at it. Realizing I had tricked him, he shook his head.

'It's good you've been on a date. Not so good you felt the need to go armed, though.' I settled on one of the kitchen chairs and rested my bottle on the table. 'You going to tell me about her?'

'You going to tell me what you're doing here?' he snapped back.

I cleared my throat and, buying some time, took a sip of my beer and glanced at my watch. 'I'm guessing by the fact it's still early she wasn't the one?'

TJ opened the refrigerator again and grabbed some pastrami and cheese. He was using delay tactics too. He leaned to the left-hand cupboard, took out two plates and placed them onto the table with a clatter. Drowning me out some more, he switched on the radio. The Nets were playing the Knicks and the sound of the crowd chanting belted out into the kitchen.

Not wanting May to wake up until I'd had time to explain everything to TJ, I leaned towards the radio and switched it off.

'What you doing? It's the Nets!' TJ threw his hands in the air.

'You might want to lower the noise a little,' I whispered.

'What are you talking about?' TJ's forehead creased in exasperation.

I nodded to the living room. My stomach flipped a little as I did.

He furrowed his brow further. TJ, pastrami limp between his fingers, opened the kitchen door and stared into the room. The moment his gaze clapped onto a sleeping May, his face dropped.

He turned to me and gave me a look I had seen a hundred times before.

With both my palms in the air, I gave him another half-smile. 'I can explain.'

TJ shut the kitchen door, quietly this time, and threw the pastrami onto the plate. 'This better be good.'

He slumped onto one of the other chairs and pushed the plate of half-prepared food away.

I ran through the day's events, while trying to read the expression on TJ's face. It wasn't hard to decipher.

'You've got to take her back to the precinct – now,' he said.

'I can't.'

'What do you mean, you can't. Jesus, Harper. You got a kid here you don't even know. Probably half the force is out there searching for her and you're keeping her stashed in my house.'

His whisper crept up to more of a bawl.

'Weren't you listening? No one had claimed her. No one was looking for her. I took her to the cops and they were about as interested in her as you are in your pastrami.'

TJ glanced at the plate. His eyes darted everywhere except at me.

I took a moment to make my case. 'Listen, I don't need to tell you how it is—'

'No, you don't.' TJ clenched his teeth and shook his head.

'Harper, if you're saying her mom didn't turn up, she could be dead down some alley for all we—'

The kitchen door opened. We both jumped, startled.

A sleepy-eyed May crept around the door and tentatively stared at TJ.

'Hey, kid. This is my friend TJ.'

May bit her lip and hung on to the door handle.

TJ unclenched his jaw and winked at her.

'Nice to meet you. You got a name?'

May glanced at me. I nodded at her.

'May,' she said, her eyes downcast.

'Well, a real pleasure to meet you. I'm TJ.' He held his hand out and finally she took it. He shook it and gave her a smile. 'You hungry?'

May nodded.

'OK, why don't you go watch some TV and I'll finish up talking to Harper here and she'll bring you in something to eat.'

May scooted back into the living room, and as soon as TJ heard the TV switch on, he leaped to his feet.

'You've got to get her back to the precinct. I'm not kidding. For one thing, you could be charged with abduction.'

'Can't you make some inquiries with your police buddies. See if anyone has called it in?' I said.

'What you want me to say? Oh, don't suppose anyone is missing a kid, are they? No? No, just wondering...'

'I mean on the QT.'

'I'm a decorated cop, for Chrissake.'

'I know.'

The heady mix of Scotch and beer wore off and the reality of the situation kicked in, and fast.

TJ and I both sat in silence for a minute, waiting for the

other to break. We'd played this game for years. Neither of us willing to give in.

TJ stood. He picked up his gun from the kitchen counter. He stepped up on his toes to a top cupboard, pulled out a box, placed the gun in it and returned the box.

I glanced around the kitchen and took in the mess.

A calendar hung on the wall. TJ had marked various days with different colored asterisks.

'Those all your dates? Good for you.'

TJ scowled. 'Changing the subject isn't going to change the facts, Harper.'

Busted.

TJ stared at me, resigned. I'd seen him look at me like that a hundred times before too. 'Get her something to eat, go play cards with her or something, and I'll make a couple of calls,' he finally said.

7

TJ grabbed the landline handset and wandered into the back-yard.

I watched as he paced to and fro, the phone next to his ear.

I opened the refrigerator door and then shut it. I flipped open the icebox and, hallelujah, I found a tub of chocolate-chip ice cream. I grabbed it, riffled through the silverware drawer for a spoon and headed into the living room.

'What you watching?' I asked May. I passed her the tub and spoon.

She shrugged, her attention diverting to the ice cream. I glanced at the TV screen. What she had found was not appropriate for a four-year-old.

I grabbed the remote from her side and flicked it over.

'Mommy don't let me stay up this late.'

'No? Let's see this as an adventure, huh?'

May nodded and shoveled her spoon into the full tub.

After what felt like an age, TJ called me into the kitchen.

'Back in a minute, kid.' I left the living room and shut the door behind me.

'You spoke to someone?' I whispered.

'Yeah. They're going to look into it.' TJ shook his head at me. 'This has got to be your stupidest move yet.'

Like I didn't know it.

'I just didn't want her spending the night with Family Services.'

TJ sighed.

'Hey, at least you can depend on me to screw up,' I said.

TJ looked me up and down. 'Sit. I'll make you something to eat.'

'I'm good.'

'Sit. You're too skinny. You've got to look after yourself more.'

TJ buttered some bread.

'I'm sorry,' I said.

'You're always sorry. When you going to learn to think before you act?' He slapped some pastrami onto the bread.

I nodded and peeled the label off my beer. He was right.

He cut the sandwich in two and slid the plate towards me.

'Eat.' Finally, he gave me a smile.

I'd taken one bite of the sandwich when we both jumped at the noise. Both of us sprang to our feet and hurtled into the living room.

Swirls of vomit covered the rug. The empty ice cream carton lay at May's feet.

'My tummy hurts,' May said.

TJ glanced from May to me, his jaw a little slack. 'You gave her the whole tub?'

The splattered contents soaking into the rug answered the question. I shrugged, regardless.

'Jesus, Harper. You go get her cleaned up. I'll deal with in here.'

I stood frozen to the spot.

'Don't just stand there, go sort her out,' TJ growled.

I picked May up and led her towards the bathroom. I peeled off her soiled dress.

'Let's get you clean, and maybe it's time for bed, huh?'

May, pale, nodded. 'I don't feel well.' A tear slid down her cheek.

'I know, sweetie, I know.' I wiped the tear away with my thumb.

Perhaps a tub of ice cream after fries and Coke and whatever other crap her so-called uncle had fed her that day wasn't the brightest idea.

I filled the tub and as soon as it was deep enough I picked her up and placed her in it.

'Here, use this.' I passed her a bar of soap from the basin.

'Mommy does it.'

My heart skipped a beat. I crouched at the side of the bath-tub, took the soap from her, dipped it in the water and washed her down.

Toweling her dry, I led her to the spare room. I rooted through a closet and found an old Nets T-shirt, dressed her in it and tucked her into bed.

'You feel a little better?' I asked.

May nodded and lay her head on the pillow.

'You get some sleep, and tomorrow we'll take you home.'

May closed her eyes and curled into Mickey.

I watched as her chest rose and fell and I was sure she was asleep.

I had promised to take this kid home and I had no idea where that was. All I could hope for right now was TJ's contact would soon be able to shed some light on this crazy situation.

As if on cue, I heard a car outside come to a stop. A moment later came a rap on the door.

I waited in the bedroom for TJ to answer. But as soon as I heard the other voice, my heart sank to the floor.

8

I stayed in the bedroom until I heard the door latch click to. Sullen, I walked down the corridor into the living area. I tried to adopt my best, breezy 'couldn't give a crap' look, but I knew the reality was I simply looked like crap.

I glanced through the front window. A patrol car parked up outside.

The voices wandered into the kitchen. The distinct low rumble of TJ's voice followed by Reggie's.

Reggie being my ex.

I walked in. The room went silent.

'Don't stop on my account,' I said.

Out the corner of my eye, I noticed Reggie raise his eyebrows at me. I avoided looking at him and instead stared straight at TJ.

'Seriously?' I said, raising my own eyebrows at TJ.

TJ shrugged.

'Of all the people you could have called, you chose him?'

'Nice to see you too, Harper,' Reggie said. His deep baritone voice made my stomach flip. *Damn.*

I placed my palm up in Reggie's direction to shush him. I threw May's vomit-covered dress into the kitchen corner and stood with my hands on my hips staring at TJ.

'What, you think I have a list of cops on speed dial that'll find out if you've abducted a kid or not,' TJ said.

I shook my head. I didn't know how to answer that.

'You need to get her to the precinct now.' Reggie clearly wasn't going to be hushed.

'So, you found her mom then, huh?' I stared at Reggie. It took all my strength not to allow memories to come flooding back.

He was six five, appoximately two hundred and thirty pounds, and most of that muscle. His blue uniform stretched across his body. His skin, the color of macadamia, was smooth and shiny. A tiny pale scar on his neck from a shaving cut stood out against the dark sheen.

I'd kissed that scar a thousand times.

'No. But if she's back at the precinct we could ask her the right questions and find her mom.'

'Back at the precinct? Are you serious? I took her to the precinct and you know what the asshole told me? Family Services.'

'You want to run through exactly what happened?' Reggie's voice was calm.

How could he be so damned cool? We hadn't seen each other in eight months and he was sat there like snow wouldn't melt on him.

To be honest, I didn't want to tell him anything. But he was a cop and right now I had a kid stashed in a room without an idea what the hell I was going to do. Any lead would be helpful at this point. My head throbbed and all I wanted was my own bed and this day to be over.

I ran through everything I could recall from the store to the precinct house.

'Hold on, hold on,' Reggie said, as I was midstream. A smirk cracked on his face. 'Let me get this straight, you were buying a dress?'

I looked from him to TJ, who was also trying not to smile.

I threw my hands up in the air.

'Are you kidding me right now? That's the part of the story you're focusing on?' Blood flushed to my cheeks.

Reggie laughed. 'Come on, you've got to admit it's funny, right?' He opened up his palm as if to invite me to join him in the joke. 'Right?' He glanced at TJ for backup.

TJ nodded and grinned.

'You want me to tell you what happened or not?' I was not amused.

Reggie covered his smirk with his hand and tried to compose himself. I wanted to slap him.

Reggie stared at my chest.

'Really? You want to hit on me now?' I snapped.

'Hell no. I was wondering what that was, that's all.' He gaped at my T-shirt. 'And what in Christ's name is that smell?' Reggie winced and held his hand up to his nose.

I glanced down. A spray of vomit had soaked into the fabric of my top.

Great. Just great.

Of all the times to see my ex, I had to have spew on me.

'Listen, why don't we all calm down.' TJ motioned for me to sit.

Ignoring them both, I stripped off my T-shirt and flung it to the floor. I stood against the kitchen counter in my jeans and bra and stared at Reggie.

It was good to see him squirm for once.

Reggie's eyes looked everywhere except at me. *Gotcha, smart-ass.*

Finding my ground, I attempted to plead my case. 'So, no one has reported her missing and you two don't find that odd?'

'No one is saying—' TJ began.

'No one is saying it isn't odd, Harp, we're saying you can't harbor a young kid here like a fugitive,' Reggie said.

I threw my hands up in exasperation. Reggie couldn't help but look at me now.

'She is not going to Family Services,' I said. I glared at them both.

'I get you're looking out—' Reggie said, his voice calm and controlled.

'You don't get shit. You never did.'

'Whoa, whoa, time out, guys.' TJ spread his arms like a wrestling referee.

'What I get…' Reggie said, a little more rage in his voice, '…is you brought a kid to a cop's house.'

'Retired cop,' I corrected.

'Retired cop's house. And involved another cop,' Reggie completed.

'I never asked you to come here.'

TJ rubbed his face in his hands. It was not like it was the first time he had seen us fight.

Reggie eyeballed me for a minute. I watched his pecs rise and fall under his uniform as he tried to control his anger.

'Did you find anything out or not?' I asked.

Reggie's Adam's apple bobbed up and down. 'There have been no reports of a missing kid that fits this description or name.'

'So?'

'So yes, I agree something isn't right, but keeping her here—'

'Keeping her here means she doesn't have to endure a night in a scary place with people she doesn't know,' I said.

'She doesn't know you, Harper.' Reggie's voice grew louder with each word.

'She trusts me,' I said lamely.

Reggie shook his head.

I kept my voice low. 'All I'm asking is for you to listen out for any information on her and maybe speak to the jerk-off security guy and see if he'll show you the camera footage from earlier.'

'So, you are asking something from me?' Reggie glared at me, took a deep breath in and looked towards TJ.

TJ raised his shoulders in a shrug.

Reggie's jawline tensed. His eyes narrowed and he pointed his finger in my direction. 'OK. First thing tomorrow, I'll go see if there's anything the cameras picked up, but after that, I'm telling you, that kid needs to go to the precinct. You hear me?'

'Sure,' I said.

'I mean it, Harper.' He prodded his finger at every word. 'If nothing crops up, I'm taking her straight in and you can explain to them why the hell you took the girl.'

9

I awoke to a sharp shrieking in my head. I curled up one way and the other. A wool blanket half on and half off me.

The wailing in my skull wasn't just the bad night's sleep on top of the alcohol I had consumed. Instead, I soon realized it was the yelling and squawking of *Woody Woodpecker* coming from the direction of the television.

Rolling back over, I opened my eyes. May was cross-legged in front of the TV watching a cartoon at what seemed like full volume.

I had, for the briefest moment, forgotten all about yesterday and now, everything flooded back in.

'Can you turn it down a bit, kid,' I murmured.

May sat, oblivious.

Lifting myself up from the couch, I wrapped the blanket over my shoulders. I stepped into the kitchen and shut the door. The screech and scream continued, but at least the door muffled it a little.

What time was it? I put the kettle on the stove and glanced at my watch.

I needed coffee. A gallon of it. Reggie's threat of hauling us into the cops weighed heavy on my chest.

I slumped in a chair, leaned my arms on the table and rested my head down on them, closing my eyes once again.

'Whatchadoing?'

I squinted one eye open.

May stood in front of me in TJ's Nets T-shirt.

Good question. What was I doing? The last twenty-four hours had me asking the same thing.

I leaned back in the chair and looked at her.

'You always up this early?' I asked.

''S'not early.'

I shrugged.

'You seen TJ?'

'He went out.'

I nodded. 'You feeling better?'

'I'm hungry.'

Clearly, she was better.

'Why don't I fix myself some coffee and I'll bring something in to you.'

May didn't take the hint. Instead, she clambered up onto one of the kitchen chairs and perched there. Waiting.

I took a deep breath in and scratched my head. Well, my attempt at food last night didn't go so well. But maybe I could find something a little more suitable.

I opened the refrigerator. Not much happening there.

I flipped open TJ's breadbox. *Amen.* There were still some slices.

Toast. I could do toast.

I opened the grill, flicked on the ignition, turned up the gas and placed the bread under the heat.

Now I could make my coffee.

'When am I going home?'

I was grateful I had my back to May when she spoke. I stirred and poured the coffee into the cup, added a couple of sugars and took a sip before I replied.

'Here, let me show you something.' I slid open one of the kitchen drawers and picked out a deck of cards.

I shuffled the deck and watched May's face.

I fanned them out.

'OK, pick one, but don't show me.'

May plucked out a card and pressed it to her chest.

'You get a good look at it?'

May nodded.

'Now pop it back in the deck. Anywhere you want it to go.'

May did as she was told. I shuffled them again and watched her eyes widen at the speed of my hands.

'Right, let's see if we can find that card of yours.' I turned each one over and shook my head. May giggled. As soon as I flipped over the Queen of Hearts and passed it to her, she gasped.

'Your card, m'lady.'

May's mouth opened in a perfect 'O'.

If there was ever a way to distract a kid, it was with magic. I'd spent many a night huddled under the freeway, too frightened to go back to whichever home they had placed me in that month. Instead, I'd hang out with the street hobos. Sit by the fire at night, listening to their stories and watching Marvin do some magic tricks. Everybody assumes because you're sleeping out on the streets, you're no good for anything. But Marvin was smart, and more than street-smart. He'd been some college professor or something. When his wife had been killed in a car accident, he turned to the bottle and that was that. He'd show me how to do these tricks and soon enough I was using my sleight of hand to work the street corners for tourists on Coney

Island, earning myself and him some food for the night, before TJ would hunt me down and take me back to the home.

'Again!' May squealed.

I shuffled the deck. As I plucked a card out from behind her ear, a screech screamed in the kitchen, louder than any *Woody Woodpecker* cartoon.

The smoke alarm.

I had forgotten about the toast. Grabbing a cloth, I pulled out the grill tray. Smoke billowed out from the charred bread.

Opening the back door and the window, I fanned the smoke towards the direction of the yard. I turned to see May bawling her eyes out. Her hands clamped over her ears.

The kitchen door swung open. TJ ran in, grocery bag and newspaper in his hand.

'What on earth are you doing?' He stared at the charred toast. Me, dressed only in bra, panties and blanket, and to May who was sobbing.

'Breakfast?' I shrugged.

Reggie placed his tall macchiato into the cup rest and leaned back into his car seat. His shoulder blades burned. Waiting for the lights to turn green, he cricked his neck. Yawning, he released the brake and pressed on the gas. The New York traffic shunted along painfully slow. The car smelled sour. The mix of drunken perps, doped-up gangbangers and whatever other trash had been hauled in the car overnight.

Reggie had barely slept last night after his shift. Feeling pumped from his run-in with Harper, he had changed into his gym kit and pressed a few weights. Something, anything, to get the knots to undo. By the time he'd crashed at home, his muscles may have burned, but he was no less pent up than when he had first arrived.

The car shifted along Gerritsen Avenue. He listened to the chatter on the police radio. A robbery near Borough Park, a crash on the I-278, but nothing regarding a missing girl.

He tensed and relaxed his fingers around the steering wheel. The events of last night played over and over in his head. He should have known when TJ called, the moment Harper's name was mentioned, the idea of sleep was going to evade him.

Who finds a kid and decides to take them home? No, not even take them home, but to a retired cop's home. Sure, he knew why she'd done it. Of course he did. But really?

After he had left TJ's, he had double-checked the logs to see no one had called it in. There wasn't a single thing about a kid being reported missing. How was it possible? Someone must have noticed her gone?

He'd checked all the logs again this morning. Nothing.

Reggie worked through Harper's story in his head one more time.

Indicating left, he swung down Avenue U towards the stores.

He pulled up. Anxious, he glanced towards his radio. He should call in his location. Requesting a brief personal half-hour, he got out of the car, adjusted his hat and made his way to the entrance.

The place heaved with pedestrians. Reggie scanned the directory board for the security-booth location. Fourth floor. He strode up to the elevator and waited for it to descend. The doors slid open. He politely smiled to a couple of women who exited. He stepped in, pressed the button and gazed out of the glass doors as the car ascended.

Reggie glanced around and spotted the booth over in the far right-hand corner. Passing La Vida Loca on the way, Reggie smirked to himself at the thought of Harper buying a dress. Not once in the three years they had been dating had he ever seen her wearing one.

Reggie approached the kiosk.

A short, heavyset guy dressed in a uniform, his shirt half tucked into his pants, stared at a bank of screens. Half a burrito in one hand, his radio in the other.

'Excuse me, sir,' Reggie said.

The security guy jumped. The radio clattered to the floor.

'Sorry. Hey. What can I do for you, officer?' Terence stood. He threw his burrito on the side, straightened his shirt and tucked it into his pants. He dragged his forearm across his mouth to clear the chilli sauce from his lips.

Reggie waited until he had finished.

'Say, I was wondering if you record what goes on, on those screens.' Reggie indicated to them with his hand.

Terence turned back to them. 'Well, yeah, for twenty-four hours. Then they're wiped clean. Something I should know about?'

'You remember a woman coming to the booth with a lost kid yesterday?'

'You mean that hot chick with the …' He gesticulated her ample breasts with his hands.

Reggie raised an eyebrow. 'Yeah, her.' He cleared his throat.

'Sure. I told her to come see you boys. Wait, hold on – she did, didn't she?'

'Yeah. We're following up on something. Can I see your footage from yesterday?'

Terence shrugged. 'Sure. What time?'

Harper had said the store was closing when she found the girl. 'What time does La Vida Loca shut?' Reggie tilted his head in the store's direction.

'Six.'

'Give me what you've got around then.'

Terence nodded. 'You want the camera over there, the one pointing at the store?' He indicated towards the ceiling. A black circular camera embedded in the wall.

Reggie followed his hand and peered across at its point of view.

'Yeah. Let's start there.'

Terence shifted to the booth door and opened it wide. Reggie entered. Empty food cartons spilled out of the trash can. A well-thumbed porn magazine lay open on the bottom shelf. Reggie shook his head.

Terence leaned over and tapped on the keyboard.

The screen on Reggie's left flickered and buzzed awake. The image focused on the La Vida Loca entrance.

'You can rewind and fast-forward using this.' Terence pointed at a console in front of him.

Reggie picked it up and rewound the footage. He slowed as he noticed Harper take the little girl from the store and walk in the direction of the security booth.

Pressing the console indicator left, he rewound some more and slowed it down. Harper entered the store. Reggie took a deep breath and clicked the instrument again.

Reggie recalled Harper saying she had been to the store twice. Once, approximately an hour earlier, when she had first set eyes on the kid and thought nothing of it.

Reggie scrolled back. He pressed pause. The footage came to a stop. Reggie leaned forward towards the screen. Terence did the same. Reggie felt Terence's breath on his neck.

'Want to give me a little room?' Reggie said.

'Yeah. Sorry.' Terence took a step back.

Reggie pressed play and peered at the screen.

'So, I was going to be a cop some time back,' Terence started.

'Oh yeah?' Reggie said, distracted.

Reggie watched a figure hold a little girl's hand. He crouched beside her, pointed towards the store entrance and patted the little girl on the back. Reggie squinted at the screen. Whoever it was wore a plain black baseball cap pulled low over their eyes. Their back to the camera. Dressed in chinos and a khaki button-up casual jacket.

Oblivious, Terence continued, 'Yeah, went the whole nine yards, and fell at the physical. Only by a little but...'

Reggie ignored him. He leaned closer to the screen.

The little girl glanced up. The person nodded. The little girl walked towards the entrance of the store. The person adjusted their hat, pulled it down and walked away.

'I thought about, y'know, retrying, lose a couple of pounds, press a few weights... Say, you must work out a lot. You're pretty ripped.'

Reggie swiveled in the chair. 'You hitting on me?'

'No! I meant—'

'I'm kidding with you, man,' Reggie said.

His attention turned back to the screen. His brow crumpled. He rewound the footage and replayed it. It was difficult to make out any distinguishing features.

'Can you play me some other cameras at this exact time?' Reggie pointed to the time code on the screen.

'You want to follow them?'

Reggie nodded.

Terence leaned over, the smell of chilli sauce on his breath. He tapped on the keyboard and stood back up.

Staring at the footage, they both followed the figure as it entered the elevator. Terence switched to the next camera on the first floor. Still with their head low, hat pulled low, the person walked out of the entrance without looking behind. Like they knew the cameras were there.

What the hell?

'Donut?' Terence asked. He shoved a box under Reggie's nose.

Distracted, Reggie shook his head.

Why would someone leave a little girl in a store and walk away?

TJ wafted the smoke out of the back door with the newspaper in his hand. When it had cleared, he threw the paper down on the table and shook his head.

He gestured to the paper and to May.

'There's nothing in there.'

May peeled her hands away from her ears and wiped her cheeks. Her face still startled by the alarm.

'You OK, kid?' I asked.

May nodded.

Anxious, I checked the time and wondered how long it would take Reggie to check the security footage.

TJ looked at May dressed in his old T-shirt. 'We need to get her cleaned up, in case, you know—'

He didn't finish the sentence, realizing I didn't want to hear him spell it out to me. It was clear neither of us was hopeful her mom was going to materialize. Which left only one option.

TJ stooped over and picked up her vomit-stained dress and the T-shirt I had thrown in the corner last night.

'You got any other laundry?' he asked me.

I shook my head, too distracted by the idea of having to hand her over to the authorities.

'You not got any dirty tissues in these pockets, have you,

kid? I don't want to be putting my fingers into any snot rags,'
TJ teased May.

May giggled and shook her head.

TJ opened up the washing machine. He dipped his hand into
the dress pockets in case.

'I thought you said there was no tiss—'

TJ tugged out a piece of paper and unfolded it.

'What the …?'

I leaned over to look.

Without a word, he passed me the note. It was on plain white
paper, approximately five by eight. It had been folded in two.
The top edge serrated as though it had been torn from a pad.

I turned the paper over. The other side, blank.

'Who the hell wrote that?' TJ said.

I shook my head.

My thoughts exactly.

IO

Written in black ink were two words.

I'm sorry.

We stared at the note and at each other.

Aware May was in the room, TJ and I said nothing more.

'I'm hungry,' May said, breaking the silence.

TJ gave me a knowing look and walked to the kitchen table. He riffled in the grocery bag.

'You like eggs, May?'

May nodded.

TJ raised his eyebrows at me and placed the note to the side. 'How about I scramble up some eggs and toast, Harper goes and gets dressed –' he looked pointedly at me, stood in my bra and a blanket wrapped over my shoulders, '– and then –' TJ dipped his hand back into the bag and pulled out a box of wax crayons and paper. 'You can do some drawing if you like.'

May's eyes widened. She took the crayons from TJ.

'What do you say?'

May looked up at TJ. 'Thank you.'

My heart ached.

'Good girl.' He rubbed the top of her head.

The fall sunshine streamed through the kitchen window. I grabbed my cellphone, flicked open the camera app and took a shot of May.

TJ nodded at me to go and get dressed. We didn't want to discuss what we had found in front of her.

I washed and whipped into TJ's bedroom, grabbed another of his T-shirts and threw on my jeans.

When I got back to the kitchen, TJ was serving up breakfast. May hummed some nonsense to herself and crouched over a piece of paper with a thick red crayon in her hand.

'What you drawing, kid?' I leaned over her shoulder.

'My house.'

TJ turned from the stove and glanced across at the picture.

It was hardly telling. A big box, with a roof, but what was curious was the squiggle next to it.

'What's that?' I pointed at it.

'A boat.'

'A boat, huh.' I raised my eyebrows in TJ's direction.

'So you live by the sea?'

'Uh-huh.'

'You live in Coney Island?' I asked.

'Beach,' May said.

If she lived by the beach, perhaps she was from Coney Island. It wasn't too far from the store I had found her in. That would make sense. It wasn't an address, but it was something at least.

As soon as May had finished her eggs, I set her up in the living room. I shifted the car magazines off the side table, brushed away the dust and laid out the paper and crayons.

'Why don't you draw something else while me and TJ clear up in the kitchen.'

With May occupied, I shut the door behind me and grabbed the note. TJ and I sat at the table staring at it.

'What the hell does "I'm sorry" even mean?' I asked. I wasn't expecting an answer, but I hoped saying it out aloud would enlighten us.

'You think her uncle wrote it?' TJ said.

I shrugged. 'You think this guy, this uncle, did do something to her?' I asked him.

'May or the mom?'

I clenched my jaw. 'Both,' I whispered.

TJ tilted back in his chair. He stared out of the window, his eyebrows knitted together in concentration.

The kitchen door opened. May wafted a piece of paper in her hand in our direction.

'What you got there?' I took the picture from her and held it up. 'A car. You do that?'

TJ looked at May and grinned. 'That's my gal.'

I smiled at both of them and shook my head.

'Hey kid, listen. You know we're looking for your mom, right?' I said.

May's face dropped a little and nodded.

'You remember the last time you saw her?'

TJ shifted in his chair.

May closed her eyes tight for a second.

'Two sleeps ago.'

Two? That meant she hadn't seen her for a day before I found her.

'Was your mommy OK when you saw her? She wasn't sick or anything?'

May shook her head and twisted her mouth. 'She was crying.'

Hairs rose on the back of my arms. My mouth went dry. I took another sip of my coffee.

'You know why she was crying?' TJ asked, seeing I was faltering.

May didn't answer. She looked down at her feet. Her bottom lip jutted out.

'You remember where you slept the night before last?'

May scrunched one of her eyes shut this time. 'In a big room, with a TV and refrigerator and I had pizza.'

'So, like a motel?' I shot a look from May to TJ.

May shrugged.

I really didn't like this sick feeling I was getting.

'And it was just you and your Uncle Orange?' TJ asked.

May nodded and glanced towards the living room, eager to get back to her crayons.

'Why don't you go draw me another car – a blue one this time – and, after, we can play cards?' TJ said.

May's head jolted up. 'Magic?' she screeched in my direction.

'Yeah, I think we can do that.' I winked at her.

We all headed into the living room.

'You ever seen this trick?' TJ said. He pulled out a nickel, placed the paper on top and crayoned over it.

May watched in amazement as the picture of Jefferson appeared.

'You know that's me on the coin, don't you, kid?' TJ said.

May looked at TJ and the coin in awe.

I must have been on my twentieth card trick by the time we heard Reggie's Cruiser pull up. I wasn't sure if it was relief to get a break from the one-woman magic show, or the fact he would hopefully have some more information to help us out. I was up and at the door before he had opened the gate.

'Harper.' Reggie nodded at me and walked through the front door.

May picked up some of the cards and attempted to shuffle them. The deck, too big for her little fingers, fluttered to the floor.

'Well, you must be Little Miss May,' Reggie said. He gave her a big grin.

He's got a good smile, I'll give him that.

May offered a shy smile back.

'I'm Reggie,' he said and crouched down.

'Are you a police officer?'

'Yes, I am, young lady.'

'Am I in trouble?' May looked from Reggie to me.

'No. Nothing like that. These are my friends and I thought I'd come say hi. I'm still working, so I won't keep them long.'

Reggie stood and motioned to us towards the kitchen. Taking the hint, I picked up the fallen cards, placed them into a deck and passed them to May.

'Why don't you keep on trying. I'm going to have a quick word with Reggie.'

May did as she was told. She clambered up onto the couch with the cards grasped into her tiny hands.

The three of us all took a seat around the kitchen table.

Before Reggie spoke, I slid the note across to him.

'We found this in one of her pockets.' I kept my voice low so May couldn't hear.

Reggie didn't pick it up. He stared at it, his brow furrowed. He looked from me to TJ.

'Hmmm,' he said almost to himself. 'Well, there's been nothing on the radio, but I did get to see the security footage.'

TJ and I leaned in, expectant, and listened to Reggie explain what he had seen.

'Why would you drop a kid somewhere where's there's clearly cameras?' TJ asked, once Reggie had finished.

Reggie shrugged. 'I don't know, but it was obvious he knew where they were. He kept his head down all the time.'

'But to drop her in such a public place?' I added.

'Guess no one would suspect anything. Everyone's too busy doing their own thing,' Reggie said.

I shrugged. 'She said the last time she saw her mom, she was crying.'

'She say that?' Reggie asked.

We both nodded.

'Are you really going to take her in?'

He clenched his jaw and took a deep breath out.

Before he could reply, May skipped through the door.

'I drawed you a picture.'

May passed Reggie the sheet of paper dangling in her hand.

'Look at that!'

May had crayoned a giant-sized stick man. His head a trace of the coin.

'Is that me?' Reggie asked.

May nodded and grinned.

'That's some real talent you got there, girl.' He said.

I stared at it for a second. Something gnawed away at the back of my mind.

'I look pretty handsome in the picture too, don't you think?' Reggie said to me. He looked in my direction.

My mind distracted, I scrambled to my feet, shot into the living room and grabbed one of May's wax crayons.

I picked up the 'I'm sorry' note and held it up to the light.

'What the hell you doing, there could be fingerprints on that?' Reggie barked.

Ignoring him, I laid it on the table and rubbed the crayon

back and forth over the whole piece of paper. Bringing it close up, I was sure I could make something out. I crayoned a little harder.

I leaned back and looked up at Reggie and TJ with a grin.

Reggie took the paper from my fingers, his eyes widened in surprise. He passed the note to TJ.

'Well, I never,' TJ said.

11

There, underneath the crayon were lines of numbers and letters. Faint, but legible.

Along the top read: SD 3334769-08/30.

Below it, what looked like: AE-017643219763-05/21. Some of the ink covered the figures, so the threes could have been eights.

Then another set of numbers written from the top left towards the bottom right. As though someone may have jotted the figures down at a different point. They read: 09/25-0716 DFW0940.

We leaned in and squinted at them.

'Phone number?' TJ said.

Reggie shook his head and took the note back from TJ. 'No. Too many digits.'

'Maybe not the top one?' I said.

Aware May was still in the room, no one said another word, but we knew what the other was thinking.

'You know how to play Snap?' TJ asked her.

May shrugged.

'Let's see if I can teach you.'

TJ led May into the living room.

'Are those dates?' I pointed to the figures with slashes.

Reggie shrugged. 'Perhaps. The top one would make it nearly four weeks ago.'

'And the twenty-fifth, would make it three days ago. May said she hadn't seen her mom for two nights.'

Reggie and I looked at each other for a moment.

I picked up my cellphone.

'You want me to call?' Reggie asked me.

I stared at the top number and took a moment.

'No, I'll do it.' I stood, picked up the note and opened the back door. The chill from outside blew in. I braced myself and paced the backyard.

I glanced back into the kitchen. Reggie stayed sat at the table, looking out at me. I turned away and dialed the number.

My body tensed the second I heard a dial tone. *So it was a phone number.*

I pressed the phone to my ear, listening to the persistent ring. Not even a voicemail kicked in.

'Dammit,' I whispered to myself.

I turned to face the kitchen window. I shook my head at Reggie and shrugged a little. I waited a couple of rings longer and headed back into the house.

'It rang out.'

I put my cellphone and the note back on the table and rubbed my arms for warmth.

Reggie frowned. He glanced at his watch and stood. 'Look, I've got to head back out, I've still got a couple more hours on my shift. Why don't I see if I can get a trace on the number and get an address.'

I nodded, distracted, and Reggie made to leave.

'Reggie—'

He stopped and turned back.

I gave him a little smile. 'Thanks.'

Reggie nodded and left.

★

May, TJ and I spent the afternoon playing cards while we waited to hear back from Reggie. Although I was keen to find out what the next step was, I was relieved she was here with us, rather than in some home with kids twice her age and twice their wits, ready to pounce. I sure as hell knew about that. I may have grown up in the system, but it still took some skill to try and beat it, before it beat you.

Not once since I was a kid had I ever tried to understand why I'd been left in care. To ask the question was futile. I figured I was simply another unwanted statistic. A result of a one-night stand in the back of a Chevy with a stranger who probably never knew I existed, never mind gave me another thought.

It was getting dark by the time Reggie called. He had finished his shift and asked me to meet him outside Ocean Parkway subway station. I left TJ to occupy May, grabbed my jacket and headed straight there.

Reggie was already waiting for me by the time I had arrived. He was dressed in his dark blue jeans, gray sweater and a fitted leather jacket. Damn, he looked good.

'You got an address?'

Reggie nodded.

'I looked it up before I came out. I think it's a wreckers' yard or something.'

I creased my face and shook my head, confused.

We walked a couple of blocks. Reggie pulled out the piece of paper he had handwritten the address and number on. He double-checked the details.

'Along here.' He pointed.

He was right, it was some sort of boat scrapyard. Chain-link fencing edged the exterior. Chunks of rusting metal in various piles in one corner, a two-story brick building in another.

I thought back to the picture May had drawn with the boat. The yard backed straight onto the water. Although it wasn't what I was expecting, I was a little optimistic.

'Lights are on,' I said, and pointed up to the building's second floor.

We followed the fencing around to the entrance. The gates were closed, a heavy iron chain wrapped around them. A padlock securing them together. I rattled it to see how much it would give.

'There any sort of intercom?' I said.

Reggie peered around and shook his head.

'Give me a boost.' I grabbed onto the chain-link fence and heaved my left leg up, placing my toes into one of the holes.

'What? No. Jeez, Harper, I'm a cop!'

I scowled at him in frustration. I scrambled my right leg up to get a hold. The fence clattered with my weight.

'Stop!' Reggie hissed. 'Let's try the number again first.'

'Hey!' A loud male voice from the far corner hollered over. A security light flooded the area. Startled, I jumped down with a thud.

Reggie shot me a look.

'What you think you doing?' The guy had an accent. He was dressed in navy overalls with a black hooded sweatshirt underneath.

'Sorry, man.' Reggie put his hands up. 'We were trying to—'

'You know this girl?' I cut in and held up the photo of May on my phone.

The guy came closer. He was late fifties, silver streaks in his black hair, salt-and-pepper whiskers on his face. His skin smudged with oil. He stared at Reggie a moment longer before switching his vision to my cellphone.

He frowned. 'I don't know no girl.'

I glanced at Reggie to see if he noticed any tells.

'Look, I'm a police officer. We've found a girl and she had this number in her pocket. Reggie showed him the piece of paper with his number and address on.

'That's my number, but I don't know no girl.'

'You live here alone?' Reggie pointed up to the lit building.

'No, I live with my wife.'

Reggie paused. 'Think we could speak to her?'

The man eyeballed Reggie and gave a sharp nod. He tugged at something in his pocket and pulled out a key. He unlocked the padlock and chain. We stepped through the gates and waited whilst he secured it.

'You have to be careful. They steal anything. Animals.' The man threw his hands up in the air as if we knew who 'they' were.

We walked to the back of the building and entered through a steel door leading to some concrete steps.

'Bajram,' he said at the top of the steps. He offered his oil-stained hand out to Reggie and me.

As soon as we entered the living area, the warmth hit me. The smell of baking filled my nostrils.

'Smells good,' I said.

'That's my wife. She's the cook.'

He led us into the kitchen.

'Rosa, these peoples want to speak to you.'

A woman, mid-forties, auburn hair loosely tied up in a bun, turned and looked startled at us as we hovered in her kitchen. Both Reggie and I gave her a disarming smile.

'We're sorry to bother you—' Reggie's eyes scanned across

at the array of food she was cooking. 'Looks incredible.' He pointed at a plate. 'That moussaka?'

'Tave kosi. You want to try?' she offered.

'No, no, sorry, ma'am. We wanted to ask you a quick question and then we'll get out of your way.'

Rosa nodded, waiting.

I cleared my throat and stepped forward, my phone at the ready.

'You ever seen this girl before?'

Bajram sidled up to his wife and peered at the photo. Rosa shook her head and squinted at it.

'No.'

'You sure?' Reggie asked.

She nodded.

Reggie and I both looked at each other, our shoulders slumping a little.

'You know anyone by the name of Brown?' I asked.

Rosa and Bajram exchanged glances and frowned at each other. They shook their heads at me.

'You sure?' I persisted.

Bajram opened up his palms and shook his head again. 'Brown? No.'

I stared at him for a beat.

Reggie cleared his throat. 'Sorry to have troubled you. Thank you for your time.' We both backed out of the kitchen.

Bajram followed us out. 'No trouble.' He walked us across the yard, the lock clanking as he wrapped it around the gate.

Reggie and I headed in the direction of the subway.

'Now what?' I said to Reggie.

He paused a moment and glanced out to the bay. 'You hungry?'

★

We jumped on the subway and headed towards Joe and Albi's pizza restaurant.

Collecting our order, we walked towards TJ's with enough takeout for the four of us.

It hit me how familiar this felt. Reggie and I picking up food, heading towards TJ's. How many nights had we done this before? Reggie's arm brushed against mine.

I don't know if it was the feeling we had headed into a dead end with May, or what could have been with Reggie, but there was a tightness in my chest that made it hard to breathe.

We walked along in silence. Both of our minds occupied.

We turned onto TJ's block.

I pulled myself out of the black fog. 'If the number isn't a phone number, what else could it be?'

Reggie took a breath and furrowed his brow. 'I don't know. Passwords. Safety-deposit numbers – it could be anything. It could have been his number, but one of his clients wrote it down.'

I shrugged, defeated. 'But she drew a boat and said she lived by the beach. It made sense we were in the right place.'

'You think they were lying?' Reggie asked.

'No, I don't. I just don't get it.'

I tried to ignore the sinking pit in my stomach. Whatever hunger I had felt a short while ago dissipated as quickly as my optimism had.

As we walked through the gate into TJ's front yard, Reggie stopped and turned to me.

'I think we've exhausted all our options, Harp. We've got to take her in.'

I stared at him, incredulous.

'I could lose my badge over this,' he said, pleading.

'Your badge? That's what you're worried about?' I couldn't

help but let my voice escalate. 'What about May? You thought about that? You really think you could sleep at night, knowing you let May fall into the system after what we think has happened to her?'

'We don't know what has happened to her?'

'Exactly,' I hissed.

Reggie shook his head.

'What?' I opened up my palms and shrugged.

'Don't you think this situation is ironic, considering?' Reggie said.

I frowned, taking a beat to understand what he meant.

I examined his face. Even in the low evening light, I detected a little hurt. We locked eyes for a moment.

The realization dawned on me: our breakup and the reasons behind it.

Seeing what he had said had landed, Reggie turned and entered the house.

Reluctant, I followed him in.

'You had a party?' I asked TJ, scanning the floor.

TJ looked around. Playing cards, open magazines with pages torn out and new drawings lay scattered on the carpet.

May pressed something from one of the magazines onto a piece of paper with her fist, glue trickling down her arm.

'Just having a little bit of fun,' TJ said.

'Harper! Look what I did.' May held up a piece of paper in my direction.

I took the collage of sorts from her to inspect closer.

'Impressive,' I said.

TJ stood up from the couch. 'Any luck?' He followed the smell of pizza into the kitchen.

We filled him in on what we'd found, or not found, more to the point.

'I told her, we've got to take her in. This has gone on too long,' Reggie said.

I couldn't look at either of them.

My cellphone beeped in my pocket. I slipped it out and read the text. It was from my editor, Richard.

The Bronx Zoo. 9 a.m.
Contact Judy Oppenheimer. Thanks.

I had completely forgotten about that.

'Everything OK?' TJ asked.

'Yeah, I ...' My mind whirred fast. 'Hey, May, come get some pizza,' I shouted through to the living room.

May's footsteps thumped as she ran into the kitchen. She sounded more like a horse bolting than a little girl.

TJ passed her a plate with a slice of margherita on.

'Thank you,' she said.

I glanced at my text again and looked up at May. 'Hey, you want to go to the zoo tomorrow?'

May gasped in her usual wondrous way. 'The zoo?'

'Harper!' Reggie snapped at me.

I ignored him and smiled at May.

'Yeah, the zoo.'

'Yeah!' May screeched. Her grin stretched from ear to ear as she jumped up and down.

Reggie shook his head and shot me a warning look.

'What?' I opened my arms up in a shrug. 'C'mon, you can't deny her a trip to the zoo ...'

12

A small table lamp illuminated the room. A woman dressed in a peach satin blouse and knee-length skirt crossed her legs. She offered the man opposite a kind smile.

The windowless room was painted a soft beige. A few insipid pictures dressed the walls. But other than a low glass table sat between the two chairs, the room was sparse.

The heavyset man shifted in his seat, tugged on the knees of his pants and cleared his throat.

'What frightens you the most?' she asked him, her voice soft.

She heard him take a deep breath in and noticed his knuckles tighten a little as they pressed on the arms of the chair.

'My wife discovering who I really am.'

The woman nodded. 'Do you think she suspects?'

The man stared at her, incredulous. 'Suspects? Are you kidding me? If she had any inkling of what I've done, she wouldn't be able to look at me. My life would be over.'

'Are you ashamed of yourself?'

The man's head sagged. His eyes closed. 'Yes,' he said in almost a whisper.

'What is it you are ashamed of?'

The man looked to his feet.

'Everyone sees me as this successful man, a wonderful

marriage, three incredible children. But they don't know me at all.'

'Are you able to tell me what the worst thing is you have done?'

He shook his head. A tear rolled down his cheek.

'Take your time.' The woman held her breath for a moment.

'My wife …' he gripped the sides of the chair, '…she was away with the kids at her mom's.' He raised his head and looked at the woman.

'Go on.'

'I don't even remember his name. I got his number off some internet site. He came over and we …' His voice trailed off. The man looked at her now. 'I'm a monster, aren't I?'

She offered him another smile. 'You're misguided. But you're here and that is the first step.'

The man nodded to himself. His eyes brimmed with tears.

'Shall we leave it there for today?' the woman asked.

He nodded again.

'Go get some rest. We can pick this up tomorrow.' She uncrossed her legs, stood, smoothed down her skirt and opened the door.

The man towered above her and held out his hand to shake hers. Obliging, she took it.

The woman closed the door and locked it. She walked to the framed picture on the wall behind her chair. She slipped it to the side, eased open a small cupboard and switched a camera off. Removing the memory card from the camera, she placed it into her leather briefcase and left the room.

13

The following morning, I walked into the kitchen to find TJ and May playing cards. He threw his hand face down on the kitchen table and pointed at May, a faux-serious look on his face.

'No cheating now, kid.' He stood and walked to the stove.

Dirty dishes with the remnants of pancakes and syrup sat on the table.

'You teaching her poker?' I said. 'You know she's four years old, right?'

TJ tipped batter from a pitcher into the frying pan. It hit the grease with a sizzle.

'It's Snap. Thought I'd start with this and work my way up.'

I poured coffee into a mug. 'You looking forward to the zoo, May?'

May nodded enthusiastically. 'Will we see monkeys?'

'Monkeys, tigers, and maybe some bears.'

The smell of butter floated up from the pan. TJ flipped the pancake and grabbed a clean plate from the cupboard. It slipped through his fingers and smashed to the floor with a clatter. Ceramic shards shot in every direction.

'Jesus Christ,' TJ shouted. He turned to May and raised his palm to apologize. 'Sorry, kid.'

May startled in her seat. TJ reached into the closet and grabbed a dustpan and brush.

'It's OK, I'll clear it up,' I said. I pulled the dustpan from him, but he snatched it back.

'It's fine, I can do it.' TJ's voice brittle.

I stood back in surrender. This wasn't like him. The situation with May must have really got him rattled.

'Sit. You've got to eat,' TJ said. His tone a little softer now.

'Not got time. I need to pick up my kit.' I glanced at my watch. The sooner this damn gig was over, the sooner I could focus on the main task in hand. I may have bought the little girl some extra time away from the authorities, but there was no way Reggie wasn't going to be on my case.

TJ ignored me. He slipped the pancake onto a new plate and pulled back a kitchen chair.

Indulging him, I sat.

'You go get your kit and I'll drive you two to the zoo,' TJ said.

'You don't mind?'

'You can do whatever it is you need to do and we can go see the animals.' He looked at May. 'See if we can't throw the lions a piece of Harper, whaddya reckon?'

May giggled.

I'm not sure I saw the funny side, but I said, 'That would be great.'

'I need to be back this afternoon, something I need to do,' TJ said.

'Oh yeah?' I asked.

'Yeah, something and nothing,' TJ muttered, not looking at me. He threw his right hand up in the air dismissively.

I took another bite of pancake, swallowed the last of my coffee and scraped back my chair.

'OK. Be back in thirty,' I shouted. I grabbed my jacket and left the kitchen.

I slipped down the front steps and through the yard, took a left and headed towards my apartment. I passed the trap house on the way. Now it was deathly quiet. The devil only seems to show himself at night.

The streets always looked different in the day. It smelled different. Sure, there was the saltiness from the bay. But the odor of spices was replaced with coffee and baked bread wafting out from the local coffee shops.

My head throbbed. Twenty-four hours ago, I thought my biggest problem was paying my rent, and now it seemed I had a kid in tow.

As I walked the couple of blocks to my home, I couldn't get the 'I'm sorry' note out of my mind. And all the numbers and letters. I didn't think the boatyard owner was lying. But the fact May said she lived by the beach and had drawn a boat had me convinced we were onto something. Perhaps Reggie was right. Any one of his clients could have taken down the number. But what did SD stand for? And the dates, if they were indeed dates – surely it wasn't a coincidence one of them was shortly before May was found?

I got to my block and slowed down.

I hesitated at the corner and peered across the street for Arty. It'd be just my luck he'd be there right now.

I needed to get into my apartment, pick up my kit and get out without being seen.

I scanned left and right, and approached.

Walt lay in his usual position. Covered in blankets, he leaned against the iron railings.

'Hey, Princess.' Walt shaded his eyes and squinted up at me. We slapped our hands together in greeting.

'Seen Arty?'

'Maybe. Maybe not.'

'Walt, you seen him or not?' Anxious, I peered around.

'You got five bucks?'

'Seriously, Walt?'

He shrugged. Walt coughed up phlegm into his mouth. He gulped it back down.

I didn't have time for this. I slipped my hand into my back pocket, pulled out a ten-dollar bill. *No way*. He may be desperate, but I was hardly Daddy Warbucks myself. I dug my hands into my front pocket and took out some loose change. There was about four bucks. I cupped out my hand to him and handed it over.

'So, you seen him?'

'Nah, not since yesterday.' Walt counted the money out onto the sidewalk.

'Good. Do me a favor and bang those railings if you see him coming, yeah?'

Walt gave me a toothless grin and shrugged again.

'You serious?'

'A guy's gotta eat, you know.' He coughed a little more.

Yeah, and I've got rent to pay. I shook my head, slipped my hand into my back pocket and gave him the ten bucks.

'You know where I'll be if anyone needs me.'

Walt held the ten bucks up into the air as if he was checking it wasn't counterfeit. 'Give TJ my best,' he said. He tucked the money into his shoe.

'Will do.' I leaped up the steps and slipped into the building.

I unlocked my front door and shut it behind me. I grabbed my bag of kit and stepped into the bedroom. Flipping open the closet doors, I pulled some extra clothes off the hangers. I opened the drawers and shoved it all into a carryall. Closing the door behind me, I nodded to the apartment as if to say goodbye.

Taking no chances, I left via the fire exit and slipped along an alley towards the main street.

By the time I got back, TJ had dressed May and brushed her hair.

'You ready?' I asked.

'As we'll ever be,' TJ said. He made to leave.

'You've got your buttons done up wrong,' I said.

TJ glanced down, noticed his shirt was jumbled up, un-buttoned the top one and stopped.

'What's the matter with you?' I walked up to him and rebuttoned the shirt in the right order.

'Nothing. Can't see, that's all,' he snapped.

Jeez, he was tetchy today.

TJ drove us in his Camaro and dropped me off at the staff entrance. The job wouldn't take more than a couple of hours.

'So, I'll meet you in the coffee shop?' I said through the open window.

TJ nodded, glanced at May in the rear seat and back at me. He left the engine running but stepped out of the car so May couldn't hear what he was about to say.

'Yeah. And then, Harper, you know we've got to take her in, right?'

I clenched my teeth and didn't dare look him in the eye.

'I mean it,' TJ said. 'You could be in a lot of trouble for this.'

I nodded.

TJ got back into the car.

I watched him drive off towards the zoo parking lot.

TJ was right, I could be in trouble, but the thing about trouble is, I'd known it all my life.

It was a familiar friend.

Better the devil you know, right?

14

TJ and May looked like your regular grandpa and grandkid queuing for the zoo. TJ wasn't concerned some officer was going to notice them, hunt them down and arrest him. He knew from what Reggie had said, she hadn't been reported missing. But what he was bothered about was what they were going to do now. He knew he'd have to accompany Harper to the precinct. At least if he went with her, he could perhaps persuade them to go a little easy on her.

TJ had spent the night tossing and turning, trying to figure out what the hell had happened to this kid. Sure, he'd seen enough juveniles wandering around the street without an adult in his time. Once, he had found a toddler in his soiled diaper. He was picking at some old burger wrapping in the gutter, without a clue where his parents were. It had taken three days to track them down, and only because the mother had awoken from her crack coma and realized her little boy was no longer in the house. But May? May was no kid from a crack-addled mom. Someone had left her at the store on purpose. She was clothed in some pretty dress. And, let's face it, before she threw up the contents of the ice-cream tub, she was neat as a pin. No, this was different, and it didn't add up.

TJ and May shuffled forward, paid for two tickets and slipped through the entrance. Families gathered, all peering at a paper map, pointing and debating where to start first. Toddlers sat atop parents' shoulders. Couples with strollers and young children in tow clustered close to a huddle of screeching elementary-school kids.

TJ opened up the map. He crouched beside May. 'Where you want to start?'

'Monkeys!' May squealed.

TJ acquiesced. He spotted a shuttle stop pointing in that direction. He took May's hand and walked over to the line.

The shuttle's brakes screeched to a halt. Children and adults clambered onto the plastic seats. TJ and May followed suit. With a ding of the bell, the shuttle pulled off, winding its way among the shrubbery on either side. They passed fenced enclosures. Groups of people pressed their noses up close. The smell of animal dung and cotton candy floated in the air.

The shuttle slowed and came to a stop. TJ and May stepped off and walked across to a large chain-link area. High atop a maze of branches, a group of orange monkeys jumped from one tree to the next.

May tugged at TJ's hand to draw him closer to the cage. She pressed her face against the metal and giggled as two monkeys groomed each other.

TJ squatted to her height and watched them with her.

'You been to the zoo before?' he asked.

She nodded. 'We saw elephants and giraffes.'

'Oh yeah. Was it your mom and dad who took you?'

'My mommy. Daddy always working.'

'That right? You know where he works?'

May shook her head.

TJ knew he'd have to tread gently. He wasn't trained in kid psychology. He left that part to the experts, but still, he knew a few things. After all, that's how he had got Harper to trust him back in the day.

Harper had been no more than eight years old when he'd first encountered her. An alert had gone out reporting there was a minor missing from one of the homes off Knapp Street. There was always some kid running off from there – TJ was surprised it hadn't been shut down long ago. It was only when he attended some robbery off Marine Park later that day, he spotted her traipsing along the street by herself. Harper clocked him in his Cruiser and sped off. She must have led him on a twenty-minute chase by the time he caught up with her. He may have been a lot fitter and faster back then, but she sure as hell gave him a run for his money. Finally catching up with her, he first noticed the bruises. Each arm had five mottled marks, the size of a dime, where someone had grabbed her hard.

'Who did that to you?' he'd asked.

Harper had said nothing. Her cheeks had flushed. She'd narrowed her eyes and stood rigid.

It didn't exactly take a police mind to work out why she'd run away.

'You hungry?' She was all skin and bones.

Again, Harper had eyed TJ warily.

TJ had pointed at a diner on the corner of Brown and U. 'I hear they do a good strawberry shake and fries.'

Harper had followed him, and despite tucking into the food like she hadn't eaten in a week, she didn't say a word.

'You know I've got to take you back,' TJ had said when she'd wolfed down her last mouthful. It was the last thing he wanted to do. But what were his options?

Harper had bit her lip and slumped in the Cruiser, the window down, her dark hair floating on the breeze.

TJ never forgot how she appeared that day. She may have said little, but he could tell by the look in her eyes, she was a kid who had already seen a lifetime of troubles. The marks on her arm may have showed him some of what she'd endured, but that was only skin-deep. It was what she kept hidden away inside of her that worried him the most.

She didn't seem any different, twenty-something years on.

May squeezed TJ's hand.

He let her lead him to the next adventure. THE WORLD OF REPTILES.

A small line formed as they entered. Voices echoed in the tunnel. The light dipped low. Left behind were the jolts and screams of the folks outside. The change in atmosphere brought the public to a whisper. They huddled over glass containers or pressed their noses against the fingerprint-smeared tanks, searching for the inhabitants.

May held on to TJ's hand. They shuffled past the displays. She gazed in fascination as an anaconda slid across a marsh-covered rock. Its tongue buzzed in and out, dipping under the water.

'See that anaconda? That's what Harper looks like when she's in a bad mood,' TJ whispered.

May's giggle echoed around the glass-covered arena. They strolled on to the next window. A huge glass-fronted box housed a large pool of murky green water as high as TJ's shoulders. Viridescent and pink-hued stalactites dripped from the surrounding rocks. The pond led all along the wall towards a shallow area.

The moment they pressed their noses against the glass, May's hand whipped away from TJ's. She darted towards the exit, scooting between the legs of the public.

'May!' TJ's voice echoed off the walls.

Folks turned to look at him in shock.

Startled, TJ followed in May's direction. He shoved past a group of kids, almost knocking a couple like bowling pins to the ground.

'Sorry,' he shouted. His eyes darted everywhere, trying to catch a glimpse of May. Losing his footing, TJ stumbled, caught himself on the wall and bolted after her.

The daylight blinded him. Shielding his eyes, he scanned the perimeter. His heart thumped in his chest. A wheeze caught in his throat. Peering down, he spotted pink sandals poking out from behind a trash can. TJ charged towards them.

May crouched behind spilled styrofoam cups and empty popcorn cartons. Safely in his sight, TJ leaned his palms down on his knees and collected his breath.

'Jeez, kid, what the hell was that about?' His words puffed and whistled through lack of oxygen. He stood back up and wiped sweat from his brow.

Hesitant, May crept out from behind the trash. 'Snap, snap.'

'Yeah, we can play it later. But why'd you go running off like that?' TJ wiped his clammy hands on his pants.

'Snap, snap,' May pointed

TJ stared at her, quizzical. He turned towards the reptile house.

'You mean the alligator?'

'Mommy say we got to run from snap, snap.'

TJ took a moment to register her words.

'You live near snap, snap?' TJ scratched his temple.

What the hell? He glanced down at May. Her pink cotton

frock poking out from under the sweater and her jelly sandals covering her feet. It may explain the outfit. But what it didn't explain was why the hell she was in New York.

15

A man headed into the elevator and pressed the keypad. The doors swished shut and descended to an underground parking lot.

He pulled the key fob out of his jacket pocket. He flicked the switch and heard the familiar beep of his blood-red Corvette unlocking. The lights flashed at the rear of the parking lot.

He was glad to be nearly home. The trip had overrun and he was tiring of being away. Right now, all he wanted was to get back, take a dip in the pool and watch the sunset.

The car door opened and closed with a satisfying clunk. The odor of leather enveloped him as he settled into the driver's seat. He loved this car. To him, it smelled of success.

He waited for the barrier to open. He slid the nose out onto the main street, tapped the button to release the roof and waited until it peeled its way back. He pressed his foot onto the gas and took off with a pleasing whoosh.

The warm breeze tousled his hair. He drove along the seafront. He never stopped appreciating the view. How far he had come. Despite the odds, he had made it. He always needed to remind himself of that. He could let the guilt kick in, but what was the use? No, he had done good and this life was his just reward.

He pressed his foot on the gas another inch. The car rocketed forward. The man smiled to himself. Yes, it was great to be home.

The car wound its way around the roads with a satisfying purr. The vibration of the powerful engine hummed as it cornered the roads. He pulled up onto his driveway and killed the engine. A loon flapped and howled high above him. He glanced up to the clear cobalt sky, blinding him for a second.

He strolled up to the porch and placed his key in the door. 'Hey?' he called out.

The house was silent.

He frowned to himself and shrugged. He threw his carryall on the marble floor with a clatter. He would sort it out later. His fine leather shoes clipped on the tiles as he stepped into the kitchen.

White floor-to-ceiling cupboards dressed the back wall. Next to them, a baby blue La Cornue stove that had rarely been used. A large granite island sat in the middle.

He walked to the bank of cupboards. He pulled out a tall crystal glass and pressed it against the refrigerator lever. Ice-cold water glugged down. Taking a sip, he meandered to the glass doors separating the kitchen from the exterior.

Manicured lawns stretched out towards the seafront. A kidney-shaped pool dominated the left-hand side. The surface barely rippled. The air was still. Little movement, other than the sprinklers blowing out a shower of water. On then off, on then off.

The man took a deep breath, loosened his tie and undid his top button.

He turned back towards the kitchen. He checked the clock above the stove. His eye caught a note on the stone island. It was leaned up against a basket of fruit. Taking another sip of water, he walked towards it and unfolded it.

His brow furrowed at first, as though to decipher the writing. But it was the words that had caught him by surprise. The crystal glass he had been holding dropped and shattered onto the tile floor. Water snaked its way across the marble, slipping into the creases of the island.

Leaning on the granite worktop for support, the man stared at the two words on the paper. Unable to hold any weight in his trembling legs, his body slumped to the floor. Water soaked into the linen of his pants.

The note fell to his side. The ink bled as it hit the puddle.

The words 'I'm sorry' faintly legible on the floor.

16

I knew TJ had something on his mind the moment I entered the coffee shop. He was nursing a drink and staring off into the distance. His brow creased. He rolled his thumb and forefinger together. Something I had seen him do a hundred times before when he worked on a case. A case he couldn't quite get his head around.

I pulled out a chair and tried hard to ignore the sound of kids shrieking, chairs scraping and plates rattling.

'You have a good time?' I asked May.

May barely took a breath before launching into all the animals she had seen.

TJ didn't say a word.

Once she'd finished, I gave TJ a quizzical look.

'You want to go see if they got some more of those coloring books?' TJ said.

May scuttled off to a play area in the right-hand corner.

He waited until May was out of earshot and told me what had happened.

'So, she's not from around here?'

TJ shrugged. He gazed back off into the distance, no doubt still trying to fathom out how or, more to the point, why she was in New York.

'I guess that'll explain the motel,' I said.

I recalled the boat she had drawn. I thought about the number on the note. We had presumed she was from New York, and when she said the beach, I had, of course, thought she meant Coney Island. So when I'd called, I had surmised the number was local. It could have needed any number of area codes at the front. If the person who'd written the number down was in that area at the time, of course they wouldn't have needed the prefix.

I tugged out my cellphone.

'What you looking at?' TJ asked.

'A map.'

'What for?'

I ignored him and rustled in my purse for a pen and paper. I passed them to TJ.

'What am I supposed to do with that?'

I pulled out the 'I'm sorry' note and pointed at the top line of numbers and letters.

'I'm going to look at places with the initials SD. Maybe that's the area code. Write them down.'

TJ took a breath and slid the pen and paper back to me. 'We could be here all day.' He shook his head.

'Humor me.' I raised my eyebrows at him. 'Or while May's playing, we could talk about your love life.'

TJ smirked. 'Or yours.'

'Exactly, so let's try work this out instead.' I indicated to my cellphone screen.

TJ took his turn to raise his eyebrows now. 'OK, but you write, my handwriting's terrible.' He stared at the pen like it was a stick of dynamite.

I scanned the map of the states to see if anything obvious

jumped out. 'We can rule out anything inland, if she lives by the beach.'

TJ and I leaned into the phone's screen.

'San Diego?' I said.

'I don't think you get many alligators in San Diego, Harp.'

I shrugged, embarrassed.

'You need to look along this side.' TJ pointed to the south-east of the map. 'Louisiana, Alabama, Mississippi, Florida, perhaps even Georgia.'

I glanced across at May in the play area, her Mickey Mouse toy grasped in her hand. She was chatting to some other young kids watched over by their mom and dad. I stared at her for a second and back at my cellphone.

'Florida,' I said, conviction in my voice.

'What makes you think that?' TJ furrowed his brow and stared at me.

'She has a Mickey Mouse toy.'

'I can get a toy like that in Queen's, for Chrissake, Harp, it doesn't mean anything. She could be from South Carolina for all we know.'

'Great. Let's start looking at Florida and then we can look at South Carolina.'

TJ opened up his left palm and frowned. 'You know I've got to leave soon.' He glanced at his watch.

I scanned down the coastline of Florida. I started at the top right-hand corner from Jacksonville.

It didn't take long before I gasped.

'What?' TJ's head flicked up.

'Look.' I zoomed in on the map. 'South Daytona. And look what's close by. Port Orange. If she's from South Daytona, maybe her Uncle Orange is from there. Could be how he got his name?' My pulse quickened.

TJ took a moment to think it through. 'That's not bad, Harp.'

I flicked off the maps and opened the internet. I typed in 'South Daytona area code'.

Grinning at TJ, I tapped in all the numbers on my cellphone and held it up to my ear.

17

The dial tone rang. I heard a click of someone picking up. My body tensed.

'Ni hao?' a woman answered.

'Hello?'

'Ni hao,' she repeated.

'Hello, who is this?' I asked.

TJ opened his palms to me to ask what they said. He leaned in towards the phone to listen.

'Loon Fa Supermarket,' the woman replied in broken English.

TJ's head drooped the same time as mine.

'Sorry. Wrong number.' I clicked off the call and flung my cellphone onto the table. 'Shit.'

TJ placed his hand on mine. 'At least you tried.'

Sick disappointment settled into my bones.

TJ checked the time again. 'Look, we've got to make a move, I need to ...' He let the sentence drift and shifted up from his seat.

Distracted, I nodded.

'Harp, we know she's not from New York. It's a start.' He offered me a gentle smile. 'We can tell the cops when we take her in.'

Blood drained from my face.

We may have been a step closer, knowing she wasn't from New York, but what we didn't know was why she'd been dumped here. Or what had happened to her in the first place. And nor, in the short term, would the cops, which would still mean she'd end up in care.

I threw the pen and paper in my purse, picked up my camera kit and walked over to May.

'We've got to make tracks, honey.' I held my hand out towards hers. I smiled at the parents of the two little boys hovering close by.

'Your daughter's so pretty,' the woman said to me.

My stomach clenched. I grabbed May's hand and shuttled her towards the exit.

TJ suggested I drive and drop him at the Hunts Point Avenue subway.

I pulled up close to the station entrance.

TJ shifted a bag over to May and stepped out of the car.

'I'll be back by five and then we'll ...' he indicated in May's direction, 'you know.'

I nodded and ignored the muscles tightening in my stomach.

As he turned to go, I hollered through the open window. 'Hey.'

TJ bent back down to the window.

'What you got going on?' I asked him and nodded towards the subway.

'None of your business,' he said. He had a jokey laugh in his voice, but I sensed he was hiding something. Figuring he had another date, I shrugged and set off back to his.

'You have fun today?' I peered in my rearview mirror to May in the back seat.

'We saw a dragon.'

'What? A real one?'

May nodded.

'Wow. Did it breathe fire?' I asked.

May squinted. 'No.'

'Are you sure? I thought dragons breathed fire.'

'No, silly.'

'What else did you see?'

'We saw a big lion and giraffes.'

'What was your favorite animal?'

'Monkeys!' May screeched.

'Is that because you're a monkey?'

'I'm not a monkey!!'

'Are you sure, because you look like one.' I stuck my tongue out at her and winked.

May wrinkled up her nose. 'You look like an anaconga.'

'An anaconda? What?'

'They stick their tongues out and Uncle TJ said you look like one.'

'Hmmm. He did, did he?' I squinted at her suspiciously. 'Well, he looks like a big bald eagle.'

May giggled and stuck her tongue out at me this time.

As we made our way towards Brooklyn, my mind drifted to the letters and numbers on the note. I really thought I was onto something when I had found the code for South Daytona.

Having crawled through the traffic, I parked up outside TJ's. I opened up the back passenger door and unclipped May from her seat belt. May slid across and tumbled out, clinging on to the bag TJ had passed her.

'What's in there?' I asked, unlocking the front door.

May handed it to me. THE BRONX ZOO was emblazoned across it in red. I dipped my hand into it. I found a coloring book with animals, a gray sweatshirt with a giraffe on the front and a pair of leopard-print leggings.

I shook my head and laughed. Only TJ.

May grabbed her crayons and jumped up onto the couch. I passed her the coloring book and headed into the kitchen.

I set my laptop up on the table. I connected the memory card from my camera and transferred the photos. I typed up a quick email to Richard, detailing the photos, and added a line asking him for more work. This job was barely going to cover what I needed.

Once I had finished, I pulled out the 'I'm sorry' note and placed it on the table in front of me. I studied each line of letters and numbers, trying to decipher anything. If I could find one more clue, at least it would lead the police in the right direction. The sooner they found May's mom and dad, the less time she would be in care.

I focused my attention on the line written from the top left towards the bottom right.

09/25-0716 DFW0940.

If 09/25 was a date, it would have been shortly before May last saw her mom.

DFW?

I leaned back in my chair and stared out of the window. I repeated the letters in my head. Nothing.

My eyes flicked back to the note.

I pulled the laptop towards me and opened up the internet browser. I typed in 'DFW' and pressed search.

Reading the links on the screen, my stomach clenched.

DFW. Dallas Fort Worth Airport.

I picked up the note and peered at the numbers next to it. *Were they flight times?*

If they were flight times, where were they from? Dallas was inland, so I discounted that being May's home.

I almost heard the workings of my brain as I tried to grasp onto any tangible thought. If I could work out what flight landed in DFW on the twenty-fifth of this month at 0940, I could be a step closer.

I opened up the flight itineraries for the airport. It might not tell me past times, but, more often than not, flights flew to regular destinations using the same schedule. I clicked on to their flight status page. My eyes swept over the hundreds of flights due to land. I scanned down to the morning flights.

The skin on my face prickled with excitement as I stared at one particular flight.

PBI 0716 – DFW 0940.

PBI. Palm Beach International.

I didn't need to look at a map to know that was on the coast or in Florida.

I clicked open another tab and typed in 'Palm Beach area code'. My hands trembled.

I stepped up, poked my head in the living room, checked May was occupied and closed the door.

I sat back at the kitchen table and tapped into my cellphone the number across the top of the note, adding the area code.

My left leg jigged up and down, with nerves and a little excitement.

'Liberty of the Mind Legacy. How may I direct your call?' a young-sounding woman said.

Liberty of the what?

'I'm sorry. What number is this?' I asked.

'You've come through to the Liberty of the Mind Legacy. How may I help you today?'

I scribbled the name on the piece of paper.

'I think I have the wrong number. Sorry.' I clicked off the call.

I was expecting it to be someone's home number, not what sounded like a corporate business. *Shit*. Maybe this was another false lead.

I typed out a text to Reggie.

Ever heard of the Liberty of the Mind Legacy???

I pressed send and looked back at the laptop.

I typed the name into the search browser. A bunch of links came up. I clicked the top one, which appeared to be for their main site.

The home page had a menu listed on the left-hand side. Their name in large letters across the top of the page, with a symbol of some sort underneath it. Below, a large photo of a group of people laughing and smiling.

I scanned the bottom of the page, where their addresses were listed. There were six in total, all across the US, including the one in Palm Beach. My eyes shot to an address in New York. That might explain why May was in the city. But none of them were in Dallas.

I leaned into the screen, browsed the menu and clicked on 'What We Do'.

The page had more photos of men and women and children smiling along the bottom. A couple of paragraphs of writing above them.

The Liberty of the Mind Legacy is a set of practices and beliefs which allow us to mine ourselves for our best potential. Whether it's the perfect relationship, the best job,

or simply peace of mind, we at the LOML will guide you to
finding the best version of you!

I scan-read the rest of the paragraphs. The elation of possibly
being a step closer drained out of me. Despondent, I clicked
open a new search tab and typed in 'Liberty of the Mind Legacy'
and 'Brown'. Nothing. It directed me back to the main site. I
clicked on another tab on the left-hand menu.

Come join us on one of our courses and unlock your
potential. Visit any one of our centers today and enroll...

I pressed the icon which said, 'Who We Are'.
A black and white photograph of a man, late fifties, dressed in
robes, addressing an audience took up half the page. Underneath,
his name: 'Svaag Dimash'.
Below, a paragraph stated:

Our Founder, Svaag Dimash, opened up the first Liberty of
the Mind Center in early 2005. Since then, he has inspired
tens of thousands of people across the world to become
the best version of themselves, by untapping the hidden
potential available in all of us. For many years, he studied
in various ashrams, before writing a testament to what he
believes is the ultimate answer to humankind.
Book a course today!

Reading this sort of baloney made my lip curl. I shook my
head and blew air out of my cheeks. *How did this place connect
to May?* I stared at the note and back at the website. I re-read
the paragraph.

Svaag Dimash.

SD.

Shit!

I peered closer at the photo of people staring up at the man in awe.

'What you doing?'

I jumped in my chair, startled. I hadn't noticed May enter the room.

She swept around the table in a dance and stopped back in front of my laptop. 'He goes to Daddy's work,' May said, pointing at the photo of Svaag.

'What?'

'That man goes to Daddy's work.'

I shot a look from May to the photo of Svaag and back to May.

'You've definitely seen him at your daddy's work?'

May nodded and twirled around the table.

'You remember when you saw him?'

May shrugged. 'We took Daddy his lunch and the man was talking to Daddy and he told me he eats peanut butter jelly sandwiches and I told him I didn't like them.'

'You sure you saw him there?'

May nodded. Her serious face mirrored mine.

'And you don't know what your daddy does at work?'

May shook her head.

She had said earlier 'he makes people happy.' Well, that sure as hell was what the website was spouting.

I watched May pirouetting in the kitchen, oblivious to what was going on.

I inhaled slowly and glanced at the clock on the wall.

15.40

TJ wouldn't be home for at least another hour.

I looked back to the address of the Palm Beach center. I knew if I was going to do this, we would need to do it right now.

'Say, May, why don't we go on a little road trip?'

18

I grabbed whatever I'd collected from my apartment and the bag with May's new clothes in and threw them all in the trunk of the Camaro. I hurried back into the house.

'Bring your crayons, kid,' I hollered to May.

I don't know why, but I reached up to the top kitchen cupboard and contemplated taking TJ's gun. I'd never fired one in my life. I slammed the cupboard shut and shuddered at the thought.

Florida was one hell of a way from New York and we couldn't exactly fly. Forget about the money, May had no ID, so it was out of the question. I wasn't sure if the Camaro would make it, but it was my one and only chance. If I didn't leave soon, TJ would be back, and when Reggie found out what I was doing, he would call it in. If we got on the road now, we could make it to South Carolina by nightfall. I'd find some motel overnight and make the last leg in the morning.

I knew as soon as TJ realized the car was gone from the front, he would figure it was me. I wrote him a note all the same. Trying to make light of it a little, I wrote two words:

I'm sorry.

I'm not sure he'd find the funny side. But I had left his gun, what more could I do?

We set off via Contelli's bakery and picked up a custard tart for May to eat on the way. I was running low on cash and for the first time I was grateful I'd done the zoo job. I could only hope Richard would rush the payment through for me knowing I was feeling some heat.

It took us fifty minutes to get onto the I-278. Bumper-to-bumper traffic. The Camaro's engine rumbled. The stench of exhaust fumes filtered through the dusty vents. Every time I pressed on the clutch, it squeaked and clunked finding the gear. I turned the knob on the radio. I found a station I liked and settled back in my seat and waited for the traffic to ease up a little. I reached into my pocket and pulled out my cellphone. Reggie hadn't replied to my earlier text. I switched it off and watched the screen go black. I leaned forward and slipped it into the glove compartment.

TJ had bought this car years ago. He'd talked about little else when he had first got it. It had been his dream and after scrimping and saving he finally bought it. The whole car had needed fixing up. It sat outside his place on bricks for months while he tampered underneath, fiddling with one thing and another.

I had long left the clutches of the state system behind me and found a room to rent. TJ no longer had to track me down and haul me back to a home. He would pop in, say he was passing by, bring me something to eat – but I knew he was still keeping an eye on me. Both he and I knew it was too easy for someone like me to fall in with what he called 'the wrong crowd'. I had skipped so much school, at one point it seemed likely I would never graduate. When I did, TJ pulled up in the rusty Camaro, long before it had a full respray, and took me out for dinner to celebrate. I'll never forget, after we'd finished eating, he handed me a box all wrapped up.

Inside it was my first camera. A Canon EOS-1Ds.

'A little something for you to show the world how you see things,' he'd said.

I don't think I had ever seen anything so beautiful in my life. I didn't know what to say. Instead, I picked it up and, after figuring out how to set the autofocus, I pointed it right at him and took his picture. I still carry it in my wallet today.

The warmth that memory brought soon turned cold with guilt. I knew he was going to get back to the house to find his precious car and both of us gone.

I should have turned off the interstate and headed straight back to TJ's. But glancing at May in the passenger seat gazing out of the window, clutching her Mickey Mouse, I knew in my gut I couldn't let what happened to me happen to her.

She noticing me staring and turned in my direction.

'Are you sad?' May said.

'What?' I creased my brow.

'You look sad.'

I shook my head. 'I'm not sad. Just tired.' I took a beat. 'Are you sad?'

May tugged the Mickey Mouse closer to her and shook her head. May peered at me for a second longer and turned back to gaze out of the car window.

The traffic thinned. I sat up, pressed on the gas and nudged May's leg.

'You know how to play "I Spy"?'

19

Reggie sat at his desk in the bullpen. He tuned out the incessant phone ringing, the printer whirring, doors opening and slamming shut. He shuffled one document on top of the next and back again.

'Y'OK there, buddy?' His partner Joey tossed a foam ball at him. Like Reggie, his uniform pulled tight against his muscles. His black hair slicked back with oil. A real Italian stallion.

Reggie looked up.

'He's not doing that thing they call filing again, is he?' Garcia, his lieutenant, hollered over.

'Yeah, yeah, real peculiar. Hold on, he's placing something in a folder,' Joey said. He held his hands up as if to still any movement in the office.

Reggie ignored them.

'You know he only gets like this when there's a woman involved,' Joey said.

'Oh yeah?' Garcia walked over to Joey's desk.

'Yeah, it's like he thinks if his paperwork is in order, he's got the situation in order.'

'That right? Guess that'll explain why it's usually in a mess.' Garcia shook his head.

'Jesus, guys, you could do with a little clean-up yourselves,' Reggie threw his hand out in the direction of their desks.

'Yeah, he gets all anal like and distracted, pretending he's doing work, when all he's thinking about is doing some chick.' Joey swayed his hips to and fro. He pulled his arms in tight to make his point.

'So, who is she? Someone we know?' Garcia asked.

Reggie didn't reply.

Joey shrugged.

'Shame, 'cause I was thinking of introducing you to my cousin. She's a nice piece of ass,' Garcia offered.

'Garcia, she's your cousin,' Joey winced.

'What? I still got eyes.' Garcia held his palms out and shrugged.

'I don't think it was your eyes that was doing the looking.' Joey waved Garcia away, like he was infected.

'Well, listen, buddy, I'm pleased for you. About time you started seeing someone new. Especially after that crazy chick,' Garcia said, strolling back to his desk.

'You want coffee?' Joey asked.

Reggie nodded.

He waited until Joey had left the office and turned to his computer screen. He opened up his phone and glanced at the text Harper had sent earlier. He tapped on his keyboard and entered the name 'Liberty of the Mind Legacy'. He wasn't expecting anything to come up.

It was approaching five p.m. He knew TJ was going to bring Harper and May in. Although he didn't relish the thought of having to explain to Garcia what he knew, he was relieved this would all be over.

The computer monitor beeped. A list of files buzzed up onto the screen.

'What?' Reggie muttered to himself and leaned in closer.

He clicked onto the first file. The computer beeped again.

File protected. No access. Password required.

'Damn.' Reggie clicked on the next file.

Same thing.

'File protected' could only mean one thing. FBI.

Reggie rubbed his chin. If the FBI was investigating them, there's no way it would share that info with the NYPD.

Reggie pushed his chair back. He slid open his desk drawer. The metal rails scraped as it opened. He took out a contact book. He thumbed through the pages and stopped at the letter 'D'. He ran his finger along the names.

Gary Davidson.

Gary had graduated from the police academy same time as Reggie. They'd started off together at the 63rd precinct, but over the years, Gary specialized. Soon enough, he was training at Quantico. Reggie had barely spoken to him since, but he guessed it was worth a punt at least.

Reggie picked up the phone and dialed the number. It took him through to the main switchboard and he asked to be put through.

'I'm afraid he's out in the field at the moment. May I leave a message?' a man said.

'Yeah, you know when he's due back?' Reggie asked.

'No. You want to leave a name and contact number?'

Reggie did. He replaced the handset and turned his attention back to the screen. Why was the FBI investigating them and what did they have to do with May?

Reggie's cellphone rang. Distracted, he picked it up from his desk.

He glanced at the screen.

TJ.

'Hey, man. You on your way?' Reggie stared back at his computer.

His head drooped the second he heard TJ sigh.

'What the hell's she gone and done now?'

20

We'd been traveling for close to five hours when we passed into Prince William County, VA. May, having tired of 'I Spy', had fallen asleep around about Washington. She was curled up in a ball, her head resting on Mickey's against the car door. I've got to say, seeing her like that made my tummy roll over. She couldn't have looked more innocent and vulnerable if she tried. Why would someone leave her? The same question had looped on my brain like a spiral ever since I'd found the kid.

Perhaps this was crazy. Me driving to Florida, when I barely had an idea what I was going to do, or where we were going to start. Sure, I had the address of the Liberty of the Mind Legacy headquarters. But who was to say they had anything to do with her? She had recognized the founder. It was all I had to go on and I was going to do my best to find her parents and discover what had happened to them.

I was reluctant to wake her. The more sleep she got, the more peace I had for thinking things through. However, I needed to stretch my legs, take a comfort break, and I figured she'd need to eat at some point.

Spotting a sign for a twenty-four-hour diner, I pulled into the parking lot and switched off the engine. Rousing May, I opened my car door and gave my legs a good stretch. My bones seemed to crunch as I eased myself out of the car.

As soon as we walked into the diner, there was the arresting smell of grilled cheese, fries and coffee. A couple of booths occupied by truckers, couples and a handful of families tucked into their food.

I glanced at a waitress behind the counter, nodded to her and slipped into a booth.

The waitress strolled over with a pot of coffee. She was dressed in a brown and white candy-striped uniform, frizzy shoulder-length blond hair and gold-colored hooped earrings. Her name badge hanging from her breast pocket read MINDY.

'Coffee?'

I nodded. I picked up the laminated menu and opened it up.

'I'll give you guys a minute.'

'It's OK, some fish sticks for her, and I'll get a regular burger and fries.'

Mindy popped the coffee pot onto the table and plucked out a pad and pen from the front of her apron.

'Any drinks with that?' She looked at May.

'She'll have an OJ.'

The waitress finished writing on her pad. She slipped it into her pocket, picked up the coffee pot and walked back off to a door which I assumed led to the kitchen.

Taking a napkin from the metal holder, I wiped away a ring of coffee left on the table.

'So, tell me about your house,' I said.

May's brow creased.

'Is it like Uncle TJ's?'

May shook her head.

'Is it a big house?'

'I got a really big bedroom.'

'You have, huh. What else you got?'

'A pool!' May screeched, excited.

'A pool?' *The kid had a pool?*

'You got a best friend?' I asked.

'Zoey was my best friend, but then she didn't want to play horses with me, so then Ryan played with me. He has a real horse, but we're not allowed to play on it as it's really big.'

'A real horse, huh.'

'He will show if you like.'

'That sounds great.' I gave her a smile.

'Have you got a best friend?' she asked me.

I paused before answering. I hadn't ever considered that.

'I don't know. I guess TJ is my best friend.'

'You can be my best friend if you like?' she said, her face so earnest.

A lump pricked my throat. 'I'd like that very much.'

'Need to pee-pee,' May said, changing the subject.

I glanced around the diner to where the restroom sign was and pointed over to it. 'Need me to take you?'

May shook her head, scrambled off her seat and headed towards it.

Mindy returned to the table with our order and placed the plates down with a clatter.

'Cute kid you got there,' Mindy said.

'Sure is.' I glanced away, unable to look her in the eye.

May returned and clambered back up onto the seat.

'Dig in, kid,' I said. I squeezed the greasy burger between my two hands and took a bite.

May looked at her plate and up at me.

'What? I order the wrong thing?' I asked.

'No. Mommy usually chops it up for me.'

'Oh, right.' I picked up a knife and broke her fish sticks into smaller pieces. 'Like this?'

May nodded. Smiling, she picked up her fork and stabbed at one of the chunks.

I leaned back in my seat. My half-eaten burger churned in my stomach, poking at my insides.

Both of us, tired from the drive, ate the rest of our food in silence. The sounds of the other diners chatting, spoons clattering against cups as they stirred in some sugar. The jangle of dirty silverware being dumped in a bucket filtered around us.

I used the restroom, paid the check on my card and got back into the Camaro. I opened the map I'd found tucked under the driver's seat. I guessed I could go another five or so hours before we needed to stop for the night. I checked the fuel gauge. Spotting it was close to empty, I turned out of the parking lot and hung a left where I'd noticed a gas station shortly before we had pulled in.

Filling up the Camaro, I told May to wait while I paid. The door beeped as I entered. Fluorescent lighting flickered above. I picked up a large pack of chip sticks, some candy, which I guessed she might like, a comic that had some sort of half-mutant superhero on and a couple bottles of soda. Seeing the crap I had bought, I added some toothbrushes and paste to the order too.

Pulling back out onto I-95, May huddled up to Mickey and occupied herself with the comic.

Night fell as we headed towards South Virginia. Tail lights dotted in the distance. The fan of headlights on the other side flew by. My vision drifted a little. I adjusted my position. We'd been on the road now a good while and every muscle in my body told me it was true.

I glanced across to May. Her head lolled to the side, her eyes closed. The lights from the interstate glowed orange against her skin.

But a couple of beats later, the orange flickered to red and blue. My vision shot back up to the rearview mirror.

Hurtling towards me was a patrol car, its lights flickering bright.

I tensed my fingers around the steering wheel and kept my foot away from the brake. *Come on, pass me, dammit.*

Ignoring my plea, its distinctive siren wailed right on my tail and, a moment later, indicated for me to pull over.

21

You know, I never believed once Reggie had found out what I had done, he would call it in. I figured he'd know how much trouble I'd be in crossing state lines. But here I was, pulling over on some interstate, a kid that didn't belong to me in the passenger seat, me at the wheel of a car I technically hadn't been given permission to drive.

As I switched off the engine, May stirred in her seat. The patrol car's light flashed bright inside ours.

'Why we stopping?' May asked. She stretched out in the seat.

'It's fine, kid. Let me handle this.' I stared in my rearview mirror. The lone cop put his hat on and stepped out of the car. My view switched to the wing mirror. I watched him approach.

I rolled down the car window with a squeak.

It may have been the night-time air, but a chill ran across my skin.

He had a swagger to his walk. His gun bounced on his hip. A pair of cuffs on his other. A curled black wire led up his shirt to a radio.

'Everything OK, officer?' I craned my neck up to look at him. Your typical blond-haired southern boy.

Silent, he swung his flashlight into the car, pointed the white glare at May and myself. He waved the beam onto the back seats.

'Driver's license and registration please, ma'am.' Yup, the southern lilt to his voice.

I flipped down the visor and passed him my documents. He took them from me, stood back up and aimed his flashlight at them.

'Where you traveling to this evening, ma'am?'

'Florida.'

'We're going home,' May shrieked. She kicked her legs excitedly on the seat.

The cop poked his head through the window and fixed his sight on May.

'That right, little lady?' He glanced back at my documents and stared at me. His eyes narrowed. 'Seems home is New York, ma'am. That's the other direction.'

Surely, if he was here to arrest me, he'd do it right now. I pressed the tips of my fingers into my thighs and, taking a chance, I replied.

'It's a surprise,' I whispered. I craned my neck in May's direction.

The cop leaned in and peered through the open window at May. He glanced towards my ring finger, saw it was empty and smiled.

If I hadn't seen that look a million times before.

'You know your tail light's out, ma'am?'

Jesus. Is that why he had pulled me over?

It took every ounce of energy in me not to high-five him right there and then.

'No, sir, I did not.' A flush of relief pumped into my cheeks.

'You need to get that fixed.'

'Yes, sir. Will do. Soon as I see a repair shop, I'll be right on it.' I smiled. And, trust me, it was genuine.

The officer passed me back my documents. 'Well, you have a good journey and get home safely now.' He winked at me and made his way back to his car.

My hands shook. I placed the license back up behind the visor.

I exhaled, accelerated onto the highway and watched him follow behind.

Waiting for my heartbeat to return to close to normal, I pressed a little harder on the gas. Not wanting to risk being stopped again, I signaled off the interstate and pulled up at the first motel I could find.

22

As places go, it wasn't so bad. It was basic, but it was clean, at least compared to some of the dives I'd stayed in.

I got May undressed and into TJ's old Nets T-shirt I'd swiped when I'd packed her stuff, and before long she was fast asleep. I turned out the light and lay on my bed, the neon of the motel vacancy sign flashing against the limp gray sheer under drape. I closed my eyes. Sleep washed over me.

The long drive combined with the fact I was lying on a real bed meant by the time May switched on the television the next morning, I had gotten a good night's rest. I opened my eyes. May was cross-legged on the bed, flicking over the pages of the comic I had bought her. Daylight poked through the gap in the drapes. I rolled across the bed and checked the time.

Still dressed from the day before, I walked into the bathroom. I grabbed my washbag and switched on the shower. The water ran lukewarm, splattering against the cracked tiles.

'I'm going to grab a shower.' *Shoot. When was the last time I had given her a wash?* 'And then it's your turn,' I added.

I cleaned myself as fast as I could. I toweled myself off, wrapped it around me and, tearing May away from the cartoon, I led her into the bathroom. I stripped off the T-shirt and dumped her in the shower. I lathered up some soap, gave her a quick washcloth down and scrubbed suds through her hair. I passed her a hand towel and helped her rub herself dry.

'Right, kid. Let's get dressed, something to eat, and we can get on the road. We've got another eight hours or so before we hit Florida.'

I opened the motel door. The balcony led out to the parking lot. A trail of ants meandered across the walkway. I turned my head towards the main motel building. I have got to say, if I'd have seen what it looked like in the daylight, I'd have thought twice about staying.

We found a nearby diner. I stuck to the coffee while May tucked into a stack of pancakes that should have taken her a week to eat.

We headed back to our room, packed our stuff and checked out.

We hit the road at rush hour. The traffic on I-95 was clogged. I figured in the next hour or so it would quieten down and we had to keep heading south. As long as there were no major problems, we could be there by mid-afternoon.

I hadn't dared turn my cellphone on since yesterday. I knew there'd be who knows how many messages from TJ and maybe Reggie too. I dreaded picking them up. But feeling some distance between us, I reached into the glove compartment and pulled it out. I waited for the cellphone to wake up. I dialed my voicemail and held it away from my ear to protect it from TJ's bawling. There were two messages. Both from TJ. The first giving me an earful about taking off, and the second, about how I needed to handle the Camaro. He seriously needed to ease up on that car. I was handling it fine.

However, now TJ was on my case, Reggie would be, too. There was no saying what he would do. He was right, if the cops found out he knew about May all this time, he could lose his badge over this. I didn't feel good about the position I'd put him in, but I had no choice. I had to think about May first. She was just a kid.

23

If you've never been to Palm Beach before, which up until this moment I hadn't, I have two words that describe it to a T.

Holy. Cow.

This was some serious real estate.

We headed down Ocean Boulevard – and no kidding – I had to make sure I didn't go straight into the back of the vehicles in front of me as I took in the view. Not only of the white sandy beaches but, more to the point, the houses. The driveways leading towards them were bigger than my block. I have to admit, if you ever find you've a missing kid on your hands, there could be worse places to be than here. Even if I was paying for this road trip on my Visa card.

The nearest I'd ever got to playing on a beach was hiding off West 16th Street in Coney Island. I was thirteen years old. Me and a friend, Cookie, had managed to steal some pizza from one of those storefronts that sell them by the slice. Tony, the owner, caught us the moment we'd got the piece in our hand. Grabbing it, we both ran, the pizza slices flapping in our palms, neither of us wanting to let the damn thing go. We lost him after the first block. Or maybe he figured he may as well give up, but we didn't stop until we got to chicken-wire fencing by the old boatyard. We jumped over and huddled up against some rock. Boy, did that pizza taste good, even if half the toppings were still a couple of blocks back. We took off our shoes and socks, tucked up our pants and paddled in the water. Later, Cookie's cousin told her a corpse had been dragged out near to where we had been. So that was the last time I paddled in the sea.

'You see anywhere you recognize you yell out, OK?' I said to May.

May leaned further out of the window. Her chestnut locks whistling around her face, sunbeams dancing on her olive skin.

May pointed to the white sands. 'The beach!' she screeched.

'Yeah, the beach. You been here before?'

May nodded.

'You have?' My foot tapped the brake.

She nodded again.

I glanced around me, not quite believing it.

I signaled to the right and pulled the car to a stop. The Liberty of the Mind Legacy Center was a couple of miles from here. I had seen a motel on the internet close by I thought we could crash in. But as we overlooked the beach, it dawned on me that if May recognized where we were, there was every chance someone would recognize May. Until I had worked out what was going on and why she'd been dumped in New York, I didn't want to risk her being spotted.

'Are we going to play on the beach?' May said.

I took a breath. 'Not yet. Maybe later.' I placed the car in gear and signaled. When the street was clear, I turned the car back around, heading in the direction we had come from.

'Where we going?' May looked at me, confused.

'We have to do something real quick.'

I recalled a short while back we had passed a boulevard of stores. I drove for another fifteen minutes or so and pulled over.

'Come on.'

I stepped out of the car and walked around to May's door. I unclipped her seat belt and took her hand.

'You ever play dress–up?' I asked.

May nodded.

'Good. Let's go get you something.'

I headed towards a small children's store. From the items in the window display, it looked like it was aimed at people with more money than sense. However, it was my only shot. The other couple of stores were a jeweler's, a florist and a ladies' boutique.

The door beeped as we entered. A stick–thin woman stood behind a sales desk and glanced at us. The smell of coconut oil wafted by from a nearby diffuser. I scanned the store for something that would suit.

May wandered up towards a toy display on a center table.

I placed a big smile on my face and walked up to the sales clerk.

She leaned up from the counter.

'Hi. Do you have any fancy-dress outfits, or shades or hats or anything?'

The woman offered me a withering look. 'Well, we have shades for little ones and a couple of hats.' She pointed over to the far right-hand side.

I turned to look.

'Is there something particular you're after?'

A disguise for a missing child?

I checked behind me to see May wasn't in hearing distance. 'Oh, it's just my daughter has a slumber party with her friends, and they wanted to do a little bit of dress-up.' I forced a laugh.

The woman's face settled into a knowing smile.

'Well, the only things we stock are, as I say, the shades and hats, but how about something like this...' She stepped out from behind the counter. She led me towards the back, where nightwear clothes were stocked.

She leaned into a shelf and pulled out a few items that made my eyes widen.

'Any good?' She looked at me and back towards the outfits.

In her hands, she held up a couple of onesies. But not just any onesies. The first, designed like a lion, with a faux-fur mane and another a monkey, complete with a hood with ears.

Before I had the chance to make my excuses and simply buy a hat and shades for her, May ran up to us.

'Monkey!' she screeched.

'I think I'll just get a hat for—'

'Monkey. I want monkey.' May tugged on my jeans.

I looked at May and to the woman, who shrugged.

'Really?' I asked her.

'You said I was a monkey,' May said. 'Please.' She gazed up at me with doleful eyes.

I rolled mine at the woman and took the item from her. I walked back towards the front of the store. I grabbed a pink floppy summer hat and a pair of shades that would have looked more suitable on a reality-TV star and placed them all on the counter.

The sales clerk slipped them into a bag, rang up the cost on the cash register and offered me a smile. 'That will be eighty-two dollars.'

How much?

Trying not to balk at the cost, I flipped out my credit card and handed it to her.

With May in one hand and the ridiculously expensive outfit in the other, I walked out of the store and headed back to the car.

★

We drove for a couple more miles and pulled into the motel parking lot. Finally, like the waves on the beach, relief washed over me. Having made it here without incident, the anxiety gripping me earlier dissipated at the possibility I was so close to taking May home.

24

We strolled up to the main front-desk area of the motel. Already the place looked ten times better than where we had stayed the previous night. A fresh coat of white paint dazzled the brickwork.

A woman, early fifties, her face freckled from the sun, gave us a smile as we approached. Sandy, as her name tag suggested, typed my details into the computer.

I leaned down to May.

'Want to go down to the sea in a bit?'

'Yeah!' May screeched.

Sandy laughed and handed me a key on a large wooden dolphin. FAIR TIDINGS MOTEL embossed in gold on the front.

'Well, aren't you a cherry pie,' Sandy said, leaning over the wooden-top counter.

May held on to my leg and hid a little.

'Your momma taking you to the beach?' Sandy continued, determined to get May to talk.

May's face crumpled. 'That's not my mommy.'

I heard my own sharp intake of breath, and from the look Sandy gave me, she did too.

My heart drummed in my chest.

'I want my mommy,' May said, and looked up at me, her eyes now brimming with tears.

'I know, kid. I know.'

'I'm sorry, I …' Sandy's voice faltered a little.

May sniveled and, with no warning, she wailed. And when I say wailed, I mean, you remember the smoke alarm that went off? Well, the New York Fire Department had nothing on this.

Sandy shot a look at me and at the three-foot bundle bawling down her lobby.

I picked May up into my arms. 'Sorry about this. I'm looking after her while her mom's away and she's got some attachment issues,' I whispered.

I didn't wait for her reaction. May's fists beat against my chest, her caterwauling echoing around the walls. I pulled on the exit door with my free hand and scurried across the lot and up the metal stairs to our room. I placed her down on the floor, swiftly unlocked the door and slammed it shut behind us.

May jumped onto a bed, her fists now beating against the comforter.

Crap! She hadn't done this before. Sure, she had welled up and, to be honest, I thought it was a little weird she hadn't kicked off more before hanging around with TJ and me. But up until now, I had been more relieved than anything. If she didn't stop soon, we'd have the rest of the motel banging on our door.

I grabbed the cellphone out of my pocket and dialed TJ's landline. *Dammit.* The line rang out. Where the hell was he when I needed him? He'd know what to do. And why didn't I even think to bring a deck of cards to distract her.

I scanned the room for the remote, located it in the bedside cabinet drawer and flicked the television on. I channel-hopped until I found a cartoon. I lay on the bed beside May and held her screeching body in my arms until she eventually relented.

May's screaming turned into hiccups. Soon enough, her tear-stained, flushed face stared towards the television.

'I want Mickey,' she whispered.

I glanced around and remembered we'd left him in the car.

'OK, I'll go get him.' I smiled at her and kissed the top of her head.

I slipped off the bed, grabbed my car keys and left the room to collect our stuff.

I tumbled down the stairway towards the Camaro. Sandy peered across at me, one hand holding a phone to her ear.

I hurried to the car, grabbed Mickey Mouse, my bag and the groceries I'd bought from the gas station. I locked the car and gave Sandy a wave. The woman who had a short while ago greeted us with a smile, stared at me. She continued talking into the phone.

Was she calling the cops?

I headed back up to our room. I leaned over the balcony, glanced towards the front desk one last time and shut the door behind me.

May lay fast asleep on the bed. I tucked Mickey under her arm. I pulled the comforter over her legs and turned the television volume down. I perched on the bed beside her.

I picked up my phone and opened the internet. I typed in the White Pages telephone directory. 'Brown' and 'Palm Beach'. There were over thirteen thousand. Even if I discounted those aged over fifty, I'd still be left with thousands to call.

I opened up a new tab in the search engine. I tapped in Svaag Dimash's name. Article after article regarding the foundation came up. I scanned each one. I scrolled down to further links.

My finger hesitated over a news story.

EXONERATED LEADER SETS UP NEW CENTER

I tapped on the story. It was dated 2005.

> Robert Janin, formerly of the God's Greater Good Church,
> praised his followers today at a press conference. After
> finally being exonerated of any wrongdoing in the fraud
> charges brought against him, he thanked his supporters for
> standing by him the past eighteen months.
>
> 'I am sorry for any upset this may have caused our
> true followers. The fact I have been cleared of all charges
> cannot take away the hurt the authorities have caused to
> not only myself, but our organization as a whole. I can only
> hope we will be left alone to continue our great work and
> we can rebuild our center brick by brick, hope by hope,
> hand in hand.'
>
> Janin, who has changed his name to Svaag Dimash,
> opened up the new center in Arizona under the name
> Liberty of the Mind Legacy with the hope that every major
> American city would one day embrace his teachings.

I clicked off the link.

I tapped in the name 'Robert Janin' and 'God's Greater Good Church'.

News articles spanning over eighteen months reported the arrest of Janin. All describing the various fraud charges amounting to millions. Photos accompanied some of the articles. He stood on the steps of what must have been the center in Arizona. His fist raised in the air in defiance. I zoomed in on the picture. It may have been a number of years since it was taken, but it barely resembled the photo on the Liberty of the

Mind Legacy website. His hair much darker and longer. He'd clearly gone for the 'Jesus' look.

I glanced at May curled up in a ball under the comforter. I was exhausted and could only imagine how she felt.

If there was ever a time I wished I'd remembered to buy a quart of whiskey, let me tell you, now was it. I placed my cellphone on to the bedside cabinet and flicked through the TV channels for something, anything, to numb my mind.

I kicked off my shoes, grabbed a pack of potato chips and a soda and settled in for the night.

Around nine, it started to get dark outside. Footsteps thumped along the walkway, heading towards our room. Thinking, or at least hoping, they'd move on, I craned my neck and waited for them to pass. Instead, a shadow hovered by the window, followed by a loud rap of knuckles on the flimsy wooden door.

It seemed the desk clerk had called the cops after all.

25

The television rumbled in the background. May stirred a little beside me.

There was no way they'd believe we weren't in here.

I slipped off the bed and eased myself to the drapes. My legs trembled. I squinted through a tiny gap.

'Open up, Harper. I know you're in there.'

Goddammit. TJ.

I swung open the door. 'Crap!'

'Yeah, my thoughts exactly,' TJ said. He raised his eyebrows at me. He arched his neck and peered inside.

'She's asleep.' I slipped out of the room and shut the door behind me. 'Seriously, what are you doing...' Before I finished the sentence, Reggie walked up the steps, motel keys jangling in his hand. 'You've got to be kidding me?' I opened up my palms in astonishment.

'Harper,' Reggie said.

I shook my head and said nothing.

Reggie handed TJ a key.

For a moment we all stood on the walkway looking over the parking lot, not saying a word.

The smell of the ocean wafted by on a gentle breeze. Sweet, salty and without a hint of the Sheepshead Bay sewage.

'So, she got you here OK, then?' TJ said. He tilted his head to the Camaro.

I couldn't help but smile at the pride in his voice. 'Yeah, she did good.'

Reggie's gaze pressed on my chest like a heavy weight.

'So, how the hell did you know which motel I was in?' I asked.

TJ shook his head a little. 'It was hardly difficult figuring out where you had gone, and there's not many '74 Camaros parked up in the nearby motels.'

I shuffled on my feet, embarrassed.

Reggie exhaled loudly.

'Something you want to say?' I said to him. 'And haven't you got a job?'

'Well, if they find out why I'm here, maybe not, Harper. But for the time being, yes. I'm due some leave and, hey, I thought why not waste it trying to save your ass?'

I heard TJ take a deep breath in, waiting for the explosion.

My jaw tightened the same time as my fists. *Count to three, Harper.*

One.

Two.

On three, I leaned into TJ and planted a kiss on his cheek.

'There's a diner a block away. Go get some rest and I'll see you tomorrow for breakfast,' I said.

I opened my motel room door and closed it behind me.

Once I heard them leave, I smashed both of my clenched fists into the pillow until my heart stopped silently screaming.

26

The man paced the floor. The television blared out in the kitchen. A twenty-four-hour news channel looped continually. He had watched it for days now. There had been no reports.

He sat at the island, flipped the switch on his laptop and opened up the search engine. He checked all the news feeds. Still nothing.

The 'I'm sorry' note with the bled words lay on top of the marble. Perhaps it wasn't what he thought. If she was with the police, he would have heard by now. Surely.

He was a sitting duck, waiting for them to swoop. Anxious every time he heard a car pass by the house.

Maybe he should cut and run. He had lain awake all night, thinking through a plan. He could go to Europe. Get away from the States. If he went now, there was every chance he could escape unnoticed.

But this wasn't him. This wasn't who he was. Or so he had managed to convince himself all these years.

He stepped off the stool and walked to the back doors. He grasped the handle and pulled it back with a satisfying swoosh. He stepped out towards the pool. He stood on the edge, his bare toes gripping on to the stone. Mosaic tiles shimmered in the sunlight.

He gazed across the land. He had done well for himself. He had worked hard for it. He couldn't lose it all now.

No. He needed to sit tight. Wait it out. Carry on as if nothing had happened. After all, he was well-practiced. He could do this.

27

The next morning, May – dressed in her monkey outfit and designer shades – raced up to TJ. She squeezed her tiny arms around his legs.

'How you doing, kid?' TJ gave her a big grin and stared at me with a 'what the hell is she wearing?' look on his face.

I shrugged at him.

'You came,' she said, her cheeks like rosy apples.

'Yeah, well, couldn't let Harper have all the fun, now could I?'

'She's my best friend,' she said, proud.

I raised my eyebrows at TJ and grinned, equally proud.

We all slipped into a booth and ordered breakfast. Well, when I say breakfast, I stuck to coffee. Strong, and lots of it. I knew I was going to get a grilling about what my big plan was and I needed some serious caffeine to wake up my brain.

As Reggie tucked into his food, I took a moment to study him. His skin soft. Slight stubble poking from his chin, his long eyelashes flickering like butterfly wings. Yup, there was no denying he was hot. You only needed to ask the waitress who had served us. Not only did she bring him his breakfast, but it so happened the top two buttons on her blouse had come undone the minute she clocked him.

'So, I thought I'd take May up the coast a little bit this

morning. Give you two time to, you know, check out the sights,' TJ said. He opened his eyes wide to give us the hint.

Great. So, TJ was planning on Reggie joining me. This was going to be fun.

Reggie pushed his empty plate away, wiped his mouth with a napkin and eyeballed me.

I dug my nails into my jeans.

'Are we going to play in the sand?' May asked.

TJ shrugged. 'I don't see why not. I thought we could drive a little bit and find a beach you've never been to before. It'd be an adventure for both of us.'

May giggled. 'Can we get ice cream?'

TJ pulled a face for a moment and stroked his chin. 'Hmmm, do monkeys eat ice cream?'

May nodded.

'I think we might be able to manage that.'

'Yeah,' May said. She wiggled in her seat, her monkey ears flopping forward a little as she did.

We paid the check and made our way back to the motel to collect our stuff.

TJ tugged me aside as we walked into the parking lot. 'You want to explain the outfit?'

'It's the best I could do. I didn't want her, you know – recognized.'

'You don't think it draws attention?' He raised his eyebrows.

I shrugged a little. 'If you can get her to lose the shades, it might work a little better.'

TJ shook his head and smirked. 'I think you're right, though. For the time being, we should keep May away from this area, until you've scoped things out.'

I glanced across at her skipping alongside Reggie and nodded.

★

We agreed to meet TJ and May later that afternoon at a diner in Lantana, approximately a twenty-minute drive from the motel. That would give Reggie and I plenty of time to check out the center.

I grabbed my camera kit from the room. I went into the bathroom and scrutinized my reflection. *Dammit.* Why was I worrying about how I looked? But something about Reggie had that effect. Or at least he did on me. Maybe it was the cutesy-pie waitress making eyes at him. Whatever it was, it annoyed me.

I pulled myself together and left the room.

Reggie leaned against the Camaro. Shades on, arms crossed, his biceps swelling out of his T-shirt sleeves.

Feeling awkward, both of us nodded to each other. We headed down Murray towards South Flagler Drive. The headquarters were approximately a ten-minute walk from here. And on this occasion, a painful ten minutes. No, make that excruciating. Clearly, I wasn't the only one who didn't know what to say. His earlier comment about the irony of the situation shifted uneasily between us. For all my bravado, and his Mr Cool exterior, both of us were tongue-tied.

Ahead of us, a large white building overlooked the seafront. Surrounded by smaller buildings, But they were not small, by any stretch of the imagination. A long driveway flanked with huge stone pillars lay on either side.

Reggie and I raised our eyebrows at one another. This was some serious money these guys had.

At the top of the driveway, Reggie placed his hand on my shoulder.

'Look, before we go in, I need to tell you something.'

My brow crumpled. 'Go on.'

'I checked these guys out at work. There's markers against them. A lot of markers.'

'What do you mean "markers"?' I pulled up my shades.

'I mean the FBI is looking into them for all sorts of crap. I don't know what, I couldn't get into the files. But we need to tread real careful, Harper. If the Feds are looking into them, they could be into some serious shit.'

I paused a moment, trying to take in what he was telling me.

Reggie stared towards the front entrance, his face pensive. Even with shades on, I knew the look he had in his eye. I'd seen it before. He and TJ were like two peas in a pod. Once they had something between their teeth, it was hard to let it go. And yes, I admit, perhaps we weren't so different after all.

We strolled up the driveway. Lush green grass edged either side, sprinklers put-putted on the lawn. Men and women wore matching navy blue T-shirts. The red logo I had seen on the website – that looked like some cheap tattoo you'd get in Brooklyn that probably meant PEACE OUT MAN – emblazoned on the front and LIBERTY OF THE MIND LEGACY written across the back.

Everyone we passed waved and gave a polite smile to say hi. People worked on the land. They were cutting the lawn, pruning fruit trees, sweeping the long driveway. Others collected on the far side in a circle, legs crossed, listening to a woman reading aloud.

On the surface, everything appeared serene. But as I peeled my vision away from the circle of people, I spied cameras placed high up in the trees. Others located along the whitewashed brick wall surrounding the property.

We approached the main entrance. Two men dressed in dark suits – who looked like they'd be more comfortable in the Special Forces – studied everyone entering and exiting the building.

28

If there was one thing we were united on, this place being everything that made our skin crawl was definitely it.

First, I admit I'm not good around money. Well, I'm clearly not good with money, but being around it makes me uneasy. Second is a group of strangers smiling at you when they don't know you. And other than the two meatheads at the entrance, they all smiled. And I mean all. You only needed to catch someone's eye. They were there ready and waiting, with that glazed look in their eye, like they were high. But high on life. I mean, who gets high on life? *Eugh*.

We walked into the lobby of the main building. It was laid out more like a hotel than anything. A front desk on the left-hand side, a coffee-shop area on the right. Another security guy hovered towards the back.

My first thought, other than I wanted to get out of here, was why would they need this much security?

Ten a.m. and already the place buzzed with people.

We stepped into the front-desk area, like regular tourists. We were, of course, greeted with yet another smile.

'Are you interested in joining one of our seminars today?' A pamphlet wafted in the young woman's hand, ready. She had the look of a farm-girl. Plump cheeks and dimples, like life couldn't get any better.

Reggie and I stole a glance at each other. I let him take the lead.

'Sure, what'd you recommend?'

'There's a complimentary introductory seminar we do, which starts in approximately half an hour. And later this afternoon we have the intermediate course beginning, for which, if you're interested, we have a couple of spaces left. This one gets real full real quick, but we have an offer on today ...'

Reggie cut in. 'Why don't we give the seminar this morning a go and see how we get on?' He gave her a smile back.

'Of course, sir. Will it just be the two of you?'

Reggie nodded.

'It begins at ten thirty, and it's in lecture hall three, which you'll find out of the building and to your right. It's the Autarky building. In the meantime, feel free to have a look around.'

'Thank you, ma'am, you've been real helpful,' Reggie replied.

We both stood in the lobby and furtively scanned the area. Hallways led off in various directions. Some doors had keypad entry, others were wide open.

We walked along one of the hallways and stood outside a room with a large window in the door. A group of young adults kneeled in a semicircle throwing a soft red ball to each other. As one caught it, they yelled out a word and threw the ball to the next person. Reggie and I both stared in silence. I shook my head and made my way back into the lobby and along another hallway. I approached a room and peered through the glass. About twenty people, men and women, sat in rows, eyes closed in some sort of meditation. At the front of the room, a woman, hair tied up in a yellow and green scarf. She faced them, her head slightly bowed, eyes also closed.

Reggie leaned over. His breath blew against my neck. Goosebumps spiked at the memory. I whipped around and pushed past him. Reggie followed behind.

We shifted down the large steps and into the yard area. Following a gravel path towards the back of the building, we made our way between grapefruit and orange trees. The scent thick in the humid Florida air. People in uniform crouched at the earth, harvesting food.

'Can you believe people pay for this sort of garbage?' I whispered.

'People will pay for anything if it makes them feel better about themselves.'

Both our heads swiveled towards some giggling. In the far right-hand corner, a group of young children burst out of a building and ran towards a play area.

Two women followed behind them. They stood to the side and watched. One of the women in a burgundy smock glanced over in our direction, leaned into the other woman and said something. They both peered across, held my eye for a moment and turned their attention back to the kids.

'See that?' I said to Reggie.

'Uh-huh.'

We walked along a little further.

'What time is it?'

Reggie checked his watch. 'Ten ten. Shall we go get a drink?'

I nodded, shot the women one more look and turned back onto the path towards the coffee shop in the lobby.

*

We both nursed a drink and studied people coming and going. *How did May fit in to all of this?*

Reggie's eyes danced around, his brain whirring, trying to work out the same.

'Let's ask to speak to Svaag,' Reggie began. 'See what he has to say?'

I leaned in towards Reggie, keeping my voice low. 'What if he's involved? What if he has something to do with her being dumped in New York?'

'If he is, we have got to call the local cops in, Harper. At least we'll get to the truth sooner and we are a step closer to finding her mom.'

I glanced off to the side, my stomach churning. 'You think her mom's alive?'

'Because she hasn't reported May missing?'

I nodded, not really wanting him to answer.

Reggie looked away. 'Honestly, I don't know.'

He strolled over to the front desk. I followed behind. We waited for a man in front to finish chatting to the young woman. As he walked away, Reggie stepped forward and gave her one of his winning smiles.

'Hey, we were wondering, is it possible to speak to Svaag Dimash?'

The woman laughed to herself, as though Reggie had asked her if she would be willing to loan him a million bucks.

'I'm afraid not.' She pulled a pitying face. 'Svaag's away on a retreat in Nepal at the moment. He isn't due back for a couple of weeks.'

'Oh. Right. When did he leave? It's just, when I called, I was told he would be running some seminars,' Reggie said.

I stared at him, curious. *He was good at this.*

'There must have been a mix-up. Svaag went on the retreat

on the twenty-ninth last month, and he's not due back for another four weeks. May I ask who you spoke to?' she said.

The twenty-ninth? The day before the date on the note.

'I don't recall. You know when he's due back, exactly?'

The young woman peered at Reggie. Her eyesight shifted towards the security guard.

'I'm afraid not, sir. We do have a talk scheduled for him in November, but it's fully booked. I'm afraid these things get full before we even announce them. I could put you on the waiting list in case we get any cancellations—'

Reggie cut in, 'Hey, don't worry about it. Thank you anyhow.'

I heard him take a deep breath as he turned to me and raised his eyebrows.

Nepal? Seriously?

29

The Autarky building, impressively large, white and dome-shaped, looked more like a chapel than an auditorium from the outside. Inside, the hall crammed with people. The plush elevated seating set out like a regular movie theater. A large stage at the front.

I turned around and clocked two free seats next to each other. I tugged Reggie's arm and we made our way down the deep red carpeted stairway and along the aisle.

Folks around us chatted to each other. Reggie and I said nothing, for fear of being overheard. A few minutes later, the lights dipped and the auditorium hushed.

A spotlight flickered.

A man, approximately mid-forties, who had spent too much time on his tan and teeth, sauntered onto the stage. The audience erupted into applause. Thick brown hair combed back. He wore khaki slacks and a crisp pale pink, long-sleeved cotton shirt.

'Please, please.' The guy held his hands up in mock surrender. 'Please, sit.' He held a microphone in his hand like he was some sort of rock star.

Compliant, they quietened, the hum of appreciation still in the air.

'Thank you. For those who don't know me, my name is Trey Garrison.' His southern voice came out like candy.

The audience whooped again. This was going to be painful.

Trey peered out into the audience. He shaded his eyes from the intense beam of light that did nothing for his perma-tan complexion.

'It's so good to see so many people here.'

Trey took a sip of water, placed the bottle on a table and rolled up his sleeves. The crowd sat in silence as though waiting for a magician to complete a trick.

When he had finished, he picked up the microphone and gazed into the crowd.

'Let me ask you a question. Who here has felt guilty about something?'

The majority of the audience raised their hands. The woman next to me arched her arm high. She glanced at me. My hands remained firm in my lap.

'Everyone, right?' Trey paced up and down the stage.

'We all feel guilt. We didn't call Mom, we didn't finish a job, we didn't go to Billy's baseball game. A relationship didn't work out. There's always something to feel bad about. But when do we feel good? When do we take the time to congratulate ourselves for calling Mom, going to the game, getting a job done. Rarely, right?'

People nodded.

'We need to stop suffering from guilt and start feeling good about ourselves. We're programmed to undergo negativity all the time. We feel bad because we earn money, we feel bad because we have a good life, we feel bad because we treated ourselves to a new car.' Trey took another sip of water. 'We have got to stop this. We have got to learn to experience good

about ourselves and this is what we at the Liberty of the Mind
Legacy help you do.'

Again, more people nodded.

'You know, recently I was in New York...'

My head spun towards Reggie. He subtly nodded at me.

'...And I got out of the subway and I looked around me,
and everyone had their heads down. They were either on their
phones, they were texting, they were bickering with someone,
they were in their own world, and you know something?'
Trey paused dramatically. 'They all looked sad. Not one person
appeared happy. They were just ... so miserable. They were mill-
ing around like ants, being crushed by life. I mean, what is that
about? Is that what we are here for?'

The audience shook their heads.

'Do we really want to be ants?' he continued.

'No!' a guy shouted out from the crowd. The audience
laughed.

'Now, I want to ask you all to do something for me.' Trey
paused. 'I want each and every one of you to close your eyes
and hold the hand of the person sat right next to you.'

A murmur emanated through the audience.

'I know, there's some of you guys out there who don't want
to hold hands, but go with me on this. As my sweet momma
used to say, "Can't never could." Words I didn't truly understand
until I came here.' Trey held his hand to his heart.

Reggie took my hand in his. Not wanting the woman next
to me thinking she could do the same, I snapped it back and
placed it on my lap.

'OK, now I want you to keep your eyes closed, and I want
you to focus your mind on your hands.'

The auditorium fell silent. I looked around and everyone was doing as they were told. Reggie and I glanced at each other. The look of horror on our faces.

'Can you feel your neighbors' pain?'

Trey perched on the stool center stage and held his palms up to the audience, his eyes shut tight.

'Let those next to you connect with your problems, feel their fear and know that from this moment on we are here to help you. We can all help each other.'

People still had their eyes shut tight. They nodded to themselves, squeezing their hands and smiling.

'When you're ready, I want you to open your eyes.' Trey kept his palms up to the audience. After what seemed like an eternity, he opened his eyes and stood from his stool.

'Now, I want to hear from you guys. Tell me, who here has lost someone they loved?'

Arms shot up across the room. *Why on earth do these people do it?*

And then I noticed it. Reggie had his hand held up high.

I swear, my jaw swung open.

Trey glanced around the audience. His eyes landed on Reggie. He nodded and smiled at him.

A young pockmarked man – dressed in one of their T-shirts, stud in his left ear – appeared at the end of our row. A microphone made its way to Reggie. A spotlight falling straight on him.

To say I wanted to die at this point doesn't come close.

What was he thinking?

Reggie stood, microphone in hand. The whole of the audience's eyes on him.

'Let me ask your name first of all,' Trey said, his voice like caramel.

Without any hesitation, Reggie replied, 'Ron.'

I bit the inside of my cheek. *Seriously? Ron?*

'Tell us your story, Ron,' Trey said.

Reggie paused. 'It was a while back now.' He took a deep breath. The auditorium was silent.

'I'd met this girl. God, she was hot.' The crowd rippled with laughter. 'The usual story. We dated, we fell in love, she was, let's say … high-maintenance.'

My body tensed.

Guys nodded as if they related.

'But she was worth it,' Reggie said. He cleared his throat.

I wanted to rip it out.

My fingernails clenched so hard into my skin, I thought they were going to tear right through.

Reggie continued. All eyes on him. 'I knew she was the one. Y'know, our future lay ahead of us, a little house, a couple of kids running around, and I don't mind admitting I was excited.' Reggie shrugged.

More nodding from the audience. *What is wrong with people?*

'Then, pow, just like that, she ended it.' He clicked his fingers.

A gasp emanated across the auditorium.

I wanted to punch him.

'She didn't want any kids.'

I closed my eyes. My teeth gritted together.

'Said she wasn't cut out to be a mom and I needed to find someone who was. I didn't even get a say in it. Next thing I know, she was gone, she didn't return my texts, my calls, nothing.'

The guy next to Reggie shook his head.

Reggie slapped his hand against his chest with a thump. 'My heart ripped out.'

I was going to kill him. Really, I was going to kill him. Slowly and painfully.

The audience was silent. Some nodded and, no shit, a couple of people wiped their eyes.

Trey stood from his stool. The audience's gaze turned to him.

'Thank you, Ron. That was truly brave of you.' Trey paused. He breathed air out of his cheeks, as if to take on the gravity of what 'Ron' had revealed.

You have got to give it to him, this guy was a real showman.

'Ron. Let me tell you, you're not alone.'

Reggie nodded and peered around at the audience. The spotlight moved off him and back to Trey.

Reggie sat, glanced in my direction and winked.

The look I shot back said everything he needed to know.

'At the Liberty of the Mind Legacy, we teach you a way to accept the obstacles we come across. Whether it's a broken heart, a serious illness, the loss of someone. No matter what the hurdle is, we can overcome it.' Trey paced the stage, his voice lifting a little like a southern preacher ready to give his Sunday sermon. 'When Svaag wrote his teachings, the first thing he said is we have to accept the obstacles, embrace them, invite them in as if they're a dear friend. Sit down at the table with them and try to understand them.'

Trey held his palms up towards the audience. 'I know, I know, you're all thinking, easier said than done, and you're right. It's not easy. That's why we take our time here at the center, listening to you, hearing exactly what you're up against. Our first course is two weeks long, and I'm not going to lie, it's not comfortable. Trust me, I've done it, and I thought to myself, is this what I've signed up for, to turn my insides out? But then –' Trey held up one finger and pointed towards the ceiling, '– once I'd laid out all my worries, my problems, my deepest secrets, things I hadn't even admitted to myself before,

I felt this lightness creep inside of me. A lightness I hadn't felt before. A space in my mind opened up, allowing me to think, see things clearly and finally take the right path.' Trey stopped center stage. He gazed over the audience. 'Who here wants to learn how to take the right path?'

Arms shot up across the audience. I couldn't believe what I was seeing.

A couple more people droned on with their sob stories. The audience listened intently to their woes. They shared saddened glances, shook their heads and hung on to Trey's every word.

Trey drew the session to a close. 'There's a few people at the back there who would love to talk to you more about the Acceptance Course, so catch one of them on your way out, and I'll hopefully see you guys real soon.'

The audience stood and applauded him. Trey waved to them and exited stage left.

The lights flicked back up. I shifted past Reggie before he had a chance to stand. There was no way I was spending another minute around him.

A woman, mid-thirties with long dark hair, stood at the exit with a clipboard in her hand.

'Hi. How did you find the seminar today?' she asked me. Again, with the smile. I wanted to strangle them all.

'Great. You tell me where the restroom is?'

'Oh. Right. It's up towards your left, but if you have a minute I wanted to …'

I didn't wait for her to finish her sentence. I headed straight to the restroom and locked the door behind me.

I stood over the basin, the cold faucet running, and stared at myself in the mirror. Rage buzzed in my veins. It was one thing trying to fit in so we could figure this out, it was another to humiliate me in front of these idiots.

I splashed water over my face. My skin flushed. I needed a moment to calm down.

When I left the bathroom, the audience had dispersed into various areas of the lobby. People huddled around staff with clipboards, chatting about the seminar. A group of women flocked around Reggie. A guy approached and shook his hand.

I was sick of this place, and the sooner I found out how May was connected, the better. I wanted out.

I slipped out from the building and walked towards the back entrance. Checking no one was close by, I tucked myself into a small walkway and waited.

Minutes later, Trey stormed out of the rear exit, his hand up to his ear on a phone call.

I pulled back and watched him from afar.

He rounded the corner. His voice rose as he spoke into the phone. But rather than having a voice like candy, it sounded agitated.

I shifted a little closer and pressed my body against the wall.

'What's that supposed to mean?' Trey snapped.

So much for 'we're here to make you feel better.'

He paused.

'There must be some trace. People don't just disappear into thin air.'

Again, another pause.

'And my documents?'

Trey threw his hands up in the air.

'How long can it take? I gave him three thousand dollars in cash, for Chrissake. You sure he's up to the job?'

Trey listened.

'Fine, keep me posted.'

He ended the call and I kept out of sight until I was sure he had gone. I waited a moment longer. But as I rounded the corner, I don't know who jumped more, me or him.

30

Both of us took a second as we caught our breath.

Trey looked me up and down before saying a word.

'Can I help you, darling?' The candy-voiced man was back.

'I'm sorry. I was ... I was in your talk a moment ago, amazing by the way ...' I tried not to choke on my own words. 'I wanted to ask, do you know how I can get hold of Svaag? I'd love to meet him.'

He sized me up before replying, taking a little too long to move his eyes away from my chest.

'Svaag is at our West Coast center at the moment.' Trey paused and licked his lips. His mouth moved into a smile, not quite reaching his eyes. 'Anything I can help you with?' Again, he eyeballed me up and down.

'No, it's fine. Thank you.' I gave him a similar smile back, turned and headed along the driveway leading towards the exit.

'Hey, wait up.'

Reggie's footsteps thumped behind me. I didn't bother to turn. Right now I needed him to stay away from me.

'Harp, wait ...' He placed his hand on my shoulder.

I spun around and, with my hands on my hips, I glared at him.

'Look, I'm sorry. I was just playing around.' Reggie held both his hands up in surrender.

'What, and you thought it'd be funny, humiliating me in front of that bunch of wackos?'

'Who said I was talking about you?' Reggie winked at me.

I refrained from punching him.

'Look, Harp, I'm sorry. Thought it would lighten the mood a little. You're right, they're wackos and I thought we could have a little fun.' Reggie paused. 'Like old times.'

My stomach flipped.

I marched out the driveway and along South Flagler.

'Can we at least be civil?' Reggie said.

I scowled at him and carried on walking.

'I'm sorry, OK?'

'See you had a horde of women flocking around you after the seminar.' I raised an eyebrow.

'Jealous?' Reggie smirked.

'No, I...' I answered too quick.

'I'm kidding. You're right, they were, and guess what they wanted? Apart from some of this.' Reggie fanned his hand across his body.

I couldn't help but smile. 'We did agree they were wackos. Go on, what did they really want?'

'To sign me up for this "enlightening acceptance course" that would help me mend my broken heart.' Reggie flicked his fingers for quotation marks.

'Oh yeah. How much it going to cost you?'

'Guess.'

'Reggie, I'm not in the mood for—'

'Four thousand dollars.'

I stopped dead on the sidewalk and swiveled towards him. 'How much?'

'Exactly. And think how many more suckers were in the hall. Now you can see how they can afford a place like that.'

I shook my head. *Four thousand dollars?*

We took a bus to Lantana and strolled towards the diner. I told Reggie about my encounter with Trey.

'You think he knows something?'

I shrugged. 'I don't know, he's just … creepy. You should have seen the way he looked at me.'

Reggie bristled.

'And, according to him, Svaag's on the West Coast. So, so much for him being on a retreat.'

Reggie and I walked a few more blocks in silence, both of us churning through the possibilities.

I have to say, there was something about seeing TJ and May together that lifted my heart. Perhaps it was a throwback to the many times TJ had taken me out for something to eat after catching me for the hundredth time running away from one of the flea-ridden hovels I was forced to stay in. 'One day at a time,' he'd always tell me. He knew it wouldn't be long before we'd be playing cat and mouse again. There was something about how he treated me, though, I'd never had before. Watching him now with May, who was half the age I was before I met him, made me think of those times.

I approached the table, leaned in and kissed him on the top of his forehead.

'Good day?' I asked.

May jumped in and told us all about the beach, the sandcastles, how TJ rolled up his pants for a paddle and still got soaked. It was good to see her giggling.

When May finished, TJ looked at both of us and sensed our body language.

'You two good?'

We both nodded.

May slipped out of her seat. She tumbled over to a cordoned-off area of the diner. It was filled with cheap plastic and foam blocks to clamber on and some wooden toys that looked like they'd come out of the Ark.

'What's going on?' TJ said.

We filled him in on what we'd discovered regarding Svaag.

'So we have no idea where he is?'

'Or if he's even connected to May,' Reggie added.

I looked across at her. 'I think Trey knows more than he's letting on.'

'About what?' TJ's face creased.

'About Svaag, and maybe May.' I told them the little I had heard from his phone call.

'That could have been about anything,' Reggie said.

I shrugged.

'So now what?' TJ asked, opening his hands up.

I glanced at TJ and at Reggie. 'I say we go back and this time we follow him.'

31

The following morning, we left TJ and May having breakfast and headed back to the lot to pick up the Camaro. The HQ may have been a short walk away, but if we were going to follow this guy, we needed to be ready.

We pulled onto the center's driveway and parked up, making sure we were in a spot where we'd be able to move fast if we needed to.

We stayed in the car, in fear of being pounced on by some loony tune wanting to sign us up for our life savings.

Reggie pointed over to the far left, where a building stood at the back. A line of young children crocodile-marched up to the front. They were supervised by the same women as yesterday. We watched and waited.

'What you think that's about?'

I shook my head. 'Their blurb said they do kids' camp? Should we go over there? Show them May's photo?'

Reggie paused. 'Not yet, we don't know what we're walking into. Let's see if we can find out in here.'

He indicated to the main lobby. We stepped out of the car and shifted up the steps towards the front desk. The same woman was manning the station. She greeted us with a smile.

'You came back. That's wonderful. I knew you would.' Her dimples creased.

My lip curled at her self-satisfied manner.

'Is that a school you got going over there?' Reggie said. He thumbed to the outside.

'Sure is. We have classes running throughout the day over the summer. And in the fall we have selected classes for some of our senior members. You have kids?'

Reggie stumbled. 'Not yet. You mean like a daycare for your workers?'

'Well, we don't describe ourselves as workers as such. More volunteers. But yes, daycare.'

'Interesting,' Reggie said. He gave her a polite nod and walked away.

Reggie and I parked ourselves in the coffee shop. I'd picked up the day's 'itinerary'. Trey had a session already ongoing and one at eleven. He wasn't scheduled for any more after that, but it didn't necessarily mean he was going anywhere.

There was no way I could face sitting in another 'poor me' lecture. Who knows what stupid trick Reggie would pull. So after we'd finished our drinks, we decided to go for a stroll around the grounds and wait until Trey made an appearance.

It felt weird to be walking among the greenery, the sweet smell of the sea combined with the citrus plants. My life had always been in New York. I had barely traveled beyond it. I loved the nitty-gritty of the city. The buildings that loomed high, shadowing out the light. The sound of the sirens, the buzz of humanity swarming around me. That to me was as close to a feeling of home as I had ever had.

*

We perched on a wooden bench in the far corner, overlooking the grounds and main building.

'What do you think draws people to this?' I asked. I was genuinely confused.

'I don't know. Sadness? Loss? Wanting to belong to something?' Reggie shrugged.

I turned to him. The sun flickered on his skin. 'Don't tell me you're falling for it?'

Reggie winced. 'No, I'm just saying life throws you off course sometimes and I guess they're looking for some sort of anchor.'

'An expensive anchor,' I said. 'Rich folk with first-world problems.'

We sat in silence, the heat beating on our faces. It was the first time since I had seen Reggie I felt relaxed. We sat like any couple, comfortable in the quiet space between us.

'Think we'll find them?' I asked.

Reggie shifted his body in my direction. 'Her parents?'

I nodded.

Reggie placed his hand on my thigh. I had to catch my breath.

'I don't know,' Reggie said. 'But I do get why this is important to you.'

He lifted up his shades and stared into my eyes. My insides crumbled. We held each other's gaze. I sensed his breath close to my face.

A door slammed at the side of the main building. Both of us sat bolt upright. Trey, a cellphone next to his ear, hurried towards a car.

Reggie and I jumped up and rushed over to the parking lot. Before I had a chance to protest, Reggie shifted into the Camaro's driving seat. Surrendering, I got in the passenger side and waited for Trey to pass.

★

Trey's car couldn't have stuck out more if he had tried. A canary-yellow Viper. The exhaust roared as he pulled out of the driveway. If he decided to press his pedal to the metal, there was no way we'd be able to tail him. He'd be gone in a shot. Lucky for us, the road hummed with traffic. Reggie stayed a couple of cars behind and headed along South Lakeside Drive.

The water from the nearby ocean glistened in the light. Boats bobbed on the waves, the sound of clinking from the yachts' sails.

I glanced at Reggie, shades on, window down, his arm sticking out. My heart hammered against my ribs.

We followed Trey for approximately ten minutes. He turned onto a side street off South Ocean Boulevard. He paused in front of an ornate iron gate, manned by a uniformed guard in a small security building. We held back towards the bottom of the street and waited. The guard opened the gate and flagged Trey in. As the tail end of his car inched through the entrance, we pulled up a little closer.

It opened up to a huge cream villa. The Viper drew onto a long driveway heading towards the building. Formal gardens edged the entrance.

'Whoever he's meeting likes a lot of security,' Reggie said. He nodded towards the cameras overlooking the property.

'It could be his place.'

'No. He had to lean in and talk to the guard.'

The iron gates closed to.

'Hold on,' Reggie said. He opened the car door, walked up to the guy and spoke with him. I peered through the window, trying to make out what was being said.

Less than a minute later, Reggie jumped back into the car.

'He's not giving us anything. Politely told me to move along, else he'd call the cops.'

'How's it feel to be on the other side of the law?' I smirked.

Reggie shook his head.

'Does it look out to the front?' I asked.

Reggie shrugged.

'Turn the car around,' I said.

'What?'

'Turn it around. Drive back to the beach.'

We slid out onto the main strip which separated the villa from the beach.

'Stop. Pull over here,' I said, and glanced up at the beachfront house.

'We're not going to be able to see anything from here. It's too far away.'

'Pull up,' I snapped.

Reggie sighed and turned in.

I leaned over onto the back seat and grabbed my purse.

'Now we can see in.' I tugged my camera out and fixed on the zoom lens.

I pointed my camera up towards the direction of the balcony. At first there were only shadows, but moments later, there he was. Trey Garrison.

Snap. Gotcha.

32

Trey sauntered up to the brick motor court and smoothed down his shirt and pants. He wiped sweat from his brow. He really didn't need this conversation.

The carved oak door opened. A butler nodded. Trey didn't bother to acknowledge him. He stepped through the main lobby. Curious, he scanned the house. A marble fountain trickled into the large font. Fish mouthed the surface of the water in search of food. Trey leaped up the stairs cascading through the center of the building. It was essential he calmed himself. Act like nothing was wrong. Like nothing couldn't be fixed. Get out and focus on his bigger plan.

When he entered the vast living area, Svaag's back was to him. He stood at the windows, gazing towards the beach. When he turned and faced Trey, Trey couldn't help but show his shock.

'Whose place is this?' Trey asked.

'A friend's. Being careful, that's all.' Svaag's voice was almost a whisper. Gentle, poetic. He offered Trey a glass of water. 'Any word?'

Trey shook his head. He surveyed the living area. A large stone fireplace on the far right-hand side. The floors, chevron-patterned oak. The glass doors leading to a coquina terrace overlooking the beach.

'I have people all over looking for her.' Trey clenched his fists and cleared his throat. 'The place is empty. All her stuff, the kid's stuff, all gone.'

'She can't have just disappeared.' Svaag paced the floor.

Trey took a deep breath and nodded. 'We'll find her.' Looking at Svaag now, it was hard to believe he had fallen for his crap all those years ago. Still, Trey couldn't slip. He had to buy time. And this was a complication he could do without.

Something had been amiss for a while. Instinct was an itch. It wriggled around in his belly like some putrid little bug. It was, after all, why he'd decided to feather his own nest. A little here, a little there. But it seemed Melissa had other plans. Had they gotten too greedy? It had been so easy for so long, perhaps they should have taken more care. But money blinds even the most paranoid of men. Did she know something they didn't? Svaag was always too caught up in his big plans, his schemes and, most importantly, himself, to realize if something was hovering on the horizon. Or was he? After all, here he was, hidden away 'being careful'.

Trey tried to assure himself he was being too suspicious. But there was no escaping the fact Melissa was missing. There was every chance she had gone to the Feds. Was it every man for himself? Should he go too? Tell them everything he knew in exchange for immunity.

No. He hadn't worked this hard to walk away from it all. Not without his just reward.

'I need you to meet someone,' Svaag said. He sipped water through a straw. 'A potential donor.'

Trey's brow creased.

'It's important. It could be a lot of money. I'd ordinarily do it, but ...' Svaag waved his hand towards his face.

Trey nodded. 'Does it hurt?'

Svaag shook his head. 'Nothing I can't handle.'

'Who do you want me to meet?'

'His name is Mackenzie. James Mackenzie. Property portfolio. His marriage is, well, not exactly solid. Lost his way. Usual story. He's been attending some of the seminars and I think he would make a good investor.'

Trey covered his smirk. *Investor*. He loved how Svaag fell for his own bullshit. When he said 'investor', he meant 'mark'. And Svaag had no qualms bleeding them for everything they had. Except this time, Trey was going to get in there first.

'Do we have an appointment?' Trey asked.

'No. He's apparently away on business. He'll call. Check him out, give him the spiel, you know the rest.'

Trey did. He pulled back the large glass door with a whoosh. He stepped out onto the expansive terrace framing the property. The warm air hit his skin. Gargantuan terracotta pots filled with lemon and orange trees edged the side, their scent infusing the air. He closed the door behind him. Trey strolled to the front and placed his briefcase on a glass and rattan yard table. He plucked an orange from a tree, proceeded to peel it and leaned against the pink brick wall and admired the view.

The white sands stretched as far as the eye could see, surrounded by palm trees dotted along the beach. It was hard to tell where the turquoise sea ended and the sky started. Never as a kid did he believe he'd be living somewhere like this. Hey, not just as a kid. He thought back to ten years ago. He'd sit in his beat-up Chevrolet, eating corn dogs from some street vendor, trying not to get grease on his cheap suit. He'd venture back out onto the sidewalks, knocking door to door to get some commission on goods no one wanted to buy.

But here he was, finally. And he would be damned if anyone was going to stop him getting what he deserved. Not him, and certainly not her.

Trey pared off an orange segment and ate it, sweet juice filling his mouth.

He heard the whoosh of the doors opening. Svaag approached from behind.

Trey turned and picked up his briefcase and removed a blue folder.

'I need your signature on a couple of things.' He pulled out an ink pen from his inside jacket pocket and passed it to Svaag.

Svaag flipped open the folder and leaned over the table. He signed the documents and checks and passed the folder back to Trey.

He placed his hand on Trey's shoulder.

'You know I trust you like a son, don't you, Trey?'

Trey found it hard to look at him and take him seriously.

'Find her,' Svaag said.

Trey nodded.

'Good boy. I know you will. I don't need to tell you what we could lose.' Svaag slapped his shoulder. He took the rest of the orange from Trey's hand and retreated into the property.

'What can you see?' Reggie said.

'Give me a minute.' I waved my finger at him.

Trey Garrison leaned with one hand on the balcony door. He was talking to someone, but it was difficult to see who.

He turned and walked to the front of the balcony ledge, looking out at the view. He wouldn't be able to spot us from this far away, but the fact I could see him still made me nervous. It appeared like he was staring right at us.

I kept my hand steady and rested the lens on the half-open window.

'Anything?' Reggie asked, impatience in his voice.

'Just wait.'

Trey turned to face someone and passed him something. I pressed the shutter. Seconds later, whoever he was with stepped forward.

'What the hell?' I muttered to myself.

'What? What is it?'

I tilted back in my seat.

Reggie leaned over and peered through the viewfinder.

'What on earth?' Reggie said.

I pushed Reggie back out of the way, and while I had the chance, I pressed the shutter again and took as many snaps as I could.

The guy Trey was talking to had bandages wrapped around his face, like he'd been in a serious car accident or something.

'Think he's been in a fight?' Reggie asked.

'One hell of a fight.'

I took a couple more snaps and pulled the lens back into the car.

'Drive back up to where you were. Let's wait and see where he goes.'

Reggie did, and before long we saw the Viper slip out of the gates and onto the main boulevard.

Cautious, we pulled out and followed him.

Trey put the car in reverse. The iron gates creaked open.

He nodded to security and pressed his foot on the gas. With a satisfying rumble, he accelerated onto the side street towards the main boulevard.

Rather than views of white sands and blue seas, all he could see in front of him right now was a long sentence in a Federal prison. Svaag's words regarding what they could lose rang in his ears.

There was no way Svaag would take the risk of going to prison. After all, wasn't that why he was hiding out in someone else's home? Perhaps it was time for him to pull the plug. Get out while he could. The situation was spiraling out of his control. But the idea of one more donor filling up his pot of gold was too good to resist.

Reggie slowed as Trey's vehicle signaled into the driveway of an apartment complex. Pausing a beat, he steered the car aside.

Trey got out of the car and walked into the building.

'Wait here,' Reggie said.

He exited the car and headed towards the entrance. He scanned the area and seeing it was clear, he pressed his face against the glass on the front door.

A minute later, he was back. The car door slammed. He turned over the engine and reversed.

'Well?' I asked.

'Well, nothing. It's a regular apartment block and he definitely lives there,' Reggie answered.

'How d'you know?'

'I could make out his name on the mailbox. Apartment sixteen.' Reggie checked the road was clear and headed in the direction of the motel.

I braced myself before I spoke. 'So I'm guessing we only have one option.'

33

'No way.' Reggie shook his head.

'You got a better idea?' I asked him.

Judging by the look he shot me, I soon regretted the question.

'Yeah. I had it in New York. Take her straight in.' Reggie, jaw clenched, kept his eyes on the road.

'If we got a look inside the apartment, we would at least be able to see if he has anything to do with it.'

'Harper, I get he was hiding something when you asked him about Svaag, but it doesn't mean he's involved.'

'So who was the guy he was seeing, the one who'd been in a fight?'

'It could have been anyone.'

Frustration rose in Reggie's voice.

'So you don't think that was Svaag?'

'I don't know.'

'Say it was Svaag, and he'd been beaten up because he's involved in something seriously shady. Trey knows that, which is why he lied to my face. It means he could know a whole lot more. If we got a look around the apartment, we would know for sure.'

Reggie signaled and steered the Camaro to the side of the

road. He waited until the stream of cars overtook him and turned to me.

'Harper, I am a cop. You understand that, right?'

I took a slow breath in and gazed out of my window.

Seeing I had nothing more to say, Reggie pulled out and headed towards our motel.

TJ called mid-afternoon to check in on us. He and May were still at the beach. Reggie and I suggested we drive up there and grab something to eat, save them catching the bus back. Having seen the extent of what appeared to be serious injuries to the unknown man's face, I was relieved TJ had taken May a little further afield. Who knows what he was involved in.

Except Trey. He was our only lead right now, and despite Reggie's reservations, I knew I had to get into his apartment.

May was tucking into a strawberry milkshake by the time we arrived at a coffee shop overlooking the bay.

'Hey, kid.' I gave her a smile.

She looked up. A smattering of pinky-white residue around her lips.

'Harper's here!' She wriggled in her seat.

'You have a good day?' I asked her.

She nodded and took another gulp of milkshake.

'Will you come to the beach tomorrow? I can show you the secret shells,' May asked me.

'Secret shells, huh?'

'That's where the fairies in the sea live sometimes.'

TJ nodded to her in agreement.

'Well, I'd love to see them. You sure you can let me in on the secret?'

May giggled. 'Yeah, but you can't tell anyone,' she whispered.

I made a zipper motion across my lips with my fingers and winked at her.

I could tell by TJ's expression he was keen to find out what had happened, but with little ears around, we knew we'd have to wait. Catching the waitress's attention, we ordered something to eat.

We settled up and wandered along the sidewalk adjacent to the beach, watching the boats bob on the bay.

Reggie walked a little to the side with May, asking her about the day. As soon as I heard her tell Reggie a story about a woman on the bus with a puppy, I knew she would be too occupied to listen in on our conversation.

'How has she been?' I asked.

'Good, considering. She was asking after her mom and dad again.'

'What did you say?'

'What could I say? I told her we were looking for them, that it was an adventure and she could help us find clues to track them down. What about you?'

I ran TJ through the events from the kids' daycare, to the bandaged man's fortress and finally to Trey's apartment.

'You think there's something in there that would give us a lead?' TJ asked, without me suggesting it.

'I don't know, but I think it's worth a shot.'

'And this guy – the one with the bandages – you think that could be Svaag?'

'It was impossible to tell, but his home was covered in security, cameras, a manned gate, you name it, just like the center.'

TJ went quiet for a moment. 'What about the apartment?'

'What about it?' I looked at TJ.

'Did you see much security?'

My pulse quickened. I shook my head.

'No. It looked like a regular apartment complex.'

'Think we could get in?' TJ asked.

I couldn't help but smile. I guessed from his question, TJ was missing the buzz of police work more than he had been letting on.

'I think I know how.'

We didn't say another word until we were back at the motel. We agreed to meet in the parking lot, once May was fast asleep. That way, we could at least talk without her hearing and keep an eye on the room at the same time.

The second we entered our room, May jumped up onto her bed. She kicked off her sandals and bounced up and down on the mattress.

'You be careful you don't make yourself sick again, kid.'

'I won't.'

I plopped myself on my bed.

'Is TJ your daddy?' May asked.

I took a beat to answer.

'No. He … he's kinda like my dad. Remember, I said he was my best friend?'

May crumpled her face in confusion.

'He looks out for me. Like we are looking out for you,' I said.

'My daddy said I'm a princess,' May said.

'He did, huh. Well, I agree.' I stood and bowed at her bedside. 'And I am your lady-in-waiting.'

May giggled.

'And we need to get this princess clean, so let's get you showered and into bed.'

I lifted her up and led her into the bathroom. I stripped her and popped her into the shower. Grains of sand collected in the pan. Running the water, I lathered some soap and, trying not to spray myself at the same time, I gave May a quick clean. The bathroom mirror misted up.

I wrapped her in a towel and dressed her in the Net's T-shirt.

'Clean teeth, ten minutes of TV and then lights out for you.' I squeezed out some paste onto the brush and passed it to her. 'You've got some serious shell finding to do tomorrow,' I said.

'You going to come with us?'

'Of course I am, kid. I can't be missing out on this secret, can I? I've got to go do something real quick in the morning, but then I want to hear all about these fairies in the sea.'

While May finished up in the bathroom, I picked up my camera and scanned through the photos I had taken. *Who was Trey talking to? And what had he passed him?* I zoomed in a little closer. *A file?*

I heard the toilet flush.

'You finished in there?' I shouted towards the bathroom.

May came out with a grin on her face.

'What's that smile for?' I asked her. I placed the camera to the side.

May giggled. 'Nothing.'

I lifted her onto the bed, tucked her up into the covers and wrapped my arm around her. The smell of soap on her skin.

I picked up my camera and flicked back through the photos. 'You ever seen this guy before?' I zoomed in on the picture of Trey.

May shook her head.

'What about this place?' I showed her a wide shot of the villa.

'No.'

'This one?' It was a photo of the Liberty of the Mind Legacy exterior.

May shrugged and yawned.

'Tired?'

May nodded and curled up under the covers. It was clear none of the photos resonated with her, or she was too exhausted to engage. Either way, it didn't take long for May to drift off.

Leaving the television on with the volume low, I crept out of the room. I walked along the balcony and knocked for TJ and Reggie.

The parking lot was empty. A young couple arrived and didn't give the three of us any attention. Regardless, we waited until their door shut.

Once it was, I told TJ and Reggie my plan.

'You cannot be serious?' Reggie butted in.

'All I'm asking you to do is look after May for a couple of hours,' I said. 'You won't be doing anything illegal.'

'Are you hearing her right now?' Reggie stared at TJ for backup.

TJ gave him a half-smile. 'It's worth a shot.'

Reggie glared at him, incredulous. 'And you're cool with this?'

'Yeah. I think if she can keep him occupied, I can be in and out in a breeze.'

Reggie took a deep breath in. 'It's too risky.' He shook his head.

'Which bit, TJ breaking in, or me keeping Trey occupied?' I raised my eyebrows at him.

'You know what I mean. If this guy is involved – and it's a big if, Harper – you're putting yourselves in serious danger.'

'I can handle myself,' TJ interjected.

Reggie paused.

'You really think you can get TJ in?' Reggie said, his demeanor softening a little.

'Easy,' I said and grinned.

34

'Pass me that, would you?' Agent Lucy Green, short, plump with dark hair, leaned forward. She was dressed in her usual pant suit. She pointed to a thick Manila file

Her partner glanced up from his computer. He looked to where she was pointing at and slid the folder across the desk towards her.

'What you looking at?' Green asked him.

He clicked on his mouse, opened up a search engine and typed in 'JMac Finance'. A list of sites appeared. He clicked the mouse. Green leaned forward towards the screen.

'Not bad, hey?' he said.

Green let out a whistle. 'Nice.' She nodded appreciatively. 'You want to make the call?'

'Why not?' He shifted in his seat and picked up the phone. 'Pass me the number.'

Green flicked through the file and lifted out a piece of paper.

He pressed in the digits and held his finger in the air to quieten Green.

'Hey. How you doing? It's been a while.' He paused, listening to the other end of the phone. Green looked up from the file. 'That's great. Well, I'm flying in tomorrow and I wondered if you wanted to meet?' He squinted a little, listening to the reply.

Green noticed her partner's brow furrow.

He picked up a pen. 'Oh, right.' He paused again. 'OK, sure, no problem.'

Green stepped up and leaned over him to read what he'd written.

'Trey Garrison? Oh yeah. I've heard him speak. Fantastic. Sounds great. I look forward to it.'

He flicked off the phone.

'He's giving me Trey.'

'So, you're not meeting him?'

'No, he says he's away.' He raised his eyebrows. 'None of our guys have seen him at the house. So he could be.' He gave a small shrug.

'Even so. Trey Garrison.' Green nodded and pursed her lips.

'Yup. Trey Garrison. Looks like we're on.'

They both grinned and slapped their palms in a high five.

35

The following morning after breakfast, we waved TJ and May off on the bus. We promised to meet them at the same location by lunchtime. Reggie and I took the Camaro and parked up at the rear of the Liberty of the Mind Legacy Center parking lot.

I left Reggie brooding in the car. I headed into the main lobby and nodded at the meatheads on the entrance. I ordered a coffee to go and, grabbing one of their leaflets, wandered back outside to one of the benches on the lawn.

Trey was scheduled to begin a seminar in half an hour.

Shortly before it was due to start, I heard the distinctive thrum of the Viper's engine enter the driveway. With the coffee and pamphlet in hand, I strolled in the direction of the parking lot. I kept the car in my peripheral vision. With my head down, appearing like I was engrossed in the reading material, I slammed straight into the path of Trey, spilling my coffee down the front of him.

'Oh no. I'm so sorry.' I looked at him, embarrassed. I patted his shirt with a tissue from my pocket.

'Damn!' Trey glanced down at his once white shirt, and up at me. His look of disagreement softened the second he checked me out. 'You?' he said. A smile curled on his lips.

'Sorry. I have a bad habit of not looking where I am going.

I'm such a klutz. I was reading one of the leaflets and I...' I shrugged. 'I guess I was so engrossed.' I fluttered my eyelashes. 'I'll pay for it to be cleaned, and oh, it's all on your jacket too.' I dabbed a little at the coffee dripping down him.

'Hey, don't worry. I've got another shirt in my office.'

'No, I need to at least get it cleaned for you.'

'Really, no need.'

'Maybe I could buy you a coffee to apologize?' I fluttered my eyelashes again.

Trey glanced at his watch and back up at me. 'That's real sweet, darling, but I've got a seminar right now.'

I looked to my feet in disappointment

Trey noticed the leaflet in my hand. 'The Open Heart Seminar. Good choice.' He paused. 'Tell you what—' Trey dazzled me with another one of his bright-white smiles. 'How about we call it evens for ruining my shirt by you agreeing to go for dinner with me tonight.' He stared at my chest as he spoke. 'I could even give you an insight into the course.' He licked his lips.

I feigned shock. 'I don't know what to say.'

'There's a nice little fish restaurant off South County Road, The Raft. It does the best oysters in the whole state.' Trey pressed his fingers to his mouth and kissed them.

'Sounds perfect.' I gave him a smile. 'Again, I'm so sorry.'

'It's nothing, really. Eight o'clock work for you?'

'Great.'

Trey checked me out one last time. 'I don't even know your name.'

I faltered for a second. 'Jenny,' I finally said.

'Trey.' He put out his hand to shake mine.

It felt clammy to the touch. I shook it and held my smile.

'The Raft. Eight o'clock,' Trey repeated and headed towards the main building.

★

Aware of the cameras, I glanced in Reggie's direction, gave him a subtle nod and walked along the driveway. I waited one block up for Reggie to pull over and I jumped into the passenger seat.

'And that is what you call magic,' I said as I dangled Trey's keys in my hand.

Reggie shook his head at me. 'Let's get them copied and back to Trey before he realizes they're gone.'

36

Trey skipped up the center steps, a smarmy grin covering his face. He didn't bother to acknowledge the security guys as he walked in. He gave the few staff members on the front desk an obligatory nod and made his way to his office to change his shirt. That hot piece of ass could throw coffee over him any time. Perhaps his luck hadn't run out after all.

He opened the closet in his office, flicked through a few shirts and picked one at random. Unbuttoning the stained one, he stared at himself in the mirror. Seeing a roll of fat spill over his pants, he breathed in and shook his head. He threw on the other shirt, combed back his hair and winked at his own reflection.

Checking himself one last time, Trey exited the office and glanced at his assistant.

'Get this cleaned would you, Stacey.' He threw the soiled laundry at a young woman sat behind a desk. 'And book me a table for two at The Raft. For eight. My usual table.'

Without losing pace, he shifted down the lobby steps and made his way to the seminar.

TJ held May's hand as they stepped off the bus and crossed the street towards the beach.

'Let's go find those secret shells,' he said.

Once they were on the sidewalk, he let go of May and smiled to himself as she raced onto the sand. The monkey's tail attached to the back of the outfit bobbed up and down.

Perhaps it was the sunshine on his face warming his skin, but TJ felt more alive today than he had done in a while. Having Harper and May around seemed to have awoken something in him he hadn't experienced in a long time. Or realized was missing until now. And yes, he would admit, despite their worries, a part of him was excited about tonight. He hadn't felt this sort of buzz since he had retired. It was this feeling that had got him out of bed in the morning and on the beat going on forty-odd years. More recently, it was difficult to motivate himself to get up, never mind get out.

TJ watched May play. She hummed to herself and placed every shell she could find into a circle beside her. TJ tugged out a handkerchief from his pants pocket and wiped sweat from his brow. Despite a little cloud cover, the heat was intense.

'Hey, kid, come drink some juice.'

May stood and took a juice box from TJ. Once she'd drunk most of it, TJ sprayed a little sunblock on her face.

'That's better.' He rubbed the last of it in.

'When's Harper coming?' May asked.

'Soon. They won't be too long.'

May ran back to her shell circle.

TJ checked his watch. He had no doubt Harper would be able to pocket Trey's keys without him noticing. After all, when she was a kid, her sleight of hand was what had got the police's attention more times than he wished to recall. If the morning went as planned, Harper had reluctantly agreed to go and buy a dress. If she was going to keep Trey distracted, short and tight was the only way to go.

★

Trey finished up his talk, left the lecture hall and headed straight back to his office.

His assistant waved for his attention. 'Arlene from Svaag's office called to say she was sending over some files Svaag had requested for you.'

The corners of Trey's mouth curled into a smile. This is what he had been waiting for.

'Oh, and someone handed these in.' She dangled a bunch of keys in front of him.

Trey stopped and stared at them. His brow furrowed.

'I think you dropped them by your car,' she added.

Trey grinned, recalling Jenny knocking into him.

'Thank you, darling.' He grabbed the keys and walked back into his own office. He took the laptop from his desk and a file of paperwork and slipped them into his briefcase.

He sauntered back out to the main area. 'I'll be on the cell if anyone needs me.'

Trey didn't bother to listen to her reply. He slipped on his shades, jumped into the car and drove back to his apartment.

Settling into his home office, Trey powered up the laptop. He pulled out the file. He flipped it open, countersigned the enclosed checks and documents and shut it to. If there was one thing Svaag had taught him, it was to ensure all the company's utilities and taxes were paid and on time. That way, there was little excuse to have any authorities sniffing around.

He clicked on his email program, opened Svaag's message and saw various attached files.

Four documents and nine movie clips. Waiting for them to download, he slipped his hand into his back pants pocket and unfolded a piece of paper. On it, he had written the address of the Villa Svaag had procured. Curious, he opened up the member's database and typed in the details.

The laptop beeped and opened up a box. The address was registered to one of their members. He clicked on their file. Trey scanned the headlines. It didn't take long for Trey to work out what leverage Svaag had on the guy.

Disgruntled Svaag had managed to get to him first, Trey's vexation soon dissipated as the laptop beeped again. Clicking onto the downloaded files, the first of Mackenzie's movie clips began to play. With excitement building, he tossed the address to the side. He settled back in his seat and watched the drama unfold on the screen.

37

TJ and Reggie knocked for me shortly after seven thirty. Both of them seemed to do a double take as they eyed up my dress. It was my idea of hell. A pale pink and white crocheted bodice, an open back with crisscross strapping. The skirt of the dress above my knee. I bought some high-heeled shoes to accompany it and hoped to God I could actually walk in them.

'Wow,' TJ said. 'Is Harper here?'

'Screw you.' I playfully punched his shoulder.

Reggie stood silent next to TJ. Lost for words, his mouth agape.

I pulled the door back fully so they could come in. May lay on the bed, face down, propped up on her elbows, crayoning.

'Ready?' TJ asked me.

I nodded.

Reggie pulled me aside. 'You sure about this?' he whispered.

'I'm sure.' I turned away from him and leaned down to May. 'Me and TJ are going out for a while, so Reggie is going to stay here with you.' I ruffled her hair a little.

'You look pretty.' May said.

I smiled at her. 'Thank you.'

'She's right. You do,' Reggie said, staring at me.

I grabbed my purse. My cheeks flushed pink.

TJ glanced at his watch and looked from me to Reggie. 'OK, let's do it.'

TJ pulled up a block from The Raft. Anxious, he looked in his rearview mirror onto the street.

'You OK?

'I'm fine,' TJ said. He tried to sound confident, but his nerves kicked in. The familiar tremor buzzed in his hands. He kept them firmly wrapped around the steering wheel. 'Are you?' he asked.

'I've got the easy part,' Harper said. 'You got your cellphone?'

TJ slipped it out of his pocket and placed it on the dashboard. 'Right here.'

'Charged?'

'It's charged,' TJ said, indignant.

'Any problems I'll text you, OK?'

TJ nodded. As he looked at her in the short dress, an uneasy feeling shifted in his stomach. 'Just be careful. If this guy is as sleazy as you say, he could try anything.'

'I'll be fine.' Harper gave him a reassuring pat on his leg. 'Ready?'

'Ready,' TJ replied.

He watched her shift out of the car and walk along the street towards the restaurant. Once she was out of view, he placed the car in gear and headed towards Trey's apartment.

38

The Raft had been recently refurbished. All the walls had been sandblasted, the glass and chrome tables of old had been replaced with heavy wood. Ornate chandeliers hung low from the ceiling. A long mahogany bar edged the back, multicolored optics decorating the wall. Glass doors that were rarely closed, except in midwinter, overlooked the bay. The restaurant attracted a particular sort of clientele. The menus no longer showed the prices. You could either afford to eat here or not.

The evening air was humid.

Trey parked up, took out a small breath freshener, sprayed his mouth, cupped his hands, checked his breath and stepped out of the car. Lifting up his shades, he skipped up the entrance of The Raft and scanned the restaurant for Jenny.

A waiter approached him. 'Good evening, sir. If you'd like to follow me.'

Trey was a regular here, either entertaining clients or women. He was a firm believer that money was the great equalizer among the sexes. Men couldn't get enough of it and women were attracted to men with it. And amen to that.

Trey stepped out onto the terracotta terrace. Rope lights twinkled around the edges. The sparkle of nearby boats in the bay.

Perfect.

He positioned himself at the table so Jenny would not only get a great view of the ocean but, more importantly, him.

'I'll get a club soda,' he said.

The waiter nodded and walked off back into the restaurant.

Trey glanced at his surroundings. He had to admit, he'd miss this. Checking the time, he peered around to see if Jenny had arrived. Seeing she hadn't, he pulled out his cellphone, opened the text messages and typed a message to his contact.

Any word on my documents?

He pressed send.

He couldn't go anywhere without those. He had been prom- ised them this week, but there had apparently been some delay. 'Hopefully tomorrow' is all his gopher, Junior, kept replying.

Noticing Jenny approach, Trey placed his cellphone to the side and stood to greet her.

'You look …' Trey whistled. 'As pretty as a peach,' he said and flashed his pearly white grin.

She looked hot. And, in that short dress, she looked more than game.

And you look sleazy.

I gritted my teeth and mirrored his smile.

The waiter pulled back my seat.

Trey waited until I was comfortable and sat opposite me. The smell of his cologne masking any chance of fresh air.

'Drink?' he asked.

I needed something strong to settle my nerves. A bead of sweat trickled down my back.

'Scotch on the rocks,' I said to the waiter who hovered by the table.

'A real drink,' Trey said, a sparkle in his eyes.

'I don't usually do this,' I said quietly.

'Go for dinner with strange men? Or drink Scotch?' Trey raised his eyebrows.

His eyeline glided along my bare legs, the skirt of the dress hitched up my thigh. He leaned forward and touched my knee.

'Don't worry, darling, I'm not so strange.' He gave me a wink, which I think was meant to disarm me.

'So, Jenny . . .' He swallowed, hard. 'Tell me, what's a pretty lady like you doing at the center?'

I took a slow breath in. 'Oh, it's a long story.' I shook my head dismissively.

'Well, we have all night,' Trey said. He stared at me for a beat too long.

The waiter approached with my Scotch and passed us both a menu.

Trey flicked his hand to usher them away. 'We'll take the oysters for two,' he said to the waiter. 'And a bottle of Dom Perignon.'

Ugh. He couldn't have been more obvious if he tried. I swigged back my drink.

'Let me guess,' Trey said. He leaned back in his seat and studied me for a moment. 'A breakup.'

I glanced towards the ocean. *This was going to be one hell of a long night.*

I gave him a quick smile and nodded.

Trey waited until the waiter had poured the champagne and picked up his glass. 'To mending broken hearts.'

I raised my glass and clinked his. 'To mending broken hearts.' *And breaking into your apartment.*

TJ parked the Camaro up a block from the address. If anyone caught him breaking in, the car was too distinctive not to notice it. He shuffled up the street and scanned both sides for oncoming pedestrians. His breath quickened.

The air still and sticky. His shirt clung to his skin.

TJ glanced up at the sky. Cumulonimbus clouds towered above him.

The apartment block was situated in a residential area. Little traffic passed by.

TJ lifted the duplicated keys out of his pocket and strolled towards the front entrance. Trying the first key, he placed it in the lock. The mechanism didn't shift. Pulling it out, he tried the second key. He felt the bolt undoing. Opening up the front door, he entered. It smelled of disinfectant. To ensure no one was behind him, he stopped and retied his shoelace. The lobby was silent. He heard the static from the overhead lights, buzzing above him. TJ stepped into the stairwell and walked to the second floor. He slipped along the corridor and counted down the apartment numbers. He headed back to the stairwell and, figuring it was on the floor above, took the next flight.

TJ heard the low murmur of voices in the corridor. He waited. Confident no one was around, he headed away from the stairwell and attempted to find the right apartment.

He arrived at number sixteen.

TJ knocked lightly. He pressed his ear to the wooden door and listened.

Nothing.

Checking left and right, TJ pulled out the key and shifted it into the lock. His hand shook a little, his fingers clamped tight.

'Come on, come on,' he muttered to himself.

He released the key, flexed his fingers and allowed blood to pump back into them. Trying once again, TJ turned the lock, pressed on the handle and slipped into the empty apartment.

'So …' Trey picked up an oyster, doused it with pepper sauce and slurped it back. 'Is that a New York accent I detect?'

'Brooklyn, born and bred,' I said. I wasn't keen on him knowing anything about me, but my accent was a clear giveaway, and I hoped mentioning Brooklyn might give me a slight tell from Trey. After all, it was where I had found May.

'A long way from home. You here on your own?' He dabbed his mouth with a napkin and took a sip of champagne. He wiped sweat from his brow.

I nodded. 'I needed to get away for a while.'

'The broken heart.'

'The broken heart,' I repeated.

'Well, he must have been one hell of a fool to let a pretty little lady like you go.'

His eyes danced from my legs to my chest.

I smiled briefly. If I was going to waste my time distracting this jerk, I needed to find out more regarding the organization. More specifically Svaag. 'You said you'd talk to me about the courses,' I said, changing the subject.

Trey looked a little disgruntled to be pulled back to the topic of work.

'Have you worked at the center long?' I continued.

'A few years.' Trey shrugged. 'Like you, I was lost for a little while, but when I discovered the center, well, it might seem clichéd, but I found myself.' He picked up the bottle of champagne. He dabbed the icy drips on the bottom and topped up my glass.

'Seems like you do great work there,' I said. I took a small

194

sip. Now the liquor had allayed my nerves, I wanted to make sure I had my wits about me.

Trey's cellphone beeped.

'Sorry, darling.' He picked it up off the table. 'I've been waiting for an urgent—' Trey stopped. His body tensed. 'Shit!'

'Everything OK?' I asked. A chill ran through my veins.

Trey shifted back his seat. 'I'm sorry. I have to go.' He stood, pulled out his wallet, riffled through some bills and threw them onto the table.

'What's going on?' I jumped up.

'My apartment's been broken into.'

39

'Let me come with you.' Jenny grabbed his arm and rubbed her hand along it.

At any other time, Trey would have happily driven some hot chick back to his apartment. But with so much at stake, his sexual appetite had slipped down as quickly as the oysters he had eaten. However, he didn't have the time to argue. Perhaps if it was a false alarm, the pair of them being at his apartment could have been worse.

The security system had gone off a number of times since he had moved in. Someone only needed to slam their door in one of the other apartments and it appeared to trigger the damned thing. But right now, he couldn't take any chances.

Jenny buckled up in the passenger seat. The skirt of her dress high above her knee as she leaned over to reach her purse. She pulled out a cellphone and appeared to type something on it. Seeing Trey watching her, she turned to him and smiled.

'Just showing off to my friend what sort of car I'm in.'

Trey gave her a brief smile. Women really were as shallow as men.

*

TJ took a moment to catch his breath. He leaned against the door and slipped the keys into his pocket. He stood still. He scanned the apartment, not noticing the tiny sensor above the doorway flashing.

The front entrance opened up onto a basic living area. The room decorated in a muted gray. A gunmetal-colored couch sat to the right, in front of an excessively large television screen. A floor-to-ceiling shelving unit against the back wall. To the right, balcony doors opened up onto a small terrace that appeared to lead along the front.

TJ shuffled along a tiny corridor. There was enough light coming through the windows to be able to see. He spotted two doors on either side. Careful not to leave prints, TJ leaned into the first. It opened up into a compact kitchen. He tapped open the door on the opposite side. A bedroom. Again, minimally decorated. He stepped forward a little more. The bathroom. The last door led into a small office. A white desk against the far wall. A laptop open on top. TJ checked behind him. Hearing nothing except his own staggered breath, he entered the room.

He tugged out a handkerchief from his pants pocket. Using it like a glove, he approached the computer and pressed on a random button. The laptop whirred to life, but a welcome screen appeared, prompting a password.

Ignoring it, TJ scanned the desk. He picked up a blue folder and flipped it open. He held it close to the laptop, using the light to illuminate the documents.

Insurance forms for the center. Utility bills and checks. Nothing out of the ordinary.

He closed it and slid open the top drawer.

Pens, paper clips, the usual crap. He opened the drawer below and poked around at some papers. He lifted them out and placed them on the desk. Fanning them across the surface, he leaned in to read them.

They appeared to be personnel files. Each document had a photograph of someone in the top right-hand corner. To the side of the photograph, what must have been the person's details, and below, a short report about them. They had all been typed. But someone had gone through each one and highlighted particular lines.

Addicted to pornography.
Inclination for prostitution.
Stolen office funds.
Pays for male escorts.

Most of the files appeared to be men's, but TJ noticed a few women's photographs, too.

Four illicit affairs.
Stripper.
Abortions.

TJ shook his head. *What is all this?*

It was approximately fifteen minutes to Trey's apartment from The Raft, but in the Viper it was more like ten. Trey slammed his foot down and shot past the other traffic. The rain that had threatened to break drummed against the windshield

They pulled into the designated parking lot. Trey peered up towards the third-floor balcony. He scanned the other cars around him. Through the downpour, he sped over to the front entrance and unlocked the door.

Jenny followed right alongside him.

They shook themselves off in the lobby.

'Nice location. You lived here long?' Jenny asked him as they walked up the stairwell. Her voice echoed on the walls.

'A year or two,' Trey answered distracted, his hand ready on his apartment key.

'You have a sea view?' She was getting louder.

Trey glanced at her and regretted not ditching her at the restaurant. If there was someone in his apartment, the last thing he needed was to have a drunken loudmouth alerting whoever it was they were there.

He whispered as they crept along the corridor. 'You need to keep your voice down.'

'Sorry.' Again her voice boomed out. 'I love the colors they painted the walls. I was thinking that maybe when I'm back in Brooklyn—' Her words sounding slurred.

Shit. She really couldn't hold her liquor.

Trey threw her a stern look. He held his finger up to his lips to shush his date and approached his front door.

TJ opened up the far drawer. Again, more papers. He pulled those out and flicked through them. Bank statements. All in the name of Peter Johnson.

Why would Trey have someone else's bank statements?

TJ scanned the figures. Large deposits coming in from all over. The balance amounted to over $2.7 million. TJ studied the statement closer. The names of the accounts depositing the money matched the files he had found.

Pulling out his pen and pad, TJ cross-referenced the figures with the names. His fingers fumbled around the pen's casing. He struggled to hold it firm in his hands.

TJ's head shot up.

Voices emanated from the outside hallway and appeared to be drawing closer. *Was that Harper?*

TJ froze.

He stepped into the apartment hallway. Hairs on his arms bristled

Footsteps.

TJ rushed back into the office, shuffled the files together and threw them in the right-hand drawer.

Again, he heard Harper's voice.

Confused, TJ patted himself down, trying to find his cellphone. If something was amiss, she would have called or texted him.

TJ tensed. His pockets were empty. *The cellphone.* He had left it on the car dashboard when she asked him if he'd charged it.

Having no time, TJ sped into the living area and headed towards the balcony. He clasped his fingers on the door handle and attempted to turn it. His hand clamped up. He heard a key in the front door. Trembling, TJ let go of the lock, opened and closed his fist and tried the door once again. His fingers slipped. Finally, he maneuvered the handle, slid the door open and stepped onto the balcony. He closed it and stood to the side. His heart battered against his ribcage. His breath short and heavy.

He strained to hear through the glass. The rain thundered around him.

'False alarm?' *Harper's voice.* He was sure of it.

Followed by Trey's. 'Yeah. Seems so.'

TJ pressed himself up against the wall. He swiveled his body a little and carefully peered into the living area.

Harper stood alone in the middle of the room. She had her high-heeled shoes in her hand, clutched like a weapon. Spotting Trey wasn't close by, he caught her attention.

Noticing him, she glared his way and indicated for him to hide.

TJ swung his body back to the wall and listened to what was going on.

Trey stood in the open doorway and surveyed the living area. His brow furrowed a little.

Nothing.

He walked in and headed up the hallway.

'False alarm?' Jenny asked.

He left her in the living area. 'Yeah. Seems so,' Trey hollered back. He walked straight to the office and scanned the desk. His laptop screen was lit up, but only the password-prompt screen showed. Still, curious the laptop had awoken. He stepped closer to the desk, noticing something on the top. A pen. He picked it up. It wasn't his. His whole body froze.

Trey glanced behind him to make sure Jenny hadn't followed. He opened one of the drawers. His breath became shallow. A cold sweat emanated up his spine.

He needed to ditch the chick and fast.

Spinning around, he glanced into the bathroom and kitchen. He walked back into the living room.

'Listen, I'm sorry, darling. I'm going to have to raincheck this evening.' Trey ushered Jenny towards the exit.

'What? No. We were just getting to know each other.' She placed her hands on his shoulders. She turned his body to face her, away from the window and stood close to him.

'I know, and trust me—' he licked his lips, 'I want to get to know you some more.' He felt her breasts brush against his chest. 'But right now, I've got things I need to take care of.'

Jenny pouted. 'Anything I can help with?' She ran her fingers through his hair.

'Honey, there's a lot you could help with, but another time.'

Jenny sighed, disappointed. 'Don't suppose you could give me a lift to my hotel? I'd walk but—' She pointed to her heels and the weather.

Really? Now?

'Where you staying, darling?' he asked, resigned.

'The Four Seasons.'

Trey raised his eyebrows. 'Well, you are full of surprises.' *The Four Seasons, huh. So the girl had money.*

Trey opened the front door, took one more look at the apartment and shut the door behind them. Her hotel was less than a five-minute drive away. The sooner he dropped her, the quicker he could be back.

Trey screeched out onto the street. His mind turning over faster than the car engine.

Who the hell had broken in? Whoever it was, they knew exactly what they were looking for. He hadn't had a chance to see if any of the files were missing, but there was no doubting they had been riffled through. And the bank statements. He could have sworn he had left them in the other drawer.

Ahead of them, lightning flickered in the sky, followed by a deafening rumble.

The oysters shifted around in Trey's gut. He could only see three options. The Feds, Svaag or one of the guys in the files.

Trey pulled out his cellphone and glanced at the screen. Still no reply from Junior regarding his documents. *Dammit.*

Trey skirted the car around the corner and pulled up at the front entrance of the hotel.

'I'm sorry about tonight. Maybe we could pick this up later on this week?' Trey said, not even sure he would be here.

Jenny unbuckled her seat belt and smiled at him. 'Sure. I'd

like that. I'll call you.' She winked at him, opened the door and shifted her bare legs out. She leaned back down to the car window, gave him one more smile and tottered up the hotel steps.

Trey shook his head, placed the car in drive and tried to refocus. He shot out of the driveway onto the main strip towards his apartment. If it was Svaag, he needed to rule him out before he started to think it was the Feds. If it was the FBI, he needed to leave now.

Anxious, he signaled and pulled to the side of the street. He picked up his cellphone and hesitated a moment. He scrolled to Svaag's number and pressed dial.

'Trey.' Svaag's voice was calm.

'I think we've got problems,' Trey said. His voice raised over the rain pounding on the car.

The other end of the line went silent.

'Someone was in my apartment,' Trey continued.

'Feds?' Svaag asked. Trey detected anxiety in his voice.

'I don't know.' Fear rumbled in Trey's stomach. If it wasn't Svaag, it left the other two options. The Feds or one of the members. He peered around him nervously. If it was the Feds, they could be tailing him right now. Paranoid, he looked up at the reflection in his rearview mirror. Other than water streaming down the window, he saw nothing.

'You think she would really go to them, after everything?' Svaag asked.

'I don't know.' Trey scanned the sidewalk and glanced back to the road.

What he saw made him do a double take.

What the fuck?

'I've got to call you back.' Trey clicked off his cellphone. He slipped low in his seat and stared across at a line of cars halted at the lights. He leaned forward to see closer through the rain. His vision locked on one car in particular. An old blue Camaro. And in the passenger seat was Jenny.

Why would she ask to be dropped off if someone was picking her up? The car didn't exactly look like an Uber. So who the hell was she with? Didn't she say she was in town on her own?

Trey peered at the driver of the vehicle. No one he recognized.

The lights changed to green. The car moved forward and turned right.

Trey waited a couple of beats. He started his car and, staying back as far as he could, he followed them along the street.

40

As TJ drove back to the motel, both of us sat silent for a while.

'I'm sorry about my cellphone,' TJ finally said.

I shook my head. 'Let's leave that bit out when we tell Reggie.'

TJ smiled a little embarrassed. 'Seems I'm a little rusty.'

I placed my hand on his thigh to reassure him. 'Thanks for picking me up.'

Even the short distance from the lot to the room had us drenched to our skin.

May was in a deep sleep by the time we got back. We quickly towelled ourselves dry and huddled in the corner with Reggie.

'Peter Johnson? Who the hell is that?' Reggie whispered.

TJ shook his head. 'I don't know. But all the bank statements were in his name and there was a lot of money in the account. It was registered overseas.'

'So where was the money coming from?' Reggie's brow furrowed.

'All sorts of places. Big deposits. They seemed to be from personal accounts, very few from business accounts,' TJ said.

'Like donations?' I asked.

'I don't think so. The files appeared to belong to center members, but there was dirt on all of them.'

'What do you mean?' Reggie asked, wrinkling his nose.

'I mean, someone had gone through and picked out really personal stuff. Stuff you wouldn't want everyone to know. I didn't get the chance to go through them all, but the ones I did see correlated with the names attached to the funds going into this Peter Johnson's account.'

I nodded. 'So you think they're being blackmailed?'

TJ shrugged. 'Looks that way.'

'Might explain why the FBI are looking at them,' Reggie said.

'I still don't get it,' I began. 'Where does May fit into it? Did any of the files have anyone called Brown on them?'

TJ shook his head. He paused and looked over to May, sleeping. 'Maybe someone kidnapped her and was holding her to ransom?' TJ shrugged.

My mind flickered back to the 'I'm sorry' note. I riffled in my bag to find it. I pulled it out and passed it to TJ, pointing at the line of numbers I hadn't deciphered.

'You think that's someone's bank details?'

TJ squinted.

AE-017643219763-05/21.

Reggie leaned in to look. 'Could be?'

'But why let May go, unless they paid the ransom, which means her mom and dad would have collected her?' I said.

'Unless…' TJ paused

'They didn't pay,' Reggie finished the sentence, quietly.

'You think someone killed them?' I lowered my voice and glanced at May. Color drained from my cheeks.

'I don't know, Harp.' Reggie placed his hand on my arm.

The solemnity of what we were all thinking seemed to suck

all the air out of the room. We stood in silence for a minute. The roar of the rain pummeling outside on the balcony.

'Why does Trey have this Peter Johnson's bank information?' Reggie finally asked.

TJ shrugged

'Did you find anything else?'

TJ shook his head. 'No. There was a folder on his desk with bills, checks, administrative stuff for the center, but I didn't get time to see anything else—'

'A folder?' My head shot up in his direction.

'Yeah, but inside were just checks for maintenance stuff, small amounts. Nothing significant.'

'What did it look like?' I asked.

TJ screwed up his face. 'An ordinary folder. Blue. Cardboard, the sort you keep your papers in.'

'Were they signed?'

'The checks? Yes, why?'

'By who?'

'Trey and Svaag. They must be the account signatories. But what's the big deal?'

Ignoring the question, my breath quickened. 'Were they dated?'

'Yeah, they were recent. Harp, what's going on?'

I shuffled over to the side of my bed, picked up my bag and pulled out the camera. 'If the checks were signed recently, it means Svaag isn't away.' I powered up the camera and flicked through the images on the memory card. Reggie and TJ both looked over to me curiously. I squinted at the small screen that allowed me to view the photographs. I stopped and walked back over to them.

'Did it look like this?'

TJ peered at the screen. I showed him the photograph I had

taken of Trey on the villa balcony passing something to the bandaged man. A blue folder.

TJ paused, looked up at me and nodded.

A smile spread across Reggie's face. 'So that was Svaag.'

'It could explain why someone had beaten the shit out of him. If you were being blackmailed, wouldn't you want to smash their face in?' I said.

'Guess that's why there's all the security.' Reggie raised his eyebrows.

'So now what?' TJ asked.

We all stared at each other for a beat.

'Why don't we see what fruit we can shake from that tree?' I looked towards Reggie.

'And what about Trey?' TJ asked.

'He can wait,' I said.

Trey had parked up in a lot adjacent to the Fair Tidings Motel. He had watched Jenny and the driver exit the car and run up the stairwell to one of the rooms. They had been in there approximately twenty minutes. He could detect shadows by the window dressed with a thin sheer under drape. Trey didn't dare leave his car. He stared up towards the room and back to the Camaro. Who the hell were they? He leaned in and had a clearer view of the car now. *New York license plates?* When the driver had run across the lit parking lot, Trey noticed the guy was maybe in his mid-sixties. So why was she sharing a room with him? *Was she a hooker?* She was hot, but no one would drive that far for ass. Or were they feds? Surely he was too old, and what was with the car? Not exactly FBI standard issue.

Trey's cellphone buzzed in his pocket. *Svaag.*

Trey hesitated before answering. He needed to play this carefully. Now he was sure it wasn't Svaag that had ordered the break-in, he didn't want to alert him to any possible dangers. Not until he was sure what was going on. If Svaag thought it was the Feds, there was no telling what he would do. Trey needed to make sure he was in the right position before any moves were made. Every man for himself.

Trey clicked on the call. 'Hey, sorry. False alarm.'

'What?' Svaag replied sharp.

'It was just some kids.'

'Are you sure?'

'Positive. They'd tried a couple of other apartments in the block. Neighbors caught them.'

Trey heard Svaag sigh with relief.

He ended the call and glanced at his watch. He took a deep breath in and slowly let the air out of his lips. He needed to get back to his apartment. He had to find out exactly what they had discovered. All he had noticed was one of the drawers to the desk was slightly ajar. The files thrown back in.

He waited another ten minutes. Confident he knew at least where they were staying, he pulled out onto the street. With anxiety streaming through his veins, and the sharp crackle of lightning above him, Trey headed back home.

We all agreed it had been a long night and we needed to rest up. Our collective brains spinning at the possibilities. Nothing was coming into clear focus.

I lay on my side, watching May tucked up under the covers fast asleep. If her mom was still alive, I couldn't begin to imagine how she felt, not knowing where her little girl was. But if she was still alive, why hadn't she or her dad reported her missing to the police? It would have been all over the local news and in the press. The sinking feeling of all the reasons they hadn't reported her gone pressed on my chest like a heavy weight.

I turned on my back, covered myself with a blanket and listened to the rain beating on the window.

It would be hours before sleep would finally come.

41

The following morning, Trey returned to the motel. The storm had passed. The air was cool. The streets damp from the deluge.

Again, he parked up in the adjacent lot. The Camaro was positioned in the same spot. The room and the car were in view, but far enough away they wouldn't see him. There was no movement from the motel room.

Trey had parked here since sunrise, wondering if the Feds were finally coming after them. Or, more specifically, coming after him. Who else could it be? He hadn't recognized her or the old guy from any of the files. Nothing was missing. And Svaag seemed as alarmed as he was.

Trey had two seminars that morning and as soon as they were out the way, he'd try and get an hour's nap. He needed to rest his brain a little so he'd be able to figure out what he should do next. He wasn't going down for this. No way. He'd do what he needed to do to protect himself. No matter what. So, if it meant getting up at dawn, so be it. He could do without these damned seminars. All false smiles and people boohooing. He was sick of it. To think he was one of those idiots once, searching for some sort of hope – the memory made him shudder. That's what a broken heart does to you. Turns you into a wet tissue. Well, not any more. It'd been a long time since he'd thought about Debbie. Whenever he did, he thought how she'd feel now, seeing him in his bespoke suits, driving a Viper. He would love to see the look on her face. He was tempted, before he drove off into the sunset, to shoot back to Millport, Alabama. He could parade himself as a 'screw you' in front of her. He would leave only the hum of his two hundred and ninety horsepower as a memory.

Looking back, he couldn't believe what a gullible jerk he'd been. But still, even until recently he had thought there was something special about Svaag. The way he looked at you, the way he made you feel, like you're the only one that counted. And yes, he'd been a father figure to him when he needed it most. He could hardly have gone to his own pa for any sort of comfort after his engagement had broken off. Not that he'd be able to find him. Probably holed up in some dive drinking Scotch until he passed out or, failing that, sleeping it off in some cell. No, he'd never been a father. Svaag had given him time, comfort, words he desperately wanted to hear. He had been patient with him and said he'd seen something special in him. No one had ever seen something special in him. He'd given him a job when he needed it most and a place to live. He felt lucky to be part of something that was helping people.

Until he realized it wasn't.

Until he realized it was all some big scam.

He'd overheard Svaag chatting to Melissa Harding, his right-hand bitch, one day. Talking about taking the organization global, and how much money they'd make. And then Svaag mentioned some wealthy donor who had been through the Liberty of the Mind Legacy programme and how they'd take him for all he had.

Trey couldn't believe he had been duped. He had actually thought they were trying to help people. Help him.

The second he discovered it was a racket, he took off. He found some bar up the coast and, like his pa, drank until he could no longer stand.

He had woken up the next morning in his beaten-up car. The smell of stale alcohol on his breath and one almighty hangover as company. He spent the day slumped in his vehicle thinking of all the times in his life he had been wronged. The sense of injustice rising like the summer heat.

And then he thought about the money. About what he could do with it. He wondered if he helped Svaag wring more dollars out of these saps, they'd let him in on it, give him a piece of the action. Screw Debbie, screw his dad. Damn, screw them all.

He'd already showed promise in front of Svaag. He'd gone from being a clipboard crony selling the latest seminar to actually running some of them. Soon enough, he had a regular spot and people loved him. People actually savored listening to him talk. Regardless of what he had discovered, Svaag had seen something in him no one else had before. And he was good at it. You had to book beforehand for some of Trey's seminars. Their numbers increased, the organization nearly doubled in equity and he was a big part of why. But did Svaag give him a piece of the pie? No. It was always 'soon'. Never today, not even tomorrow. Well, he had gotten sick of waiting until tomorrow. Like he told the hundreds of fools that trudged through their doors, he had to seize the day. Own his life. Take what he deserved. *Can't never could.*

And so he had. Slowly but surely, he began to skim off funds. Svaag had finally put him in charge of the accounts. He had minions that crunched the numbers. But with a few sweeteners here and there, they turned a blind eye to the movement of funds. Once Trey's eyes had been opened, he had learned one key lesson. Humans are all the same. They lost their morals when it came to money. They were fulfilling their own American dream.

Trey's cellphone beeped.

A text message from Svaag.

Trey stretched out in his car seat and pressed the open message command.

Mackenzie meet 1 p.m. today. HQ.

Trey fist-pumped the air.

His fingers hesitated over the keys. He typed a message back.

Leave it to me.

He scanned his messages and texted Junior. He couldn't go anywhere without his new IDs. How long can it take?

There was no doubt Trey needed to cut loose. He'd siphoned off enough, slowly but surely. He had a sizeable pot waiting for him. But with the promise of a big donor on the horizon, what harm would it do to see if he could squeeze a little more while he waited for his documents to come through? At least now he was one step ahead of the Feds. Jenny may have fooled him once with her short dress, but fool him twice, not a chance.

Shortly after eight thirty, the motel door opened. Jenny stepped out onto the balcony. *So she definitely wasn't staying at the Four Seasons.* She moved along the balcony and knocked on another door. *Who was she calling for?* The older man answered the door. The driver of the car he had followed. *So they weren't sharing.*

Trey watched her chat to him for a little while and finally go back to her room. The man locked the door and made his way down the steps.

Trey leaned in closer to his windshield. This guy was way too old to be a Fed, surely.

The old guy strolled out onto the parking lot and along the sidewalk, headed in the direction of town.

Trey slipped out of his car, kept a good distance back and followed him.

The man walked up a couple of blocks and went into a car-repair store. Trey stood on the corner and waited. Ten or so minutes later, he left the store and crossed the street to a diner.

Trey waited until the old guy perched himself in a booth. He pulled out his cellphone, flicked through his contacts and pressed dial.

The guy on the other end picked up immediately.

'Hey, boss. I got your text. The documents will be with you real soon,' Junior said.

'Good. But I need you to do something else for me.'

'Sure thing. Tell me where and when.'

42

Junior jumped up off the bed and tugged up his shorts. Blood rushed to his skull.

The girl he'd brought back last night lay comatose beneath the sheets, no doubt in some drugged brain fog.

Junior stepped into the bathroom, ran the cold faucet and splashed water over his face. A half-used wrap lay on the bathroom counter. He glanced at his watch and figured a quick line wouldn't hurt. It'd wake him up at least. Tipping out the white powder, he scraped it into a decent line, snorted it back and smacked his cheeks.

He knew exactly where Joe's Diner was. It would only take him five minutes by foot. He figured he would have plenty of time. He could grab something to eat himself, settle his stomach a little. But as the high of the white hit his veins, his appetite disappeared.

Early mornings were not his thing. But still, he would make a nice amount of money for this job. Easy cash too. Trey always paid well. He would get this over and done with and be back in bed before noon with that night's party money already in hand. Not a bad day's work.

★

At approximately 9.15, Junior entered the diner. The smell of grits and bacon filled his nostrils.

He scanned the booths and clocked his target.

The clientele were mainly lone men. Probably salesmen, filling up before they hit the road. But in the corner by the window sat an older man. The only thing was, he was sat with a kid. Trey hadn't mentioned anything about a kid. Junior studied the diner again. He fitted the description all right. But the kid was an added complication.

With a clear view of his target, Junior slipped into a booth close to the exit. He ordered himself a coffee and settled back in his seat.

Kid or no kid, he'd get the job done.

43

I knocked for TJ early morning.

He was anxious to fix the tail light before we got pulled over by the cops. I decided not to tell him I already had. The less he knew about my close shaves, the better right now.

He'd spotted a repair store a couple of blocks from the motel. We agreed he'd go get the bulb and I'd return my dress and take May to get a couple more clothes. The onesie was fine for a few days, but it wasn't exactly beachwear, and if more storms were due, she would need a change of outfit. My Visa bill was going to make some interesting reading. I figured that was another problem for another day. My head was way calmer when I stuck it in the Palm Beach sand.

I promised TJ we would be quick. I would drop her off at the diner, and they could head to the beach further up the coast, while Reggie and I went back to the villa.

May and I headed into town towards the stores. She kicked at the puddles that collected along the street. I held tight on to her hand. There was something about the close proximity of the stores to the Liberty of the Mind Legacy Center that made me anxious. Monkey outfit or not.

'Do you have a mommy and a daddy?' May said.

My fingers tensed in hers. No one had ever asked me that before.

'I guess so.'

'But you don't live with them?' May's face was set in a question mark.

'Well, when you're as old as me, you don't really live with mommies and daddies.'

May shrugged, let go of my hand and skipped ahead of me on the sidewalk. I caught up with her and took her hand back in mine.

'Do you know where my mommy is?' She arched her neck to look up at me.

My jaw clenched. After what we may have discovered last night, I couldn't bear the thought of answering.

'Not yet. But we will.'

May's lip jutted out a little.

'It's like a game of hide-and-seek. You ever play that?' I added quickly. The last thing I needed was for May to have another meltdown in public.

May nodded. 'Sometimes I play it with my friend Lily when I go for a slumber party. Her house is bigger than mine and we can hide and no one can find us.'

'There you go, you see. Your mommy is probably in a really big house somewhere and we've got to keep looking.'

'Like a really, really, really big house?'

'Exactly.' I winked. 'Now let's see if we can get you a couple more things to wear. And then TJ is going to take you to the beach.' I pressed on the door of a children's clothes store, relieved to change the subject.

★

Once I'd dropped May back with TJ, I collected my camera from the motel room. I exchanged the memory card for a new one and replaced the batteries. Fully prepared, Reggie and I took the car and headed over to the villa.

Reggie drove to the seafront and parked up. I clipped on the zoom lens to my camera and squinted through it. There was no movement on the balcony, but there were shadows shifting through the glass doors. Someone was at home.

'You really think she could have been kidnapped?' I asked Reggie.

Reggie shrugged and peered pensively out of the car window. The possibilities of why they would have let her go hovered in the air. 'If that's why the FBI are looking into them, we really do need to be careful, Harp.'

We exchanged glances and looked around us. There was no one around.

After an hour and little movement, we moved the car around the corner. We parked far enough away from the security gate, but close enough to watch.

Finally, it paid off. The gates swept open. A ruby black Mercedes Maybach nosed out of the driveway. These guys didn't mind flaunting their wealth. Giving it a beat, Reggie waited. Again, he kept a couple of cars behind.

The Maybach headed in the direction of the city.

Reggie and I stayed silent. We cautiously followed them through the increasingly busy lanes of traffic.

The car came to a stop. Reggie did the same. He switched off the engine. Both of us leaned forward. I glanced around me. We had pulled into a bustling street surrounded by what looked like office blocks. Grilles covered an underground parking lot to the left of us. There were no obvious signs of why we were here.

The Maybach's driver's door opened. A beefy guy – buzz cut, dressed in a suit, crisp white shirt with no tie – slipped out of his seat. He moved around to the sidewalk. He opened the rear door and nodded to the passenger. The man we had seen on the balcony. His face still covered in bandages. He stepped out of the car and approached a doorway to the side. He pressed a buzzer on a panel in front of him. He wore cream linen pants and a white collarless shirt. A large gold watch glistened on his left wrist.

The driver stood close by until the man entered the building. Once he had, the buzz cut stepped to the driver's side and disappeared back into the car.

I opened my door, and before Reggie could respond, I sidled over to the same building. I glanced down to the car. The driver flicked through his cellphone. He didn't notice me looking in.

I stood at the doorway and read the names on the intercom directory. It wasn't hard to work out where he had gone.

ClearView Medical Clinic.

So he was having his injuries treated privately. Another way of avoiding the authorities.

I pressed the buzzer above it. It read BEAGLEY & JAMES LAW PRACTICE. I glanced back towards Reggie. He opened his arms to say, 'What the hell?'

'Yeah,' a man's voice answered.

'Delivery,' I said.

The door buzzed.

I turned, shrugged at Reggie and pushed open the unlocked door to the lobby.

ClearView Medical Clinic was based on the third floor.

Entering the front-desk area, a clinical smell hit me. A water cooler bubbled away gently in the corner. A waiting room furnished with low black leather couches and an ankle-height table covered in magazines. A small front-desk area towards the back.

I walked towards it. While the woman, whose name tag said NORMA, finished a phone call, I turned and stole a glance at the guy. He was sat in the corner, reading.

He was slight with bony hands, covered in liver spots. He leaned in to read a newspaper. If I had to take a guess, I'd say this guy was late sixties.

'May I help you?' the receptionist asked.

I swiveled back around at the sound of her voice

'I was wanting to book an appointment?' I leaned in towards her and spoke in a low voice. I had to pretend I was here for something.

'Of course.' Norma attached a form to a clipboard and passed it to me with a pen. 'If you wouldn't mind filling in a few details first of all, I can book you in for a consultation.'

Distracted, I took the form. I sat opposite him. With my head bowed to appear like I was reading, I eyed him up and down.

A door opened along the hallway and a tall man – mousy hair, dressed in a white coat – stepped into the reception area. With a brief smile my way, he shook the bandaged man's hand. 'I'll just be a second,' he said to him.

The man approached Norma. 'Try and get hold of Eric. I've been calling him and I'm not getting a reply. Tell him it's urgent.'

Norma nodded.

The man turned on his heels back to his patient and led him down a corridor. 'Svaag, good to see you. How have you been getting on?'

My jaw tensed. *So it was him.*

'All done?' the receptionist asked.

'Sorry?'

'The form. You finished?'

Distracted, I shook my head. Buying time before Svaag exited, I filled in my details at the top.

'It's OK if you're not sure at this stage. You can always talk to Mr Anderson about it when you have your initial consultation,' Norma said.

'Not sure about what?' I looked up, confused.

Norma frowned briefly. 'What procedure you would like.'

I slowly took in her words and looked down at the form. Below the personal details section were a number of tick boxes.

My eyes widened as I read them.

Laser Skincare
Breast Augmentation
Fat Transfer
Lower Body Lift
Rhinoplasty

The list went on.

My mouth dropped open.

This wasn't a private medical practice. This was a cosmetic surgery clinic.

Norma held her hand towards me to collect the form. 'Finished?'

My mind whirring, I randomly ticked a box and handed it back to her.

'Now, when would you like an appointment? I've got a cancellation on Thursday, but we're pretty booked up at the moment. Unfortunately, Mr Anderson's partner is away, so there's a little bit of a waiting list.'

'Thursday's fine,' I answered. It wasn't as if I was actually going to come. I thought back to the newspaper article I had read regarding Svaag. I pulled out my cellphone and scanned through my internet history. He used to be called Robert Janin. So maybe he was 'Peter Johnson'.

'Well, let's pop you in, Miss ...' Norma glanced at the details on the form, 'Stein, and we can take it from there.' She grabbed a piece of paper from the printer and handed it to me.

I took it from her and slipped it into my purse.

I gave her a polite nod goodbye and exited the office.

I sped down the stairwell and stepped out of the main lobby back onto the street.

Reggie stood at the side of the Camaro.

'Get in the car,' I said.

Both of us jumped in. I grabbed my camera, ready.

'What's going on?' Reggie asked.

'Wait. You'll see.'

Approximately twenty minutes later, the lobby door opened. The driver of the Maybach ran around to the sidewalk, opening the rear passenger door.

The man exited the building. His bruised face no longer covered in bandages. He placed on some shades, looked left and right and stepped into the car.

Reggie leaned forward to the windshield and stared at the guy. 'Who is he?'

With my finger on the shutter, I took snap after snap.

As the Maybach drove off up the street, I turned to Reggie.

'That look like Svaag Dimash to you?'

'No. Should it?'

'No. He's changing his identity.'

44

Junior was a hulk of a man. His back, broad. Arms, thick and meaty. His gnarled hands, like jaw buckets on a JCB, rarely needed a weapon in their grasp. He would look more comfortable in a ring with Mil Mascaras. Instead, he skulked in his booth and watched his target pay the check. He left a ten-dollar bill under his own coffee cup and made his way out to the sidewalk. Ordinarily, he'd have cut and run. Why pay for something when you didn't need to? But he didn't want to attract any unnecessary attention. So, he paid with a tip and waited until the old man and the kid left the diner.

Junior lit a cigarette and hung back, keeping them in sight. The old guy pointed with one hand and took the young kid's with the other.

Junior lit a cigarette and waited, keeping them in sight.

Finally far enough ahead of him, Junior stubbed out the half-smoked tab with the heel of his shoe. He crept behind them along the main boulevard. He knew these streets well, and when to make the move.

They headed in the direction of the bus station. He needed them to go a little further, where an alley led down the back, away from the queuing passengers.

Seeing them approach the corner, Junior's pace sped up.

TJ didn't get a chance to register the sound of footsteps.

Junior grabbed TJ's arm tight and shoved him into the alley. The full force of his body slamming TJ to the ground with a thud.

The crack of TJ's skull pounding the asphalt echoed on the brick walls.

May stood silent in shock.

As TJ lay motionless, she finally let out an almighty scream.

'Mierda.' Junior turned and tugged May into the alley and smacked one hand around her mouth, his thick sweaty fingers covering her face.

Coming to, TJ rolled over towards May and strained his right arm in her direction. He stumbled to his feet. With his left fist, he took a swing at Junior, who must have been a good ten inches taller than him.

Adrenaline and coke pumped in Junior's veins. Letting go of May, he whacked TJ into the wall with a thump.

Junior sneered down at the kid. 'You want some of that, you carry on whining.'

May stood to the side, hiccuping back tears. Her cheeks mottled by his fingers. Her eyes filled but not a squeak came out of her.

TJ groaned and attempted to move.

Junior held his hand against TJ's chest, leaned close to him, slipped his other hand in TJ's pocket and tugged out his wallet. 'Don't fucking move.' He stared at TJ with bloodshot eyes, spittle in the corners of his mouth. His breath stank of decay.

Flipping the wallet open, Junior slipped out TJ's driver's license. He noted his details. His eyes narrowed. He spotted another card behind it. *TJ's retired cop ID*. Reading it, Junior scowled. He shoved it in his pocket. He grabbed whatever cash was in the wallet and threw the rest to the floor. He snatched

TJ's cellphone and smashed it on the ground. He crunched the shattered pieces with his foot.

'Don't even think about calling the cops.' Junior pressed his face close to TJ's. He backed up, keeping his eyes on them. He glanced behind him, and seeing the coast was clear, he took off along the main boulevard. The thud of his heavy frame disappearing into the distance.

TJ grabbed May and hugged her to him. The second he had her in his arms, May sobbed. Tears and snot streaming down her face.

'It's OK. It's OK. He's gone.' TJ wasn't sure if it was his body shaking or hers.

His vision blurred. He rested against the brick wall a little longer. He held her close until her sobs became hiccups and she eventually stopped.

TJ pulled out a handkerchief from his pants pocket and wiped her face. The marks from Junior's hand still clear on her cheeks. 'How 'bout we just go back to the motel, kid?' TJ heard a tremor in his own voice.

May nodded, the monkey ears flopping on her head.

He touched the back of his skull. His fingertips smudged with blood.

Not wanting to let May go, TJ clung on to her, made his way along the street and headed straight back to the motel.

How could he be so stupid as to get mugged? He knew why, but he wasn't ready to face that yet.

45

Trey wound his way through the crowd of people eager to speak to him. Another seminar over. He pumped a couple more hands and patted a few more backs. He slipped into the main building and along the hallway to his office. His face ached from smiling. Once the door shut, Trey slid open his desk drawer and pulled out a bottle of hand sanitizer. He doused his hands in it and rubbed them together. He was sick to death of everything. Soon he would be free of all this.

Trey checked his cellphone. No word from Junior. Trey's shoulders tensed.

He slumped into his large black leather office chair. He popped the hand sanitizer back into the drawer and, allowing himself a moment of joy, he pulled out a magazine. He eyed the front cover he had looked at so many times and briefly flicked through it. Page after page of cerulean seas and white sands. But not the ones here in Palm Beach. No, this was a million miles away. Well, five hundred and sixteen to be exact. The Cayman Islands. Which was not so far. But far enough away from here, and far enough from the Feds and Uncle Sam.

Trey glanced at his watch. Mackenzie should be here shortly.

He afforded himself a little smug smile. He flicked on the laptop. The computer beeped.

He pointed his mouse at the search button and typed in 'James Mackenzie'. A number of websites popped up. He had already done his research on this guy, but still, it felt good to be looking at his meal ticket.

He clicked onto a profile of his company, JMAC Finance.

There he was, the CEO. His portfolio was impressive. Trey clicked on a few other links. This guy was rolling in it. If you were to look at him, you'd think he was your ordinary Joe that had done real good for himself. But Trey had seen his files. And they showed a whole lot more. Trey couldn't help but smile to himself. Whether this guy liked it or not, he would be donating a large sum of money. It was up to him if he wanted to do it the easy way or the hard way. Either option, it needed to be quick.

Trey stood back up and walked over to the mirror on the far wall. He picked up a comb and brushed it through his hair. He opened his mouth and ran his tongue around his pearly white teeth. He looked good. He leaned down towards a small cupboard. He took out a bottle of cologne, dipped some on his palm and patted it onto his neck and cheeks. Grinning at his reflection, he gave himself his usual wink and waited for the intercom to buzz. Anticipation hummed in his veins.

Finally, his assistant called through. Trey checked himself one more time. He took a deep breath and walked along the hallway towards the front desk.

A man stood staring out of the entrance, his back to Trey.

Trey took a second to eye up his mark. Despite his portly figure, the charcoal gray suit he wore fitted him perfectly. That was no off-the-rack number. His shoes clearly Italian leather.

Trey approached.

'James?' Trey said. The smile already on his face.

The guy turned and matched his grin.

Trey couldn't help but notice the heavy gold watch on Mackenzie's wrist as he shook his hand. That was quite a grip he had there.

'First, let me apologize, Svaag couldn't meet you. He's away at the moment, so you're left with me.' Trey shrugged and masked his smirk.

'No, it's such a pleasure to meet you,' Mackenzie said. 'I've seen your seminars and wow, just wow.'

Trey grinned and, with his usual mock surrender, he held up his palms.

'Would you like me to give you a tour?' Trey offered.

'Oh, sure. I'd love it.'

This guy really was pumped. What a schmuck. It'd be like taking candy from a baby. He looked like a putz too. For someone who was worth in the region of half a billion, this guy needed to spend more time in the sun. His skin was sallow and dark brown rings nestled beneath his eyes. But, hey, if working hard meant a pasty complexion, and millions in his pocket, who was he to argue.

Trey led him towards the therapy rooms. 'This is the heart of what we do. Am I right in thinking you were at our California center?'

Mackenzie peered into the rooms. 'Yeah. I have a beach house over in Malibu and, well, after everything…' Mackenzie's voice trailed off.

Trey placed his hand gently on Mackenzie's shoulder. 'I'm only glad we could help you,' Trey said.

Mackenzie nodded. 'I'm so relieved I found you guys. I don't know what I'd have done without you.'

Trey led him outside to the gardens. He slipped down his shades. 'Well, thankfully you don't need to worry about that. I guess it's the people who don't know about us that keeps me awake at night.' Trey shook his head almost to himself.

Mackenzie said nothing.

Had he gone in too quick? Trey led them up through the citrus trees. He smiled and waved at the volunteers as he passed them by. Deferential, they all looked towards him.

'It's an impressive setup you have here,' Mackenzie said.

'Well, it's getting there. We just want to reach as many people as we can.'

Mackenzie nodded. 'And you think I could help?'

Trey had to hold his breath before replying. He couldn't sound too keen.

'Sure. We love to get our members involved.' *Don't pounce, Trey. Don't pounce.*

'Svaag mentioned something about opening a center in the Midwest?'

Trey turned to him. 'Oh well, that's a long way off. It's the dream, but it'll cost us money we unfortunately don't have.'

Silence stood between them a moment.

Trey literally led Mackenzie along the yard path towards the back entrance of the building.

'Well, I'm hoping I could help you there,' Mackenzie said.

Trey flipped up his shades and furrowed his brow. 'How do you mean?'

'I'd like to donate to your organization, maybe get that center up and running.'

Trey feigned shock. 'Oh no, no. That's really good of you, James, but unfortunately for this sort of setup we're talking in the millions. We'd need a number of donors to even break ground.'

'Why don't you send me the details and I'll see what I can do.' Mackenzie smiled at him. 'If it means helping people, like you guys helped me.' Mackenzie threw his hands up in the air.

Trey couldn't believe his luck. 'Are you serious, because if you are, we've a piece of land we've had our eye on for quite a while now and, well, between you and me, I think it would be the perfect location.'

Trey's palms clammed up. Heat rose up his neck. Beads of sweat popped on his forehead.

'Of course I'm being serious. I would need to get a few ducks in a row business-wise. Send over the details, let me take a look at it and I'll see what I can do.' Mackenzie smiled at him. 'I mean it, you guys saved me.'

'I don't know what to say.' And he didn't. Trey couldn't believe his luck. 'Thing is ...' Trey winced. 'If we are going to make a bid for this land, we have to move real quick. There's a lot of competition for it.' Trey shook his head.

'How quick?'

'Well, that's just it. Our lawyers said the sellers have had a few offers and they're wanting to close the deal, so we're talking a day, or two days at the most.' Trey held his breath.

Mackenzie glanced off to the side.

Trey went in for the punch. 'Look, I appreciate you wanting to help, but maybe we have got to say goodbye to this center for the time being. Find somewhere else ...'

'No. If you think it's perfect—'

'It is,' Trey cut in.

'Then let's not waste any more time. Get the figures over to me, I'll get my guys to crunch the numbers, and let's make an offer they can't resist. So long as the figures add up, we can transfer funds straight away.'

'You serious?' Trey gaped at him, astonished.

'As I said, I don't know where I'd be if I hadn't have had Svaag's help when I needed it. The more people you can reach, the better.'

Trey and Mackenzie strolled towards the parking lot.

'I'll send you everything you need. You'll have it by this afternoon.' Trey pumped Mackenzie's hand once again.

He stood and watched Mackenzie walk over towards a white Bugatti Veyron. Trey's jaw dropped. *Was this actually happening?*

As Mackenzie pulled out of the drive, Trey virtually skipped up the steps to the front lobby and headed towards his office.

Once the door was shut, Trey fist-pumped the air.

He collapsed into his chair and threw his feet up onto the desk, his hands entwined behind his head.

After reading Mackenzie's file, Trey had no doubt in his mind he would be able to persuade him to deposit the money into an account of his choosing.

All he needed to do now was stall Svaag and by the end of the week he would be out of here.

Smiling to himself, he heard his cellphone ring.

Junior.

Trey pressed the answer button and listened to him speak.

It didn't take long for the grin to disappear from his face.

46

Green heard the growl of the Bugatti outside the office. She stepped out, walked up to it and placed her hands on her hips. 'Well, look at you.'

Her partner, Agent Mackenzie, shrugged mockingly. 'What can I say, I was made for this life.'

Green laughed. 'I'm guessing it went well.'

'He nearly made out with me.'

'Shit. If I wasn't married, I'd make out with you in this.' Green ran her finger along the hood.

'Want to go for a spin, we've got it until the end of the day,' Mackenzie said.

'Be rude not to.' She opened the passenger door and closed it with a satisfying clunk. 'Sweet.'

'I know, right.' Mackenzie grinned.

'How come you get all the glamorous parts of the job?' Green asked.

'Are you kidding me? I had to endure one of their courses for this.'

Green fastened her seat belt. The second it clicked into place, Mackenzie pressed his foot onto the gas. The car surged forward with such speed, Green screamed and clasped her hand onto Mackenzie's leg.

'Told you, I'm a chick magnet.'

Green let out a guttural laugh. 'I'm not sure your wife would agree.'

Mackenzie shrugged and raised his eyebrows. He overtook a lane of traffic with ease and headed along the coast toward Briny Breezes.

'Want to slow down a bit? I'm feeling my breakfast coming up.'

'She's a beaut, huh?' Mackenzie said.

Green stared at him, too nauseous to answer.

Mackenzie turned towards her and grinned. He pressed his foot gently on the brake, signaled right and pulled up alongside the harbor.

Color flushed back into Green's cheeks. 'So, what did he say?'

'The guy was a clown. He tried to be all "Oh no, we can't accept your money, and if we did we'd need millions."'

'You have got to give it to him.'

'You should have seen his face when he clocked this baby.'

Green shook her head.

'So now what?'

'He's going to send the details over. Told him I needed to sort a few things and I'd be in touch.'

'You don't think he suspected anything?'

'Nope. Guys like him are all the same. They're blinded by the money.'

'It's not just guys. You read Melissa Harding's testimony? That woman has more balls than the Florida Gators.'

'She's one hell of a rat, huh.'

'Deserting the sinking ship. You see she got Teresa Mendoza as her attorney. Bulldogs in the pound together.' Green stared out of her open window. She watched some Barbie doll totter along the sidewalk with a dog the size of a hamster. Barbie gaped at Mackenzie at the wheel and winked at him.

Mackenzie ogled Barbie in his rearview.

'Case in point. Blinded by money,' Green said.

'Jealous?'

'Sure. I can't keep my hands off you,' Green replied, deadpan.

'Want to get some lunch?'

Green shrugged. 'Taking me somewhere fancy?'

'Subway?' Mackenzie said.

Green shook her head.

'What? They didn't say I could cover lunch expenses.'

'Just drive,' Green said. 'Then let's ditch the chick magnet and see what Trey's up to.'

'Oh, but Mom!' Mackenzie whined.

'Five more minutes, then toys away.'

Mackenzie grinned and slammed his foot on the gas.

47

'You're not going to like this, boss.' Junior's accent still carried a Mexican lilt even though he'd lived here since a young boy.

'Tell me,' Trey snapped.

'He's an ex-cop.'

'Ex-cop?'

'Yeah. From New York.'

Perhaps they were Feds after all.

'One other thing.'

Trey didn't like the sound of this either.

'There was a kid.'

'What do you mean a kid? Where?'

'With the cop. A little kid.'

'What do you mean? How old?' *Shit.*

'It was kind of hard to tell.'

'What?' Trey snapped at him. 'Was it a boy? Girl?'

'Well, that's the thing. I couldn't see.'

'What do you mean you couldn't see? Was there a kid or not?'

'Yeah. It's just they were dressed like a monkey, so you know—'

'Are you fucking on something?'

'No.'

Trey didn't say anything for a beat. His mind too busy whirring, calculating, worrying. *A kid? Jesus!*

Finally, Trey spoke. 'You made it look like a robbery, right?'

'Yeah. Don't worry. I know what I'm doing.'

Trey doubted that. He blew air out of his cheeks.

'Need anything else?' Junior asked.

'No. That's fine. Actually, wait up …'

'Yes, boss.'

'My documents. I need them today. You hear me?'

'I'll do my best, boss,' Junior said.

Without another word, Trey ended the call. A sick dread crawled into his stomach. Checking the time, he quickly clicked the mouse. He scanned the computer for a file regarding the bogus land in Chicago. Locating it, he flicked open his email. He hastily typed in James Mackenzie's address, attached the document and typed out a short accompanying note.

James,
I think you'll agree, the attached land is a great investment for the center. We have a lot of big plans for the place, which we are real excited about. However, I've spoken to our lawyers and they are keen we make a cash offer in the next 24 hours – if we are to secure it.
Trey.

Trey scanned through it one more time and pressed send.

He picked up his cellphone and typed out a message to Svaag.

Met with Mackenzie.
He'll get back to us in the next week or two.

Trey sent the message.

He had no intention of waiting a week or two. The net was closing in. He needed that money fast and he was going to make damned sure he got it. Trey's mind wandered back to what Junior had told him. Grabbing his jacket and keys, Trey left his office. He jumped into his car and made his way back to the Fair Tidings Motel.

48

Green slumped in the driver's seat of their usual sedan, slurping on a large Diet Coke through a straw. Mackenzie stepped out of their hotel lobby. Now dressed in his usual cargo pants, green polo shirt and a baseball cap pulled low, he slipped into the passenger seat.

He glanced around the car, noticing the cheap plastic dashboard and uncomfortable seats. 'The dream really is over.' He clipped in his seat belt. 'Back to reality.'

'Yup,' Green said. She placed her drink in the tray, pulled out, drove down the hotel driveway and back onto the main strip. 'Let's start at the HQ and see if he's around and take it from there.'

Mackenzie nodded, fiddled with his cap and wound down his window.

They pulled up a block from the HQ. Mackenzie jumped out of the car. He walked over to a drinks stand and waited for his partner to check out the center's parking lot.

Green drove up the main driveway. Trey's Viper was parked close to the entrance. Green drove back out of the center. She accelerated onto the boulevard, picked Mackenzie back up and parked up close enough to watch the entrance.

Mackenzie passed Green another Diet Coke. She flicked her hand in the air. 'No more, else I need to pee.'

Mackenzie clicked open his can and guzzled half of it down in one.

Both settled in their seats, watching their wing mirrors for any movement.

They heard Trey's car before they saw it. The undeniable thrum of the Viper's engine. Spotting the hood poking out, Green allowed Trey and a couple of other cars to pass and carefully followed behind.

They had only driven a couple of blocks when they spotted him indicate and turn into the rear of a motel parking lot.

'What you think he's up to?' Mackenzie said.

Green, her brow creased, shook her head. She pulled up in an adjacent parking lot.

Both of them peered across. Trey didn't move from his car.

'Maybe he's on a call?' Green said.

Mackenzie leaned into the back, tucked his hand under the seat and tugged out a small pair of binoculars. Lifting them up to his eyes, his fingers adjusted the focus and zoom.

'Nope. He's just sitting there,' Mackenzie said.

Mackenzie passed Green the binoculars. She peered through the viewfinder.

'He could be waiting for someone,' she said.

Green handed Mackenzie the binoculars back.

Mackenzie shrugged. They both settled in their seats and waited.

The door of the Viper eventually opened. Trey stepped out of the car.

'Here we go,' Mackenzie said.

Green leaned forward.

They watched Trey shift up the steps to a second-floor balcony, check behind him and approach one of the motel rooms.

Trey surveilled the motel for any movement. He had dialed a pizza place as soon as he had arrived and made an order to be sent to the room. He watched as the delivery guy arrived and got no response.

The area was pretty quiet. The only other people around were men in cheap suits, returning looking creased and weary after a day's work. Some with a six-pack and a takeout burger in their hands, ready to slump into their pit. No doubt flicking through the porn channels to find something to their liking. It seemed a lifetime ago, that had once been him.

Although he had parked at the back of the lot, Trey crouched in his seat just in case. It's not like you wouldn't notice his car. If he ever was going to split, he needed to get something new, something less flashy. He could do that. He was getting tired of it anyhow. He would trade it in soon enough. But that Bugatti was real nice.

Confident there was no one in Jenny's room, he exited the car. As casually as possible, he sauntered up the stairwell to the second floor. Peering left and right, he plucked out a small steel pick from his suit pocket. He fiddled it to and fro in the lock. The mechanism popped. Cautious, he turned the handle. He glanced around and slipped into the room, shutting the door behind him.

The room was, as he expected, pretty basic. It smelled of damp and soap suds. Twin beds took up the majority of the space. A small bathroom at the back. Empty soda cans on the side cabinet. A large paper bag lay on the bed. Trey poked his finger into it. Clothes. He pulled out a small red T-shirt. Trey's brow furrowed. He looked across at a side table. A pad and crayons lay on the side. *So, there was a kid here.*

Trey scanned the rest of the room. A small tan leather carryall poked out from under the bed. He crouched and tugged it out. He opened it. Inside, clothes and a canvas camera bag. Trey placed the camera bag onto the bed. He unzipped it. *Empty.* He dipped his fingers into the small pockets and, feeling something, he lifted it out. A memory card. Curious, he slipped it into his inner suit pocket. He riffled through the rest of the carryall. Clothes, toiletries. No paperwork, nothing.

Trey scanned the room one last time, saw little else of interest and headed towards the door. He peeked through the drapes and checked the walkway was clear. Spotting no one around, he slipped out of the room and walked as quick as he could to his car.

'What's he doing?' Green asked.

Mackenzie squinted through the binoculars. 'He's getting something out of … Shit.'

'What?' Green said.

'He's breaking into one of the rooms.'

Green screwed up her face and leaned further forward.

Mackenzie lowered the binoculars. 'What the hell's he up to?'

Green snatched the binoculars from him and focused them on the door.

'Think we should go in?' Mackenzie said. 'Call a local unit?'

'Let's see what happens. We don't want to blow anything.'

Five minutes later, the door to the motel opened. Trey glanced left and right, pulled the door shut and hastily made his way back to the car.

'You want to follow him?'

'Yeah. We can always come back, find out whose room it is.'

Seconds later, the Viper was back on the boulevard, heading towards the HQ.

Staying close behind, Mackenzie and Green followed. They pulled to the side, as Trey turned into the center's drive.

'What d'you think?' Mackenzie asked.

'I reckon they're another bunch of idiots who have fallen for this shit, and he was searching for dirt on them.'

49

I could tell something was up with TJ the moment we walked into the diner. He seemed older than he had this morning. And instead of playing Snap with May, or watching her color in her pictures, he stared out of the window. His face pale and drawn.

'What's going on?' I said, as soon as we got to the table.

I slipped into my seat and grabbed TJ's hand. It shook underneath mine.

'It's nothing.'

I looked at May. She appeared equally drawn. 'What's happened?' I glanced at Reggie, who, like me, stared at TJ, his eyebrows knitted together. He could tell a difference in them too.

'I got robbed by some punk.' TJ's head dipped to his chest.

'You what?' Reggie and I both asked in unison.

'It's OK. I'm fine. It's little May here who was the brave one.'

I pulled her in close. She tucked her head under my chin. 'You OK?' I asked her.

May blinked and nodded. 'He was a nasty man.'

My blood started to rise. I tugged her little body into mine.

'You get hurt?' I asked TJ. My eyes flicked between him and May.

'No, like I say, it was some jackass punk. Should have seen him coming.' TJ's jaw clenched tight.

'He banged his head,' May said. She blinked at TJ.

'It's nothing, kid, don't you worry.' TJ winked at her.

'Why didn't you call us?' Reggie asked.

'He smashed my damned phone.'

Every single atom in my body was ready to hunt down that son of a bitch, whoever he was, and tear him apart. Reggie placed his hand on my arm to calm me. I don't know whether it was my rage or the comfort of his touch, but my eyes welled up.

'Feel like a fool more than anything. Should have seen him coming,' TJ said.

'What did he look like?' I asked.

TJ shook his head. 'Like any other. Probably from some gang, hustling.' He shrugged.

'Why do you think he's from a gang?'

'Tattoo on his wrist. JL 16, JM 16 or something.'

Reggie shook his head. I clutched on to TJ's hand. There was still a faint shake underneath mine. I gave it a squeeze and he gripped mine back.

Sensing a need for a change of mood, Reggie clapped his hands and rubbed them together.

'Well, I say we start with the knickerbocker glory and move on to the fudge brownie, and maybe if there's room afterward, a piece of pie. What do you say, May?'

May giggled. 'Silly.'

'What?' Reggie said. He furrowed his brow and opened up his palms to fake his confusion.

'You can't start with dessert, silly,' May said.

'That so?'

May giggled some more.

TJ looked at her, smiled and glanced at me. 'Let's eat,' he said. He squeezed my hand and raised his other to one of the waitresses.

Once we'd finished our food, TJ appeared a little more relaxed. Color flushed back into his cheeks. Even so, I hadn't seen him look this vulnerable before and it bothered me.

'Is he your boyfriend?' May said the second she finished her second dessert.

Whoa. Well, that jolted me out of my thoughts.

'Hey, what?' I did a double take.

'Is he your boyfriend?' She pointed at Reggie.

Reggie gave the biggest grin. He shrugged at me.

'No,' I said. Color now flushed into my cheeks too.

May leaned over to me and placed a cupped hand around her mouth.

'You should be boyfriend and girlfriend,' she whispered in a way only a kid can whisper. Loud.

Jesus. That kid.

Reggie and TJ laughed.

'She's talking sense if you ask me,' Reggie said.

I raised my eyebrows at him and shook my head. I'm not going to lie, that threw me. My head was buzzing right now. I needed sleep. And a stiff drink.

'Come on, let's make a move.' I raised my hand for the check.

TJ got his empty wallet out.

'This is on me,' Reggie said.

'I can put it on my card. At least the punk didn't take that.'

'Let me get it,' I offered, not wanting to think about the money.

'No. My treat.' Reggie pulled out his own wallet, leafed through some bills and placed them on the check.

Despite it being fall, the evening air was warm on my skin. There was one thing you could say for Florida – at least you didn't freeze your ass off half the time. Still, I couldn't wait to be home. Wherever the hell that would be. Even when I had figured all this out, I still owed Arty his rent – and that's if he hadn't already thrown my stuff out onto the street.

Reggie and May raced to the wall that edged the beachside and played tag, chasing each other along the sand.

'Watch she doesn't get sick. She's just eaten, for Chrissake,' I shouted over.

'Listen to you,' TJ said with pride in his voice.

'Well, I'll be the one clearing it up off my motel room floor.'

TJ gave me a look to show me he wasn't convinced by my excuse.

'You're good with her,' he said.

'She's a sweet kid.'

'I knew one of them.' TJ raised his eyebrows at me.

I laughed. 'Sweet was not how you described me.'

'You were. Troubled, but sweet.' He shrugged and raised his palms.

I walked alongside him and placed my arm inside his, pulling him close to me.

'Really. You OK?' I asked.

'Yeah. Ego's bruised more than anything.' He pursed his lips and smiled at me. A beat later, the smile dropped. His face serious all of a sudden. 'But you know I'm not always going to be around, Harp ...'

I let go of his arm and stood directly in front of him.

'What's that supposed to mean? Listen, I know I got you into this…'

'That's not what I'm talking about. I'm just saying, you know…' He shrugged a little. 'I'm not getting any younger.'

'Look, I know today shook you up. Jeez, it'd shake any of us…'

'No, I'm serious. I'm worried about you.'

'Me? What the hell you got to be worried about me for?'

TJ raised his eyebrows at me. 'When don't I need to worry about you?'

I slapped his arm playfully.

'Hey, watch it, I got jumped, remember.'

He looped his arm back in mine. We watched as Reggie threw himself on the ground, May running at him, both of them giggling loudly.

'I don't know what happened between you two. It's not any of my business,' TJ said.

'TJ, I…'

'I know, I know. But hear me out. You two were good. Real good. And I don't know what happened, like I said, but you got to remember, the past is exactly that, the past. You're not a kid no more, Harp, and not everyone is going to abandon you.'

I shook my head to protest.

'Make an old man happy and let me see you settled.'

'You're talking like you're about to cash in your chips. Is there something you're not telling me?'

'No. I'm saying, you could do worse than him.' He waved in Reggie's direction.

'Come on, let's get this old man home.'

'Hey, I'm the only one that can call myself an old man. Right?'

'Right.' I smiled at him. I leaned in and kissed him on the cheek.

Reggie carried May the rest of the way back on his shoulders. By the time we got to the motel, her head had slumped over, having fallen fast asleep. Reggie lugged her up the steps towards my room. I kissed TJ again on the cheek and wished him goodnight.

I followed Reggie up the stairs and plucked out the key to my door. Opening it, I let Reggie walk in first and place May on the bed.

'Wait up,' I said. A cold shiver passed through me. I stood rigid in the doorway.

'What?' Reggie said.

'Someone's been in here.'

I glanced around the room.

'Probably the maid or someone,' Reggie said.

I placed my hand up to him, to tell him not to move.

'You smell that?' I said.

Reggie sniffed the air. 'What?'

'Cologne.'

I crouched down. My bag was under the bed. But something didn't feel right. Whether it was years of growing up in shared homes, where kids would riffle through your shit, or the distinct smell of cologne in the room, I didn't know. But something was definitely up.

I tugged out the bag. Nothing appeared out of place. I pulled out my camera bag. It was unzipped. I dipped my hand into the side pocket. 'What the hell?' I checked the other pockets. 'The photos. They're gone.' My jaw clenched.

Reggie swiveled. 'Anything else missing?'

I took a quick scan of the room. 'No.'

Reggie stared at me.

I glanced towards May, fast asleep on top of the bed. 'We need to get her out of here.'

50

Trey poured himself a bourbon. He had barely slept. The cubes of ice crackled as the amber liquor cascaded down. He took a large gulp. The burn melted down his throat. It may be early morning, but he needed something to take the edge off his nerves.

He heard a rustle by the front door. Jumping, he froze.

Silence.

He waited a moment longer, walked out of his study and noticed an envelope had been pushed underneath the door. Opening it up, Trey let out a breath of relief.

Finally, his new identity.

Glancing at the driver's license, he took out his wallet, slipped it in there and placed it back in his jacket pocket.

He walked back into the study and perched in front of the laptop.

The light from the screen reflected on his face.

A weight pressed on his chest.

He clicked to open the memory-card file.

Small icons appeared in a box. He tapped on the first one. It was a shot of the HQ. He flicked to the next. More shots of the center. He clicked forward and stopped.

There he was on the balcony of Svaag's villa.

He scrolled his mouse to zoom in on his own face. *Was that fear in his eyes?* Trey shook his head and pressed on the next image. His head, half turned on this one, looking towards the balcony door. He clicked on the next. *Svaag.*

Trey scanned through a few more. Each one making him increasingly nauseous. He had spent the night staring at these images, and the more he did, his panic grew. *Who the hell was she and what did she want?*

Trey stood and helped himself to another large glass of bourbon. He gulped it in one and poured himself another. He rubbed his clammy neck. It felt like a noose was tightening around it.

Trey pulled the cellphone out of his pants pocket and hesitated. He shook his head. He couldn't wait any longer. He needed Mackenzie's money now. Once that was in, he was ready to go.

Trey didn't want to arouse suspicion. But still, time was running out.

He took another sip of his drink, dialed Mackenzie's number and waited for him to answer.

51

'You think it was definitely Trey?' Reggie stood close to my bed, watching me pack up May's stuff. I hadn't slept all night.

'I'd gag on that cologne any time.' I winced at the memory. 'It's too dangerous keeping her here.' I walked to the window, pulled the drape back a little and peered down to the lot. I scanned the cars. A businessman in a crumpled suit heaved himself out of a vehicle and approached the front desk. I turned back to Reggie. I lowered my voice and glanced towards the bathroom, where May was peeing. 'We need to find another motel.'

I picked up her Mickey Mouse toy and crayons and placed them in a bag.

TJ jumped as the toilet flushed. Yesterday's events fresh in his mind. None of us believed it was a coincidence they had been attacked the day before.

'Maybe I should drive her back?' TJ said.

'Back where?' I asked.

'To New York.' TJ shrugged. 'At least we know she'd be safe there. The further away, the better.'

My stomach flipped. I glanced at Reggie. 'What do you think?'

He opened his palms and considered it. 'Guess she'd be out of harm's way.'

'You'd be OK with that?' I looked to TJ.

'I'd be happier if we all went back. But yeah.' He nodded.

'And you're fine to stay?' I asked Reggie.

He stared at me a beat and smiled softly. 'Sure I am.'

TJ turned to leave. 'I'll go get my stuff together and meet you in the lot.'

Mackenzie parked up at the Fair Tidings Motel and waited for Green to return to the car. He gnawed on a quarter-pounder squashed between his fat fingers, the onion spilling out onto the waxed paper.

Green exited the lobby. She opened the car door and jumped into the passenger side.

'Seriously? For breakfast?' Green said. She gurned at him.

'What? It's a very balanced meal.'

Green winced.

Mackenzie chewed and spoke at the same time. Mayonnaise sat in the creases of his lips. 'So what they say?' Mackenzie pointed with the burger in the direction of the lobby.

'Three rooms. A woman and a kid in one. And two guys in the others. She seemed to think they were on vacation. She said the kid wasn't the woman's, but she was looking after her.' Green pulled out a small notepad. 'I've got their names. Can run them later if we need to.'

They both leaned forward. A young dark-haired woman exited the same room Trey had broken into. She walked along the balcony and tapped on another door.

Mackenzie lifted the binoculars.

'What can you see?' Green asked.

'Nice rack.'

'Apart from that?'

'She's talking to some old guy.'

Mackenzie watched him walk back into the room, return and exit with a bag. He locked the door behind him. The woman returned to her room and came back out with a young child. They shifted down the steps and huddled in the parking lot.

Another door opened. A tall black guy exited.

The old guy strolled towards the front desk. The woman crouched to the young girl and embraced her. The black guy leaned against a car.

'You read the license plate?' Green asked.

'Yeah. New York. 31-078.'

Green wrote it down.

'Neat ride,' Mackenzie said.

'What is it with you guys and cars?'

'What? It's a classic.'

'Anything else stick out?'

Mackenzie peered through the viewfinder. 'Other than the fact she's got great tits on her, no. Looks like the kid and the old guy are going.' Mackenzie shook his head. 'They'll be some chumps who've gone to one of the seminars.'

'Let's call in the car and see what comes up,' Green said.

Mackenzie and Green watched the Camaro pull out onto the road and shrugged at each other.

Mackenzie's cellphone trilled.

Mackenzie took it out of his pocket. He kept his eye on the couple in the parking lot. As soon as he glanced at his phone, his attention turned.

'It's Trey,' Mackenzie said.

Green's eyes lit up. A smile jumped onto her lips.

Mackenzie clicked on the cellphone. 'Hey.'

Green leaned in closer.

'Oh hey, Trey. How are you?' Mackenzie pushed Green away.

'Sure. I was going to call you.' Mackenzie listened to the response.

'No, great to meet you too.' Mackenzie rolled his eyes. 'Listen, I'm really sorry. I had a look over the figures you sent me, and I don't think I can make that investment right now.' Mackenzie's eyes widened at Trey's response.

'I know, I know. And I'm sorry. It doesn't feel like the right time.' Mackenzie gesticulated with his pumped fist what he thought of him.

Green's attention momentarily shifted. She watched the couple from the motel split. The woman headed off in the opposite direction to the guy. Seeing them walk off, she turned back to Mackenzie.

'I don't understand,' Mackenzie said, feigning confusion. He cupped his hand over the mouthpiece. 'Here we go,' he mouthed to Green.

'Sure. OK. But I don't see how meeting you is going to change my mind. The figures don't really add up.' He paused to listen to the response.

'Fine. I won't be back in town until tomorrow.' Mackenzie raised his eyebrows at Green. 'I'll call you when I land.'

Mackenzie finally clicked off the call.

Green opened her palms in anticipation.

Mackenzie placed his cellphone to the side and high-fived his partner. He turned over the engine and pulled the car out onto the main strip. 'Let's get everyone in place. Seems we're finally on.'

As we waited by the Camaro for TJ to check out, I crouched down to May and held her face in my hands.

'I want you to take care of TJ for me, OK?'

May nodded. 'You're not coming?' Her face dropped.

I glanced at Reggie a second before I replied.

'No. We've got to take care of some business first and we'll be back before you know it. We still need to find your Mommy.'

'Hide-and-seek?'

'Exactly. Hide-and-seek.' I squeezed her tight. 'Don't you worry, kid. We'll find her.'

It was Reggie's turn to glance at me now. *What was I supposed to say?*

TJ sauntered over to the Camaro and threw his bag in the trunk. He slammed it shut.

He shook Reggie's hand and pulled him in close, patting him on the back.

I walked towards him. A lump stabbed in my throat. Tears filled my eyes. I hugged him, the warmth of his body against mine. Letting go, I pulled back and quickly wiped my cheek.

I squatted back towards May and kissed the top of her head. More tears stung my eyes. I gave her a big smile.

'Don't you go giving him any trouble now.' I winked at her.

'You ready for an adventure, kid?' TJ said. He opened the car door. May tumbled in. TJ fastened her belt. 'Now we'll show you how this baby really drives,' TJ said to May. He shut the passenger door.

He walked around to the other side and, with a nod, he got into the car.

The engine roared to life. With a honk on the horn, he pulled away onto the main strip. Reggie and I stood alone on the lot, gazing at the blue Camaro racing off into the distance.

52

We both stood still for a moment, the realization it was the two of us now.

'Why don't I go get us a rental?' Reggie said, breaking the silence.

'Sure. Meet you back here. I'll get us an iced coffee.'

Reggie headed off towards the downtown area.

I walked to the diner and, with the last of my cash, I ordered us our drinks to take out and made my way back to the room.

For all my bravado, I was relieved Reggie had stayed. The thought someone had been here unnerved me.

Knowing Reggie would be a while, I took the opportunity to take a shower before we packed up and found ourselves another motel.

I stood under the warm water for a good ten minutes. It was the first time I had been alone since I had found May. It seemed a lifetime ago. I had got so used to having her around. The thought of her humming away in the background or wittering on about some nonsense made me smile. She had only just gone and I missed her already.

I stepped out of the shower and, as I glanced through the mist, my heart skipped a beat. On the mirror, she had drawn a heart and, next to it, the letter *M* and the letter *H* on either side. So that's why she had come out of the bathroom grinning like a Cheshire cat that time.

Wrapping a towel around me, ready to dry my hair, I heard a knock on the motel door.

'Reggie, it's open,' I shouted. I brushed through my wet hair and turned on the blow-dryer.

The mist dissipated with the heat. I glanced back at the mirror, attempting to catch the drawing one last time. The heart sketch had already disappeared.

Instead, all I saw in the reflection was Trey standing right behind me.

53

Trey snapped his arm around my neck, jolted me back and threw me into the bedroom. I slammed into the corner of the bed. A searing pain shot through my side and along my arm.

Trey pinned my legs down with his. With one arm, he tugged my hands above my head and slapped me sharp across my mouth with the other. My jaw popped.

Lying on top of my near-naked body, I smelled liquor on his breath. He licked his lips.

'Well, look at you, darling, all dressed up for me.' His eyes traveled across my scarcely covered breasts.

My chest tightened. I tried to speak. My jaw throbbed. A trickle of blood from my lip slipped down my chin.

Trey leaned back. He ran his right index finger along the side of my face, across my throat, around my breasts and down to my hip.

'Such a shame our date was cut short before, don't you think?' He looked to where his hand lay, close to my thigh. His eyes glazed from the liquor.

The towel slipped open.

Clearly enjoying the power he had over me, Trey removed his jacket and took his time carefully folding it. He placed it to the side as I lay frozen underneath his weight.

'Now we can get to know each other a little more, don't you think?' He unbuttoned the top of his shirt and unbuckled his belt.

'What do you want?' I managed to whisper.

'Well, funny you should ask that...' His hand wandered back up towards my breasts.

I screwed my eyes up tight. My heart trembled against my aching ribs.

'I was going to ask you the same question,' he continued.

I opened my eyes and stared at him. I was not going to let him do this.

'What do you want?' I repeated with more venom in my voice.

Trey leaned back now. The sick grin on his face disappearing. 'What I want – *Jenny* – is to know,' he spat his words at me, 'who the fuck you're working for?'

No candy voice now.

I tried to move my jaw. It felt like it had come loose from the rest of my skull. The taste of iron in my throat.

'I said, who you working for?' He pressed his face to mine.

I attempted to squirm my way out from under him, but he must have been an easy fifty pounds heavier than me. I shifted my head to the side to breathe a little easier.

'Where's May's mom?' My words sounded woolly.

He leaned back, his weight easing a little. Trey's face creased in confusion. 'What the fuck you say?'

A high-pitched tone screamed in my ear from where the side of my head had hit the floor. 'Where is she? Why'd you dump her in New York?'

'Dump who?' He leaned forward, the weight of his body crushing mine. 'Who the fuck is May?'

Was he bluffing?

'I can't breathe.'

He pressed down further. My ribs screamed in pain.

The door flew open. Reggie soared across the room and jerked his arm around Trey's throat. Reggie yanked him off me, clenched his fist and punched him on the nose with a crack. The acute sound of knuckles against bone. Blood splattered across the motel wall. Trey shook his head to stabilize himself and jumped to his feet. Reggie, in full combat mode now, shifted onto his toes and thumped him hard in the gut. Trey gasped for air. Reggie lifted Trey by his shirt, whacked him against the wall. His back slammed into it with an almighty thud.

Trey collected himself and swiveled his head to the side. He kicked up his left leg, his knee catching Reggie straight in the balls.

'Motherfucker.' Reggie took a sharp breath in.

In that split second, Trey – a trail of blood spurting from his nose – freed himself from Reggie's grasp and sprinted out of the room. The sound of his footsteps pounded down the stairwell.

Reggie doubled over. He took another breath and, cupping his hand between his legs, he hobbled to the door after him. He peered over the balcony and watched Trey scramble to his car.

I heard the screech of rubber as Trey shot out of the lot at full pelt.

Reggie spun around.

'Jesus Christ, Harp ...' He sped towards me and kneeled. He placed my head in his hands. 'Did he touch you?'

'I'm OK.' I shook my head, but my whole body was trembling.

'You're not OK.' Reggie covered me with a blanket. He looked at the cut on my lip. 'We need to clean this up. Stay right there.'

I tried to move, but the agonizing pain in my ribs pierced my side.

Reggie raced to the bathroom and grabbed a towel. He doused it in cool water, wrung it out and gently pressed it to my lip.

'I know,' Reggie said, as I winced at the pain. 'Hold that there. I'm going to get some ice.'

Reggie jumped back up and, seizing a bucket from the side, he ran out of the room.

I eased myself onto the bed and leaned against the headboard. Damn, my skull was pounding.

Reggie walked back in and shut the door. Taking the bloodied towel from me, he snatched another from the bathroom. He wrapped it around some ice and held it next to my face and gave me a gentle smile.

'You all right?' I mumbled.

'Shhhh. Don't talk. I'm fine.' He held the ice up to my lip.

'Is this your way of keeping me quiet?' I said. I tried to smile, but it hurt even more.

'Well, if it was, it's not working.'

We sat there for a moment, contemplating each other, as if no time had passed at all.

He pulled away the iced towel, leaned forward to look at my lip and kissed it.

Butterflies fluttered in my stomach.

'The cut doing it for you?' I said.

'Always with the sarcasm,' Reggie kissed me again.

I winced. 'OK, you're going to have to be a bit more careful than that,' I mumbled.

'How about here instead?' Reggie leaned in towards my neck.

'Perfect.' In my mind, I tried to say it soft and seductive. The reality sounded a little more different. My lip ballooning by the minute.

Reggie laughed and nuzzled my neck. Despite the throbbing of my mouth and the aching of my ribs, I actually felt better than I had in a long while. Reggie could do that to me. I had tried to forget it. But now, as he held me, it was impossible to ignore.

Reggie peeled off his clothes.

The warmth of his skin next to mine. His familiar smell, the softness of his lips against my breasts, made me forget all at once what it was like to feel like I was battling the world. Instead, we melted into each other. There was no hesitancy. We knew instinctively how to be with each other, like no time had passed at all. Our bodies moved in unison. My ribs ignored the pain.

Reggie rolled towards me with a grin on his face like he'd unwrapped his favorite toy.

'What?' I said, again through a cotton mouth.

Reggie shook his head and shrugged. 'Nothing. It's nice, that's all.'

He interlaced his fingers with mine. We lay there for a while, studying each other, feeling the rhythm of the other's breath.

'Who'd have thought a kid would have brought us back together?' Reggie said.

I took a deep breath. I leaned over and lay on my back, flinching at the stabbing cramp in my side.

'Seriously, you're real good with her, you know.' Reggie stroked my stomach with the tips of his fingers. His fingernails, perfect ivory crescents against his skin.

My muscles tightened. I closed my eyes. I wanted to hold on to this feeling for a moment longer.

'I get why you left, Harp. But surely you can see you're good with kids.'

Boom. There it was. Like a pin in a balloon, the air seemed to disappear from the room. The feeling had gone.

I jumped off the bed and didn't care about the pain screeching through my nerves.

'You couldn't let it go, could you?' My eyes filled with tears.

Reggie shot bolt upright on the bed.

'What did I say?' He held his palms open.

I grabbed my pants and T-shirt and scrabbled to the bathroom, slamming the door shut.

'Just go!' I screamed. I keeled over the basin in agony. I shouldn't have moved so quick. Something was squeezing my lungs in their fists. My breath shallow.

'What is wrong with you?' Reggie shouted through the closed door.

My head pounded. I thrust the door back open.

'What is wrong with me? We're together, what, five minutes and already you're talking about kids again? Seriously?'

Reggie's mouth opened. No words came out. He stood in front of me butt naked.

'Go.' My hands trembled at my sides.

'I was only saying you're good—'

'I know what you're saying.'

'No. No you don't, Harper. Because, as ever, you don't listen. Always the same ol' Harper, doing her own thing. Doing what she wants.' Reggie grabbed his pants and T-shirt and threw them on.

'That right?' The throbbing moved from my lip to my throat. I was damned if I was going to cry in front of him. 'Screw you, Reggie.'

'Oh right, screw me. Fine. You don't want me around? Then I'll go. I came here to save your ass, and yeah, I wanted to make it work, and yes, I'm sorry for complimenting you on how you are with May, but it seems like I'm the fool.' Reggie flipped his hands up in the air.

I shook my head. I didn't want to look at him right now.

'You know what? You can do this on your own.' Reggie tugged the car keys out of his pocket and hurled them on the bed. He pointed his finger at me. 'Next time you want help, call some other gullible asshole.' He stopped for a moment. He glared at me one last time and headed to the door, slamming it behind him.

I stood half in the bathroom, half in the motel room. My eyes scanned the walls covered in cold coffee and bloodstains, the furniture set askew from the fight, and back at the door.

Come on, Reggie.

But the door remained shut. My body trembled. With no one in the room to see me, hot tears flowed down my cheeks, stinging the cut on my lip.

How did it go from feeling so glorious to so crap in such a short space of time?

I knew the answer. Me. It's like I have 'self-destruct' tattooed all over me. Why couldn't I have taken what he said as a compliment? And why didn't I chase after him and tell him I'm sorry?

He was right. And I hated it.

For months before we split, Reggie took every opportunity to talk about the future. About having kids. At first I ignored it, was early days, but I could tell he was getting more serious and I knew, just knew, it wasn't for me. I wasn't cut out to be a mom. Hell, I could barely look after myself, never mind kids. How was I supposed to know what to do when I hadn't had a parent myself?

I explained my reasons why. But as the words tumbled out my mouth, the look in his eye told me he thought he'd still be able to convince me. The thought of being a soccer mom, shouting and cheering from the sidelines, unpacking Tupperware boxes, with warmed homemade cookies, or worse still, staying awake until the small hours, sewing a costume for Book Day, because someone else's parent had managed to make an outfit fit for a movie set, made me shudder.

I hadn't meant to walk out on him. But I knew in my heart he wouldn't stop until he had kids – and the way Reggie was jabbering on about it, he wanted a whole team of them. He needed to find someone else, someone who felt the same, someone who would be good with them. That wasn't me.

So I did what I usually do. I ran. I ran away from him. I ran away from the problem, and until today I had kept on running.

Fresh tears stung my eyes. I don't know if it was the adrenaline of being with Reggie, or from the fight, but whatever it was, it fell fast. The pain cascaded in. I searched in my bag and found some Advil.

I ran the cold faucet. I cupped my hand, swallowed the pill and drank some water.

My mind wandered back to Trey. *Why had he sounded so confused about May?* It made no sense.

I dipped a towel into the water. I pressed my face against it and stared at myself in the mirror. I'm surprised the damn thing didn't crack, the way I looked. My eyes red-raw from crying, my cheeks flushed, and the cut on my lip had swollen to about three times its size.

I leaned in closer to the mirror. The cut was deep. I needed a stitch.

The towel dropped out of my hand.

A stitch. How could I have been so stupid?

May had nothing to do with Svaag or Trey. The phone

number I'd found. Yes, it was his. But someone had taken that number down. And the date. The day after Svaag had allegedly gone on a retreat. The date could have been for the cosmetic surgery.

Hadn't May said she had seen that man at her daddy's work?

Goddammit.

Like the cut on my lip, it had been right under my nose all this time.

54

It didn't take long for Reggie to pack up the few items he had brought to Florida. He checked out of the motel and, rather than wait for a cab, he decided to walk along the front and hail one from there. His mind raced. He needed to walk off his mood. Only Harper could get him this wound up. He was not only mad with her, but angry with himself for considering they could give it a go again. What had he been thinking? But, as ever, she had got under his skin. His first mistake was telling TJ he would come over and help. He knew seeing her would mean trouble and that was just in terms of his heart, never mind all the other crap she brought along with her.

He spotted a cab hurtling towards him, raised his hand and waited for it to slow.

'Airport,' Reggie said.

The driver nodded. Reggie jumped in the back.

For all his anger, Reggie needed to know Harper was safe.

It was only a ten-minute ride to the airport. Once he was out of the cab and out of earshot of the driver, he would phone the office and see if his buddy Gary Davidson had returned his call.

*

The cab pulled up.

Reggie paid the fare and stepped through the large glass entrance into the airport. He glanced up to the screens. A flight to JFK was boarding in ten minutes, another a half-hour later to Newark. Spotting the ticket office, he hurried over and purchased a ticket for the next flight. Grabbing his carry-on bag, he walked towards the security gate. A small line wound its way around the plastic poles. He tugged his cellphone out of his pants and dialed his office number.

'Hey, Marie, it's Reggie. You put me through to my desk?'

'Sure thing. I hear you're living it up in Florida. You bringing me home some sun-drenched hottie?'

'I'll do my best, Marie. I'll do my best.'

''S'all I can ask.'

He heard her dial the extension and waited as it rang out.

'Garcia,' his buddy growled.

'Hey, it's Reggie. You keeping the streets safe?'

'Well, if it isn't Mister Vacay. You still sunning yourself on the beach while some of us do a hard day's work.'

'Yeah, yeah, something like that, except who d'you know doing the hard work?'

'Funny, wise guy. What you doing calling? You missing us?'

Reggie heard Joey shout something across the office.

'Yeah, he says he's found himself in Florida and he's finally come out,' Garcia hollered back to him.

''Bout time too,' Joey shouted.

'Yeah, as much as I'd love to listen to Abbott and Costello, I wondered if you'd check if there's been some messages for me.'

'What am I, your secretary now?'

'You've always been my bitch, you know that, Garcia.'

'Don't I know it. Hold on, hold on.'

The phone clunked in Reggie's ear as it hit the desk.

The line in front of him shuffled forward.

'Hey, Reggie.' It was Joey. 'When you going to introduce us to your new boyfriend then, uh?'

'Thought you'd met your dad,' Reggie said without a pause. 'And there was me missing you.'

'Give me that…' Garcia took the phone. 'You got a couple of messages from Mrs Bianchi 'bout the four eighty you were looking into. And, ah…' Paper shuffled in the background. '…A message from, shit, I can't read Joey's writing. Jesus, retard, you skip handwriting lessons?' he shouted out. 'Hold on, a Gary Davidson returning your call? Doesn't say what…'

'That's what I'm after. He leave a number?' Reggie's head flicked up.

'Yeah. You got a pen?'

Reggie dropped his bag on the ground. He patted his pockets. *Damn*. No, he didn't.

'Text it to me, will you?' Reggie moved closer to the security check.

'Yes, sir!'

'And that's why you're my favorite bitch.' Reggie ended the call and smiled to himself. He missed those guys.

A couple more people lined up in front of him.

He placed his cellphone, wallet, belt, shoes and bag onto the conveyor belt and walked through the barrier. As he waited for his tray to come through, the tannoy announced the final boarding call for his flight. Reggie grabbed his stuff, shoved his shoes on and tried to loop his belt through his pants. He sped to the gate and stepped onto the plane.

Settling into his seat, his cellphone pinged. He opened up a text. It was Gary's number from Garcia.

Seeing as the plane was still stationary, he dialed it.

A young blond woman dressed in a red uniform, hair perfectly in place, approached Reggie. She tapped his arm. 'Excuse me, sir. Could you turn your cellphone off, please?'

'I'll only be a ...' Reggie threw one hand up in the air.

'Please, sir.' The woman gave him a polite smile.

Reggie pulled the cellphone away from his ear and cut off the call.

He switched it to airplane mode, placed it in his pocket and fastened his seat belt. The flight was less than three hours. He would have to wait until then.

He only hoped Harper could keep herself out of trouble in the meantime.

55

Could that really be it? That the person who left the 'I'm sorry' note was the cosmetic surgeon? It made sense that the number I had found to the center was Svaag's. The date on the note was nearly four weeks before we had found her. The day after he had supposedly gone on his retreat – which may have been the date of the surgery. And the number I hadn't figured out could have been bank details for the procedure.

But how did the cosmetic surgeon connect to May? The brief moment I saw him at the clinic, he was going about business as though nothing was wrong.

I wracked my brain, trying to recall every single moment of being in the clinic. I walked myself through it. I'd entered the lobby and saw Svaag. The cosmetic surgeon had appeared and spoke to Norma. He took Svaag into his office and … *Hold on. Wait up.* The surgeon had said something to Norma about trying to reach someone urgently. Norma had said one of the partners was away. So perhaps it was the partner who was connected? Was it his flight to Dallas I had found?

Stumbling into the bedroom, I clutched my ribs and searched for my cellphone. Scanning the room, my eye caught something on the floor. It was Trey's jacket. I picked it up. A snakeskin wallet fell to the floor. I flipped it open and riffled through it.

A wad of cash filled the main pocket, and not small bills either. There must have been a thousand bucks there, easy. I slipped out the driver's license. A photo of Trey staring straight into the camera, a smarmy look on his face. But the name next to it read Peter Johnson. I pulled out bank cards. All under the name Peter Johnson.

So that explained the bank statements in his apartment.

I placed the wallet in my purse and found my cellphone.

I flicked onto the internet. What was the name of the cosmetic clinic? Clear Day? *ClearView* – that was it. I typed it in the search browser and up popped their website.

Welcome to ClearView Medical Clinic

Scott Anderson and Eric Diaz have successfully run the ClearView Medical Clinic for four years. We are nationally renowned in cosmetic surgery. If you'd like to book a consultation for free, dial our toll-free number 800 BEAUTY or fill in a form below.

Anderson. Diaz. No mention of the name Brown.

I clicked some of the pages on the menu. Adverts for Brazilian butt lifts. Breast Augmentations. Botox. All at *'great prices'*. *Jesus*. I clicked the 'Testimonies' page.

'Amazing.' '5 Stars.' 'Wow, I look so much younger.'

I moved on to the 'Meet our Doctors' page. There was a section for Scott Anderson and one for his partner Eric Diaz.

No photos, dammit.

Eric Diaz. That's who was away. The guy Svaag's surgeon needed to get hold of.

I scan-read his profile. But my eyeline caught something below, in Scott Anderson's biography.

It stated Anderson had run a clinic in New York. Was that a

coincidence? Was he 'Uncle Orange'? I needed a photo of him to send it over to TJ to see if May recognized him. Perhaps her dad worked in the clinic as one of the surgery staff.

I clicked off their website and typed 'Scott Anderson' into the search engine.

A bunch of sites came up. References to medical papers he'd written. A few links for conferences he was speaking at and, in the *Medical News*, a profile piece on him from a year ago.

Shit. Still no photo.

I scan-read the article, searching for any clues. Nothing.

As a last attempt, I tried typing his name into Facebook. A whole host of guys popped up with the same name. I recalled he had mousy blond hair, but still I couldn't quite picture him. It could be any of them.

I jumped off the bed. Pain shot through my chest, across my stomach and down my legs. Even trying to breathe sent a hundred shock waves through me.

If Scott Anderson was 'Uncle Orange', why in the hell was he carrying on his business like nothing was amiss? She had seen him herself at the clinic. He hardly acted like a man who'd dumped a four-year-old kid in New York. And why had he left her there?

More importantly, who was her dad, where was he and where was her mom? Had Scott Anderson done something with them too?

I needed to talk to Reggie. Why had I gotten into such a stupid fight? All he had done was compliment me. And he was right, I wasn't so bad with May. I missed having her small hand in mine. Like protecting the kid gave me an invisible shield I never knew I had.

I scrolled through to Reggie's number. My thumb hesitated

over the call button. I pressed it and held the cellphone up to my ear. It went straight to his voicemail.

I stepped out onto the balcony, knocked on his motel door and waited. *Nothing*. Perhaps he was walking off our argument and, if I was lucky, there'd soon be a knock on my door.

I went back to my room, my pulse racing.

TJ would still be on the road. I would have to wait to talk to him and May. Regardless, I called his landline and left a message for him to call me the second he got back home.

With little choice, I navigated back to the ClearView Medical Clinic website. Bracing myself, I dialed their number.

56

Reggie had his cellphone in his hand the minute he stepped off the plane. The whole journey back, he had become increasingly anxious. Seeing Harper, her face smashed up, looking so vulnerable, made him sick. How could any man do that to a woman? A question he had asked himself so many times on the hundreds of callouts he'd had for domestic violence. But seeing someone he knew – and, yes, loved, despite himself – bruised and battered, made his blood boil. There was no way Trey Garrison was going to get away with touching her. If it meant Harper having to worm her way out of trouble with the cops, so be it. He needed her to be safe, and Trey needed to be behind bars.

Reggie switched on the cellphone. The moment he passed through JFK passport control, he called the number Garcia had texted him.

'Ya, Davidson.'

'Gary, it's Reggie Lamont.'

'Hey, man. How are you?'

'I'm good, I'm good. What's it like in the dizzy heights of the Bureau?'

'Well, you know that's classified information,' Gary laughed.

'I bet how many sugars you take in your coffee is too. Must be real fun working up there. If you can call it work.'

'Still walking the mean streets?'

'Sure am. You know, real police work,' Reggie said.

'I'm sure you didn't call to bust my balls. What can I do for you?'

'Listen, I came across something on a case I've been working on and I saw your boys were on it.'

'Go on.'

'There's something called the Liberty of the Mind Legacy and...'

'Oh yeah, I know about them,' Gary scoffed.

'Oh yeah?'

'Yeah. Not my case, but I know a couple of guys who are real excited about a lead they have. Seems they've picked up a canary.'

'Right. You know what the canary's singing?' Reggie's heart picked up pace.

'Why you ask?'

'No reason really.' Reggie faltered. He was on shaky ground. 'Their name came up with a CI of mine and when I looked them up, I saw they had Fed fingerprints all over them.'

'Well, think they've been following them for a while. Extortion, blackmail. You name it, these creeps have been at it. But I think one of the honchos got cold feet and she came running to us. You know how we like to be a shoulder to cry on.'

'Oh sure, real sympathetic, you guys,' Reggie laughed, trying to keep the conversation light.

'Yeah, I like to think of us as counselors, with guns and warrants and a nice little place you can stay that happens to have bars on the windows.'

'Say, they didn't mention anything about a missing kid, did they?' Reggie waited with bated breath.

'A kid? No, don't think so. I can check. As I say, it's not my case, but…'

'No. Don't worry. Probably crossed wires.' Reggie's mind whirred. He needed Harper to be safe, but he couldn't risk her being locked up. 'Listen, it may be nothing, but my CI mentioned a couple of names and something about them flying, so whatever your canary's singing, I'd swing by their nest pretty quick.'

'Shit. OK, I think they're keeping pretty close tabs on them, but I'll pass it on. Say, who's this CI?'

Reggie snorted. 'You know I can't tell you that, man. Classified information.'

'Touché. Gee, so, did your CI…' Gary had a sarcastic tone in his voice now, '…say what made him think they were going to fly?'

'I think one of them, a Svaag Dimash…' Reggie tried to sound vague, '…is trying to change his identity. Had a lot of work done at ClearView Medical Clinic down in Palm Beach. And another guy – Trey Garrison? Sounds like he's a real nasty piece of work.'

'Seems your CI knows quite a lot.' Gary sounded a little suspicious.

'Why – you think I recruited him?' Reggie said, trying to put him off the scent.

'I hear you. What's the name of that clinic again?'

'ClearView Medical Clinic.'

'Well, man, thanks for the heads-up. I'll pass it on. Say, next time I'm up in New York, let's go for a beer.'

'Yeah, I'd like that.'

'And thanks again for the lead. Appreciate it.' Gary sounded a little more buoyant now.

'Any time,' Reggie said.

Reggie finished the call. As frustrated as he was with Harper right now, at least now he knew she would be safe.

57

I pressed the ClearView Medical Clinic intercom buzzer and waited to be let into the building. I took the elevator this time as every muscle in my body seemed to ache.

Unable to get an appointment until the afternoon, I had spent the day reading and rereading every article I could regarding the two guys, trying to find a tangible link to May and anyone connected to the clinic with the last name 'Brown'. I came up blank. Every article referred to the surgeons' medical work, with not a hint about their personal lives or staff.

I entered the main front-desk area and scanned the space to see if anyone else was around. No one. I strolled up to the desk and waited until Norma, the desk clerk, glanced up. I forgot for a second my face resembled something pulverized with a frying pan. That was until her mouth fell open.

'It looks worse than it is,' I mumbled. Yeah, I was real convincing. I tried to smile. The skin on my distended lip stretched tight. 'I have an appointment. Harper Stein. I called earlier about my consultation.'

She gave me a pitying smile. 'Sure. Take a seat. He's just with a client and then Mr Anderson will be right with you.'

I had my cellphone in my hand ready to take a discreet photo.

'Is his partner still away?' I asked

'Eric? Yes, he had a close family bereavement sadly, so he's out of the country at the moment. Would you have preferred a consultation with him?'

I shook my head. I paused.

'When Mr Anderson does his surgery, does he use regular surgical staff?'

Norma looked a little taken aback. 'Well, we try. They're often agency staff. But we only use the highest skilled people.'

I felt the urge to ask her if any of them had the last name Brown, but I didn't want to alert her to anything before I had the opportunity to work out the link to Scott Anderson and if he really was 'Uncle Orange'. Whoever 'Uncle Orange' was, he had dumped a young kid in New York City and I needed to understand why. Once I had sent a photo of Anderson over to TJ and May, I could begin asking questions.

I stood by the chairs. Sitting would mean having to get up and my ribs pleaded with me to stay still. Instead, I paced a little, my mind whirring as to how this all fitted together.

An office door opened. A woman who was bronzed like a statue sashayed out into the lobby. Her breasts the size of basketballs and lips so large, they made my current situation look like a paper cut.

I think the statue gave Norma a smile, but her face barely moved, so it was difficult to tell.

'Miss Stein?' a man's voice called out.

My head shot in the direction of the open door.

Scott Anderson – around six two, approximately a hundred and sixty pounds, sandy blond hair – approached me. His hand outstretched to shake mine.

'Come this way.' He gave me a smile and led me along the hallway.

Mackenzie watched as Green hunched over her desk, a phone pressed next to her ear.

'What CI?' Green creased her face up.

Mackenzie mouthed at her, '*What?*'

She shook her head and ignored him.

'Uh-huh.' Green scribbled on a pad. 'So what makes him think he's going to be in the wind?' She furrowed her brow some more. 'Clear what? And that's some kind of cosmetic surgery clinic? Shit.' She pointed at the laptop. Mackenzie turned it towards her. Green nodded and tapped on the keyboard. 'We'll check it out. Thanks for the call, Gary.'

Green switched off the cellphone and clicked on a link for ClearView Medical Clinic.

'You going to tell me what's going on?' asked Mackenzie.

Green scribbled down an address and grabbed her jacket. 'Get the keys, come on.'

Mackenzie picked up the sedan's keys and followed Green out of the door.

'Hello. Want to tell me where we're going?' Mackenzie shouted.

'I'll tell you in the car. You look up that Camaro by the way?'

'Yeah, it's registered to a Thomas Jefferson O'Neill. Same as the name on the motel room. An ex-cop, apparently, if you can believe it.'

Green and Mackenzie exited the office and placed on their shades. Green held out her palm to Mackenzie. He passed her the keys.

'An ex-cop?' She unlocked the car.

'Yeah. New York.' Mackenzie shook his head to himself. 'Promise me something?'

Green turned over the engine and pulled out. 'Go on.'

'If when I retire I turn to some crazy cult looking for answers, you shoot me.'

Green looked at him and grinned. 'You got it.'

Mackenzie shook his head soberly. 'You'd think a cop would know better.'

Green shrugged. 'It takes all kinda crazy.'

Mackenzie fastened his seat belt. 'So where we're heading?'

She kept one hand on the wheel and grabbed his stomach with her other. 'That was your wife on the phone. She asked me to get you a tummy tuck.'

'Real funny.'

58

I followed Anderson into his clinic.

If you'd have asked me to describe a murderer or child snatcher, he wouldn't have been it. He had the bearing of a preppy schoolboy. His face smooth and tanned, flaxen hair tousled slightly, piercing blue eyes. But what does a killer look like?

I scanned the room. A large mahogany desk took up the left-hand side of the office. A comfortable plum leather chair on either side. A brass and emerald glass lamp sat on the desk next to the computer. I spotted a photo frame with its back to me. Towards the right of the room, a draped-off area for changing. In the adjacent corner, a surgical bed – presumably for checkups – positioned next to a large steel cabinet.

The office overlooked the beach and nearby harbor.

'Sorry to keep you waiting. Normally there'd be two of us handling the consultations, but my partner is away, so it's just me. I take it Norma told you there's quite a wait for surgery at the moment?'

I nodded.

'Please, take a seat.'

I sat opposite him. The desk between us.

I tried to shift my chair a little so I could snatch a glimpse of the photo.

'That's quite a view.' I indicated to the windows, hoping he would turn around for a moment and I'd be able to take a peek. He didn't. Instead, he peered at me curiously, his blue eyes scanning my face.

'And, if you don't mind my saying, it's quite a cut you have there.' He stood and made his way around to my seat. He leaned on the edge of the desk, blocking my view.

So much for my plan.

'Mind if I take a look?' He edged closer towards me.

I shook my head. I didn't know what else to do.

'May I ask how this happened?' He squinted as he peered at the cut.

'It was nothing,' I mumbled.

'Well, nothing sure as hell did a number on you.' He stood, his imposing frame close to mine. 'Please. If you wouldn't mind sitting over here a second.' He indicated to the bed at the far wall.

I rose slowly and tried hard to mask the pain screaming through my bruised ribs. I edged over to the bed and perched on the end.

Anderson followed. He pulled out a small flashlight from his top pocket and stepped closer. 'I don't ordinarily do this, but if you give me a minute, I could pop a stitch in that and clean it up a bit.'

'No, really, it's OK.' I waved him off.

Anderson stepped over to the steel drawers. They opened with a screech. He plucked out a few items, placed them on a metal tray and stood close to me.

'I noticed from the form you filled in you're considering breast augmentation?' Anderson searched the tray for something. He picked it up and leaned into my face.

I had forgotten about the form. Why the hell had I ticked

that box? Why couldn't I have ticked Botox or, yeah, even lip fillers. The irony.

'Well, I don't...'

'Keep still.' He pulled at a bright light hanging by a swinging arm and flicked it on, blinding me. He rubbed a sanitized wipe across my lip. He held my chin in his one hand and picked up a syringe in the other.

I jolted my head back.

'It's to take the pain away. You'll feel a slight scratch.' I smelled coffee on his breath.

'Jes—' The needle pricked my skin.

'There. It'll take a minute to work its way in and we'll have a stitch in there in no time.' He leaned up. 'Now, in terms of breast augmentation, there's a number of options.'

I was in hell. Whatever I had done over the years that was wrong, it was now coming back to haunt me.

Anderson strolled over to the cabinet and opened up another drawer. 'Do you have any idea what size you were looking for?'

Please. Someone save me.

'I'll need to examine your breasts, discuss the various shapes and sizes, and often I find clients like to go away and think about it further before deciding. But I have a range here which will give you some idea of what you might be after.'

If my mouth hadn't already been made numb, I'd have been struck dumb.

'Now, let's look at this lip.' He placed his hand up to my jaw. 'There, can you feel that?'

I felt nothing but the need to get out of this office and fast. I shook my head.

He picked up a needle from the tray, and I guess from the dull tug on my lip, he was sewing the flap together.

A snip of the scissors and a flick of the light switch and he seemed to be done.

'Right, why don't you sit yourself down and let's talk about shapes and sizes and then let's examine you. I'm going to wash up and I'll be right with you. I'd ask Norma to get you a drink, but you may need to let your lip settle.' He smiled at me.

Anderson exited the room.

I whipped around to his side of the desk and picked up the photo frame.

Shit. There it was.

'Excuse me?' Anderson said. His voice brittle.

I jumped. I hadn't heard him come back in. Alarmed, I stared at him and towards the photo.

A woman, long platinum blond hair, sat next to Anderson, and on his lap was none other than May.

He wasn't 'Uncle Orange'. He was May's dad, or stepdad at least.

Anderson whipped the picture out of my hand. He glanced at the photo and, instead of propping it back up, he slammed it face down on the desk.

And there was a look in his eye now I really didn't like.

The phone buzzed, startling both of us.

His eyes still focused on me, he picked up the handset. 'Yes?' He turned away. 'Who's here?'

He looked back at me. Anderson's face paled. His body visibly shaken. 'Give me a minute.'

Anderson replaced the handset. 'You need to leave.'

Before I had a chance to reply, he led me to the door and hastily shut it behind me.

59

Green and Mackenzie stepped into the elevator and ascended to the third floor.

Walking to the front desk, Green slipped her fingers into her jacket pocket. She tugged out a black leather card holder and flipped it open.

'FBI. I'm Agent Green, this here is Agent Mackenzie. We'd like to talk to someone who dealt with a client of yours. A Mr Svaag Dimash?'

Norma sat bolt upright. This was her first time dealing with someone from the law, apart from that speeding ticket she'd gotten eight months back.

'Well, the only person here is Scott Anderson, he's one of the partners, but I don't think he can ...'

'I know, I know, client confidentiality and all that,' Mackenzie jumped in. He waved his hand in the air. 'If you could call through to him, that would great.' He stared at Norma with the 'don't screw with me' look he'd perfected over the years.

Norma, flustered, picked up her phone and pressed the digits to ring through to her boss's office.

Green raised her eyebrows at Mackenzie.

'Scott, I'm sorry, but there's a ...' She faltered, forgetting their names.

'Agent Green,' Green prompted.

'Agent Green from the FBI here to speak to you.' Norma's throat constricted as she swallowed. 'The FBI,' she repeated. There was a pause. 'Of course.' She replaced the handset. 'He asked if you wouldn't mind taking a seat. He'll be just a minute.'

Green motioned towards the leather couches. Mackenzie followed her and, tugging on the knees of his pants, he sat.

'Ease up a little, will you? She looked like you were about to take her to the chair,' Green said to him.

Mackenzie cocked his head and smirked. 'Didn't want to waste our time with any of the "do you have a warrant" bullshit.'

Green leaned forward and picked up a pamphlet from the table in the middle. She glanced up towards a woman leaving the surgeon's office. She looked like she'd lost an MMA fight; her face bruised, her lip swollen.

'Let's hope that's the before look,' Green said through gritted teeth.

Mackenzie raised his eyebrows in acknowledgment. There was something about her that looked familiar.

60

Scott Anderson finally walked down the corridor. Mackenzie shook his hand. Anderson's palms were sweaty.

'Only a couple of questions, won't take long,' Green said.

'Please come through,' Anderson offered.

Anderson showed them into his office. Green scanned the room. A large wooden desk, sparse other than a computer and a green art deco lamp. On the other side of the room, what looked like a regular doctor's office.

'Nice view,' Green said, walking towards the expensive glass panes.

'Shit, we don't even get a window looking out onto a parking lot,' Mackenzie said to no one in particular.

Anderson wiped his palms on his pants. A bead of sweat curled along his temple.

'Relax, we simply want to ask you a couple of questions regarding a Svaag Dimash. I believe he's a client of yours?' Mackenzie started.

Anderson's moist brow furrowed.

'Look, we could go to a judge, get a warrant, search through your files, but I'm guessing that would disrupt your clinic. Or you could answer a few simple questions.'

Anderson's Adam's apple bobbed up and down.

'Sure. What do you want to know?'

'What kind of work is he having?'

'May I ask why you're interested in him?'

'I'm afraid I can't tell you that information.' Mackenzie offered him a 'whaddya gonna do about it' shrug.

Anderson invited them to sit. He opened his desk drawer, riffled through some files and pulled out a Manila folder. He flipped it open and slid it across the desk.

Mackenzie and Green both leaned forward.

'Son of a gun. You're some kind of Van Gogh,' Mackenzie said. He peered closer at the before and after photos.

Anderson said nothing.

'They look like two totally different people,' Green said. She shook her head in disbelief.

'Is he in some kind of trouble?' Anderson asked.

'You could say that,' Mackenzie mumbled. 'Say, can we take these?' He lifted the folder.

Anderson nodded. 'I'll ask Norma to get you a copy. Was there anything else?' Anderson stood, ready to lead them out.

'No, that'll do,' Mackenzie said. He got up from his seat. Green followed. They walked towards the lobby.

Green and Mackenzie descended in the elevator, the newly copied file in their paws.

'Think he seemed a little edgy?' Green said.

'Don't they all?'

Green shrugged. 'Guess so.'

'Well, I guess our lead was right.' Mackenzie tapped the file. 'Want to make the call?'

'Damn straight.' Mackenzie pressed against the door opening onto the street. They strolled to their car. Leaning against the hood, Mackenzie flipped out his cellphone. He dialed the number and waited for an answer.

It didn't take long.

'Hey, Trey, it's James Mackenzie. I wanted to confirm I was back in town.'

Mackenzie paused, listening.

'OK, well, I'll come to the center for ...' Mackenzie stopped. He took out a pen and small notebook from the inside of his jacket pocket.

'Sure, I'll see you there then.' He finished writing down an address and ended the call.

'He wants to meet at his apartment.'

61

As soon as I hit the street, an overwhelming feeling of nausea swept over me. I think the fresh air, combined with the past twenty-four hours and now the realization I had actually found the connection to May, hit me all at once. I needed to sit and gather my thoughts. On one hand, none of this made any sense, on another, it made perfect sense.

I found a nearby coffee shop and ordered myself an iced tea. I figured any more coffee was going to send me over the edge and I wasn't sure I wasn't going to dribble it down me. My lip still numb. My head foggy. I needed to clear it and go through the facts.

The surgeon had lived in New York. The articles I had read said as much. May was left in New York. But there was the question of May's mom. Where was she? And why was May's last name 'Brown'? Was Anderson her stepdad? Was he 'Uncle Orange'? Had he killed her mom and dumped May? I parked at a table by the window and took out my cellphone. I needed to book another appointment. I should have done it the second I left his office, but I was so shaken, I just needed to get out.

Realizing my consultation had been cut short, Norma squeezed me in for the following day. That gave me less than twenty-four hours to work out what the hell was going on.

I opened up the internet app and typed in 'Bay View Stores' and 'child'. All that came up were places to buy kids' stuff. I typed in 'child found', 'girl found', 'girl missing'. News stories filled the page, but nothing that related to May. I typed in 'Scott Anderson' and 'child'. Still nothing. I typed in 'Scott + Anderson + Brown'. It took me to a link for a gala dinner article. I scan-read the words and froze as I scrolled to a photo. Anderson, dressed in a dinner suit, had his arms around the woman I had seen in the photo in his office. She wore a tight-fitting claret cocktail dress. Underneath, a caption, 'Scott and Charlotte Anderson Brown'. *Shit.* So they were married. I had asked May what her *last name* was. She was right. It was Brown. I hadn't banked on her having a double-barreled surname. Anderson must have kept his single name for professional purposes. So if he was her dad, what the hell had he gone and done? And who else was involved?

I stared at the press picture and thought about the photo on his desk. There was something that was bugging me. Sure, it was one of those regular pics against some insipid background, a family huddled together, giving some phony grin, while a fella behind the camera charged a wad of bucks for it. The sort of photo you see hanging up in every regular American home. A trophy to say 'Hey, look at us, aren't we great?' But it wasn't that that was bothering me. It was something else.

62

Scott Anderson paced the floor of his clinic. He loosened his tie and undid the top button of his crisp white shirt. He took a sip of water. He glanced at his trembling hands. He needed to get a grip. His next client was due in fifteen minutes. But the more he tried to pull himself together, the more he unraveled.

Anderson slumped in his chair. He took a deep breath and opened up his desk drawer. He removed the photo he had hidden from the FBI. His jaw clenched. His eyes watered. He shut them tight and rubbed his face. He opened them up and glugged the rest of the water.

He couldn't sit here any more, hoping it would all go away. Waiting for the knock on the door. No, he had to act fast. How had he ever thought he could get away with it for so long? But, as time passed and life unfolded, he had lulled himself into a false sense of security. How could he have been so stupid? He couldn't go to prison. He looked at his hands once again. His nails perfectly buffed and manicured. His skin soft. These were hands that had done so much good. Isn't that what he thought he was, deep down? Good? Anderson shook his head. His mouth dry. He pulled his phone towards him. He had no choice.

He placed the receiver to his ear and dialed the number. Anderson's breath became shallow.

Panicked, he slammed down the receiver. No, he couldn't. What would he say?

He grabbed the phone again, dialed the number, and with his eyes shut tight, he listened to the ringtone. His stomach lurched the second Eric picked up.

Eric Diaz and Scott Anderson had set up ClearView Medical Clinic four years ago. Scott had met Eric a number of times before that at various conferences. Both were leading surgeons in their field. When the opportunity came up for them to practice as a partnership, they jumped at it. Their reputation was outstanding. It was a perfect match. They worked well together and had become good buddies. They played squash two nights a week. Eric had joined Scott and his wife for a regular Thursday dinner. He told stories of his extended family in Mexico that terrified Scott. Lowly farmers that had joined La Eme. He entertained them with tales of shoot-outs, drug cartels, bloodshed and massacres. Scott didn't believe the stories were real. But, either way, they were entertaining.

'Hey, man,' Eric answered.

The lump in Scott's throat burned.

'Hey,' Eric repeated.

Scott shook his head to pull himself together. 'I've been trying to call you. How is it going?'

Eric's uncle had passed away.

There was a pause. 'You know how it is. I've just landed. I was going to go home, but if you need me at the clinic?'

'Yeah?' Scott said quietly. *Come on, dammit. Just say it.*

'Everything OK?' Eric asked.

Scott cleared his throat, the lump barely shifting. 'Listen, I know it's a bad time, but I really need to talk to you.'

Another pause. 'Oh yeah?'

'Yeah, yeah, it's something…' Scott paused, '…personal.' He glanced at his watch. His client was due any minute.

'Look, I have to go through security—' Eric started.

'It's really important,' Scott interrupted.

Scott's stomach clenched. Eric was his only way out. For all his tales of Mexican bandits, now he needed them to be true. He had to have his help to get him out of here.

'I'm listening,' Eric said.

'No, I need to talk to you in person.' Scott stared out of the window. Yachts bobbed and twinkled on the water. 'It's sensitive,' he whispered. The fear of being overheard. A sense of his phone being tapped gripped him with anxiety.

'I'll come to the office as soon as I'm through. Let's talk then,' Eric said.

'No. Come to the house. I need to speak in private.' Scott lowered his voice as if, miraculously, Norma could hear him through the office door.

'I need to go,' Eric said.

Tears pierced Scott's eyes. 'OK, man.'

He heard the call disconnect. Scott held the receiver to his ear a moment longer, afraid to be in the room on his own. Slowly he placed it back in its cradle. Taking a deep breath, he wiped his eyes and rubbed his face.

Scott rushed into his bathroom, closed and locked the door. Moments later, he threw up. Vomit splattered across the basin, the mirror and the ceramic floor. Trying to catch his breath, he placed the lid down on the toilet and squatted, his head between his knees, a bitter taste on his lips.

Scott caught his reflection in the mirror. His skin pallid, dark rings framed his eyes.

He couldn't go on like this. *The FBI?* What the hell did they really want? Was it some sort of ruse, asking after a client? He wiped sweat from around his eyes, ran the cold faucet and swilled the basin of vomit. He tore off his white coat, threw it in the corner and grabbed his car keys.

Tearing along the corridor, Scott turned to Norma. 'I'm not feeling so good. Cancel my appointments.'

Before Norma could respond, Scott stepped into the elevator, made his way to the underground parking lot and jumped into his Corvette.

63

Even though there was still another hour or so before the clinic closed, I spotted the electric grilles below the building opening.

A red Corvette revved its engine. *Crap, it was him.*

I grabbed my purse and sprinted out of the coffee shop. I fumbled in my pocket for my keys. My rental was only across the road, but already his car had turned onto the boulevard.

My eyes half on him, and half on getting the car started, I failed to notice a motorcycle hurtling down the street. The horn blared. I slammed on my brakes, waited a moment, checked my mirror and pulled out. I screeched down the road, got to the junction and scanned left and right. I vaguely made out a red car in the distance. Figuring it must be him, I accelerated at speed, my wheels spinning on the asphalt. Pedestrians shot me a look. I shot them my finger. I raced along the road and turned right. There he was. Two vehicles in front at the lights.

I kept back as far back as possible without losing him. He might not be looking for a tail, but he sure as hell would spot a chick with a cut lip who had been in his office not an hour before, driving right behind him.

I followed for about twenty minutes.

We turned into a suburban area.

Again, the real estate here was mind-blowing. Mansions with

land at the front that had more square footage than my whole apartment block, never mind what was at the back.

His car slowed the further he ventured into the quiet streets. I crawled behind, letting him get ahead. I pressed the brake and waited.

After a short while, I set off. I scanned the driveways for his car.

On the left-hand side, a bright red Corvette parked up on a terracotta brick drive. I pulled across and surveyed the property. A large white Italian-style villa. On the front porch, a yellow tricycle with silver tassels dangling from the handlebars. The Corvette, the only vehicle on the drive. A large double garage sat to the side.

I reached over to the back seat and grabbed my camera. I fixed on the zoom lens, lifted it up and rested it on the half-wound-down window. Squinting into the viewfinder, I peeked into the house. On the second floor was movement. The shades were up, but at this angle it was difficult to see. A shadow moved from left to right and back again.

About thirty minutes later, a green Nissan approached the driveway. I slipped my camera back in from the window and slid down my seat.

A dark-haired man – white pants, pink shirt – exited the driver's side, walked up to the door and rang the bell.

I flicked my camera back up and took a few snaps. Closer up, he looked Mexican. The door opened. Anderson ushered him in and shut it. I grabbed a few shots of the stranger's car and license plate.

Scanning the windows, the men appeared to be on the first floor. From what I could make out, they were in the kitchen. The darker man was talking to Anderson, sat at an island, his head in his hands. The stranger placed his hand on Anderson's shoulder as if to comfort him. Finally, they stood.

Moments later, the front door opened. They shook hands. The stranger made his way to the Nissan and pulled out onto the street and sped off in the opposite direction.

Where was Anderson's wife? And who the hell was this other guy?

Through my viewfinder, I followed Anderson in the windows. He was now back up on the second floor.

'Excuse me, ma'am.'

A man, sixties, bald other than tufts of pearl-gray hair either side of his ears, peered in through my passenger curbside window. *Dammit, a neighbor.*

My mouth opened and shut like a goldfish. My tongue too dry to speak.

'Ma'am, what are you doing?' He stared at me and at my camera. He scanned the car's interior. His eyes narrowed. He leaned back up and looked over in the direction of Anderson's home. It wasn't hard to figure what he was thinking. I looked like a horror-movie extra checking out the joint.

Panicked, I threw the camera onto my lap. Firing up the engine, I rammed the gear into drive, slammed my foot to the gas and left nothing but the smell of rubber in his face. Daring to look in my rearview mirror, I watched as the man strolled across the road and made his way over to Anderson's house.

64

Scott politely thanked his neighbor Gerry for letting him know about the woman in the car. He assured him he'd call the cops and inform them of the suspicious activity. He closed the door with one final polite smile.

Listening to Gerry's footsteps descend the drive, Scott pressed his forehead against the oak door and shut his eyes. He knew exactly who had been watching the house. It was hardly difficult to work that out from the description he gave. But what he couldn't figure was who she was and why she was intent on following him? Was she with the FBI? If she was, why had she gone to the clinic before the others had arrived?

Scott took a sharp intake of breath. His pulse quickened. His face flushed. He couldn't think straight.

It may have been years since Scott last poured himself a drink, but right now he didn't care. He opened up the liquor cabinet. He grabbed a bottle of unopened gin and, without bothering to get a glass, he unscrewed the cap with a satisfying click and gulped it back. His friends probably assumed he was a reformed alcoholic whenever he declined the offer of alcohol. But only he knew the real reason behind his now sober state.

Scott slid down the wall, bottle in hand, and sobbed. Not a

small sob, but a guttural cry that echoed around the walls. He'd managed to keep himself together for so many years. Every ounce of guilt, pain and fear finally surged out of his pores.

Scott lifted the bottle and took another large slug. As the alcohol hit his bloodstream, his body relaxed a little. Silent tears poured down his cheeks. He swiped the back of his forearm across his face. Mucus trailed and soaked into his shirt. How had he become so pitiful and pathetic? Scott shook his head. He took a deep breath and thought through the conversation he'd had with Eric.

He had taken the news well. Better than Scott could have imagined. If he was ever grateful to have a friend in him, now was the time. And it felt good to finally tell someone. To be honest for once. Eric told him to stay calm. He had assured him he'd help. He'd make inquiries back at home. Perhaps set up a clinic there. He needed to lay low for a few days. He suggested he sign the business over to him. That way, the authorities wouldn't figure out where Scott was. Eric would get the papers drawn up. The sooner they transferred the business, the quicker he could flee.

But even with the business sorted, his move to Mexico, it still didn't answer where May was.

After everything, could he really leave without her?

65

By the time I pulled into the motel lot, I was so beat, I stayed in the car for a while, dazed and staring out onto the asphalt. There were so many questions buzzing around in my head, I couldn't grasp one of them. It was like swatting flies. The second I put my hand up to grab it, it moved.

I eased myself out of the car. Not only did my ribs ache, but now the anaesthetic had worn off, my upper lip throbbed. I clasped my purse and hobbled up the stairwell to my room, opened it up and collapsed onto the bed.

Bloodstains covered one wall. The stench of cold coffee embedded itself into the already musty carpet. If anything could sum up how I was feeling, I would pretty much say this room was it.

I lay on the bed and snatched the camera from my purse. I flicked through the shots. I scoured the images, trying to see something I hadn't noticed before. I scrutinized every detail – the house, the visitor comforting Anderson, the cars, the license plates. Nothing seemed to stick out except the fact there was no wife.

Why had I been stupid enough to get caught by the neighbor? Now the old man was likely on the phone to the cops and, worse, he probably had taken down my license plate. It's not as if they wouldn't be able to track me down, what with me having a rental car.

I collapsed into the pillow and tried to slow my breathing.

Exhausted, I closed my eyes, hoping somehow all the answers would come to me. Instead, without realizing it, the only thing that came was sleep.

Trey, a bruised jaw, broken nose, scraped knuckles and a black eye that seemed to change color every hour, paced up and down his apartment living area. Every sinew was pumping with adrenaline. James Mackenzie was due to arrive shortly. He had seen this scenario countless times before. Once they knew they were cornered, they first showed shock. As it dawned on them they had little choice, they vented their anger, and finally realizing there was no way out, they relented and gave over the money.

He had the video file ready to show Mackenzie. Trey knew he had the winning hand, but still, he was nervous. Mackenzie was a good twenty pounds heavier than him. Trey was already reeling from his earlier beating. The sooner this was done, the better.

Only one final hurdle and he was ready to bolt. His new identity had been set up. Greg Barnes, his rather creative accountant buddy, had called to assure him that not only were 'Peter Johnson's' accounts set up in the Cayman Islands, but there was no way they could be traced back to a Trey Garrison. There was nothing more holding him back.

Trey checked the time. A thought occurred to him that made his pulse tremble. What if Mackenzie had told Svaag he had been summoned by Trey? Trey had already told Svaag that Mackenzie wasn't going to be in touch for a couple of weeks. Svaag would know he was being duped. Needing to get ahead of the game, Trey dialed Svaag's cellphone. If Svaag knew what Trey was up to, he wouldn't be able to help himself but tell Trey what he thought of him. If there was anything that tripped Svaag up, it was his ego. That had always been his downfall. After all, isn't that why he'd had a nose job, or chemical peel or whatever the hell it was he had undergone recently.

Svaag's number didn't ring out. It simply went to a disconnect tone.

An automated message followed. '*This number is no longer in service.*'

Trey stared at his cellphone, tried the number again and got the same result. Why wasn't it going through? An uneasy feeling shifted in Trey's stomach.

He glanced at his watch. Mackenzie was due any minute.

Anxious, Trey patted his pockets. *Empty*. Confused, he wandered into the study. Where was his wallet? Trey pulled open the desk drawers. There was nothing in there other than the files.

Goddamn! The fight. He had left his jacket. The bitch must have it in her motel. All his new identity was in there. Driver's license, bank cards, everything he needed to access his accounts and get the hell out of this godforsaken place.

Trey's eyes darted around the room. He needed to think fast. There was no way he could risk going back to the motel to get into another fight. And he still hadn't figured out who the hell Jenny really was.

No, he needed to be smart. He couldn't afford to mess things up when he was so close.

He picked up his cellphone and this time dialed a different number.

I don't know what time it was when I heard the phone chirping. It took me a minute to register where I was. I didn't realize I had fallen asleep. I scrabbled around on the bed in the direction of the ringtone and located my cellphone.

'Hello?'

'Miss Stein?' A woman's voice.

'Yeah?'

'This is Norma from ClearView Medical Clinic. I'm so sorry to call so late. You have an appointment booked with Mr Anderson tomorrow. I'm afraid I'm going to have to cancel your appointment.'

OK, that woke me up.

'What? Sorry?'

'Mr Anderson is sick. He's asked me to cancel his schedule. I'm going to have to call you when I've had a chance to look at the appoint—'

I ended the call before she had a chance to finish the sentence.

I jumped up off the bed, forgetting the pain in my ribs, and rushed to the bathroom. I ran the cold faucet and splashed water on my face. I needed to wake up and fast. I caught myself in the mirror. It was not by any stretch of the imagination a pretty sight. The bruising had spread across the left-hand side of my jaw. My lip appeared a little less puffy than before, but however you looked at it, I was not going to be modeling any time soon. I lifted my T-shirt and, along the right side, a large bruise had spread across my torso and back. That guy was a real piece of work.

I threw some more water onto my cheeks. Figuring I was as alert as I was going to be, I scanned the room, grabbed my purse, camera and keys and opened the door.

A huge Latino guy in a crumpled suit stood in the walkway.

'Excuse me, ma'am. Agent Martinez, FBI. Could I have a quick word?'

66

Dammit. So, the neighbor had called the police. But FBI? Shit, if the Feds wanted to talk to me, it must mean they knew about May. Or, more to the point, they knew I knew about May.

Now was not the time. If I didn't leave this second, who knew where Anderson could be. Whether the FBI was involved now or not, I didn't care.

I stepped forward to try and get out of the door.

'I need to ask you a few questions, ma'am.' His accent had a Spanish lilt. His body rigid in the doorway, blocking me.

His suit, a claret number, hung cheaply on his broad shoulders. His shirt had clearly not seen an iron.

I stood with my hand on my hip. 'You'll have to ask me later, I need to …'

'Lady, there ain't no time for later. This'll take a minute.'

I hadn't got a minute, for Chrissake. A clock ticked in my ear.

'Trey Garrison. You know him?'

I was expecting him to ask about May or Anderson, not that piece of crap.

'Listen, let's not waste any time, I know you know him.' The giant rolled his tongue around his teeth. I could smell his putrid breath. He placed his fleshy hand high on the doorway. The cuff of his shirt and suit pulled up a little. His eyes scanned my body, his sight falling on to my breasts. But my sight fell somewhere else. His wrist.

He was no Fed.

I knew exactly who this douchebag was. My nostrils flared in anger. What was he after? To finish the job?

'We're not interested in you, lady. My colleagues tell me he was here. I need to check if he left anything behind. Anything belonging to him that could help us track him down.'

For a thug, he was smooth.

Just not smooth enough. I knew what he was after and I also knew how I was going to exact my revenge.

I smiled, although I'm not sure my face moved.

'Oh sure, Agent…'

'Martinez,' he said.

'You mean his wallet?'

Douchebag's eyes lit up.

'It's in my car. Want me to go get it?'

Douchebag eyed me suspiciously.

'I'll come with you.'

I pulled the motel room door to and walked down the steps towards the rental.

The evening sun bounced an ocher glow on the car windows. I flicked the lock open. Douchebag hovered close by.

'Would you mind?' I made a point of wincing and finding it hard to move. 'I got into a fight.' I shrugged a little to explain. I opened the door. 'It's in the glove compartment.'

The guy leaned in towards it, the JM 16 tattoo showing clearly on his wrist. I slammed the car door onto his side, smashing his exposed arm against the metal. The sound of bone crunching barely making it through his scream. I shoved him to the ground, his hefty body collapsing into the fetal position. Grabbing his arm, he rolled over and gasped for breath.

'And this is for TJ, you piece of shit.' I kicked him so hard in the balls, my own knee buckled in agony. But, God, it was worth it.

Jumping into the driver's seat, I started the car and tore out of the parking lot. A wave of exhaust fumes spitting into his face.

If that douchebag made me lose Anderson, he'd better make damned sure he wasn't still lying there when I returned.

67

Green and Mackenzie sat hunched up in the van. The windows were tinted, so it was impossible for passers-by to peer in. From the outside, it looked like your regular electric-repair company vehicle. White, with the logo GENELECTRICS emblazoned across the side.

Instead, on the inside, not only were Green and Mackenzie squashed in together with the A/C on full, but they were accompanied by four other Federal agents.

A similar setup was stationed at Svaag Dimash's house. Although his arrest warrant was in the name of Wyatt Browning. His actual name. The one given to him at birth, before he'd changed it to Robert Janin and then, of course, Svaag Dimash. Although he hadn't been spotted at the property, they were going to rip the place apart searching for any evidence.

Vans were also parked up across the states outside the five other Liberty of the Mind Legacy Centers. Which, on Mackenzie's nod, were to be invaded by the team of Federal agents.

Mackenzie and Green had been waiting for this moment for almost four months. They could almost feel and smell their homes waiting for them. Green had been away from her husband more than she had been with him since they got married.

She had gone from one case to the next and she swore every time she would take a break. But that hadn't happened as yet. Luckily for her, Sam also worked at the Bureau. His was a desk job at least, so it meant one of them could stay home and look after Buzz, their seven-month-old mutt. But when it came to her getting pregnant, she knew she would have to take a break, or at least a desk job, until she had the baby. Although it seemed laughable now, her being pregnant. What with her barely having time to see her husband, never mind have sex with him.

Mackenzie remained still while a tech guy fiddled with a wire. He looped it through the back of Mackenzie's jacket, tucked it under the collar and attached it close to a button. A monitor buzzed nearby.

The technician flicked a couple of switches and the image of him leaning over Mackenzie appeared on the screen.

Green lifted up a pair of headphones and placed them to her ears. 'OK, give it a go.'

'I can't wait to go home to fuck my wife,' Mackenzie said as a sound test.

Green winced. 'Yeah, I think the sound's fine.'

After four months, countless testimonies and the crowning glory of one of the key members of the organization coming forward and giving evidence in exchange for immunity, the time had come to bring the vultures home to roost.

Mackenzie exited the van and buzzed up to apartment sixteen. Trey was quick to let him in. Walking up the stairwell, Mackenzie cleared his throat, braced himself and knocked on the door.

★

'Well, come on in,' Trey said, pulling back the door. 'Drink?' Trey walked over to the shelving unit and poured himself a Scotch.

Mackenzie stood close by. 'I'm good, thanks.'

Trey shrugged. 'Take a seat.'

Mackenzie obliged. 'What happened to your face?'

'It's nothing.' Trey shook it off with a smile. 'I've got to be honest with you, James.' He settled opposite Mackenzie and took a swig of his drink. 'I was mighty disappointed to hear you couldn't invest.'

'Well, like I said on the phone, Trey, the numbers didn't work for me.'

'Yeah. Mighty disappointing.'

Mackenzie noticed a sheen of sweat appearing across Trey's forehead.

'Thing is …' Trey continued. 'We really needed that money.'

Mackenzie gave him a conciliatory shrug.

Trey shook his head solemnly. 'Really needed the money. So, it pains me to do this.' Trey stood.

Mackenzie leaned forward, adjusted his jacket and waited.

'Do what?' Mackenzie said.

Trey walked along the living area and into his office. He returned with his laptop in his hands. He placed it on the small table in front of Mackenzie.

'I think you'll be interested to see this,' Trey said.

Mackenzie cleared his throat and waited.

Trey moved the mouse on the keyboard. A video file appeared on the screen. Trey tapped play.

Mackenzie watched himself appear on screen. He leaned back and took a deep breath.

Trey hovered to his side.

'Are you ashamed of yourself?'

Mackenzie's head sagged. His eyes closed. 'Yes,' he said in almost a whisper.

'What is it you are ashamed of?'

'Everyone sees me as this successful man, a wonderful marriage, three incredible children. But they don't know me at all.'

'Are you able to tell me what the worst thing is you have done?'

Mackenzie's eyes stayed shut. He shook his head. A tear rolled down his cheek.

'Take your time.' The woman held her breath for a moment.

'My wife ...' Mackenzie gripped the sides of the chair, '...she was away with the kids at her mom's.' He raised his head and looked at the woman.

'Go on.'

'I don't even remember his name. I got his number off some internet site. He came over and we ...' His voice trailed off. Mackenzie looked directly at her now. 'I'm a monster, aren't I?'

Trey leaned over to the laptop and pressed pause. He shut the lid and sat opposite Mackenzie.

'I don't understand,' Mackenzie said.

Trey gave him a thin-lipped smile. 'I think you do.'

'Why have you got that video?'

Trey paused and shrugged. 'Insurance.'

Mackenzie frowned and waited a beat. 'You're blackmailing me?'

Trey leaned back in his chair and adjusted his pants. 'James, I wish we could have done this another way, but you left me no choice.'

'And if I refuse?'

Trey let out a little laugh. 'Really? You want the world to know what a deviant little fuck you are? Your wife, your children, your business associates?'

Mackenzie stared at Trey directly now. 'How much?'

'Five million dollars should cover it.'

Mackenzie raised his eyebrows and stood. 'You're blackmailing me for five million bucks?'

'Make the transfer tonight and the video file is yours.' Trey grinned. 'You have my word.'

'How 'bout I do it right now?' Mackenzie placed his right hand into the inside of his suit jacket. Instead of pulling out his checkbook, he flipped out his badge.

It was Mackenzie's turn to smile now. 'FBI. Turn around and place your hands behind your back.'

68

I gripped the steering wheel as I cornered the roads. I was driving so fast, I felt as though the tires were lifting into the air. I had no time to lose. I ignored the beep of horns and finger salutes from the other drivers and, narrowly missing a pedestrian, I headed towards Anderson's house.

Dusk settled in the sky.

I slowed the car the closer I got into the suburban streets. The last thing I needed was to hit someone, or get pulled over by the cops. For all I knew, they were already out there looking for my license plate.

Driving carefully, I scanned the sidewalks and pulled up approximately a hundred yards from Anderson's house. His car was parked on the driveway. The trunk was open, but there was no sign of him.

I watched and waited.

It wasn't long before I spotted movement. Hauling a large black suitcase from the house, Anderson wheeled it down the driveway. The thump, thump, thump of the wheels hitting the terracotta paving. Struggling to lift it, he rested the luggage's lip onto his thigh and wrestled it into the trunk. He slammed it shut and shot back into the house. He came out with another carryall, locked the front door, threw the bag into the car and jumped in the driving seat.

I watched him pull off the driveway. As he turned left, I figured I only had one clear choice.

Once Scott had signed the clinic papers over to Eric, he packed what little he needed for both him and May. Eric had loaned him some cash to tide him over in the meantime. Once he was over the border, Eric assured him he would sort out the share of finances for the clinic. Now was not the time to be worrying about the property he owned.

He threw his passport into his briefcase, opened up the safe and emptied what cash and jewels were in there.

Scott was damned if he wasn't going to find May, somehow. If she was with the authorities, he was sure it would have been all over the press by now. Once he was safe, he would ask Eric's family to help search for her. Surely they had ways and means of tracking people? After all, isn't that why people feared La Eme. Scott almost laughed to himself. How had he gone from a promising cosmetic surgeon to now not only thinking about involving the Mexican Mafia in his troubles, but hoping they would help him? How had his life come to this? And what if Eric's fantastical tales were just that?

Scott heaved his suitcase into the trunk, locked the house and got into his car.

Anxious, he pulled out of his driveway and, within minutes, spotted a car behind him.

Scott signaled left and peered into his rearview mirror. The car followed. He took a right. His heartbeat quickened. The car was still on his tail. Scott squinted closer in his rearview.

It was Harper Stein.

Had it simply been a coincidence she had visited his office

shortly before the FBI visit? Or were the Feds trying to trick him? If she was a Fed, she sure as hell didn't look like one. Which begged the question, who was she?

He glanced into his mirror. She was definitely tailing him.

Ice-cold fear streamed through his veins. His breath became shallow.

He could try and make a run for it, slam down the pedal and show her exactly what a Corvette could do.

Or, there was another option.

I attempted to stay as far back as possible, but the suburban streets made it difficult to find many vehicles to hide behind.

It wasn't long before we were back on the main drag with a little more traffic to use as cover. I checked my fuel gauge. It was three quarters full. He could be planning to drive anywhere across the country. We were heading in the direction of I-95, so there was every chance he was going to jump on that.

Except he didn't.

Instead, he hung a left onto the 704, towards town.

I followed behind, my mind trying to figure out his next move. He took another left, driving in the direction of his clinic.

I cruised along and, turning into the street, I scanned the area. Spotting it was clear, I figured he'd taken the car into the underground parking lot. I parked up and walked the rest of the way on foot.

I waited close by. If the electric gates opened, I could run back to my car and follow him.

I stood across the street from the entrance. The interior lobby was lit. A young woman exited out of the elevator and stepped onto the sidewalk, the entrance door closing behind her. Seizing the chance, I ran across the road. I grabbed the door at the last minute and paused, clutching my side to catch my breath. Not easy when it felt close to someone clasping a fist around your lungs.

I crept up the stairwell to the third floor and eased the office door open a little. I peered through the crack. The lobby was empty.

I opened the door wider, squeezed in and shut it behind me.

I stood and listened.

It was deathly quiet. I heard my own staggered breath.

Tiptoeing towards the corridor which led to his office, I strained my ears to pick up any sound. Any indication to where he was.

I pressed my back up against the wall. Fingers clenched tight, my fingernails piercing into the palm of my hand.

I tensed and stood rigid.

Footsteps thundered towards me.

A dull thud of what seemed like a paperweight smashed into my left temple with a sharp crack.

Like me, it tumbled to the floor. Collapsing to my knees, my vision blurred and swiftly blackened.

TJ had been on the road for almost twelve hours. Shortly after they had set off, he had found a grocery store and bought a picnic for the car. He wanted to get as many miles behind him as he could before they stopped for the night. They'd managed to get to Fernandina Beach before May said she needed the bathroom. He refueled the both of them and the Camaro and carried on up I-95. Around Rocky Mount, he experienced tingling in his legs. He thought little of it. He'd been driving for the whole day. Of course they would be aching. He pulled up in a motel parking lot and, rather than book a room, he sat there for a while. May was fast asleep next to him and it seemed silly to wake her. He only needed a couple of hours' rest and he'd be as right as rain.

He'd spent many years as a cop, stuck in his car on a stakeout or a long shift, his body was used to it.

He slipped out of the Camaro and stretched his legs. The cool evening fresh air on his skin. He walked over to the corner of the lot, and checking no one was looking, he relieved his bladder. Getting back in the car, he lowered the driver's seat, closed his eyes and woke up a few hours later to a noise outside the window. A young couple strolled past. Their voices loud. He watched as they stopped in the parking lot, kissed and finally walked towards their room.

TJ glanced at the time. It was shortly after eleven p.m. May was still curled up, having barely moved. He wiggled his toes around. They seemed fine. The tingling had gone. Opening and closing his fists, TJ decided the rest had done him good. He felt OK to drive a while longer. If he drove through the night, he figured, with a good wind behind them, he could avoid the commuter traffic and be home by six. If May awoke, they could always stop at a diner, get a bathroom break and fuel up with coffee.

Pulling back out on I-95, it didn't take long for TJ to feel the tremors return in his hands. Ignoring it, he gripped the steering wheel and carried on heading north.

Easing my head up, light crept in. A lamp illuminated the lobby. I lifted my head a little more and saw through the window, it was pitch-black outside.

How long had I been out?

My temple pounded from the blow. My ribs on fire. I turned my neck and heard a noise to my left. Anderson stood from one of the leather seats and hovered over me.

In his right hand, a shiny bright sliver of steel waved through the air.

A scalpel.

'Who are you?' The scalpel twitched in his hand. His shirt sodden with sweat.

I scrunched up my eyes and opened them, hoping it would clear the blur.

He pressed his face close to mine. He repeated it, this time with more venom. 'Who are you?'

Before I had the chance to answer, he grabbed my ankles and yanked me across the floor. He dragged me into his office. The burn of my T-shirt against the carpet tore at the skin on my shoulders.

He let go of my legs and slammed the door behind him.

Taking a breath, I watched him as he paced his office floor. 'What have you done with May's mom?' I hissed.

Anderson gasped. He examined my face, searching for clues. His brow knitted. My vision cleared a little. The scalpel flailed around in his hand.

'Where's my daughter?' He leaned into my face.

I smelled gin on his breath. 'She's safe. That's all you need to know,' I said.

'What do you want?' His eyes looked at me, pleading. Like I was the one threatening him.

I shook my head at him in confusion. Not a good idea. Circles swirled in front of my eyes. My body shook. My nerves kicked in.

He frowned and turned to look behind him. He stood, whip-sharp, and scrambled over to the metal cabinet.

I scanned the floor for my purse. I must have dropped it when he hit me.

Anderson grabbed my ankles and hauled me over to the

surgical bed. Seizing bandages from the metal drawer, he wrapped them around my wrists and tied me to the legs of the bed.

Finally securing me, he crouched down and held the tip of the blade, sharp against my throat.

69

Call me naive, but it was only now, with my wrists bound tight, a scalpel digging into my skin, it dawned on me – this could be it. This is how my life ends.

'What are you going to do with me?' I managed to ask. My voice trembled.

Anderson brushed his free hand through his hair. He moved the scalpel away and rested his arms on his knees. 'I just need time to think.' His head sagged forward. 'I'm sorry,' he whispered.

Did I hear right?

I tilted my head a little and looked towards him. My face screwed up in confusion.

'I never wanted this. I'm sorry. I panicked. I didn't mean …' His voice barely audible. Tears sprang from his eyes.

Was he talking about his wife or me? Is that what was in his trunk? Her body? I couldn't think this way. I needed to focus. I needed him to untie me.

I took concerted breaths to try and slow my pulse.

Keep yourself calm.

'It's OK,' I whispered.

More tears fell into his lap.

We sat in silence.

I cleared my throat. My mouth and lips dry. 'Can I get some water?'

Anderson pulled himself out of his daze. He walked into the lobby area and returned with a full glass. He kneeled in front of me and placed it next to my lips. I took small sips and, finally, some gulps until the glass was empty.

He didn't dare look me in the eye.

'Where's your wife?' I finally said.

He shook his head. With his free hand, he wiped his face and stared at me. His eyes red-raw.

Seeing him there, his hands shaking beside him, he appeared pitiful.

'Please untie me. You don't want to do this.' I said it softly, hoping he would finally relent.

He glanced up, a hangdog look on his face. 'Where's May?'

'Untie me and I'll tell you,' I lied.

Anderson stood and walked over to his desk, slid open the drawer and pulled out the photo.

'Where's her mom?' I asked again.

Anderson frowned and looked down at the photo. He smiled a second, as though caught up in a memory. 'She was the most beautiful tiny baby.' The smile dropped. 'My wife found it so difficult. I should have seen the signs. I should have known.'

I raised my eyebrows. *Keep listening, Harper. Keep him talking.* I tugged on my wrists. The bandages were too tight. I stretched my fingers and attempted to find the knot against the metal leg.

'I was always away, some conference or other.' He walked back over to me, the photo frame in his hand.

My fingertips detected a lump of gauze. I wriggled them, trying to discern where the bow began and ended.

'She abandoned her once. She walked out of the house and

left her. A neighbor heard May crying and called me. We found my wife on a park bench. May was in the house alone.'

'She had postpartum depression?'

Anderson peered at me. 'I guess.' He shrugged and gazed back at the photo.

'What happened?' I asked. My fingernails plucked at the knot.

'I thought maybe it was a one-off. She was overtired. It was all too much. She seemed better for a while.' Anderson shook his head. 'Then it happened again, but worse this time. She left her at a supermarket and drove away.'

'Who found her?'

'One of the staff. They found a prescription for her in the stroller and our address. I begged them not to tell the authorities. I explained what my wife was going through.' Anderson peered at me, scrutinizing my face. 'I'm guessing she left her again?'

It was my turn to examine his face now. I knew whoever 'Uncle Orange' was had dumped her at the store. But Anderson was clearly running from something. And there was no sign of his wife. Had her so-called uncle discovered Anderson had murdered his wife and taken May to relative safety? If I questioned him about 'Uncle Orange', perhaps he would suspect May was in New York. It wasn't a risk I was ready to take.

'When was the last time you spoke to your wife?'

Anderson's eyes narrowed. 'I can't remember. I've been away. I had a conference in Dallas.'

'And you've had no contact with her?' Something didn't add up.

'She was away visiting friends.'

'You didn't think it strange you hadn't heard from her?'

Anderson clenched his jaw.

'I was worried she had done it again,' he finally said. He

placed the photo frame on the bed above my head. He slumped on the floor and rested his back against the cabinet.

'So why didn't you call the cops?'

Anderson looked at me, shocked. 'I couldn't. Don't you see? If I'd called the cops, they'd have taken May away from us. I knew as soon as I could talk to her, we could get her some help. I didn't know for sure she had left her. I thought she needed some space.' A tear snaked down his cheek. He wiped it away with his arm, the scalpel clutched in his hand catching the light.

We sat awhile, neither of us saying a word. Anderson's head bowed, mine thumping.

A phone rang in the distance. Both of us jumped.

My cellphone.

I don't know how much time had passed, but the first signs of light slipped through the windows. It must have been nearly dawn.

Anderson's neck whipped around towards the sound. He looked back at me and, checking I couldn't move, he pulled the office door open and rushed into the corridor. He walked back in with my cellphone in his hand, the ringing now stopped. He stared at it and placed it to the side.

His eyes darted about. Thinking, pacing.

Finally he spoke. 'Where is she?'

There was no way I was telling him where May was.

I shook my head.

'I need to know where she is.' His words more forceful now. The scalpel twitched in his hand.

'What have you done to your wife?' I didn't believe a word he had said. No one who thought their wife was having a breakdown would act like this.

'I told you.' His voice became increasingly agitated. Anderson's chest rose and fell. His jawline tightened.

A tone beeped from my phone. *A voicemail.*

He picked my cellphone back up. Pressing a button, he pulled it to his ear.

Even from where I lay, I heard the distinct New York growl of TJ's voice saying they were home. And from the look on Anderson's face, the way his breathing changed, I could tell the next voice was May's.

Anderson strode over to his desk and flicked his fingers across the keyboard. Whatever had come up on the screen made him smile. Without giving me a second look, he cut the landline with the scalpel, grabbed his keys and my cellphone and marched out of the office, slamming the door behind him.

70

Scott floored the pedal the moment the grilles to the parking lot opened. He threw Harper's cellphone onto the passenger seat and grappled for his own. He scrolled through to Eric's number and dialed.

Hearing the tone ring out, Scott slammed his fist against the steering wheel. Where was he? He hadn't heard from him since they had transferred the paperwork. Surely Eric would know that he needed to speak to him.

Scott slid his window open. He needed fresh air on his face. What had he gone and done? How had he gone from fleeing to now abducting and tying up a woman? Shame filled every part of him. This is not who he was.

But evidently it was.

Turning left towards the airport, Scott flinched. He caught his reflection in the rearview mirror. His pale skin dotted with perspiration, red rings framed the glazed look of his eyes, stubble peppered his face. He barely recognized himself. Looking away, he took in the view. The turquoise ocean, white sands dotted with palms, hibiscus bushes lining the streets. The sweet smell of success becoming further out of his reach.

The red Corvette pulled into the long-term parking lot. Scott wiped his face, grabbed a comb from his inner jacket pocket and ran it through his hair. He needed to look like a regular guy boarding a plane. Not a soon-to-be fugitive.

Opening the trunk, he grabbed a few items from the suitcase, placed them into a small carryall, picked up his briefcase and left everything else in the car. With a beep of the alarm, Scott walked away from his old life and headed into the airport.

Standing in the line at the ticket office, Scott's mind wandered to Eric again. Why wasn't he calling him back? He recalled the conversation they'd had at the house, when he had told him the truth. Eric didn't seem as taken aback as he would have expected. At the time, he was relieved Eric hadn't bolted and called the cops. But now, his reaction seemed almost forced. Faked, even.

Scott shuffled forward and purchased a one-way ticket to Newark. He would have preferred to catch the plane to JFK, but that would mean another half-hour delay. He needed to get out of Palm Beach and to New York as soon as possible. With the boarding pass in his hand, Scott made his way through to security. There was no way they could possibly know that only a short while ago he'd tied up an innocent woman and threatened her with a scalpel. He needed to act calm. Look professional, appear sober, smile at the airport staff, get on the plane and get out of there.

71

I heard only the deafening sound of my own heartbeat. My stomach muscles clenched so tight, I barely felt the bruising of my ribs.

I had to pull myself together. I needed to think and I needed to somehow move my arms.

I forced the weight of my body to the side. The gauze dug in deeper. My breath desperate. But I was not going to fail. I leaned onto my knees until I was able to sit up.

I shifted my bound wrists to and fro, rocking the metal bed. Finally tipping it onto its edge, the photo frame crashed to the floor, the glass shattering on the ground.

I propelled my torso forward and dragged the bed with me, until I was in fingertip reach of a sliver of glass. Stretching out my fingers, the gauze dug into my skin. Tears crept out of my eyes, blurring my vision. I took a deep breath and, with my fingertips, I pinched a jagged shard in my bound hands. As soon as I grasped it between my forefinger and thumb, it tore at my skin and slipped to the floor. My hands sticky with blood.

Once again, I attempted to lift the shard. I needed to flip it towards my wrist and saw through the gauze.

I grasped the bloodied glass and shifted it back and forth. Even this tiny gesture took every ounce of my energy. I maneuvered the blade and cut deeper into the fabric. With one last tug, I flicked the shard to the lower part of the tie, slashed the threads of it loose and finally freed myself from the bed.

I lifted myself up and staggered across the room to his mahogany desk.

Scanning the computer screen, any color left in my face drained away. There in front of me was my address. The consultation form I had filled in, now neatly typed into boxes.

Stretching my fingers to gain movement, I ran to the metal drawers and grabbed wads of bandages. I wrapped one around my bloodied hands and shoved the rest in my pockets. Spotting the shattered photo of May on the floor, I snatched my purse, shifted down the stairs and out onto the busy sidewalk.

Passers-by stared at me, their faces aghast. Ignoring them, I fumbled with my keys, opened the car door and slammed the vehicle into drive. I screeched out onto the street in the direction of the airport.

I hit some red lights and caught my reflection in the rearview mirror. *Jesus.* No wonder I had gotten some stares. Clotted blood dried against my hair and skin.

Moistening a tissue, I rubbed at my face and adjusted the bandages on my hand. If Anderson made it to the airport and boarded a plane before I managed to find him, I would need to catch a flight too. The way I was currently looking, there was no way I wasn't going to attract attention.

The lights turned to green. I released the brake and shot out of the junction. I figured I'd clean up at the airport. My priority right now was getting there and fast.

I turned into the airport.

Ignoring the signs for parking, I headed straight along the route for taxicab drop-offs. Now was not the time for abiding by the rules.

I screeched the car to the curb. Someone hollered over I was in the wrong place. Ignoring them, I jumped out of the car and left the keys in the ignition.

I scanned the entrance. Anderson had a good ten minutes on me. A flight for Newark's gate had just closed. He was either going through security or had boarded a plane already. The next flight to New York was in twenty minutes, going direct to JFK. I checked the area, and seeing it was clear, I made my way to the bathroom. Running the hot faucet, I rinsed my hands and face clean, re-bandaged my fingers and brushed my hair forward over the cut on my temple.

Satisfied, I sped to the ticket desk.

With only one person in front of me, I kept my eyes peeled for any sign of him. Maybe he had got the Newark flight. It wasn't the nearest, but it would mean he would be en route. With a cab ride, I figured it would take him an hour to get to my address. I knew May and TJ weren't there, but still, it was close enough.

Scott sat by the window, peering out onto a life he once knew. The aircraft was only half full when it took off. With little else to do, his mind churned. One thought leading to the next. One second, he was picturing what he had done to Harper Stein, the next, he tried to grasp onto everything Eric had said to him. Finally, it flitted to New York, to his little girl, to him finally getting her back.

Before Harper had been on his tail, he had thought he was going to drive down to Mexico. Eric said he would meet him on the other side of the border and take him somewhere safe. From there, he would co-ordinate a search for May. Eric had assured him he would be able to buy him a new identity. They would set up a clinic together. Eric would be near his family, so of course he didn't mind resettling. But now Scott had a moment to think, it was all too good to be true. How could he have been such a fool? As ever, he had been blinded by love. First it was love for his wife, then his love for May. And now believing his friendship with Eric was genuine, he had fallen for the lies.

Fear settled across Scott's shoulders. Catching himself, he sat up. He adjusted his safety belt and, with every ounce of energy he could muster, he resolved he wouldn't be beaten. Not after everything he had sacrificed.

He would find May and somehow he would bring her home, wherever that would be.

I stepped forward, reached into my purse and pulled out my wallet.

'How may I help you today?' The woman at the desk's eyes widened as she took in the state of my face and hand.

I slapped my Visa card onto the desk. 'Direct flight to JFK. Departing now.'

The woman, dressed as neat as a pin in a cream satin shirt, bright red lipstick and a bun pulled so tight, her eyes looked close to popping out of her skull, picked up my card and stared at it.

'Seriously?' I placed my ID onto the desk too. 'See. It's me. My card. My money.' I shook my head.

The woman typed on her keyboard. Her matching lacquered red fingernails tapping each key. 'Would you prefer an aisle or a window seat, ma'am?'

And breathe, Harper.

Realizing I wasn't going to answer, she tapped a few more times on the keyboard. 'That's all done for you. That will be

$186.' She once again picked up my Visa card and pressed it into the machine.

Come on, come on. I needed to get through security and onto that plane.

'I'm sorry, ma'am, I'm afraid the card has been rejected.'

My stomach dropped. 'What?'

'The card hasn't been accepted. Do you have another way of payment? Another card, perhaps?'

This cannot be happening. Tears welled up again.

The woman gave me a sympathetic look and peered over my shoulder to the customer standing behind me.

'Please. You don't understand, I have to get this flight.' I passed her the credit card again, as if somehow it would work this time. I couldn't have hit my limit. Not now.

The woman shook her head and shrugged. 'I'm sorry, ma'am, unless you have some other form of pay—'

I didn't wait around to hear the rest. I snatched back my card and ID.

This couldn't be happening. More to the point, I couldn't let this happen. I steadied myself on a nearby seat. I needed to call TJ to warn him. I reached into my purse. But, of course, my cellphone with his number in wasn't there.

Anderson had taken it.

With no way of warning TJ, and no chance of getting on the plane, every ounce of energy drained from my body.

72

I slumped into the seat. My stomach churned like I had eaten a pound of lead.

I scanned the departures board. My flight was boarding.

I had no choice. I had to call the cops.

I stood and walked over to the help desk. I would have to use their phone.

I had done all I could to prevent May going into care. But now after everything, after this one phone call, I knew it was game over.

Hot tears rolled down my cheeks. I reached into my purse for a tissue.

My eye caught something at the bottom.

Trey's wallet.

I had thrown it in there when I had found it in my room.

I tugged it out and riffled through the bills. There was more than enough.

Taking the wad of cash, I threw the wallet and his identity cards in the nearby trash can. Trey's smug face landed exactly where it belonged. I couldn't help but let a wry smile rest on my busted lip.

I rushed back to the ticket desk. The guy who had been waiting behind me stood at the front.

'I have it. I have the money,' I shouted to the woman over the guy's shoulder.

She stared at me in shock.

The customer turned without actually looking at me. 'Excuse me. There's a line, lady.' He shook his head.

'Please, sir. I need to get on the next flight. I am begging you.'

The man swiveled around. The second he saw my face, the anger in him dissipated.

'Sure, look, you go ahead.' He held his hands up in surrender.

I gave him a smile. And I really meant it.

'Thank you.'

'JFK, wasn't it?' the woman said. She tapped quickly on the keyboard.

I nodded. My eyes stung with relief. I passed her the cash.

'Gate 4. You're going to have to be quick. They're boarding right now.' She slipped me my boarding pass and ticket.

I didn't waste a second. I scrambled towards security. I flashed my ticket towards the first staff member. He waved me through to the front of the line.

I sprinted to the gate and finally I made it onto the plane.

73

Reggie awoke to a message on his phone from TJ to say he and May were finally home.

When he had returned the previous afternoon, he'd decided to pop into the precinct, see the guys and take whatever wise-cracks were coming his way for going on leave. Once they'd finished their shift, they all went out for a few beers and blew off some steam. He needed something to distract him from Harper.

Reggie shook his head. He could curse himself for bringing up May and how she'd been with her. Yes, of course, he was only complimenting her. But experience should have told him, it was going to light the touchpaper. The word 'kids' to Harper was a red rag to a bull.

And now they'd gotten into yet another fight.

Reggie sighed at the memory, lifted himself out of bed and took a long hot shower. Wanting to check in with TJ and May, he dressed and headed over to his house.

TJ answered the door, his hands covered in flour.

'Hey,' TJ said. He looked over Reggie's shoulder. 'No Harp?'

Reggie shook his head.

'Don't tell me.'

Reggie shrugged. 'You don't want to know.' He raised his eyebrows. 'You OK? You look tired.'

TJ nodded. 'Long drive and Little Miss Monkey in there slept most the way, so she's wide awake now.' He smiled and shook his head. 'I'm too old for this game.'

'You want me to take over?' Reggie asked.

TJ gave him a half-shrug. 'I'll try get a nap in later.'

Reggie walked in the kitchen, spied May at the kitchen table, her hands covered in gluey dough.

'We're doing some baking,' TJ explained.

'Hey, kid.' He tousled her hair.

'Reggie!' May grinned and wrapped her doughy hands around him. She pulled back, the smile no longer on her face. 'Where's Harper?' May said, peering behind him.

Reggie cleared his throat. 'She's—'

'Playing hide-and-seek?' May asked.

Reggie and TJ exchanged looks.

'Playing hide-and-seek,' Reggie said, nodding.

TJ washed his hands under the faucet. 'We need to let the dough get some sleep. Why don't we go for a walk to the park and give it some peace?' he said to May. He turned to Reggie and leaned in. 'And we can talk without little ears around.'

When the wheels finally touched the runway, I felt it had been the longest three hours of my life. The whole flight, my mind had raced from one thought to the next. My heart thrummed in my chest. My body ached all over. I ignored the pitiful looks I received from the stewards and fellow passengers. Whatever they were thinking, I really didn't care.

As we dawdled through the security line, my panic rose. I was barely able to keep it together. Finally, on the other side, I pushed past the throng of people in front of me and zigzag-ran through to the front of the building.

The glass doors whooshed open.

I scanned left and right and spotted another line for the cabs. There was no way I had time to wait. Seeing the first car in the rank drive off, I waited until the line of people shuffled forward. As a family were about to embark, I shoved them out of the way and pushed my way into the vehicle.

'Please. I need you to step on it.' I fluttered the leftover cash from Trey's wallet at the driver.

He glanced at the money, shrugged, turned and grabbed it.

Checking his rearview, he pulled out and left the queuing family open-mouthed and cursing.

'Tourists,' he muttered to me and shrugged.

I nodded and told him the address. I settled back in my seat and stared out of the window as we whisked through the concrete landscape that had always been my home.

74

Scott felt like a foreigner in his own land. He had been brought up in Takoma Park, near Washington, but once he began his first residency at Mount Sinai, New York soon became his home. His life had been good. He loved the pace and feel of this city. He'd graduated here, he had set up his first practice here, he had met his wife here. But now? Now it was like he no longer belonged. Long gone were the summer evenings when he and his wife would walk through Central Park, stop at Chez Patrice for dinner and stroll back to their Manhattan apartment.

All because of one stupid mistake.

And now look at him. How had it come to this?

Maybe he should stop the cab now. Turn around. Go back to the airport and flee. But how could he leave her?

No, he needed to see this through. *One more step and it'll all be over.*

The cab wound its way through the bumper-to-bumper traffic and across Goethals Bridge to Staten Island.

Scott plucked Harper's cellphone out of his pocket and once again listened to the voicemail.

Hearing May's voice, his eyes welled up. This was why he had to take the final step.

Placing the cellphone back in his pocket, he pulled out his own. His finger hovered over Eric's number.

'Can I get some privacy back here?' Scott called through the perspex window. The driver nodded and closed the vent.

He waited for his cellphone to fire up.

He dialed his voicemail. There were no recent messages.

His hands shaking, Scott called Eric's number in the faint hope he would pick up.

With one hand on the steering wheel and the other on his girlfriend's knee, Eric listened to the familiar chirping of his phone. His fingers felt her body tense a little.

'What if he comes looking for us?' Her voice was soft, almost a whisper.

Eric shrugged. 'He'll never find us. I told you, *mi cielito*, you're safe. We're safe.'

Eric took his hand off her knee. He pressed the button to unwind the window, dipped his fingers into his pants pocket, plucked out the cellphone and threw it onto the bare earth. Winding up the window, he placed his hand back on her knee and gently squeezed it.

'No one will ever let anything happen to you. To either of you.' He lifted his hand and placed it on her belly. His fingers detecting the warmth of her skin under the sheer top.

The woman smiled. Tears filled her eyes. Placing her hand over his, she pressed it tight against her body.

'We are a family now, *mi cielito*.'

Eric smiled at her, leaned over and kissed her cheek. She smelled so good.

Turning his attention back to the road, he pressed his foot on the pedal. He wound the car through the Mexican mountains and headed back home.

★

Scott's stomach clenched as the phone simply rang out. Could it really be possible? Had they planned this all along? How could he be so blind? If it was true, where would he go? He would be trapped. He couldn't flee to Mexico. But if he had May, perhaps he could head to Canada, Europe even. If he had her, and got away fast enough, he would go anywhere.

Except someone was onto him. Whoever Harper Stein was, she knew. She might not know the whole story, but she knew.

Scott's jaw clenched tight. How had he got to a place where he had beaten and tied a woman up? He didn't recognize this man. His life in the US was over. He needed to get May and go.

Scott leaned forward and tapped the perspex window. 'There a quicker route from here?'

'Nah. It's clogged up all the way back from the I-278. Some smash or something. Once we're over the bridge, I'll see if I can find a shortcut.'

Scott leaned back into the seat, a waft of orange air freshener filled his lungs, reminding him of his old home.

Finally, the cab turned into the street.

'Hey, here will do,' Scott said.

The cab pulled up on the corner.

Scott passed him the fare and sidled out of the car. Once the cab had driven away, Scott stood on the sidewalk a moment, scanning left and right.

An elderly woman walked by, barely noticing him. She turned onto Emmons. The street was empty. Scott slipped the piece of paper out of his pocket and checked the address.

He strolled up alongside the apartment blocks as casually as he could muster, clocking the names as he went.

Towards the end of the block, Scott spotted the rusted sign

hanging loosely on chipped brickwork. This was it. An old warehouse that had been converted. His eyes scanned the front of the building. Six floors. Stone steps led up to the main entrance.

At the foot of the steps, a bum wrapped up in soiled blankets stirred at the sound of Scott approaching. A navy blue knit cap pulled down to his eyelids.

The bum turned and stared as Scott stepped up to the front entrance.

'Looking for someone in particular, son?' the bum hollered over.

Scott ignored him. He peered at the intercom button, willing himself to press it.

The bum simply watched and shook his head. He was used to people blanking him.

Scott pressed the buzzer, stepped back onto the lower step and glanced up along the windows. After no reply, he pressed the button harder.

The bum shoved the blankets from his legs. Grabbing the iron railings for support, he yanked himself up onto his feet. 'I'm Walt, the concierge. If you need some assistance, you only need to say.' Walt bowed, almost toppling over. Seizing hold of the iron railings to steady himself, he finished with a toothless grin.

Again, Scott ignored him. He pressed the buzzer again. He wasn't sure what he was going to say if someone answered. He'd make out he was delivering a package, something, anything, to get into the building. Once whoever it was answered the door, he'd force himself in if he had to.

'She ain't in.' Walt shook his head and wagged his finger.

Scott's neck whipped around in his direction. 'What?'

'She ain't there. You're wasting your time, son.'

Walt hovered at the bottom of the steps.

Scott eyed him up. The bum's coat hung off his bones. His pants too short for his legs.

'Know where I can find her?' Scott knew exactly where *she* was, but whoever had May might still be in the building.

'Might do,' Walt said. He eyed Scott suspiciously. 'You ain't no authorities, are you?'

'What?'

'You're all dressed up in your fancy pants. You some kind of lawyer?' Walt's nose wrinkled.

'Look, do you know where she is or not?' Scott shook his head. He really didn't need this. If May wasn't here, he had no idea what to do. He had come in the hope that whoever had left the voicemail that said they were 'home', it meant here. He still had the cellphone. He could call it. Say he found it and wanted to return it. But what if the guy asked how come it was in New York?

Seeing as he had little option, Scott's demeanor softened. 'Look, I'm a friend of hers. She left her cellphone with me and I wanted to return it.' He slipped Harper's cellphone out of his pocket.

Walt eyed him up and down.

'Shit. Look—' Scott pulled out his wallet and thumbed through some notes. He pulled out a fifty-dollar bill and waved it in front of Walt. 'I simply want to return her phone. Do you know where she is or not?'

Walt glanced from the bill to the man's face and back to the bill. He leaned in, snatched it from Scott's manicured fingers and held it up to the light. Satisfied, Walt turned to the man and offered him a nod.

'That I do, sir, that I do.'

Scott glared at him. 'So?'

'You good at directions?'

★

May skipped ahead of Reggie and TJ, jumping over the cracked uneven paving stones on the sidewalk.

'She left a message for me to call her when we got home. Sounded urgent. I phoned as soon as we got back, but she was probably asleep.' TJ looked at Reggie. 'That's why I called you. You think she's still in Palm Beach?'

Reggie nodded. 'Guess so.' He said it almost apologetically. 'Maybe she was calling to tell you about the fight.' Reggie shook his head to himself.

TJ took in a long deep breath. 'So you think she's safe?'

'I don't think Trey will be coming back in a hurry.'

Reggie relayed his conversation with Gary Davidson.

'And what about May?' TJ nodded in her direction.

'I don't know.' Reggie sighed. 'Maybe now the Feds are involved, they'll be able to work something out.'

'Harp's not going to be happy with that,' TJ said. 'You blame her?'

Reggie shook his head.

May ran back up the sidewalk approaching TJ. 'Mickey!' she screeched.

'What about him, kid?'

'I want Mickey.'

'We can bring him next time.'

May's voice trembled a little. 'Mickey.' Her bottom lip jutted out.

'Really?' TJ said.

May nodded.

TJ sighed and looked at Reggie.

'You take her up to the swings and I'll meet you back here.'

Reggie laughed. TJ was such a soft touch.

TJ rolled his eyes at May. 'OK, you win. I'll go get Mickey. Anything else, m'lady?'

May giggled and shook her head.

TJ turned and walked back towards his street. That kid had him wrapped around his little finger.

Scott ran the four blocks to the address, without stopping. He knew there was a possibility the bum had fleeced him. But with little choice, he was willing to give it a chance.

Scott leaned over and rested his hands on his thighs to draw breath.

A vehicle drove past. The bass of a stereo echoed on the wooden house walls.

Counting down the numbers, Scott figured the house with a blue car parked up front was the one he was looking for.

His pulse quickened. His nerves jangled. He needed to find his little girl.

Scott slipped through the gate into the front yard, walked up the porch steps and knocked on the door.

Again, there was no answer. Had the bum deceived him?

Scott glanced into the front side window. He pressed his face against the pane of glass and cupped his hand over his face to cover the light.

His stomach clenched.

There on the couch was her toy. Mickey Mouse. He had given her that toy last summer. They had all gone to Orlando for the weekend. Scott shook the memory away.

His breath quivered. The heat of his gasp misted the window. Scott's hands trembled.

He peered around. The street was empty.

Why would May be here?

Scott shuffled down the steps and into the front yard. He

leaned to the side and clocked a fence leading to the rear of the house.

Checking the coast was clear, Scott shot up the back, tugged at the wooden gate and found it locked. He grabbed a trash can, scraped it along the concrete floor, pulled it up to the gate and clambered on top, peeping into the backyard.

The small space had seen better days. Grass bled through every crack in the concrete. White plastic chairs covered in moss stacked up on one side, a rusted BBQ close by.

Scott lifted himself up. He jumped over the top of the gate and fell into the yard with a thud. Patting himself off, he stood still, listening. His eyes darted everywhere. A dog yelped a couple of houses down.

Wasting no time, Scott eased himself around to the back door. Once again, he cupped his hand around his eyes, staring in through the window. There was no movement. Nothing. Scott, feeling brave or foolish, placed his hand on the back door handle. *Locked*. Of course it was.

He spotted the kitchen window frame jutting out, its lip not quite fitting the frame. He pressed his fingertips across the bottom. It gave a little. Squeezing his fingers into the groove a little more, Scott yanked the window back. It came away with surprising ease. Positioning his butt against the wooden frame, he yanked himself up and swung his legs into the empty house.

A kitchen table flecked in flour and a cloth-covered lump of dough in the middle.

Scott tiptoed across the kitchen. His heart thumped against his chest. He craned his neck into the living room. Seeing May's toy, he couldn't help but grab it. He clutched it close to him. The smell. It was her. His baby girl.

Scott's eyes watered. His hands still trembled. Taking the toy, he eased open the living room door. To the left, the front door, to the right, a corridor leading towards the back, with three doors leading off it. Scott stood at the bottom, checking his bearings.

He stepped along the corridor and opened the first. A bathroom.

A little further up, the next door was ajar. The drapes drawn. The room, dark. An unmade bed. Men's clothes strewn across it. On the bedside table, an alarm clock, a glass of water, a bottle of pills and a car magazine.

Scott's brow furrowed. *Whose house was this?*

He stepped inside the bedroom and randomly opened the closet and the bedside drawers, searching for clues.

He walked back to the hallway.

Scott pushed the final door open and gasped. May's pink dress hung on the back of the closet door. His legs buckled beneath him. Steadying himself, he crouched on the single mattress.

But as he rested for a moment, the hairs on his arms and neck bristled at the sound of a key jangling in a lock.

75

TJ winced as he attempted to ease the key in the lock. His fingers weren't doing as they should.

'Jesus Christ,' he snapped at himself.

He'd felt it again when they were making the dough. The tingling sensation. He'd tried to kid himself it was all the driving he'd done over the past twenty-four hours. He simply needed a proper sleep. He was exhausted. But he knew exactly what it was. They had warned him about this. It wasn't the first time, but it was worse than it had been before.

As he tried to turn the lock, he felt weak, he felt old and he felt the reality of his predicament setting in.

Swapping hands, he finally turned the key and opened the door.

Scott tensed rigid on the bed. He was vulnerable sitting down, but too afraid to make a sound, he had little choice. He leaned a little in the direction of the open doorway. He heard only one set of footsteps. *No May.* He'd recognize those footsteps anywhere. For a forty-pound four-year-old, she could still make the sound of a herd of elephants.

The noise stopped.

Scott held his breath.

★

TJ scanned the living area. There was no sign of the toy. Figuring she must have left it on her bed, he made his way to her bedroom.

Perhaps he was distracted with thoughts of his hand. Or the pain he had felt in his legs, but whatever it was, TJ's usual razor-sharp sensors weren't working quite like they once had.

It was only as he entered the spare room and caught a shadow in his peripheral vision did he finally react.

It was too late.

Anderson jumped onto TJ's back and pushed him to the floor. TJ toppled forward, narrowly missing cracking his skull on the open closet door.

The wooden floor thundered with the weight of two men smashing to the ground.

TJ struggled to breathe. The guy must have been an easy one hundred and sixty pounds. His knees dug hard into TJ's spine. The pressure increased. His breath thinned. His lungs squeezed out what little air was left in them. He blinked, but colors shifted and floated in front of him. As much as he tried, he could no longer focus. Drool seeped out from the side of his mouth.

A gunshot ricocheted around the room.

The ear-piercing bang seemed for a moment to still any movement.

Fearing his last breath, TJ had little choice but to let his body relent and wait for death to come.

76

The weight that had only a millisecond ago crushed every ounce of TJ tumbled to the side.

With a gasp, air finally flowed back into TJ's lungs.

Easing his head to the side, TJ looked up.

A blurred shadow hovered in the open doorway. He blinked hard and tried to readjust his vision. Moving his neck a little more, he spotted a pool of claret easing its way across the wooden floor. He squeezed his eyes tight and opened them again. He shifted onto his elbow and lifted himself up. The simple movement of sitting allowed more oxygen to ease its way in, his vision clearing.

Harper stood motionless at the entrance of the room, TJ's Glock 19 hanging by her side. Her vision locked on the blood snaking into the cracks of the floor. TJ turned. The man who had jumped him clutched at his shoulder. Blood streamed through the wound, soaking his shirt, dripping down his arm.

TJ turned back to Harper. Her skin blanched in shock. Her empty hand bandaged. A large mottled bump on her temple. Dried blood in her hairline.

'Jesus, what happened to you?' TJ balked at the sight.

Harper didn't reply.

TJ tried to ease himself up a little more, but his legs refused. Instead, he propped himself up against the closet.

'Pass me that, will ya?' TJ barked.

She barely acknowledged him, the gun quivering in her hand.

TJ guessed she must have grabbed the gun from the kitchen cupboard. 'Hey, Harp, give it here.' He reached out his hand.

The sound of her name pulled her out of her daze. She frowned a little, glanced towards the gun and to TJ. Noticing his outstretched hand, she followed his order.

TJ took the gun. 'Cover your ears.' He wiped the gun with his T-shirt.

'What?' It was the first word Harper had spoken since entering the house.

'Cover them.'

Harper did as she was told.

TJ fired the gun into the ceiling. Plasterboard splintered down on to him and Anderson.

'What the hell are you doing?' Harper whispered.

'You're not licensed to use it. I am. Just making sure it's got my prints and residue on me.'

Both Harper and TJ stared at Anderson.

'What are you going to do to me?' Anderson's voice barely audible.

'Who is this guy?' TJ asked Harper.

'May's father.'

TJ's face fell. He stared at Anderson, incredulous.

'Please, tell me she's OK,' Anderson said. He clasped his shoulder and tried to prop himself up. Blood oozed onto his fingers.

Harper looked to TJ for the answer.

'It's all right. She's with Reggie.'

Harper let air trickle out of her mouth in relief.

'You want to tell me what's going on?' TJ asked. He shot a look from Harper to Anderson. The Glock trembled in TJ's hand.

Harper stepped into the room a little further. 'Where's her mom? What have you done to her?' Harper stared at Anderson, but her sight flickered back to TJ.

It was understandable her hand would shake in shock, it was the first time she had ever fired a gun. But TJ's? He was an ex-cop. *Why would he be trembling?*

Anderson's brow knitted. Again, he tried to move. Wincing in pain, he gave up. 'I don't know.'

'Where is she?' Harper asked again.

'I told you, I don't know. I haven't done anything to her, you have to believe me.'

'You kidding me? Believe you? You beat and tie me up, you try to kill him ...' Harper thumbed towards TJ, '...and you're telling me to believe you've not killed her?'

Tears fell from Anderson's cheeks, his skin ashen. 'I would never hurt her. I love her.'

Harper snorted.

'That's what this has all been about.' Anderson's head bowed in shame.

'What?' Harper kicked his foot.

'May.' The word fell off Anderson's lips in a whisper.

Harper frowned and glanced at TJ.

TJ shook his head at her and shrugged.

'What about May?' Harper asked.

A faint sound of sirens approaching echoed through the house.

Anderson looked up. 'She's not our daughter.'

77

Scott's wife Charlotte settled back into her car seat. She slipped off her sandals, her feet bare on the floor. She squeezed Eric's hand tight against her belly and gazed out of the car window at the mountains. Deep red dust billowed behind the car. Charlotte's blond hair danced around her face. Beneath her shades, her eyes glassy with both fear and excitement.

She was in her first trimester, but already she noticed changes in her body. Her breasts had swollen, her energy levels waned and, of course, she had suffered the obligatory nausea. But Charlotte had felt this increase in sickness was due to her nerves more than anything. She must have been four weeks gone when she realized she was pregnant. After all the procedures she and Scott had gone through over the years, when her monthly didn't arrive, a pregnancy test was merely a formality. It was easy to hide the secret from Scott. He was barely there. Always at the clinic or away at one seminar or another, and it was hardly like they had sex any more. But she knew there was only so long before things became complicated. Even more complicated than they were already.

Like any other couple embarking on an affair, she had not set out to hurt anyone. The three words often drawn out when trying to explain – 'it just happened' – were oh so true in their case. Yes, Eric could often be equally busy at times, but at least when he was free he appeared connected to her. He would listen to her, soothe her and comfort her. Scott would willingly avoid her. They had been through more heartbreak than most couples, but their secret was something that both bound them and tore them apart.

When she had met Scott, their future was laid out. He was already honing a reputation as an eminent surgeon. They both came from privileged families. They owned a townhouse in Manhattan, where she would happily cook for his colleagues and their friends. They planned the nursery for when their firstborn would arrive. They looked to the future with a breath of hope only the young can have. But when the baby didn't happen, they paid for the best doctors, assuring themselves it was a small obstacle. Pills and potions and patience would in the end win out. It was only when Scott's sperm count came back low, their hopes were dashed. The map they had drawn themselves soon became torn and tattered.

No matter how much she assured him she loved him, she knew he noticed her tear-reddened eyes and the already drunk glasses of wine when he returned from work. It was clear to both of them she was not taking the news so well.

And so, it happened. A night where the line was drawn. A decision made in the blink of an eye. Fate, they would call it. And for a while they believed it to be true.

But there was only so long before the hand of guilt would grip on her insides and clasp them tight. The fingernails digging into her soul.

78

Stunned, I rested myself on the edge of the bed, my brow set in confusion.

Anderson sighed. His body slumped, almost in relief. He glanced towards TJ, the gun still pointing at him. 'Have you seen anyone about that?' He motioned towards TJ's trembling hand.

TJ's eyes flickered to me. 'Never mind me, what d'you mean she's not your daughter?'

Anderson swallowed. He bit the inside of his cheek. The room fell silent.

'I was driving home one night, some conference in Atlanta. I'd had a couple of drinks on the plane.' Anderson paused.

'Go on,' I said.

Anderson nodded again at TJ. 'You know you should see someone. They can at least help the tremors.'

'What's he talking about?' I shot a look towards TJ.

'It's nothing. He's trying to buy time.' TJ scowled at Anderson.

I stared at TJ, unconvinced. *What had I missed?*

'So, you had a couple of drinks?' TJ lowered the gun into his lap.

Anderson nodded. 'We ... my wife and I, we'd been having some difficulties.' Anderson waved his bloodied hand in the air. 'I had a couple to take the edge off before I got home. It'd been a long week.' He covered the seeping wound with his hand. 'Listen, can I get something to wrap around this?'

I glanced at TJ. He nodded.

Confident TJ had the gun, I ran into the bathroom and grabbed a towel. I stepped back into the bedroom and kneeled beside Anderson.

'You move and I swear to God I'll blow your brains out.' TJ picked up the Glock again and wielded it in Anderson's direction.

Anderson winced as I wrapped the towel across and around his shoulder, tucking it under his arm.

Leaning back, I rested on the bed.

TJ waved the gun in the air. 'You were saying.'

Anderson paused and briefly closed his eyes. 'I got in the car. It was late, must have gone two a.m. So, I figured it'd take me a half-hour to get home. I didn't feel drunk.'

There seemed to be a collective sigh in the room in anticipation of what was coming next.

'I didn't see it coming. He was driving like a lunatic, you have to believe me,' Anderson pleaded.

'So, what happened?' I asked, my voice low. Tension gripped my bruised chest.

'Their car must have rolled, two, maybe three times.'

'Who was in it?' TJ growled.

Sirens screamed a little closer now. Someone must have heard the gunshots and called the cops.

'I got out of the car and, man, it was a mess. I couldn't believe anyone could survive that.'

'So, did you call the cops? Ambulance?' I asked, already knowing the answer.

Anderson swallowed. His lips dry. 'The driver, he was ...' He closed his eyes. His jawline tensed. 'There was nothing anyone could do. The lady …' He swallowed again. 'I felt for a pulse and there was nothing. I didn't know what to do. I mean, the guy had come out of nowhere, right, but I knew they'd test me for alcohol. My medical license would be gone. I could even go to prison. My marriage would be over.'

'You just walked away?' TJ asked, incredulous.

'I was going to,' Anderson said.

I leaned forward.

'I'd checked no one was around and I was about to get in my car.' Sweat popped on Anderson's forehead. His complexion almost transparent. A vein like a piece of twine pulsed on the side of his neck. 'And that's when I heard her.'

I closed my eyes.

'I didn't know she was there. I swear. I didn't. I wouldn't have gone to drive away if I had known.'

'You took her?' TJ snapped.

'I panicked. I'd had a drink. I don't know what I thought. They were dead and there she was, the cutest little baby.' A tear streamed down his cheek. 'She was in the back seat in a carrier. She couldn't have been more than a couple of days old. I didn't know what to do.' Anderson's voice, garbled. 'I looked at her parents, they were dirt poor. You only had to look at the car to see that. It was no wonder it crushed like an aluminum can. I thought she'd be taken into care. Because of me. Because of what I'd done.'

'But what if she had other family?' I opened my palms in exasperation.

Anderson looked to the floor. 'I was drunk. I had crashed the car. I wasn't thinking straight. You've got to believe me.'

TJ and I said nothing for a while.

'So how the hell did you explain you had a baby?' TJ finally asked.

Anderson took a deep breath.

'I got home. My wife was asleep. I brought May ... that's what we ended up calling her ... that was the month I'd found her ... into the house. She had somehow fallen back to sleep on the way home. But the minute I got back, she started crying. She must have been hungry or something—'

'Or missing her parents who you had just killed.' It was my turn to snap now.

Anderson's head drooped. 'My wife must have heard her and she came down. I told her everything.'

'What? And she agreed to keep her?' TJ's teeth gnashed together.

Anderson nodded. 'You have to understand, a baby meant the world to her.'

'But it wasn't hers,' I said.

'I thought the baby's parents were dead.'

'Whaddya mean you thought they were dead, you said they were dead,' TJ shouted.

Anderson clenched his jaw. 'My wife and I decided to keep her. We thought we could offer her a good life. We did give her a good life.' He mumbled the last statement to himself. 'We made a plan that night. She would go to Florida with May. I would shut up shop in New York and follow her down. We told our families Charlotte was heavily pregnant and she needed a warmer climate. We were always so busy with our lives, we hadn't seen them for months.'

'So – what – you faked her birth? How did you even get a certificate for her?' TJ asked.

'I'm a doctor. It's not that hard. We told them she'd had a home birth and we registered her with the authorities.'

'That still doesn't answer why you said you thought they

were dead.' TJ's voice deadpan. He jabbed his finger in the air in Anderson's direction. Again, it quivered.

The sirens came closer.

'My wife left the next morning. We couldn't risk her being seen with a baby in New York, not until we had sorted every-thing out. So, she drove to Florida. We rented a small house until we could settle. But ...' Anderson pointed to TJ's hand. 'Listen, I could suggest a few guys for you to go see who—'

'Just finish the story.' TJ's voice trembled now. He didn't look at me.

Anderson nodded. 'The next day, there was an appeal on the news for witnesses to the accident.' Anderson bit his lip. 'They said the driver had been killed, but the lady ...' his chest rose and fell, '...the lady was in a coma.'

'So she wasn't dead?' My jaw dropped open.

Anderson shook his head and closed his eyes.

'May's real mother is alive?'

TJ and I stared at each other and back to Anderson.

'She was in the coma for over three months. I didn't know if she'd pull through. I couldn't tell my wife. By then I'd moved to Florida, we had settled into a routine. For the first time in a long time, my wife actually seemed happy.'

'So, what, you live happily ever after while her mom, her real mom, is lying in some hospital somewhere?' Heat rose in my cheeks.

Shame swept over Anderson's face. 'This wasn't meant to happen.'

'Goddamn straight it wasn't. So where is May's real mom now?' TJ asked.

Anderson took a long deep breath in. 'I followed the story. There was nothing reported in Florida. After all, it was just an auto crash in New York. But I checked on the internet. When she awoke, she asked them about her baby.'

'The police didn't know?' I asked.

Anderson shook his head. 'She didn't seem to have any immediate family. They'd driven up from Indianapolis or something, looking for work, and...'

TJ shook his head. 'You didn't think then you should confess?'

'How could I? It was too late.'

'And your wife didn't know May's mom was still alive?'

'Not at first. Everything seemed great at the beginning. We had a beautiful girl, my wife was happy, but – I don't know, maybe it was the guilt – there was something that didn't work. May wouldn't stop crying. Charlotte would try feeding her, changing her, soothing her, but May kept on crying. I was out working my ass off, trying to establish a new clinic, and I think she found it too much.'

TJ clicked his tongue. He rolled it around on the inside of his mouth.

'I think the guilt, you know, got to her. I'd come home and Charlotte would be in tears. It was like before we had May. I tried to tell her it would be OK, that she was a great mom. But she wouldn't listen. I'd come back and May would be staying at a neighbor's or another playmate's. It was like Charlotte couldn't stand being around her.'

'Guess that explains why she was so easy in our company.' I shook my head.

'I thought it would pass. And then it was all over the news.'

TJ's brow furrowed the same time as mine.

'It was May's third birthday. Her mom put out an appeal. To say she was still searching for her. And I guess Charlotte must have seen it. She didn't know until then she was alive.' Anderson's head drooped at the memory. 'I did everything to reassure her we wouldn't be found out. How could anyone suspect? We'd had her for three years. We were in Florida. We were a respected couple with a kid.'

I blinked, trying to nudge a memory into the forefront of my mind.

The photo. The photo I had seen on Anderson's desk. That's why it had bugged me. It wasn't the sickly smiles of parents clutching their child. It was that May didn't really look like them.

'So what did your wife do?' I asked.

79

Charlotte placed her hand on Eric's thigh. The breeze blew on her skin.

Once she knew she was carrying Eric's baby, there was little choice. It had been everything she had once wished for. After all, isn't that how May had arrived in their life – because of what she wished for?

May didn't belong to Charlotte, and from the moment Scott brought her home, she should have known it wouldn't work. It was all well and good 'playing' at being her mom, but it was as if May knew too. The bond wasn't there.

It had taken every ounce of bravery she could muster when she finally admitted the truth to Eric. She decided to soften the blow by revealing her pregnancy first. He was, of course, elated. He knew this would change everything. He had been waiting for her to leave Scott for some time, never understanding her reason for staying.

But once she divulged the full story to him, the reality and gravity of their situation hit home.

Of course he was angry. He had every right to be. She had led him to believe that because they were in love, there were no secrets. She pleaded with him to understand how hard it had been for her to keep this from him. But now she was carrying his baby, she had little choice but to tell him.

He didn't know who to be angry with the most. Yes, he was having an affair with Scott's wife. But after what he had done, what he had involved her in, could he be surprised she had looked to another man for support?

There was no way Eric could agree to keeping May. It was one thing taking on someone else's child, it was another when it was a crime.

They had spent many nights together discussing what they could do. It was best for May, they told themselves. It was best for May's mom.

And Charlotte knew to unburden herself from this guilt, it was best for her.

They researched her real mom. They followed all the leads they could find to track her down. She wasn't difficult to trace. She had left a trail on purpose, so one day, if her daughter was still alive, she would be able to find her.

Once they knew where May's mom worked, Eric and Charlotte concocted a plan. Scott was due to present a paper at another conference. Eric had lied to him, saying his uncle in Mexico was sick, waiting for the opportune time for them to flee. Once their plan was set in place, there was no going back.

They had investigated the clothes store three weeks earlier. Charlotte had told Scott she was visiting a friend for the weekend. May had been dropped at a playmate's house, as per usual. Both Charlotte and Eric left for New York and visited the area together. They scanned to see where the cameras were and which floor the store was on. Sensing Charlotte's frayed nerves, Eric volunteered to see if May's real mom definitely worked there. Confirming she did, he took Charlotte's hand and led her away.

When Scott left for Dallas, Eric drove May to New York. Once they had arrived, he wasted no time getting to the store.

Eric watched closely. He spotted May's real mom at the cash desk. Eric crouched with May. He stole a moment and watched as she laughed and joked with a colleague, oblivious her life was about to change. How could Scott have stolen a baby from her?

Eric hugged May tight and, patting her on the head, he pointed to the store and told her to wait inside for her mom.

As soon as May entered, Eric stood. With his head bowed, cap pulled down low, he left without once turning back.

80

Other than the cacophonous sirens that screeched as they entered TJ's street, we all sat in the spare room in silence. Anderson slumped up against the bed, clutching onto the slug in his shoulder. TJ leaned against the closet, the Glock in his lap, all of us caught up in our thoughts.

It was impossible to comprehend. But not as unbearable as the thought of what was to become of May. Of course, I knew she would finally be reunited with her real mom. But how do you explain that to a little girl?

What Anderson had done was beyond belief, but dare I say a part of me understood it, understood him. Faced with watching a child taken into care or offering it a home, what would I have done?

All of us jumped as the front door was kicked in.

'Police. Drop your weapons.'

TJ responded first.

'In here. Weapons down. Ambulance needed.'

Footsteps thundered along the hallway.

TJ already had his hands in the air. I raised mine. A young female cop entered the room, sweeping the air with her gun. She scanned our faces, noticed the pool of blood below Anderson and followed it up to the wound.

With her gun still pointed at us, she used her other hand to press onto her radio and call for medical assistance.

'I want you to slowly slide the weapon towards me,' she said to TJ, her gun pointing in his direction.

TJ lifted the gun, placed it on the floor and slid it towards the police officer.

Once again, I stared at TJ, trying to get a read on why he was trembling. His eyes shifted towards me and quickly looked away. The officer blocked the gun with her foot and swept it into the hallway.

The sounds of other cops swarming into the house.

'Down here,' the officer shouted. 'OK, slowly I want you to stand up, keep your hands in the air.' She kept her gun pointed at us.

TJ and I both did as we were told.

'I can't,' Anderson said. He motioned to his arm and looked up to her.

'OK. Don't move.' The officer patted us down. 'Who needs medical assistance?'

'Just him,' I said. I indicated in Anderson's direction.

The officer nodded, lowered her gun and shifted out of the way for the EMT to get through.

'You sure you don't need looking at?' she said to me.

I shook my head. 'I'm fine.'

She kept her eyes locked on mine for a second. 'Want to tell me what's been going on?'

Both TJ and I made a brief statement. We were — to say the least — a little scant regarding the details. But there was no getting past the fact May was in our care, and we had discovered who she really was.

We perched on the front porch steps. Anderson was led in

handcuffs towards the ambulance. As he stepped out of the yard, both our heads shot up.

'Daddy!'

May, wrapped in Reggie's arms, approached the house. Swinging her down, Reggie let go. She charged at Anderson.

'Daddy!'

Anderson swept around, crouched and tried to open his arms to hug her tight. His hands in cuffs, he eased his wrists over her head and pulled her to him. Her tiny arms swept around his neck. My stomach lurched at the sight.

Reggie, open-mouthed, stared at TJ and me in turn. 'What the hell?'

I shook my head, lost for words.

'I was heading back. I didn't know where you'd got to,' Reggie said to TJ.

Leaning on the railing, TJ heaved himself up, blowing air out of his cheeks.

We all stood watching May and Anderson. The female cop approached him. Anderson leaned into May, kissed her forehead, nodded and stood.

May blinked, first at her dad, turned to the three of us and blinked again. Confusion all over her face.

I stood and walked towards her. My vision flicked from May to Anderson. His eyes red and glassy, his skin pale, his heart clearly aching.

I took May's tiny warm hand in mine.

Anderson stepped into the back of the ambulance, accompanied by another uniformed cop. As the door slammed shut, I clutched her hand, feeling like someone was squeezing it around my heart.

I turned to see Reggie stood close behind us. The flutter of blue and red lights silhouetted against his skin.

TJ joined the three of us and, as the ambulance tore down the street, he took May into his arms.

Unable to hold it together any longer, I fell against Reggie's warm chest and sobbed.

81

We were all taken to the precinct house to make a formal statement. Reggie called ahead to his lieutenant to give him the heads-up and by the look on his face, the news hadn't gone down well.

Hopefully, the fact we had 'found' May superseded anything we could have said. Her disappearance over the past four years had left more than a few officers baffled and to have her finally 'home' was going to be for them a much-needed PR coup.

Everything we told them seemed to corroborate Anderson's story. A BOLO had been issued for his wife and business partner, but the likelihood was they had already crossed the border into Mexico, and extradition would take time.

For all the jubilation around me, I have to say I felt nothing but anxiety. May huddled up to me in the back of the patrol car, tucked under my arm. She had barely said two words since she had seen her 'daddy' being led away in the ambulance. To be honest, I didn't have many words myself. I knew a call was going to be placed to her real mom, which I guess should be joyous, but I couldn't help but worry how this was going to affect a little girl.

★

After I finished making my statement, they placed May and I in a small room at the back of the precinct, which by the looks of it was a discarded rec room. It reeked of coffee and stale cigarettes.

A soiled dark brown couch took up the back wall, an ankle-height table covered in magazines from around four years ago in the middle, and a small portable TV which looked like it belonged in the 1970s, a wire coat hanger sticking out of the top, hung in the corner of the room. Reggie had been hauled in by his superiors and TJ had gone to talk to some of his old buddies out front, with the promise of returning with coffee, and a soda for May.

I fiddled with the television, pressing the digits to find a station suitable for May, and settled into the couch. I wrapped my arm around her and pulled her in tight, feeling like I never wanted to let her go.

Maria Sanchez had only just returned home from her shift at La Vida Loca when the phone call came.

As ever, when she entered into the kitchen, she kissed her two fingers and gently touched a small dog-eared photo of a newborn baby in a crocheted lemon hat, pinned with a magnet to the refrigerator.

She piled her groceries up onto the table ready to put away, but needing to take the weight off her feet for a short while, she slumped back into the wooden kitchen chair. She kicked off her high-heeled shoes and lifted her feet up onto a nearby stool.

Rolling down her stockings, she thought about her plans for the evening. She wasn't due back in work until the following afternoon. She would make herself something light to eat, have a long bath and, if her feet worked again, she would head to her friend Isabel's with a chilled bottle of wine.

When her cellphone rang, she was inclined to ignore it. She had spent the day talking nonstop to customers and all she wanted was a short moment of peace before she headed out for the evening. Wondering if it was Isabel calling, she shoved the groceries out of the way, located her purse and pulled out her cellphone.

Only a few moments later, Maria stood in her kitchen clutching the photo from the refrigerator, stockings ruched at her ankles, tears streaming down her flushed cheeks.

82

We had been waiting at the precinct for almost two hours when a woman – late fifties, silvery hair tied back into a ponytail – entered the room. She was dressed in a cheap brindle-colored pantsuit and a cream silk blouse. A small gold St Christopher pendant dangled from her neck.

TJ stood as she entered.

She gave both May and I a big smile and outstretched her hand.

'My name is Linda Kramer. I'm a child psychologist.' She crouched to May's height. 'And you must be May.' She gave her a warm smile.

May pressed her body into mine.

Linda stayed squatted, her hands resting on her knees. A small gold band on her wedding finger.

'I wondered if we could play a few games, May.' She raised her eyebrows and gave May another smile.

May looked up to me. Her dark brown eyes questioning mine.

A lump in my throat pricked and burned. Biting my lip to hold in my tears, I nodded at May, encouraging her to play.

'What do you think?' Linda asked her.

May shuffled forward a little.

'You need us to leave?' My words were almost a whisper.

'If you could give us a short while, that would be great.'

I squeezed May's hand and winked at her. 'We're just going to be out there, OK?'

May glanced at me and up towards Linda.

'They won't be going far. And it'll give us the chance to get to know each other,' Linda said.

TJ left the room first.

Reggie hovered in the hallway. I stood from the couch and, with a slight nod to Linda, I turned and smiled at May. My breath quivered as I did.

Reggie took my hand and led me towards the coffee machine. As we walked along, a woman with long dark hair sat in a side room. Her eyes glassy with tears, a chewed-up tissue clutched in her right hand. I recognized her from the day I had found May. She was the older store clerk who had left. Reggie, sensing my shock, squeezed my hand to encourage me to keep walking.

'I'll catch up with you,' TJ said. He waved over to someone he knew and headed over to him.

'Let's get some fresh air,' Reggie said.

I walked alongside him, my hand grasped in his, and approached the front entrance to the precinct.

I leaned against the brick wall for support. My adrenaline had finally peaked. Exhaustion crept into my tender bones.

'What happened?' I asked him.

'I got my ass handed to me on a plate is what happened.' Reggie shrugged. 'I'm suspended pending an investigation.'

Hot tears tumbled on to my cheeks.

'You OK?' Reggie asked.

I knew he wasn't really looking for an answer. I nodded and tensed my jaw. He leaned in and brushed his lips against

377

my tears. Kissing them away, Reggie pulled me in tight and wrapped his arms around my bruised body, tugging me close to his.

It was dark outside by the time we were called back in. Linda took me aside and explained what would happen next.

May's birth mom squatted on a bench, along the corridor, her purse clutched on her lap. She fiddled with the straps of the purse, her bloodshot eyes darting around at any movement.

I was ushered back in with May, who sat cross-legged on the floor, a puzzle laid out in front of her.

TJ and Reggie hovered outside.

The woman, whose name I found out was Maria, quietly stepped into the room. Transfixed by the puzzle, May barely acknowledged her presence. Linda knelt beside May and whispered in her ear. May turned and, with her mouth slightly crooked, she gazed, wide-eyed, up at Maria. May stared at her a little while and looked towards me. It took every ounce of energy to stop myself visibly shaking. I offered May a smile and nodded at her encouragingly.

Maria crouched down. Her cheeks wet with tears. She gasped as she stared at her little girl. Opening her arms wide, she finally called her name.

'*Mi bebe*, Sophia.'

83

The following morning, I awoke to jackhammering on my skull. Reggie lay naked, fast asleep next to me. Adjusting my eyes, I leaned up, the ache in my muscles ever-present. Squinting, I tried to detect where the thumping was coming from. I slipped from under the sheets and gently kissed Reggie's chest. I threw on his T-shirt and some panties and shuffled along the hallway.

The drumming resonated on the wooden walls.

I opened the kitchen door. TJ stood in the backyard, a black rubber-handled hammer in one hand, the edge of the window frame in the other. The radio played out full blast.

'Hey, pass me that, will ya?' TJ pointed to a spirit level on the countertop.

Shivering, I passed it to him. 'Finally, you're fixing it.'

'Yeah, well, you never know what hoodlums will break in.' He raised his eyebrows pointedly at me.

'You mean my *Dukes of Hazzard* days are over?' I opened up the palms of my hands and winked at him. 'Coffee?'

TJ nodded.

I put the kettle on the stove and grabbed the coffee pot. The calendar on the wall caught my eye. I glanced at the asterisks TJ had marked up. My stomach dropped.

'They're not dates, are they?' I turned and caught TJ's eye.

He placed the spirit level down and hammered the edge of the frame.

'You going to tell me what's really going on?' I nodded towards his hands.

TJ tapped the frame again, pressed the window shut and stood back, admiring his work. Unable to ignore me any longer, he opened up the back door, stomped his feet on the mat and walked in.

I leaned against the counter, waiting. I glanced up at the calendar again. 'They're hospital appointments,' I said. The penny finally dropping.

TJ sat at the kitchen table. 'It's nothing.'

I slumped into the seat opposite him.

Grabbing his hands in mine, I stared directly at him. TJ wouldn't catch my eye. His fingers cold to the touch from being outside.

'It's not nothing. TJ, tell me what's going on.' I clenched my jaw and braced myself.

His eyeline flickered up to mine. He bit his lip and took a breath. 'It's ALS.'

I furrowed my brow. 'What the hell is ALS?' The muscles in my stomach tightened.

'It's neurological.' He waved one of his hands in the air dismissively.

I squeezed his other hand tighter, warming it in mine. 'They can do something, can't they?'

TJ's jaw tensed.

I jumped up off my seat, shaking my head.

I poured the grains into the French press and slopped the boiling water into the pitcher. My own hands trembled now. *Not TJ. It couldn't happen to him. He was my rock.*

'Surely there's something they...'

'Harp ... sit down, will you?'

I stirred the pitcher of coffee, the spoon clanked against the glass. I kept my back to him, trying to compose myself.

The kitchen door opened.

'Hey,' Reggie said.

I turned. I pressed my lips together, forced a smile and looked at TJ.

'What's going on?' Reggie asked. His eyes narrowed.

Pouring us all a cup, I finally sat back at the table.

'I got ALS,' TJ repeated.

Reggie leaned back in his chair and looked from TJ to me. 'Shoot.'

'Well, stop staring at me as if I've just kicked the bucket, will you?' TJ barked at me. 'I can still outrun you, kid.'

I couldn't help but laugh.

I arched around towards the newly mended window. 'You see he's locked me out the back?'

'About time too,' Reggie said. A grin on both their faces.

I shook my head and took a sip of my coffee. 'So now what?'

TJ paused before replying. 'How 'bout we take it one day at a time?'

84

Even after a couple of weeks, May's story dominated the headlines. For once it was weird to be on the other side, with others looking in.

Anderson and his wife's photo emblazoned the front page, next to the photo of May as a baby in a crocheted hat. It had obviously been agreed that, for now, her current identity would be concealed.

Due to the nature of the case and the press attention it was receiving, DNA results were rushed in to confirm the identity of both May and her birth mother. But the police knew from everything Anderson had told them, it was her.

Overjoyed at finding her daughter, Maria Sanchez released a press statement thanking everyone, but asked for privacy at this sensitive time.

Since the story broke, my cellphone hadn't stopped ringing. Voicemail after voicemail, begging me to tell my side of the story, with the promise of big bucks in return. I ignored them all. I switched my cellphone off and hunkered down at Reggie's place, waiting for the attention to subside.

We called for TJ mid-morning. As we waited for him to get ready, my eyes scanned the newspaper on the kitchen table.

Next to May's story, an article reported the continued search for Wyatt Browning. A photo of his *before* and *after* surgery positioned next to it.

TJ entered the kitchen dressed smartly in a navy blue sports jacket and suit pants.

'Look at you!' I said, grinning his way.

'Well, we've an important date. Got to make the effort.'

I glanced down at my usual leather jacket, jeans and boots. 'What are you trying to say?'

Reggie and TJ raised their eyebrows at me, smiled and shook their heads.

'Ready?' Reggie asked.

I nodded.

'I'll be right with you,' TJ said. He walked towards the bathroom.

Reggie and I stepped down the porch steps.

I leaned up against the Camaro. Reggie pressed himself into me, tucked my hair behind my ears and leaned in for a kiss.

'I've decided something,' I said.

'Oh yeah?' He traced his index finger along my cheekbone and under my chin, lifting my face up towards his.

I pecked his lips gently. He smelled so good.

'I'm thinking of looking for my mom.'

Reggie's eyes widened.

I knew that would shock him. To be honest, it surprised me. Until the words fell out of my mouth, I don't think I had fully decided.

'OK,' he said.

I sensed his caution. 'Will you help me?'

Reggie's concern turned to a smile. ''Course I will, baby.'

Both of us glanced towards the house. TJ exited and tugged

the front door shut. A piece of plywood covered the hole where the cops had kicked it in.

TJ stepped into the front yard.

'Want me to drive?' I asked. I held my hands out for the keys.

TJ scowled at me and laughed. 'I'm not a cripple yet, kid. Now hop in the back.'

TJ turned down Haring Street and switched on the radio.

'...All six Liberty of the Mind Centers were closed, with members protesting to police. Wyatt Browning, reportedly using the name Svaag Dimash, fled his home and is currently still on the run. Police released a recent photograph which shows Browning having undergone extensive facial surgery. They are appealing to the public to keep an eye out and to call their local police with any sightings. His associate Trey Garrison has been charged for extortion, blackmail and racketeering. We will be reporting more on that story on our special at six p.m. Keep tuned to SBFM.'

A jingle hollered out of the tinny speakers. TJ turned the volume down low.

The three of us sat in silence the rest of the way. My mind full of TJ and his illness, the idea of searching for my mom and, of course, what we were about to find.

'Here we are,' TJ finally said. He pulled the car to the side.

My stomach flipped, but before I could register my fears, May ran out along a strip of lawn at the front of an apartment block, a tub of bubbles and a lime green plastic hoop in her hands. Too occupied chasing the rainbows in the air, she hadn't noticed us approach.

One by one, we stepped out of the car.

On some nearby concrete steps sat Linda and, next to her, Maria.

Both of them stood at the same time. Finally spotting us, May scrambled over, conflicted who to hug first. Squeezing her in my arms, I heard her squeal.

Maria walked over to me, her arms open wide. I slipped May down and watched her dart over to TJ. I opened my arms too and hugged Maria tight.

'*Gracias,*' she said. She smiled at me and kissed me on both cheeks, her gaze dreamily drifting to May.

We all stayed in the front yard playing with May. I knew Linda's presence was part of the package and for once I didn't resent it. To see May settling in was the best gift I could have.

There was no way I was selling my story – or, more to the point, May's story – to the press, no matter how much they were willing to pay. I would find another way of making my rent.

Maria chased her daughter around the yard, catching and tickling her. Their giggles floated like the bubbles freely through the air.

Lifting my camera, I peered with glassy eyes through the viewfinder and, pressing the shutter, I finally captured May's family.

Acknowledgements

Huge thanks to my editor, Emad Akhtar. Not only did you show great faith in me, but you have got to be one of the kindest, most thoughtful and incisive people I have had the pleasure to work with. Fellow writers, never underestimate the value of an illustrious editor. I am not worthy.

My glamorous agent, Maggie Hanbury – you have the ability to both make me belly-laugh and stand up straight with fear. Thank you for all you do. Never stop making me giggle. You are magnificent!

Lucy Frederick at Orion, the Gilmore Girl who is going places. You rock!

Bill Massey, for your terrifying, yet annoyingly accurate notes on my first draft.

Jon Appleton for his copyedit.

The whole team at Orion who have worked tirelessly behind the scenes making this happen. Your hard work is very much appreciated.

Jackie 'Onassis' Dolman, who has been there every Tuesday, Wednesday and Thursday.

Lilya & Igor, for your insightful comments as you purr and pad across my keyboard, demanding my full attention.

And last, but most definitely not least, the Querulous Lobster, Tig. My dear friend and muse.

Credits

Alex Hart and Orion Fiction would like to thank everyone at Orion who worked on the publication of *Take Me Home* in the UK.

Editorial
Emad Akhtar
Lucy Frederick

Copy editor
Jon Appleton

Proof reader
Jade Craddock

Audio
Paul Stark
Amber Bates

Design
Debbie Holmes
Joanna Ridley
Nick May

Editorial Management
Charlie Panayiotou
Jane Hughes
Alice Davis

Production
Ruth Sharvell

Marketing
Brittany Sankey

Publicity
Alainna Hadjigeorgiou

Finance
Jasdip Nandra
Afeera Ahmed
Elizabeth Beaumont
Sue Baker

Rights
Susan Howe
Krystyna Kujawinska
Jessica Purdue
Richard King
Louise Henderson

Operations
Jo Jacobs
Sharon Willis
Lisa Pryde
Lucy Brem

Sales
Jen Wilson
Esther Waters
Victoria Laws
Rachael Hum
Ellie Kyrke-Smith
Frances Doyle
Georgina Cutler

Contracts
Anne Goddard
Paul Bulos
Jake Alderson